NO WAY OUT

"PRAY YOU'RE NOT CHOSEN!"

DC BROCKWELL

First published in 2020 by Bloodhound Books

www.bloodhoundbooks.com

978-1-913419-64-6

I would like to thank my wife, Beks for all her hard work listening to my ideas, proofreading the manuscript and encouraging me to go for it. Thank you for all you do for me. Xxxxx

—

Day 2 Friday, 12th January

Detective Constable Nasreen Maqsood sat down next to her supervisor, Detective Sergeant Terrence Johnson. Having successfully secured a confession out of a serial rapist who'd been stalking their streets and parks, she'd been asked to join Terrence for a briefing on their next investigation.

The rapist had managed to elude them for over three months, but by using every resource they had at their disposal, they'd managed to identify the suspect before he'd struck for a sixth time; Nasreen only wished they'd been able to identify him sooner.

Sitting across from her and her supervisor was Detective Chief Superintendent Clive Adams. She'd heard a lot about Adams throughout her career, but as of a year earlier – when she'd been selected as detective constable – he was now her boss's boss's boss. It was unusual for such a senior officer to be giving them their investigation dossiers. Due to budgetary constraints, illness and other factors beyond the department's control, their inspectors and chief inspector were out of action; now it was up to DCS Adams to perform three officers' roles.

While he had a reputation as a harsh but fair man, so far, fortunately, she'd only seen the fair side of him – except for her very first day as a detective, that was, when he'd expressed his concern over her selection; he'd been honest enough to tell her that she'd been chosen, not because she was the most qualified, or had scored highest in her exam, but rather because her ethnicity was desirable. In the past year, she'd worked hard to allay those concerns, had proven her worth, and had consequently become an integral part of the team.

Nasreen listened patiently to the usual niceties, remaining quiet while Johnson and Adams spoke briefly about their families.

Adams was a well-built man in his late fifties, with a head full of grey hair. Not for the first time, as Nasreen stared at him, she noticed how big his ears were in comparison with the rest of his head – long, rather than big. He wasn't an unattractive man, but she wouldn't say he was exactly attractive either.

Her supervisor, on the other hand, was a strapping black man with a booming voice and a contagious laugh. Now, *he* was a good-looking man, one who could charm anyone into anything. In fact, about six months earlier, Terrence had charmed a female suspect into confessing to a double murder; she'd not been the brightest spark, it was true, however it had been Terrence's charm that had won her over and brought out the unexpected confession.

Once the civilities were over, Adams picked up two A4 folders, handing one each to her and Terrence before leaning back in his chair. "I've had to juggle things about a bit. You'll be running with this for the next couple of days; I've had to pull Watts and O'Hara off it because they're testifying in the Hamilton trial."

"That's okay, sir," Terrence replied in his deep voice.

"All the preliminary work's in there," Adams continued, nodding at the folders. "It's already a day old, so you'll be picking up where they left off."

Nasreen opened the folder and skimmed over the top sheet of paper, a form giving the details of the missing person: Daniel Rose. She gasped, then hoped they hadn't heard. It couldn't be *her* Danny, could it? It had to be another poor soul with the same name.

She could hear Adams and Terrence talking about the case, but she wasn't listening. She looked at the address details: they neither confirmed nor denied her worst fears; she no longer knew where he lived anyway.

Glancing through the personal section of the form, she noticed the date of birth was a match! Shit! She flipped over to the next page, and there it was: a picture of her Danny.

It was funny how she had two very conflicting histories with Danny. On the one hand, she had stacks of memories of her primary and secondary school years, years Danny spent bullying her, calling her and her friends the P-word and giving her the general verbal abuse she'd become accustomed to. Then, on the flip side, she had lovely memories of him as her boyfriend, when he'd been loving, kind, and generous.

When she was twenty – going through a rebellious phase against her parents – Nasreen and Danny bumped into one another in the high street of their hometown and he'd apologised for his behaviour in the past. They'd popped into a pub nearby and had spent the rest of the afternoon and evening catching up. When they were saying their goodbyes, they'd arranged to go out on a real date.

She looked at the picture of Danny for what felt like hours. He was such a good-looking man, with a full head of dark hair that rested slightly over his face. She remembered his smile, the smile that had made her knees tremble. She'd always wondered why such a great-looking guy had been interested in her; she wasn't ugly, but she'd never considered herself to be pretty either. Still, there she'd been for a little over a year, in a great relationship with a gorgeous man.

All these memories kept flashing through her mind while her bosses continued discussing the investigation, oblivious to her distress.

Glancing through Danny's employment history, she found that he'd worked for a company called Nagel and Nagel – a male escort agency – which had gone bust two years earlier; since then he'd taken his services private. A sudden rush of anger enveloped her as she thought of all those women paying to have sex with him.

Not wanting her bosses to know how angry she was, Nasreen breathed in and out until she felt a little calmer. She just couldn't understand how Danny could have sold his body for money, though there was no denying he'd have made a lot doing it; he had a great body and he really knew how to treat women. But to actually go and sell sex for money? What was he thinking!

Before they'd broken up – the hardest break-up Nasreen had ever experienced – he'd shown her his paintings, which were amazing. Danny had always wanted to be an artist, and to make money by selling his art in galleries was his dream. He had such talent, and such promise; he wasn't supposed to be a prostitute. What had gone wrong in his life to make him decide that selling his body was the best course of action?

Poor Danny, she thought. Something really bad must have happened to him.

Tuning into her bosses' conversation again, Nasreen heard Terrence and Adams talking about Danny's family.

He didn't have any to speak of. His mum and dad had both died when he was sixteen, and thanks to his older sister agreeing to house him, he'd just managed to avoid being taken into care. Then, when Danny was twenty, his sister had moved to Ottawa, Canada, with her new husband. There was no one else.

"Nasreen, is everything all right?"

At Terrence's voice she looked up from her file to find him and Adams both looking at her, waiting for a response. A quiet "Huh?" was all she could muster.

"Are you okay?" Adams asked, sounding concerned. "You look pale; are you feeling all right?"

"I'm fine. Sorry, what were you saying? I was just reading through the file and must've got distracted." As Nasreen stared at her superiors, she noticed their looks of concern disappear, quickly turning to expressions of confusion.

"Are you sure?" asked Adams.

She tried to keep her voice level. "Honestly, I'm fine."

Still not looking entirely convinced, Adams and Terrence went back to discussing the investigation.

Nasreen had to decide whether she should come clean and inform her superiors that she'd had a relationship with the victim; it was force protocol to inform them, so she was professionally obligated to do so. There was something holding her back though.

She knew of a fellow officer, back when she'd been a uniformed constable, whose boyfriend had disappeared, and he had not been allowed to have anything to do with the case. She wanted – *needed* – to help find Danny.

"I suggest you go right back to the beginning, see if a fresh pair of eyes – or two – will help. Watts and O'Hara interviewed..." Adams looked down at his copy of the file, "Rita Abbott yesterday; she initiated the missing persons report and we think she was the last person to see him. I'd start there."

"We're on it," Nasreen replied, closing the file and standing up. Terrence followed suit.

As she and her supervisor walked out of the office, she thought about telling Terrence privately – letting him know about her relationship to the missing person – and seeing if he thought she should tell Adams. There really was no question that she should have told them both from the beginning. There was no way she was going to let them reassign her to a different case...

2

Day 5 Monday, 15th January

Daniel Rose stirred.

His head hurt, he felt nauseous, and when he tried to rub his face, something prevented his arms from moving. He was bound by something.

Gradually, he opened his eyes.

The first thing he saw was a white ceiling, worrying considering his bedroom's was an off-white, beige. It was then he realised he wasn't at home.

Looking to his right he saw a bare white wall; to his left, the same. He could feel something around his neck, and he could smell the strong scent of leather.

Raising his head as far as the leather neck cuff would allow, he looked forwards. He was naked atop white sheets, his ankles and wrists chained and bound by leather restraints. He tried to move again, but the restraints were too tight.

Where the fuck was he? Was this one of his clients' bedrooms? It wasn't a room he'd seen before; maybe it was one of their spare rooms he hadn't been in yet?

He continued scanning the room, his head throbbing. There was a door in front of him, set to the right, and it looked heavy – made of metal maybe, painted red. There was a letterbox in the door, about five feet up; it couldn't have been a letterbox at all. It could have been a peephole, but it certainly wasn't a normal one; it looked like something you would see in a prison door.

Danny winced at his pounding head.

This wasn't funny, whatever it was. *Wherever* he was.

Just what the hell was going on?

In the middle of the front wall, to the left of the red door and slightly higher up, was what appeared to be an air conditioning unit. The flaps were open and the machine was making a strange whirring sound. At least it was comfortable, temperature-wise.

Danny suddenly realised that on his scan of the room he hadn't seen any windows. He looked to the left and right again. Nope. A windowless room meant he was either in the middle of a big complex, or underground. A basement, perhaps? None of his clients had basements – at least, not to his knowledge. He looked more closely at the walls, seeing two vents near the top of both the left and right walls.

He had to get out of here, he thought as he pulled on the wrist restraints.

"Help!" he shouted, panicked, as he continued to pull as tight as he could on his wrists, all the while wrenching his neck against the tough leather. "Anybody? Please?"

The letterbox hatch slid sideways from the outside.

As Danny found himself staring at a pair of eyes peering at him through the slot, he stopped tugging at his wrists. Who was it? If it *was* one of his clients, he was going to go straight to the police.

The hatch closed.

"Please! Untie me and let me go!" he shouted, yet again

tugging at his wrist restraints. "I haven't done anything wrong! I just want to go home, please!"

Nothing.

He listened for any noises: nothing. Either there was nothing happening outside the room, or the walls and doors were really thick – soundproofed, perhaps?

Glancing to his right, he saw there was a chest of drawers next to the bed. There was nothing on the top, but what about inside the drawers? His clothes could be in there, and maybe his mobile phone too.

He needed to get the phone and call for help; all he had to do was get out of these restraints, find his, or another, phone and call the police.

"Mr Rose, you'll tire yourself out," said a female voice. "Please relax, and don't be alarmed. I'll be with you shortly to debrief you on your situation."

Unable to work out where the voice had come from, Danny scanned the room again, hoping to see something he'd missed before. He thought the voice had come from above. Looking closer, he couldn't see any technology capable of...

Oh wait, there it was: above the air conditioning unit there was a glass ball, a camera. Someone was watching him.

How long had he been here, being watched? The thought made his head hurt.

He took the voice's advice and lay still, trying to think back to the last thing he could remember, although that was easier said than done with his head being so fuzzy; it felt like someone had stuffed it with cotton wool.

The last thing he remembered was leaving Rita Abbott – his client – asleep in her bed, and then he'd walked through the park, back to his townhouse. He remembered walking past some bloke in the dark. A big stocky guy in a bomber jacket.

So that was how he'd ended up here! That bloke must've

smashed him over the head with something, probably a baton or maybe something smaller that he hadn't seen until it was too late.

But why would he want to knock him unconscious and bring him here? And where *was* here? And whose voice was that earlier? None of it made any sense.

There were far too many questions for Danny's battered brain to comprehend. Loads of questions, with no answers. He wished he could clear his head.

Danny heard what sounded like a key in the door; his heart stopping as it opened and a woman in her late thirties – maybe early forties – walked in, flanked by a bullish man wearing shirt and trousers. Trailing them came a sweet-looking petite young Asian girl. Danny's pulse quickened as the three new arrivals stood observing him in his naked state.

Danny had never been shy. Tied up, he felt very vulnerable.

"Daniel Rose," said the woman in her late thirties. She stepped forwards and stood in front of his bed. "Finally, we meet."

Looking at her through the fogginess, some song lyrics suddenly popped into Danny's head. It couldn't really be Jolene, could it? His head throbbed as he watched her walk up closer.

Whoever she was, she sure was beautiful. He couldn't help but notice that she was wearing what appeared to be a bathrobe – a classy velvet number. "You're not one of my clients!" he exclaimed. "Please untie me. I don't deserve this; I haven't done anything wrong."

"Danny," she said softly, "this isn't about you doing anything wrong." She continued walking around the side of his bed before sitting down next to him. "I can call you Danny, can't I? I heard that's what you prefer."

He felt the bed sink as she sat down. "Look, lady," he said, panicking again, "I don't know what the fuck this is, please–"

"Shhh." She placed a finger over his lips. "Oh Danny, you're not *supposed* to know what this is." She smiled, glancing pointedly around the sparse room. "I haven't told you yet."

She had a lovely manner about her, disarming. Her smile was glorious and her long red hair topped off the whole package. Danny loved redheads. When she smiled, dimples formed, accentuating her piercing green eyes.

"You're our guest," she said, reaching out her right hand to rest on his leg. "Our newest bee."

When Daniel felt her hand gently stroking his lower calf, he asked, "Can I have my clothes, please?"

"Shhh! Shhh! It's okay, Danny. You have nothing to be embarrassed about. On the contrary," she added, raising her eyebrows, "I've heard a lot of complimentary things about you."

Trying to avoid thinking about the woman's touch, Danny glanced over at the bullish man, standing very straight in his white shirt and black trousers, his hands clasped neatly in front of him. He wasn't paying any attention to what was going on – or at least, he didn't seem to be.

The petite Asian girl stood beside the bull tried to look away.

He looked back up at the woman, feeling her steady gaze on him. "Who the fuck are you people? What do you want from me?"

"You see, Danny, we need your expertise," she replied, stroking his inner thigh.

"Expertise?" He tried to ignore the woman's fingers on his skin. "What the fuck are you talking about? I think you've got the wrong guy; I'm an artist, I can paint you a picture if you want... all you have to do is ask, you don't need to–"

"Not that kind of expertise," she said, cutting him off with a smile. "I've heard your skills with a brush pale in comparison to your... other areas of expertise."

"I don't even know what you're talking about." His mind was

fuzzy. He was still none-the-wiser why he was strapped to this bed.

Her fingers were closing in on his crotch. "I'm talking about your other skills, Danny, you know what I'm talking about."

Danny closed his eyes briefly, trying to think. His fuzzy head was making him crazy. What was going on? Where was he? And what was this woman on about? "Look, tell me what's going on!" he shouted. "Who the fuck *are* you? Why am I tied up? And where the hell is this place? Why can't I have my clothes?"

The woman stopped stroking him. "All in good time, New Bee," she replied, smiling. "You can call me Beattie, or Bea, and I own this establishment. My husband and I own it. Behind me is Walter, my number two, and the stunning young lady next to him is Kimiko. She's here to look after you, so whatever you need, just ask Kimiko."

The woman called Beattie stood up.

"How long have I been here?"

"Four days, I think." She stared into the distance for a moment. "No, this is day five."

Danny looked up at her as she walked over to him, then bent down and kissed him tenderly on the forehead. "Five days?" He couldn't believe he'd been out of it for so long; it felt as though he'd walked through the park just hours before.

Beattie's soft expression changed. "You're going live tomorrow; four of my best clients are just dying to make your acquaintance. Don't worry though, Kimiko will see to your needs."

Beattie paused.

"Please impress our customers, Danny, like you would with your own."

"What do you mean, 'our customers'?"

With a look of exasperation on her face, she shouted, "What do you think this is? You work for me now! And tomorrow you're going to service four of my wealthiest customers and you're going to be as charming and virile as you would be with your own. Do you understand? Do I need to explain this to you some more?"

"You mean fuck them?" He was beginning to understand what was being asked of him. It was too surreal to comprehend, yet here he was, bound naked to a bed in a windowless room.

She tutted, shaking her head. "Yes, I mean you're going to fuck them! And you will, like your life depends on it, because," she answered in that same harsh tone, "it really does. And I wish you wouldn't use that foul language in front of me – I hate it. You're an intelligent man; intelligent men don't need to use profanity."

"So, this is some kind of brothel, a whorehouse?" he said to himself.

"Whorehouse is such a derogatory term. This is an exclusive club, Danny, and you're my New Bee. And my hope is that you'll become my Star Bee."

"Wait! I can't just fuck on demand like a performing seal," he said, watching her fiddle with her robe belt.

"Of course you can," she replied, stepping up to the bed and looking down at him. "Your life literally depends on it. We give our 'New Bees' time to adjust, but after that, if you don't perform, if you don't impress our clients, we have ways of punishing you that you won't much like." She pointed at the wall. "You see those two vents up there? And those over there?"

Danny looked up at where she was pointing.

"They aren't air vents. We can knock you out with the push of a button... and we can put you to sleep permanently just as easily. You *do not* want to test me, Danny!"

She was right over him, an accusatory finger pointed at his face merely an inch from his nose. As quickly as she'd vented her anger, however, she recovered, her face affable and charming again. "Anyway, I'm sure tomorrow will be a success. And I'm rooting for you; you've come highly recommended."

"Who? Who recommended me?"

"One of your former clients actually. She said you'd make an excellent addition to my team. And I do hope she's right."

Danny watched as Beattie untied her belt. She opened her robe, revealing a tight and toned body. She was the whole package. "What're you doing?"

Beattie let the robe fall to the floor. "I have to sample the goods, Danny. What kind of proprietor would I be if I haven't tried you for myself? You'll find I take my job very seriously. So seriously, in fact, our in-house doctor has conducted a barrage of tests on you while you were out. I can promise my clients you're as clean as they come."

He didn't know what to make of this news. It was like being in a waking nightmare. The girl, Kimiko, had her head down, as did the guard. And there was nothing Danny could do to stop Beattie mounting him.

"Walter! Kimiko! Leave us now," demanded Beattie, straddling him. "It's time to see if you're as good as I hope..."

3

After Beattie had tested him, put on her robe and left the room, Kimiko wheeled in a trolley loaded with cleaning materials.

What the hell had just happened? He was supposed to "service" four women the next day. He was expected to just play along, no questions asked? Danny could feel the anger building up in his chest, and knowing he had to expel it, he shouted out, "Fuck you!" He pulled at his ankle, wrist, and neck restraints again – flailing left and right, up and down.

"Please, stop, you make her angry," pleaded Kimiko, hurrying over to his side. She pointed up to the camera above the air conditioning unit. "She watch from office. It has microphone. Please, stop!"

After thrashing about on his bed in anger for several more seconds, he finally gave in, exhausted. He was covered in perspiration. He took several deep breaths until he felt a little calmer, and seeing how anxious the woman was, he asked, "What was your name? Kom..."

"Kimiko."

"Please, Kimiko, go through those drawers," he pleaded,

pointing at them as best he could with his restrained hand. "See if my mobile phone's in there... please!"

"It not in there. Your clothes and phone are gone."

For the first time, Danny noticed how sweet her voice was. She was so petite, so cute, he couldn't believe someone like her would be a part of this. "What's in the drawers?"

Kimiko walked over to her trolley and wheeled it over to him before soaking a sponge in a bowl of hot soapy water. She then wiped him down, starting with his face. "They empty," she answered as she went about her work, "for now. They can soon be filled with your belongings. Bea leave drawers to show you that you can earn possessions."

"*Earn* possessions?"

Kimiko continued washing Danny and he lay back, trying to relax.

"Yes, if you are top bee on B Wing, you get to buy anything you want for a hundred pound," Kimiko explained. "All bees are graded by customer, out of ten. At end of week, bee with most point get money to buy thing."

Danny raised his eyebrows. Wait, top bee? "How many bees," he said, before correcting himself, "sorry – *people* – are there here?"

"Ten on B Wing, and ten on A Wing. Bea runs B Wing, Alan runs A Wing. There another area for naughty bees. C Wing not really wing but you don't want go there."

Danny shuddered. No, he didn't think he wanted to go to C Wing.

Kimiko answered his questions – not that it gave him any more of an idea as to what was going on. She was helpful and attentive, and in spite of where they'd met, he liked her immediately. After all, she was an innocent, so harmless and pretty, who wouldn't like her?

If he had any chance of persuading someone to help him escape, it was Kimiko...

4

In her office, Beatrice "Beattie" Harrison watched as Kimiko cleaned Danny, listening to their every word. Even though there was a bank of monitors sat on top of her desk, she could only listen in to one room at a time. As she was confident that she had broken down the other nine bees, she now had to focus on breaking Danny down, to get him to bend to her will.

Sitting back in her swivel chair, she sighed, content. She hadn't enjoyed testing a bee that much since her first test, all those years ago, back in 2002. She and her husband had bought the ten-acre farmhouse in 2000 and it had taken them a year and a half to renovate the bunker into twenty-five separate rooms, all three metres by three metres.

When she and Alan had been advised to look at the farmhouse by her father, the great William Rothstein, they'd loved the house, despite the amount of work it needed. The clincher though, had been the underground bunker and all the opportunities it offered. William had been insistent on renovating it and turning it into a high-end underground brothel, and Beattie's husband, Alan, had gone along with the idea; he wasn't one for arguing with her father. After all, Alan knew what William did for a living, and Alan knew even better how her father dealt with problems.

William Rothstein was a revered name up and down the country; he had appeared in all the national newspapers and news channels over the years, and never for anything good.

He was often referred to as a gangster by the press. Beattie didn't think of him like that; he was her dad, he loved her. And while it was true that in his younger years he'd earned an obscene amount of money through less than savoury means – prostitution, drugs, extortion, to name a few – now he was a legitimate businessman, a property developer. She was sure he had profitable "sidelines", not that he ever spoke of them to her. In fact, he never spoke about any of his other business dealings with her. She had, however, known (or at least suspected) what he did for a living from a young age.

Over the years, she had – more or less – come to terms with it.

It was through her father's property developing skills that they'd managed to renovate the bunker without alerting the authorities, and the first thing they'd had to do was erect a barn around the hatch leading down a flight of thirty steps to the future brothel. Once they'd covered the hatch they'd started work on the renovation, using only known and trusted construction workers. They'd all been paid for their work under the table and off the books, and they'd been paid handsomely to keep the project to themselves.

While the construction of the bunker was ongoing, she'd been busy with renovating the main house. It had twelve bedrooms in total, a huge lounge and separate dining room, two studies, a library, five bathrooms and a large professional kitchen; most restaurants didn't have a kitchen as big as hers. It had taken her five years to furnish, paint, and decorate the house to her standard and it had been an enjoyable experience for her.

She and Alan still shared a bedroom, although their relationship was more or less platonic these days; their marriage merely a façade, used to make them look respectable to outside eyes. They hadn't slept together in over two years; at first she'd thought it was because they had sex on tap, day and night, but later she realised they didn't love each other the way they once had. They were still good friends, however, and they kept up the pretence for the sake of the business.

She thought back to 2002. She'd been twenty-seven when they started the business and at first they only had two bees, a male and a female. They'd decided that Alan would look after the females and she would look after the males, a system that worked well for them. Her father had found their customers through his contacts; there was no shortage of men prepared to pay to have sex – or anything else they wanted for an extra charge. When they'd started out, Beattie and Alan charged five hundred an hour, and with six customers a day that meant they could make three thousand per bee. Now they had twenty bees servicing six customers each, earning them in excess of sixty thousand a day, in cash.

Every evening, at nine o'clock, a courier would come and collect the money, neatly stack it in a suitcase, and then drive it back to her father, who handled the rest. She didn't know how her father laundered the money; if truth be known, she didn't want to know. She and Alan then received their share – twenty percent – in clean transfers into their joint account. To make it appear legitimate, she and Alan were on the payroll of her father's property development company; her husband was a vice president to her interior designer.

If there was one thing she loved more than anything else, it was money, which was a shame because she never thought they had enough, even though they had over two million in their joint account. She knew what they were doing was wrong, immoral, and – above all – highly illegal, but the love of money overpowered any feeling of conscience or guilt she may have had to start with. Her bees were simply a way of making her more money; she didn't care about them. Well, no more than she cared about the starving masses in Africa, or refugees fleeing war-torn countries.

They were there to do a job – it was as simple as that – and God help them if they failed!

In spite of her and her husband's relationship not being based on love, she loved her life – and more specifically, her *lifestyle.* She was a member of an elite country club, where she played tennis with her girlfriends once a week; she regularly sailed with her yacht club; and she went horse riding whenever she wanted – there was a fully licenced stable on their farm, which they rented out to horse owners who couldn't afford a stable of their own. She had pretty much everything she'd ever wanted.

And the only reason she could afford this lavish lifestyle was because they had the twenty bees busily servicing their clients. Secretly servicing their clients. She had to admit, it turned her on to think that nobody – except their customers – knew what was going on below their farm; it was like leading a double life.

"How's it going, honey?" Alan was leaning against the door frame, having snuck in while she was reminiscing.

"I must have nodded off," she replied, pulling the robe belt tighter around her waist. "What time is it?"

"Half five. How did your bee test go? Is he going to make the grade?"

She stood and faced her husband. "I should say so."

"That good, huh?"

If Beattie didn't know any better, she'd say he was jealous, which was strange because Alan didn't do jealousy; it wasn't in his genetic make-up. "Why, honey, are you jealous?" she asked, teasing him with an elbow to the rib.

"Don't be daft."

"He'll work out fine. He just needs a bit of time to adjust to his new environment." Her smile widened. "I've got a good feeling about Danny. In fact, we might be able to charge a little extra for him once he's properly settled in."

She watched as Alan nodded and turned to leave. "How's your day been?" she asked. "Are they all behaving themselves?" Alan often came into her office for these little chats. She never asked him about his sexual exploits with his All-Stars, what he called his bees, and he never offered her his experience – not that she really cared, if the truth be told. She was happy to remain professional when talking about his side of the business.

"Nothing to report here. It's been quiet."

There had been a time when she'd loved *him* more than money. Stupid, now she thought about it. After all, a man couldn't buy you the clothes you wanted, the make-up you wanted, or the dream home you yearned for. Money bought all those things, so why love a man when you should really love money? She would have done anything for him in those early days. Now, he was only interested in testing his girls, his All-Stars. Still he was a good friend and confidant, and she was happy he was here.

While glancing over the monitors one last time before she had to go and freshen up for a charity gala, Beattie noticed some commotion on camera five. Frederick was throwing things about in his room. Pressing a button that linked her to the internal speaker, she asked, "Frederick, what are you *doing*?" Her tone was intentionally hostile.

She watched as he stopped throwing his belongings and looked up at the camera.

"Let me the fuck out of here!" he hissed. "I'm going to rip your fucking head off, you bitch! Let me out!"

She stood and paused, watching him rage inside his three-by-three cell. Looking at him, it was only a matter of time before he completely broke down, which was sad, yet not entirely unexpected. After all, he was her (current) oldest bee; he'd been with her for five and a half years, and the record was five years and eight months. Since his time with her, he'd caught three sexually transmitted diseases – which her doctor had treated him for – he'd been beaten black and blue three times, and he'd lost both of his little fingers. Bees didn't have a long shelf life, unfortunately. Oh well, it looked like she would be sending Walter out to replace him sooner than she'd hoped. "Calm down, Freddie, you don't want to test me today; I'm not in the mood," she said through the speaker. "You know what comes next."

"Fuck you!"

"Not when you're like this," she replied, angrily pushing a button on a separate control panel, then watching as smoke started filling his room. He'd asked for it. He knew what would happen, and she'd have to deal with him in the morning.

"*Bitch!*" he shouted while coughing and spluttering.

Once the monitor had gone cloudy – and she could be sure, therefore, that he was unconscious – she pressed the red stop button. "Damn you for making me do this," she snapped. "Now I'm going to have to think about an appropriate punishment..."

5

Lennox Garvey drove his Mitsubishi Shogun along the snowy narrow road leading to the Harrison farmhouse. At five to nine in the evening, the half-mile-long road was deserted; the Harrisons' customers were always gone by half eight at the latest, and the road only led to the farm. It was more of a dirt track than a road – lined with potholes and ditches – but he'd traversed this lane so many times it didn't bother him.

As he pulled up and parked outside the farmhouse, Lennox could feel the crunch of snow under his tyres. His boss, William Rothstein, had informed him that Alan and Beattie were out for the evening, so he would have to let himself in to make the pickup, which wasn't unusual given the couple's rich social life.

Lennox opened his door, pulled himself out, and walked around to the boot to retrieve the suitcase. It always amazed him how much money the "blood bunker" – as he called it – took on a daily basis; most days he had to count and sort about sixty grand in denominations of fifties, twenties, and tens. It always took him about half an hour to count, bind, and place the cash in the suitcase.

With the suitcase in one hand and a torch in the other,

Lennox walked past the house and along the two-hundred-metre path until he came to the barn, his journey lit only by the glow from his torch.

With the temperature at about minus five, he'd made sure he was wearing suitable clothing: Caterpillar boots, jeans, a thick comfy jumper and a Parka jacket lined with fur. He missed his home country's warmth – even after living in the UK for ten years, he still wasn't used to the cold. What he would give to be back in his home city of Montego Bay, Jamaica. But his employment with William Rothstein had been part of a drug alliance between Rothstein and Lennox's uncle, and he hadn't been able to turn the job down.

Removing the thick plank of wood locking the barn doors, he leaned it upright against a wall to the right of the door. Then, picking up his suitcase, he opened the right-side door and walked into the large dark barn, the sound of breaking glass under his boots filling the room. Fumbling around on the wall next to the door, he found the light switch and flicked it on.

As there was a Land Rover parked over the hatch that led down to the basement, Lennox had to get in the four-by-four, start it up, and reverse it until it was clear of the hatch. It was something he had to do a lot; the Harrisons used the car as an insurance policy, in case one of the captives managed to escape their cells – and they were, quite literally cells. If one of them managed to get as far as the hatch, well, they certainly wouldn't be going any further with a heavy Land Rover parked over them, or the glass strewn over the floor. The bees were banned from owning footwear.

After opening the hatch, Lennox walked down about eight steps until he felt for another light switch on the wall, and when he flicked it on the basement lit up, revealing its horrific secret.

He couldn't help but shudder. The entire set-up had never sat right with him; he knew what went on down here, but who was he to argue with his boss? Who was he to tell him how he should run his affairs? It was true, he'd done some pretty horrible things in his time working for his uncle but kidnapping people and making them have sex with five or six people a day – while keeping them held captive – was wrong on so many levels.

And then there was all the other nasty shit that went on down here too. Lennox knew what Alan and Beattie did to these poor people once they had served their purpose (obviously there was no way they were going to let them go) and he knew how they did it too. The whole set-up left a bad taste in his mouth. After all, these were ordinary people who'd been plucked off the street and subjected to vile actions by even viler people. He'd been able to choose his life, and everyone else in his business had chosen theirs. They knew the risks that came with their lifestyle choices, but the poor men and women locked in this dungeon didn't have a choice.

Yeah, it left a very bad taste.

Still, for a dungeon, it was plush. When he descended all thirty steps, he came to the reception area, complete with a fully stocked bar and several comfy sofas and armchairs. The Harrisons sometimes entertained their clients down here while the poor bastards were locked away, listening to the parties, the laughter.

The cells were situated along the left and right walls – Alan's All-Stars to the left and Bea's Bees to the right – ten rooms on each side. At the far end of the bunker was an old furnace room, and next to that was the main office. At the other end, off to the left, was a row of five more rooms, nicknamed C Wing; it was in those rooms that the really vile shit happened. Opposite that were the restrooms – if you could call them that. There were five lavatories and showers, alternating shower, toilet, shower, toilet, and all open-plan so they could be seen taking a shit and showering. Further along there was space for sundries, such as bed sheets, towels, and everything else the Harrisons needed to run their business as hygienically as they could.

Lennox walked past the rooms – which were all eerily quiet – until he came to the fifth room on the right. There were angry frustrated cries coming from that room, and intrigued, he pulled the peephole shutter across to look inside: a man was lying naked on the bed, his wrists, ankles, and neck bound by chains that were linked to thick brown leather cuffs. He could see that the man had had both his little fingers removed. He was thrashing about violently, writhing in pain and anger. Kimiko was in there talking to the man, trying to calm him down. Lennox couldn't hear what she was saying.

He loved his exchanges with Kimiko. She was easy to talk to, and stunning to look at; it was a shame she was off-limits. He closed the peephole as Kimiko started walking towards the door, then he waited for her to leave the room.

Lennox stood back as she closed the door behind her, as though she were trying not to wake a baby. Everything she did was so graceful and elegant; it was one of the things he liked about Kimiko. She only spoke when necessary, never for the sake of it. He guessed it was part of her upbringing in Okinawa.

"I try calm him, but nothing I say work," she whispered.

"Nothing can help him," Lennox replied in his thick Jamaican accent. "You take on too much responsibility, Kimiko. Go on up to your room and relax. And stop worrying; that guy's too far gone to be helped."

He watched as she walked along the room and up the stairs, her long Japanese kimono covering her feet and giving the illusion she was gliding. She was cute, he thought, as he picked up the suitcase and torch and walked the rest of the way to the main office.

When he got to the door, he reached inside his jacket and pulled out a set of keys, slipping a small silver key in the lock and letting himself in. After switching on the lights, he walked straight over to the wall safe and used a different key – this one long and thin – to unlock it.

Sat neatly on the top shelf of the safe were stacks of money sorted into fifties, twenties, and tens, and taking the stacks out, he placed them carefully on the desk in front of the bank of monitors. He checked the monitors to find that the nineteen prisoners were quiet, either watching TV, asleep, or nakedly restrained; he only saw two in restraints, the one he'd just checked on and another man he'd not seen before, who looked asleep.

Before Lennox started counting the money, he glanced at a photo of Beattie Harrison sat on a shelf on the wall to his right. Every time he came here to collect the takings, he took a long look at that photo of Beattie, showing her sat by the edge of a pool in some hotel resort. She was wearing a bikini, sat with both legs slightly raised, her arms leaning on her knees. He only wished he'd known her back then.

Who was he kidding, anyway? He knew Beattie was off-limits; her father would kill him if he so much as touched her, that was for certain. In fact, when he'd moved over here from Montego Bay, William Rothstein had read him the riot act on that very matter. Rothstein had even said that he didn't care whose nephew he was; if he so much as looked at his daughter a certain way, he'd be a dead man, alliance or no alliance. Rothstein had also said that his daughter's business was worth too much to him to disrupt it over an affair, or worse. Rothstein didn't really care about his daughter; he was far more concerned with keeping his cash cow milked.

Lennox often thought that Rothstein was far more dangerous than his uncle could ever be, and his uncle was the single biggest exporter of heroin and cocaine on the island, having his fair share of problems that had ended in wars with rival dealers. All this death and destruction was nothing, however, compared to Rothstein's legacy; he had heard countless stories of his boss's exploits as a younger man, stories that made him wince.

When he'd first flown over to join Rothstein's network, Lennox had been the only black man on Rothstein's payroll, which had brought its fair share of trials and tribulations. He'd had to work twice as hard to prove both his competence and his loyalty, yet on the other hand he'd found hooking up with women to be much easier in the UK.

He'd had many run-ins with Rothstein's white employees but none that he couldn't work out – except one that had been resolved by him caving a man's head in with a hammer. He remembered how the claw end had wedged itself in the man's skull and he'd had to yank on it twice to release it. Instead of being angry, Rothstein had congratulated him, saying that he never really trusted or liked the guy anyway.

Lennox took a final glance at the photo of Beattie, and got to work counting the day's takings. He would be done by ten, when he'd drive back to Rothstein's home to deliver the suitcase. After that, Lennox would be meeting his date for a bite to eat. He'd be there by quarter to eleven.

He glanced at the photo of Beattie again...

6

Day 6
Tuesday, 16th January

Kimiko missed home; she so badly wanted to be back there, where she could embrace her mother and father. Most of all, she missed her younger sister, Fumiko, whom she adored. As Kimiko showered she tried hard not to cry, tried not to remember playing with Fumiko in the fields behind their home. This country was horrible and dirty.

Although she hated living here, she was grateful to Mrs Harrison for the chance to work and earn money – money that she sent back home to her parents through the Harrisons as soon as she'd earned it. Her family were so poor they needed every penny she sent them, and it made her feel good that she was able to help them – *really* help them.

After stepping out of the shower and reaching across for a towel, Kimiko wiped her face, her arms, her chest, her tummy, and finally her legs and feet.

She knew she had to pull herself together; Mrs Harrison would be angry if she thought she wasn't happy – grateful even – to be here. And she certainly didn't want to make her employer angry, not for a second.

"Kimiko, honey, are you almost ready? We've got a lot to do this morning," Mrs. Harrison's voice asked through the door.

"I be ready soon," she replied, her voice strained. "Five minute."

She had to hurry. Mrs Harrison hated to be kept waiting. Kimiko had to admit she didn't like her employer as a person – and would even go as far as saying she disliked her. Even more than disliking Mrs Harrison, Kimiko was afraid of her, which made her want to be all the more obedient.

Kimiko knew it could be a lot worse for her, however, as she could have been placed in the adjoining house with the support staff who were mostly Eastern European, hailing from the Czech Republic, Slovakia, Serbia, and other poorer countries. They were made to sleep in a two-bedroom cottage next to the farmhouse in horrible squalid conditions, while she had her own bedroom, access to the whole house, and the freedom to come and go as she pleased – not that she ever left the farm considering she had no access to transport.

More importantly, she could have been placed in one of the bee rooms, forced to have sex with as many paying customers as Mrs Harrison deemed fit, and Kimiko was grateful to have escaped that particular fate; if she'd been put in there she would be dead by now, her body incinerated in the huge furnace.

No, compared to the rest of the support staff and the bees, she lived a more or less pleasant life – other than the tasks she was asked to perform.

Finding her turquoise kimono in the wardrobe, she tied it around her waist, slipped on some black plimsolls, and quickly walked out of her bedroom, along the landing and down the stairs. Kimiko walked with speed, knowing that she and Mrs Harrison had chores to do before the customers started arriving. She had to wash and prepare the New Bee, Danny, and then help with Frederick.

Kimiko had a horrible feeling that something bad was going to happen to Freddie today, which was why she'd tried to calm him down the previous night. She had grown fond of Freddie since he'd arrived over five years earlier, but she had worked for Mrs Harrison long enough to know the end was coming.

In fact, it was sixteen long years since Kimiko had first arrived here, having been persuaded to come and work for the Harrisons. Had it really been so long? Where had the time gone? Fumiko would be twenty-one, she thought, imagining a beautiful, strong, intelligent young lady. Kimiko smiled, just about managing to hold back the tears.

Sixteen years earlier, Kimiko met the Harrisons when they were holidaying on her island; she'd been selling fruit on her father's stall in the centre of her village, and Mr and Mrs Harrison – who'd both been carrying backpacks and were in the process of sightseeing – stopped at her stall and bought apples for their journey. She remembered Mrs Harrison being so beautiful and glamorous, yet also friendly, and they'd soon struck up a conversation in Japanese. Her father had come over, impressed that white Westerners could speak his language so fluently, and after a long conversation, he offered them supper at their family home, as well as a place to stay for the night.

The Harrisons had been so pleasant, affable, and interesting back then. The fact they were able to speak her language fluently made them even more appealing.

A week later the Harrisons had returned, asking her father if Kimiko would be allowed to travel with them to England, to work for them. Her father – who immediately liked the idea – had asked her if she'd like to go, and although she'd steadfastly refused at the time (not wanting to leave her much younger sister) her father had persuaded Kimiko that she must go, that the extra money was needed and that this was a great opportunity for her to leave behind the poverty she'd been born into. Her mother had mirrored her father's wishes, so reluctantly Kimiko had agreed. Just one week later she'd arrived at the farmhouse.

Her adjustment to her new situation was slow, and she'd felt homesick for months after the move, although the Harrisons had been very gentle and understanding – at least for the first couple of months. Her duties back then had been those of housekeeper and maid, essentially. She'd been warned never to go into the barn, to stay in the house and around the farm. She'd groomed the horses in the stable and had mucked them out, and she'd also helped Mrs Harrison with the fruit and vegetable allotments; it had been a relatively peaceful existence during those early days. Even so, she soon noticed people parking up outside the house, the activity around the barn having increased over those first couple of months.

Then one day, Mrs Harrison asked her to follow her into the barn, and it was on that day that she realised what was going on deep under the farm. Yes, it was on that day that her true duties were revealed; she finally understood why she'd been invited to work for them.

Mrs Harrison had broken her into her new role gently, first of all just cleaning the reception area, then helping to greet customers behind the bar and getting them refreshments. Then came the real work: preparing Mrs Harrison's bees, as she called them. Kimiko was responsible for washing New Bees, and for preparing them for their customers' arrival.

The first time she'd had to prepare one of the bees, she hadn't wanted to at first. Mrs Harrison had been insistent, and when Kimiko had refused, Mrs Harrison became really angry, slapping Kimiko so hard on her cheek that her ears rang. She'd cried, not that it helped. When Mrs Harrison grabbed her and forced her to do the preparations, Kimiko knew what her future life would entail.

She'd found it disgusting at first, making sure she rinsed her mouth for at least ten minutes after. Over time, however, she'd acclimatised to preparing them. Now she did it without hesitation, sometimes even enjoying the response she received from the bees. Fortunately, she only had to prepare New Bees while they were tied up. Once they demonstrated that they would behave, they were released from their shackles and her assistance was no longer required. If a bee asked her to, it was still her duty to help them, and she always did as she was asked. How could she refuse? This was her life now.

Kimiko followed Mrs Harrison out of the house, along the paved path behind the building and over to the barn before heading down the thirty steps to the reception area. Walter and two guards were stood by the bar, as they normally did when the bees were getting ready for their first customers of the day. The support staff were busy changing the bed sheets and cleaning the rooms while the bees were showering and readying themselves for the day ahead.

"Go and get your trolley, and meet me in room five," said Mrs Harrison as she carried on walking.

"Yes, Bea," Kimiko replied dutifully.

She continued walking to the storeroom on the right, past the showers and toilets where three guards were watching some of the bees shower and relieve themselves. She left Mrs Harrison outside room five where Kimiko heard her boss slide open the hatch. She so desperately wanted Freddie to be back to normal; she hoped he had calmed down.

Having filled her plastic basin with hot soapy water, she

wheeled the trolley back along the corridor, past the toilets and showers and past the bee rooms until she reached room five.

The door was open, and Kimiko could see Mrs Harrison stood talking to Freddie.

"I'll ask that again, Freddie, are you going to behave today?"

Kimiko watched as Freddie's whole body erupted violently, convulsing as he fought against his restraints. It was like every part of him was moving at the same time; it startled her. He looked like he was having a fit, or seizure.

"Fuck you, you fucking bitch!" He coughed then spat, saliva spraying over his face and chest. "I'd rather fucking die than spend another minute here, you hear me?"

Kimiko jumped, startled, when Freddie spat in Mrs Harrison's face.

Kimiko watched as Mrs Harrison wiped her face with the sleeve of her blouse. She knew something bad was about to happen, when her employer lunged forward and slapped his face, hard. His head snapped to the side.

Hearing the commotion, Walter rushed into the room. "There a problem in here, Bea?"

To Kimiko's surprise, Mrs Harrison didn't reply; she stood there, contemplating.

Walter reached into his trouser pocket and pulled out a pair of secateurs. He then walked around to the right side of the bed, took Freddie's ring finger, and placed it inside the garden cutters. "Say the word..."

Kimiko waited for Mrs Harrison to respond. Instead of replying, her employer stood there, thinking. Kimiko didn't want to be in the room when Walter was given the green light, and she was sure Mrs Harrison would oblige. Kimiko could see how angry she was by the expression on her face; she had a slight red glow and her eyes were searching for something.

"No!" replied Mrs Harrison, finally. "We're past that now... It won't do any good."

A moment of relief swept over Kimiko as Walter relinquished his grip on the secateurs, releasing Freddie's finger. Then, however, it dawned on her what that meant.

"Kimiko, go and make a start on prepping Danny for his first customer; I'll be in shortly."

Kimiko nodded, pushing her trolley through the doorway. The last thing she heard before she left was Mrs Harrison saying, "You're going to regret that, Frederick..."

7

"Mrs Singh, I know you're in there. Please open up; I need to talk to you about your missing neighbour."

Nasreen knocked on the door one more time. Mrs Singh was the last neighbour living in the row of townhouses that she needed to speak to about Danny's disappearance.

"I don't know nothing about it," came a heavily accented voice through the door. "Don't know him. Go away!"

She turned away in frustration; it wasn't as though she was going to get any more from Mrs Singh than she had from any of the other neighbours. Danny apparently had no interaction with any of them – never said hello in passing, and never had any conversations or arguments with either of his immediate neighbours. It was a dead-end line of enquiry. Nasreen hoped Terrence had had more luck going further up the road, although she doubted it.

Nasreen glanced at her watch: eight thirty. Her partner had suggested making an early start to catch Danny's neighbours before they went to work, and it had proven fruitful (to a degree), as she'd managed to speak to all his neighbours except Mrs Singh.

It had been a frustrating four days – with only a couple of leads to follow up – and ever since being given the case, she'd thought about nothing but Danny. She didn't want her memories to be the only thing she had left of him; she wanted to find him, talk to him, to find out what had happened to him to force him to sell his body for money.

Terrence met her at the bottom of the steps.

They walked along the road toward their unmarked pool car.

"Anything?" Terrence asked, a hint of optimism in his voice.

"Nada."

Anyone walking past them would be forgiven for not thinking they worked for the police; in their navy-blue two-piece suits they could be door-to-door salespeople. Terrence was a lot taller than Nasreen; he was six feet to her five feet five. He was the kind of person the PC brigade would feel immensely proud of. He was also a very competent detective, the kind she looked up to.

Nasreen, on the other hand, had to prove she had what it took to make detective constable. Being female, Pakistani and a Muslim wasn't going to make it easy, especially as she knew the top brass would be watching her career with interest.

Only a year earlier, on her first day on the job after her promotion, she'd been told by Detective Chief Superintendent Adams that the only reason she'd been promoted was to placate the same PC brigade who were so proud of Terrence. Her promotion, therefore, was effectively an exercise in public relations; she hadn't scored the highest in the test, and he'd had several candidates who were more capable of doing the job, but their ethnicity wasn't what the top brass needed. The super had told her that she had to prove she was worthy of being called a detective and that he hoped she wouldn't let him down.

So, since day one, she'd been the first to arrive at the office every day and the last to leave. In a year, she had successfully helped close thirteen cases, including that of a serial rapist who had attacked five women; that case had garnered national media coverage, and her name had been printed in all the major newspapers. It wasn't a bad record for year one in her new role, according to her super.

"Where to now?" she asked Terrence.

"Back to the station. Adams phoned me just now to say we have a walk-in." Terrence took out his car key and held it as he walked alongside her.

"A witness?"

"He wouldn't say. He just said to get back and interview her."

When they got to their car and Terrence started driving them back, Nasreen reached inside her suit jacket pocket and pulled out her notebook. "I don't get why Danny didn't speak to any of his–"

"Danny? Did you know him?"

She cursed under her breath at her loose lips. When she'd seen the name of the victim in the briefing, her heart had literally stopped for a second. She was surprised Terrence hadn't known something was wrong by her pale face; he was a detective, after all. "I knew him a little," she replied, her head down, as if in disgrace.

"A little?" Terrence repeated, staring at her. "What does that mean? You either know him or you don't."

"We were in school together. We weren't friends or anything."

"You weren't friends?"

"Not until after school. We got together after college, when we were about twenty–"

"Jesus, you got together with him? What, like girlfriend-boyfriend together?"

"For about a year, yeah. I'm so sorry I didn't tell you earlier; I thought Adams would take me off the case if I did – I just want to help find him."

Terrence leaned back in his seat, blowing air out audibly. "Bloody hell, Nas, you should've told me before now."

"I know, I'm so sorry. Please don't write me up for this; I want to help. He's my friend; you understand that, don't you?"

"I've got to be able to trust you, Nas, you're my partner." Terrence drove around the park and stopped at some traffic lights.

"You *can* trust me. I know I was wrong to keep it from you, and I get it. I should've told you about our relationship, but I really did think I was doing the right thing at the time. I need to find him."

"Okay, I get it... I suppose I might do the same thing in your shoes," he replied, overtaking an elderly driver in front. "Promise me you won't hide anything from me again. Full disclosure, all right? I can't work with a partner I don't trust."

"I promise," she replied, gratitude etched in her voice as she sat back in the passenger seat and thought about the case. "Full disclosure."

Finally, there might be something of substance. Since Rita Abbott had phoned in Danny's disappearance five days earlier, the most they'd found were traces of blood on the other side of the park from Rita's house, and the blood could belong to anyone – or any animal for that matter. They were still waiting on forensics to confirm if it was his blood or not; they had his DNA on record after he was arrested for assault three years earlier. The blood they'd found was awaiting analysis and the results should be with them soon, according to the forensics lab.

So far, they'd managed to track most of his movements for the week leading up to his disappearance. They knew that the last person to see him was Rita Abbott. They also knew that he'd walked from his home on the other side of the park to Rita's to pick her up and that they'd taken a taxi from Rita Abbott's home into town. Rita had told them that she'd heard him leave the house at roughly half three, maybe quarter to four. They'd then surmised that he would have walked back home through the park. They had walked the quickest route to his home, which is where they'd found the blood. Nasreen hoped the DNA results came back positive, giving them something to go on.

She had to be realistic: Danny was a high-risk victim, given his line of work, as male escorts were almost as high-risk as female sex workers. However, he was a high-end male escort – meaning that it was less probable that he would come into contact with unsavoury characters – plus he was a well-built physically fit man in his thirties, so he could probably take care of himself. She'd seen his work history at the briefing; he'd started his escort business with Nagel and Nagel, which had gone bust two years earlier; since then he had taken his escorting freelance, asking his N and N clients to go with him.

They'd spoken to Claire and Eric Nagel about Danny and his work with them, and they'd been as helpful as they could be under the circumstances – up to a point. When Terrence had asked them for a client list, Eric Nagel had declined, saying that information regarding their clients was protected (especially given the kind of work they did) and that their ex-clients would probably lie to protect their reputations; after all, these were often lonely, vulnerable, and wealthy older ladies. Terrence had then informed the Nagels that he would apply to the courts for a search warrant and that they should be more concerned about their former employee. The interview had not ended well. Eric Nagel had terminated the conversation by saying "good luck in retrieving deleted data"; he'd told them that they'd shredded all documentation and deleted any digital data concerning their business.

Inside Danny's townhouse – an expensive piece of property

located in a good neighbourhood – they hadn't found much to go on. He kept a clean and tidy home, which made searching it easier than usual. Unfortunately, they'd not found anything they could use. Finding a mobile phone would have been useful, but he would probably have had his with him when he was abducted – if, in fact, he'd been abducted at all. They still couldn't be certain.

If they took the time that Rita Abbott claimed Daniel left her home as the approximate time of his disappearance, it meant that he'd been missing for six days. Nasreen had been taught that if missing people weren't found within forty-eight hours, chances were they wouldn't be found at all, or that a body would be found later – sometimes much, much later. Time, therefore, was running out; her super was already hinting at putting the Rose case on the back-burner in favour of more pressing cases that would yield closure and help bolster their force's clearance rate.

The drive to the station from Danny's address took twenty minutes in peak-time traffic, and when they got there Nasreen followed Terrence into the lift, up to the second floor, and along three corridors until they arrived at interview room five...

8

Danny's head felt much clearer. He wasn't in charge of his situation, and there was nothing he could do about it while he was chained to this stupid bed. It made him want to scream. Instead, he tried to remain calm. Danny prided himself on being a pragmatist and a problem solver.

The previous night he'd got to thinking that the main thing he needed to do was to get the lay of the land; he needed to see what was outside this room. He couldn't do that while he was chained up, so the first thing he needed to do was get out of his chains, and Kimiko had told him that Beattie let her bees out of the restraints once she believed they would behave. Since there was a rating system in place, he had to do a convincing job. There was no skating around the fact.

With his vast experience of pleasuring ladies, he had no doubt he could please anyone who paid for his services. With that in mind, he had to face facts: he had to please whoever Beattie needed him to. He hated being so helpless – while he could fight Beattie, he was a pragmatist at heart. And besides, he hated pain; he would do anything to avoid it.

The previous night he'd gone through so many different emotions; he felt like he'd gone through the various stages of grief in a matter of hours. He'd gone through shock and denial, anger and bargaining, depression and despair. He was now at acceptance; if he took any longer he would make Beattie angry and consequently incur some horrific torturous punishment, and he really didn't want that.

After hours of thinking things over, he came up with his escape plan.

Stage one was to make Beattie believe he was playing along so she felt confident enough to release his chains, and he knew he could do it; after all, he had so much experience of playing people. He played most of his clients, making them believe he loved them.

He could do this, he kept telling himself.

Stage two was to get outside that door and see what he was dealing with, to see if he could find an exit strategy. It was only part of a plan, but it was all he had.

He heard a key jiggle outside before the door opened and Kimiko wheeled in her trolley. She was dressed in a different coloured kimono from the previous day, this one turquoise with white Japanese writing. She looked freshly showered, with her slightly damp hair tied back in a ponytail. With a clearer head, she was even prettier than he remembered.

"Good morning, Danny," she said in her heavily accented voice. "I here to prepare you for first customer."

He watched as she wheeled the trolley to the left side of his bed, dipped her sponge in the warm water and wiped him down.

"Morning. How are you today?"

Kimiko wiped his chest. "I very well, thank you. How you feel today?"

"I feel fine."

"Bea here soon. You need be ready when she arrive."

"I'm all yours." He smiled, thinking that phase one was in play. He was going to charm the pants off everyone...

9

"So, tell me how you came to see this man dragging a body across the road?" Terrence asked the interviewee.

Nasreen was sat next to her superior, her notepad on the table that separated them from the witness, Valerie Chapman. She observed Valerie: she was a pretty blonde in her early twenties, well dressed, with three earrings in both ears and a silver nose stud.

"My boyfriend was dropping me home on Thursday morning–"

"What time was this?" Terrence asked, poised with his pen.

"About quarter to four. Can I continue?"

"Please do."

"We were on our way to my parents' house, going past the park, when I saw a man dragging another man across the street and into a white van. At least I think it was white, I guess it could've been beige..."

"What kind of van?"

"A white one, I just said..."

"I mean type of van; what *type* of van was it?" Terrence asked. "Was it a transit van? Something else?"

Nasreen watched the confusion form on Valerie's face. "It's helpful to know everything we can about what you saw," Nasreen told her gently.

Valerie nodded. "A transit van, I guess..."

"How many doors? Three, five?"

"How many doors? How would I know that? I'm not a van expert!"

"A three-door will open from the rear, a five-door opens from both sides and the rear. Did this man put the body in the rear or the side?" Terrence asked.

"Oh, the side. I saw it from a side angle. I think there was another man in the back of the van helping to pull the body in, but I didn't see him clearly..."

"Does that mean you saw the first man clearly?" Nasreen asked, hope in her voice. They really needed a good solid witness testimony.

"As clearly as I could, being..." Valerie's voice trailed off.

"Being what, Valerie?"

There was a long pause as Valerie looked into the distance, thinking. "My boyfriend didn't want me to come in; he doesn't even know I'm here."

Nasreen thought she knew what was troubling their witness. She'd seen it so many times before, so she tried to reassure her. "Valerie, we only want to know what you saw. We don't care if, say, you were inebriated or high on drugs at the time, okay? I promise you're not in any trouble."

Valerie took a deep breath before answering. "We went clubbing that night, so I took something. And I had some drinks too. That's why I didn't come in before. At first I thought I'd dreamt it, until I saw the missing person profile on Facebook; that's when I put two and two together."

"Please tell us about this man you saw," Nasreen pleaded.

"Okay, so I saw him dragging another man across the road as

we approached the van, only from the side. But as we passed the van, the man turned and I saw his face. He was about five foot ten, maybe six foot. He had a bald head on top but dark hair on the sides, a craggy face. He was wearing a black leather jacket and jeans... I remember he had a mean-looking face and he was well-built, stocky. Dean said he wouldn't mess with him."

"Is that everything?" Terrence was busy writing everything down.

"I think so," she replied. "Like I said, I saw a shadow in the back of the van, but I couldn't say that I saw him – not to describe anyway. I'm sorry I took so long getting here."

"Don't worry about it," Nasreen replied with a smile. "Thank you so much; you've been a big help."

She showed Valerie out of the interview room before going back and sitting down at the table. Nasreen was excited. "That's great news! We know what we're looking for now."

"I know how much this case means to you, but don't get your hopes up, Nas." Terrence was still sifting through his notes. "We've got something to go on, sure, but realistically all we have is a testimony from a wasted witness. We can't rely too much on her story."

"But the time and place fits, and she's even described the suspect."

"Hey, I'm with you, I am. All I'm saying is don't get your hopes up." His eyes told her what he thought.

She nodded her understanding. "We've got cameras all around the park, above the traffic lights. Shall we start looking for this white van?"

"Knock yourself out. I've got a meeting with Adams, so you make a start and I'll join you when I'm done..."

10

Beattie was incensed. She decided enough was enough; it was time to put an end to her ungrateful bee. Freddie had been given enough chances. It was time to find another New Bee to replace this worn-out pathetic excuse for one in front of her.

As she watched him writhe on his bed like a man possessed, anger welled up in her gut. She wanted to pummel him, to pound on him. Knowing it wasn't becoming of a lady, she instead turned to Walter. "Bring him through to the furnace room."

As Beattie strode out of the room and past cells six to ten until she reached the furnace room door, she could hear her thankless bee protesting, fighting his chains while being wheeled after her. She signalled two of her guards who were stood by the bar to help, and they obeyed, following her.

She yanked the heavy metal door to the left, her face stern, still hearing the ungrateful bee's fuming cries behind her. The two guards walked past her, went up to the huge furnace, opened the doors and stood back, waiting for Walter to wheel in the bed.

Beattie stood looking at the eight-foot long, six-foot wide

furnace, remembering the first time she'd seen it. She remembered thinking how you could probably fit three people in there, it was so big. It had been there since before World War Two and it still worked – it was even hooked up to the gas mains and would explode into life with the push of a button.

Walter wheeled the bed in and brought it to rest in front of the furnace.

Beattie listened to the bee's cries and pleas for leniency with no emotion – it happened every time. She didn't feel pity for him; she felt nothing but anger and resentment at his lack of gratitude. She could have made his life so much worse here, but no, she'd given him decent customers to service and let him live a life of luxury in his three-by-three room. Thinking about it made her even angrier.

She nodded at Walter and the two guards. They proceeded to unclip the main part of the bed from the legs. The beds in each room had been specially designed for this very purpose – to be able to slide the base into the furnace at a moment's notice.

The bee's angry cries increased in fervour as his bed slid into the massive oven, the two guards standing back as Walter closed the doors and latched it, trapping the bee inside.

As Beattie watched the bee's fingers grip the oven's slats – trying to pry it open with brute force – a smile crept over her. "Not so cocky now, are you?"

The bee went berserk trying to open the door.

Then, suddenly he stopped.

It was unnerving for Beattie, who looked at Walter.

Freddie started laughing – it was crazy, maniacal laughter.

What could he possibly have to laugh at?

The bee's laugh grated on her nerves. She couldn't remember the last time she'd felt such rage. "What the hell are you laughing at?" Her voice was bitter, angry.

The bee, however, was so busy laughing he didn't answer. He

was lying on his back, looking up at the blackened ceiling of the furnace.

She strode up to the oven as she screamed, "Tell me what's so fucking funny!" She hated swearing. It was the anger forcing her.

"In a minute I'll be dead, but I'll be rid of you!" Freddie replied.

It was in that split second – the moment directly after he said "rid of you" – that Beattie realised she couldn't go through with igniting the furnace. She had to think of what to do next, and it had to be something worse – far worse than burning him alive. He was right: it would only take a minute or two for him to die, and then it would all be over. She wanted him to suffer. But what could she do?

Then it hit her.

A smile crept over her lips again, as she turned to face the ungrateful bee. Crouching, she stared at him through the slats of the oven. "I've changed my mind," she said with a smile. "You're not going anywhere." Standing up, Beattie turned to face Walter. "Prepare a room on C Wing..."

11

Finally, Nasreen had something concrete to go on.

She was sat at her desk looking over the notes she'd made in the interview with Valerie. Nasreen needed CCTV footage of last Wednesday morning, and from as many angles as possible. The van had to have been caught on at least one of the cameras, although she tried not to get her hopes up.

When she found the number she needed, she picked up the phone and dialled. All the CCTV cameras she needed footage from were owned by the council, so using her job title she requested the digital footage be sent to her email address. She hated wading through hours of video surveillance, but she hoped the search would yield results. She wanted to see this suspect for herself.

Without hesitation, the female council worker agreed to send Nasreen the data she'd asked for. She said it would take about half an hour to collate, and send through. Nasreen thanked her and hung up.

Back in her chair, she glanced over at a photo of her daughter, Mina. The photo had been taken just one month before Ashraf – her husband – had died suddenly from a brain haemorrhage. She'd found out three months after his death that he'd known of his brain abnormality and had hidden it from her. It hurt that her partner in life felt he couldn't confide in her about something so important, so life changing. That was three years earlier.

The photo was of Nasreen holding Mina on her daughter's first birthday, by a professional photographer Ashraf had paid for as a surprise. It was a lovely photo of both her and her daughter smiling happily with no knowledge that a month later both their lives would be cruelly torn apart.

Nasreen looked at her own smiling face. She'd had a lot to be thankful for back then; she didn't now. She wanted to get back to a good place, but since Ashraf's death, nothing really had any meaning, except for Mina, and her job. Nasreen thanked Allah for her work; after the funeral she'd thrown all she had into her career. She wasn't supposed to be a widow at thirty-three – life just wasn't fair.

On the one hand, she didn't want to have to think about dating yet; on the other, she wasn't getting any younger. She was thirty-six and people had begun asking her when she was going to start dating again. The thought filled her with dread; it was bad enough before she'd met Ashraf, much less now she was a mum, and a detective.

"Any luck with the CCTV footage?"

She jolted back to reality in her chair, placing the picture back on the table. "Er, yeah, it should be coming through to my email any minute," she replied, embarrassed that she'd been caught daydreaming. "How did it go with Adams?"

"As expected, this is our last chance on the Rose case," Terrence replied. "We've had two stabbings come through Adams wants us to investigate; he thinks they're gang-related. He wants us to attend the briefing in half an hour."

"But what about the footage?"

"It's okay, I'll attend the briefing; you stay here and see what you can find. I'll brief you after. Tomorrow we're taking over from the blues."

The blues was how Terrence referred to uniformed police officers. It wasn't derogatory, just a way for him to talk about them without calling them uniforms, or bobbies. She had only been a plain-clothed officer for a year, and she'd already started talking about the blues in a less than respectful manner; it was par for the course in a hierarchical institution such as the police force.

"And if I find something, do you think he'll let us carry on investigating this case?"

"I don't know," Terrence replied, somewhat perplexed. "I know he's your friend, but you know the odds of finding him now – they're slim to none."

Nasreen shook her head. She wouldn't accept that. She had to find him; the alternative wasn't an option...

"What's going on out there?" Danny strained, trying to see what was happening.

Kimiko walked over to the door and closed it quickly.

He thought she looked nervous.

"Nothing," she replied, walking back to his bed. "Bee get ready."

It didn't sound like nothing – he'd heard a bloke screaming. When Kimiko turned her back on him, he knew he wasn't going to get anything out of her.

Instead, he leaned back and relaxed as she looked at her watch.

"It time get you ready," she said, beginning to prepare him.

"Morning, Danny," came Beattie's voice.

He hadn't heard the door open – what with enjoying

Kimiko's attention – and when he opened his eyes Kimiko stopped, stood up straight, and wiped her mouth with the back of her hand.

"Five minutes until show time," Beattie said, walking to the side of his bed and looking down at him. "How're you feeling today? I see he's up and raring to go."

"I'm fine," he replied with a smile, more from Kimiko's tongue action than as part of his plan. Either way, he was determined to charm his kidnapper. "I had a lot of time to think last night; you won't have any trouble from me."

"That's good," she said. "I understand the adjustment takes time. But I promise, if you do a good job you'll be well rewarded."

"It appears you have me in a bit of a bind," he joked, jingling his wrist chains, "so it's in my best interest to work with you here."

He saw her smile at his joke, always a good sign of rapport building. He needed her to believe him. If he went along with what she wanted, he might be out of these chains soon. Then he could work on getting out of this room and look for a way out. "So, if I'm good and perform well, how long until I get out of these chains?"

"We'll see. Soon, hopefully," she replied with a smile. "Most New Bees are out of their chains within ten days, but if you're as good as you say you will be, it could be even sooner."

"That's great news," he said, smiling inwardly.

"Two minutes to go," she said, glancing at her watch.

"Anything I should know about my first client?"

"She's really nice, but don't talk to her, it puts her off. She's very much an 'in and out' client. If you talk to her, she'll mark you down; she's done it before and I want – no, expect – you to get top marks."

"No chit-chat, got it."

"Oh, and Danny, if you get in trouble – if 'he' falls asleep – remember to think sexy thoughts, okay?"

"Got it," he said, clinking his wrist chains. "I would do a double thumbs up, but…"

He saw her smile again as she walked over to the door. Before she left, she turned to Kimiko and said, "Finish prepping him, please; he's falling asleep."

Kimiko did as she was instructed.

When there was a knock on the door, she glided over to it, opened it and greeted the woman with a bow, and then she turned to him and smiled, a good luck smile.

Danny took a deep breath.

It was time for his first official performance; he had a lot riding on it.

His first client was a woman in her early fifties. She had long brown hair hanging past her shoulders, brown eyes, and was of average looks. He couldn't tell what her body was like under the white robe she was wearing.

She untied the belt of her robe, opened the gown, and let it drop to the floor.

The woman approached his bed, climbed on, and walked on her knees until she was hovering over him…

Beattie was in her office with Walter. She'd been delighted by Danny's attitude, however she wasn't entirely convinced; it normally took bees longer than one night to adjust. She'd seen so many bees come and go that she was naturally suspicious of them all. So, she would monitor his performance. If he was genuine, he would be a big asset to the business.

Whatever happened with Danny, she still had to make sure Freddie suffered; that was what her meeting with Walter was about.

"The room's ready, the boys know what to do," he said.

Beattie nodded. "So, every three hours then. Just make sure he regrets calling me a bitch and spitting in my face." She actually hated him calling her that more than she minded him spitting at her.

"Oh, he'll regret it. You have my word on that."

"And your word means a lot to me." She squeezed his shoulder.

If there was one person she trusted, it was Walter. He'd been with them from the beginning, and he had also been involved in the nastier side of the business, something she couldn't have done without him.

Walter was from Bavaria originally. He'd moved to the UK as a teenager with his parents and two brothers. He'd been a handful as a teenager, which resulted in the inevitable run-ins with the law; he'd been arrested for assault when he was seventeen, and in his late teens he'd been arrested for burglary and then separately for affray. He'd spent a year inside for the burglary, although charges were never raised against him with regards to the assault or affray arrests. Ever since then he'd been clean.

She and Alan had allowed Walter to recruit five guards, who all lived up on the third floor of the house. Walter had recruited two friends from Slovakia, Kachmar and Filip, and three from Croatia, Borislav, Slavomir and Tomislav. All five of the recruited guards were first-generation immigrants who'd decided to move to the UK to earn money for their families still living over in their respective countries.

It was the job of these six guards to keep the bees and support staff in line; they had to chain the support staff up every evening so they didn't run off in the middle of the night; they had to check they did their jobs properly and they had to watch the bees between customers to make sure they didn't chat amongst themselves while showering and using the toilets. They performed their duties well.

Beattie had every confidence in her security team, even when they were two men down; every now and then Walter and Filip had to leave the farm to go and pick up a New Bee. It didn't happen very often – when it did, it meant the remaining guards had to pull together and pick up the slack when they were gone.

She always felt uneasy on these infrequent occasions, often expecting an escape attempt, yet in the sixteen years the business had been operating they'd only had one escape, and the bee hadn't made it out of the barn before Borislav had pounced on him. In the name of punishment, she'd ordered her guards to beat him to within an inch of his life.

The bee spent a week recovering before she'd forced him back to work, and he'd gone on to earn her money for another two years. In the end, when he'd outrun his usefulness, she'd accepted a hefty sum for a colleague of her father's to have some fun with him. Back then the violence had turned her stomach. She hadn't liked the look of the tools her father's colleague had taken in with him to the room on C Wing. The screams of that afternoon still haunted her.

"Hi, Beattie, I just wanted to thank you," came a voice from the doorway. "That was just what I needed."

She turned to find Donna Clarkson stood in her robe, her face rosy. Beattie accepted the envelope Donna handed to her. "You're welcome! How was he?"

"Worth every penny." Donna was still smiling. "That boy has talents."

Beattie smiled back. "Like I said."

"I'd like to book him for next week, if that's possible? I know you've probably told all your customers about him by now, so I don't expect to have him every week."

"We'll always find a space for you, Donna; you're my number one customer, you know that!"

Donna nodded. "I need to ask a favour though. Can he always be tied?"

"Of course! Let's set your next appointment right now."

Beattie opened her calendar to book Donna in, made some small talk, and then said goodbye. Once Donna had left, Beattie turned to the bank of monitors on her desk and looked at monitor two: Danny was busy getting washed by Kimiko, and he looked fine. Better than fine actually – he was smiling, and it looked like he was chatting away with Kimiko.

Beattie walked through to Danny's room. "I'm impressed," she said, going over to his bed. "Well done! I think one could say you impressed Donna; she's booked you in for next week, so if you play your cards right, she could be your first regular client. I have to warn you though, she's asked that you be chained up every time she visits."

"Hey," he said cautiously, "hang on a minute..."

"Relax! It's just for Donna; you're well on your way to getting those chains off. I, for one, want to see how impressed our clients will be when you start using your hands and tongue."

"Don't you want to see for yourself?"

"Worker bees don't get to touch the Queen Bee," she replied, her smile waning. "It's just the way it is. And anyway, it's your clients you need to impress; you do that and I'm impressed."

Danny nodded.

She sighed. Then she smiled again. "Anyway, I wanted to congratulate you on a good job. I'll let you finish up with Kimiko; you've got three more clients to go before we get the champagne out. The next one's in an hour and a half..."

12

It was four thirty in the afternoon before Nasreen looked up at the clock on the office wall.

The email she'd been waiting for had arrived, and she'd spent the rest of the morning searching the footage for the white transit van. Fortunately, there'd been a set of traffic lights with a camera sat on top up the road from where the suspects had parked. There was a problem: the van had been quite far away from the lights. Nasreen had seen a man dragging a body across the road, but she couldn't clearly see the suspect.

She'd asked a specialist officer if he could clean up the screen – make it crisper or zoom in – he said it was too far away. The best they'd managed to get was a blurry image of the suspect as he stared up the road towards the traffic lights.

One exciting development, which gave her hope, was identifying the van's number plate. Terrence had got straight on that, only to find out the van had been torched and left in a field five miles away. As there was a chance that trace evidence – DNA, saliva – might have been left on the van, they'd sent a forensics officer to the impound where the van had been taken. They would have to wait for the results. Terrence had told her not to get her hopes up, again. She was sick of hearing that.

The following day she would drive out to the field where the van was found, take a look around and search the area for any cameras, see if she could get a better picture of the driver and/or the passenger. The only problem was her super putting the brakes on the investigation; she and Terrence were taking over the stabbing cases as of the next day.

An additional email had been sent to her address by Claire Nagel; in it was a short message and an attachment with a client list, broken down by employee and client. The short message was an apology about her husband's behaviour.

Knowing that she'd have to investigate under the radar (and on her own time), Nasreen had written down the names of Danny's clients on a piece of paper. She'd then used the Police National Computer, PNC, to obtain their addresses. She'd managed to phone one of Danny's clients and arrange a meeting for five thirty. She had an hour to get to that address...

"That's four for four," said Beattie, carrying two glasses of champagne.

Danny smiled up at his kidnapper as she sat on the edge of his bed, putting her glass on the chest of drawers and holding the other glass to his lips.

"I have to say, you're working out better than I'd ever dreamed," Beattie said as she gave him another sip. "You now have four regulars, and all with top ratings."

It was working; it wouldn't be long now before she removed these cuffs, he thought. Then he could start planning his next move, his escape. So far, he'd seen what he took to be five guards – they were all big blokes, all Eastern European, he thought, and all wore the same black trousers and white shirts. They looked tough, and Danny could only hope he would somehow be able to find a way out of this shit situation. Yes, he still had hope.

"It's like I said earlier, Bea, I'm not going to cause you any trouble," he reiterated, as genuinely as he could. "I just want out of these chains; I want to be able to use a toilet, not the bowl and bottle anymore. I want to start feeling human again."

"Keep this up and you'll be out of these in no time," she said, offering him another sip of champagne.

It grated on his nerves that she was so attractive. He wanted to really hate her, but her smile was so engaging, so disarming, that he found himself wanting to please her.

What the hell was he thinking? This was a dangerous woman; he had to hate her.

The three customers after Donna had been a challenge. It was nothing that he and Kimiko's prepping couldn't handle – they were simply something he had to endure to get to the next stage of his plan.

"I'm really proud of you," Beattie said, offering him the last of the champagne. "This doesn't happen very often, but I guess you've adjusted quicker than I thought you would. Good for you!"

He smiled up at her. "I'm glad you're pleased."

Why did she have to be so attractive? It wasn't fair! he thought, watching her.

A part of him felt disappointed when she rose from the bed and picked up both glasses. "Wait, you're going?" he asked.

"I'm afraid so," she replied, walking to the door. "I've got a lot to do this evening. I'll see you in the morning. Good night, Danny."

He laid back and thought about escaping. He had made significant inroads with Kimiko that afternoon – he'd made her smile on several occasions and even laugh once. He was getting to know her, getting closer to asking for her help...

Beattie walked from Danny's room to the second room on C Wing. After placing the two empty champagne flutes on the floor, she pulled the latch across and peered inside. She could see Freddie curled up in a ball in the corner of the room.

The room was a three-by-three, just like the others, except this one had no furniture. The only items in the room were the wrist chains dangling from the ceiling and the ankle chains attached to the floor. Over the years the cold stony room had turned a reddish colour from all the bloodstains created by its former visitors. Beattie remembered one stain coming from the bee who'd tried escaping; her father's colleague had enjoyed that experience, but the bee had left the room in a terrible state. It had taken three of the support staff an entire day just to mop up the blood, much less actually clean it.

She couldn't resist opening the door and stepping inside.

Her face expressionless, she looked down at the bloody and bruised bee. He had bruises on his arms, legs, and ribs, and burn marks on his shoulders. He buried his head in his arms, as though protecting himself, and she could hear him crying.

"Won't be calling me a bitch again, will you?"

"Just kill me," she heard through the cries.

Crouching only a foot away, she studied him. Although he was unchained and the door was open, he was no threat to her. "Now where would the fun be in that?" she asked, with no pity or sympathy.

"I'm sorry," whispered the bee. "I'll be good. Please let me back..."

"Oh, it's too late for that." She looked down at his pathetic trembling body. "No, this is your life now."

She walked back over to the door, turned, and said, "You brought this on yourself, you know. You won't see me again. Goodbye, Freddie."

With a twist of satisfaction, she locked the door and walked past the rooms to the bar where Walter and Borislav were enjoying a pint of lager together. The four other guards were in the support staff house, shackling them in for the night.

As she walked behind the bar and poured herself a Scotch on the rocks, she caught Walter's attention. "Step up the frequency of your visits to Freddie's room, would you..."

13

Day 15
Thursday, 25th January

Kimiko helped Danny out of bed. The previous night he'd had his chains removed, and although he'd been weak at first, he enjoyed his first night of freedom to move around.

Kimiko was growing fonder and fonder of Danny by the day. She'd not met anyone like him before; he'd handled his imprisonment so well, it was almost suspicious. His adjustment seemed to delight Mrs Harrison, which was good for everyone since Freddie had died in his cell five days earlier. Freddie's body had been incinerated the following morning.

Danny was funny and seemed genuinely interested in Kimiko's story. She'd told him where she came from in Okinawa, and he asked her if she would take him there one day, when they left this wretched place. She'd smiled, telling him she would, knowing it was a lie.

She told him about how she'd met the Harrisons, about their courting her father and how she'd consequently flown over here to earn money for her family. She told him that, for the most part, the Harrisons had lived up to their word; they just hadn't told her what she would be doing for work, or that she'd be isolated on a farm, miles from civilisation. She whispered the latter part, in case Mrs Harrison was listening in her office.

Mostly though, Kimiko told him of her life growing up in Okinawa, of her parents' fruit and vegetable stall, and of course her beautiful sister, Fumiko. She tried not to cry when she spoke of her sister, but it was hard. That was all in another life. She knew she'd never be able to leave this place, not having seen what went on here.

She enjoyed spending time with Danny so much that she'd started drawing out her cleaning duties by at least half an hour – not that Mrs Harrison had noticed or cared; she seemed so smitten with Danny's progress that she didn't appear to notice Kimiko's growing fondness for the latest bee.

"Good morning, my star," said Mrs Harrison as she walked into the room, a big smile on her face. "How are you feeling today? Glad to be out of bed finally, I bet."

"You'd better believe it." He stood with her assistance.

"You've earned it. You've had an excellent few days and because of that you've demonstrated to me that you deserve a prize. Tell me what you want, and I'll get it for you – within reason, of course. And don't be asking for a phone."

"Of course not." He moved one foot, then the other. "I'd love some clothes. And a clock; I hate not knowing the time."

"Done. I'll have Kimiko get you some clothes while you're showering. Have a think and tell me what else you want. I'll get whatever you need – TV, DVD player... whatever will make your time here more comfortable."

"Thanks, I'll think about it..."

Danny's feet hurt; the pressure from finally having blood rushing to his feet was immense. It took so much energy to lift his legs, he felt as though he would never walk unaided again. He was glad to have some help, even if it was from Beattie. Trying not to smell her hair, he instead focused on Kimiko, who had been a delight ever since he'd arrived.

He felt so sorry for her; she was as much a prisoner as he was. Over the last ten days he'd tried to find out as much about her as he could, which hadn't been easy. Kimiko wasn't a natural talker, although over the last couple of days she had really opened up, telling him all about her life in Okinawa, and her subsequent life here on the farm, if it could be called a "life".

Fondness was growing, on both sides; he could tell she was growing to like him by how much more she smiled – and laughed. When he'd first arrived, her face had been deadpan, almost miserable; now it was like she was a different person, and it seemed that she carried out her duties in his room slower than she had a few days earlier.

"You know the rules, don't you?" Beattie asked. "No talking to the other bees, or the guards. You go to the loo, shower, and come straight back here. The guards won't stand for any talking."

"It's okay, I got it." Danny replied as they approached the doorway.

This was what he'd waited ten days for; he was finally going to get to see outside his room. Phase two of his plan was in play.

With Kimiko holding him on his left, and Beattie on his right, he managed to reach the doorway.

It appeared that he was in the second room in a row of ten,

and there were ten more rooms opposite. To his left was another room, then the staircase leading up to freedom, and a plush-looking bar next to it. There were a number of comfortable-looking sofas and armchairs situated in front of the bar.

To his right were eight more rooms, and right at the back of the room was a closed metal door and a smaller room that he took to be an office, which must have been where Beattie kept the monitors. It appeared that there was an offshoot on either side.

He took slow small steps, trying to take in his surroundings. He'd seen the two guards by the bar keeping an eye on him. That was the best place for guards, Danny thought. So far, no signs of weakness that he could see.

As they reached the last room – cell – on his right, he could see that the room had an extension on both sides. He tried to picture it in his head and realised that the room was T-shaped. "What's down there?" he asked, looking down the corridor and seeing five doors.

"That C wing," replied Kimiko. "You not want go inside; it very dirty."

"That's right," said Beattie. "You don't want to get put in C Wing. Carry on doing what you're doing, and you won't have to, eh?"

Danny suddenly felt a heavy feeling of dread. What were they, torture chambers? He didn't want to find out.

As they approached the toilets and showers, he asked, "And that? What's over there?"

"My, you really are curious, aren't you!" exclaimed Beattie.

"The furnace room," added Kimiko. "In winter, very good have."

By now he had a complete picture in his head of the layout, and he thought he could work with it. He wondered if the guards always stood by the bar... he guessed they would. The stairs were the only means of escape, so he would need to get the guards away from the bar area if he was to make his getaway.

"There's a free shower over there," suggested Beattie.

He took his time getting there, still observing. There were five showers and five toilets, and finally, he arrived at the fourth, having passed one woman sitting on the toilet, her head down, naked.

He sat down on the toilet and sighed. "Are they gonna watch me while I take a shit?" he asked, indicating the four guards who stood with their backs against the wall.

"They're guards, Danny, it's what they do," replied Beattie.

"But does he have to stare like that? I'm doing pretty personal things here."

He watched as Beattie turned to the guard. She made some gesture, though he couldn't see what, and the guard put his head down.

"There, happy?"

"Happy."

"You'll be okay getting yourself in the shower, won't you." It sounded more like a statement than question. "Kimiko's going to get some clothes for you. I'll see you later. Enjoy your shower, my star."

Danny watched as Kimiko and Beattie walked back in the direction of the bar, then, as he sat on the toilet, he thought how he could use this new knowledge to his advantage. He had to manufacture a way of getting the guards down this side of the room, giving him the chance to leg it up the stairs and out of this place. Once he could actually leg it, of course.

He wasn't free yet, but hope filled his heart; he would get out of here, somehow...

. . .

Beattie had calmed down considerably since Freddie's death. While she'd hoped that his suffering would last longer than a few days, she also understood that everyone had their breaking point, and Freddie's weak mental state had had a knock-on effect on his body, causing it to shut down. Her in-house physician had said as much when he'd been called to assist. The look of distaste on the doctor's face had not gone unnoticed, but she didn't care; Freddie had deserved his punishment.

While she'd lost one bee, she'd found a far more superior bee in Danny. She was still suspicious of his speedy adjustment – he seemed too eager to please, in her opinion – but she was playing along with him in any case. After all, he was earning her more money than the other bees, Beattie having increased his hourly fee by two hundred pounds an hour; to seven hundred, which her clients were more than willing to pay.

She'd had an eventful and busy few days with work, and on top of that she'd had a charity fundraiser to organise through the country club she was a member of; God only knew how she'd managed to get roped into that. Her father had always recommended getting involved in charitable causes; it made them seem more like regular people, and her family were far from regular folk.

In addition to that, she had a hen party to attend for a friend at the club, though she used the term "friend" loosely – she was a fellow member and not exactly someone she would invite round for afternoon tea.

She could feel the distance between her and Alan growing. It seemed like he was talking less these days and testing his girls more. His social life had been hectic too; he'd only slept at home three nights out of ten, a record. Beattie had been forewarned of the sleepovers in advance, but alarm bells were ringing; just because she knew of his sleeping arrangements, it didn't mean he wasn't sleeping with someone else.

If she were being honest with herself, it wouldn't kill her to find out he was having an affair. In fact, it might even be a blessing; she'd be able to kick him out of their home and business, and every penny they earned would go in her pocket, not their joint account. Then again, running both sides of the business would be pushing it somewhat – the stress of organising twenty bees would kill her.

Her father had visited the previous night, and stayed for supper. He'd brought along Lennox Garvey, his right-hand man, who'd used the time to have dinner and collect the day's take. While Lennox was out counting the takings, her father had informed her that he'd received a warning from an insider that an investigation had been launched by the National Crime Agency against his businesses; they were apparently looking into all his ventures – legitimate and the not-so-legitimate.

She had asked her father if they were in any trouble, and he allayed her concerns with a simple wave of his hand, telling her not to worry. He'd then asked them to keep an eye out for anything unusual – cars following them, suspect phone calls and the like – as a precaution; it didn't hurt to be extra vigilant, he'd told her. He had also said to be careful when accepting new customers, and even went on to add that he would personally vet every new customer from now on; the last thing they wanted was an undercover cop under the barn.

It wasn't long before Beattie was walking Danny back to his room, and when she got there she saw that Kimiko had folded a pair of jeans, a T-shirt, some pants and some socks, leaving them neatly displayed on his bed. The look of joy on his face upon seeing the clothes amused her. It was the simple things, she thought.

She watched Danny dress himself. "You know you'll be getting out of those in less than an hour," she said, noting that the time was eight thirty. "And you'll be tied up for this one; it's Donna's weekly visit."

"I know. I'm just getting used to wearing them again, that's all."

She nodded. "Okay then, enjoy your clothes. I'll get more sent down later; get you a wardrobe together. You can look through some catalogues too. And remember, anything else you need, let me know and I'll get them delivered..."

14

Lennox Garvey felt Gemma's warm body beside him. When his mobile phone buzzed on the bedside cabinet, he picked it up, glanced at the caller, and then noted the time. It was quarter to nine and he wasn't due to meet Rothstein until midday; he wasn't late for anything.

"Mornin', what's up?"

"I know you were supposed to go to the farmhouse tonight, but there's been a change of plan. I need you here for eight, okay?"

He listened carefully, though he really wanted to just lie-in with the previous night's pickup. "Sure thing, what's at eight?"

"A friend of ours has a proposition. He says we won't want to miss out. He made it sound worth our time; just something in the way he said it. I want you here in case it has anything to do with your uncle."

"You got it. Do you still want me over at noon?"

"No, have the rest of the day off. See you at eight."

Lennox hung up and placed his phone back on the chest of drawers next to his bed. Then he settled back down under the duvet.

Gemma groaned softly, rousing herself. "Who was that?" she asked, her voice sleepy.

"No one; my boss. Go back to sleep."

He'd had a busy few days helping Rothstein with finding a dealer who owed him money. This particular associate was a high-value customer, and up until a couple of days earlier, he'd always paid in full and on time. Rothstein had been more concerned than angry, not believing his customer would be so stupid as to steal from him. So, Lennox had been dispatched to find him.

Two days earlier Lennox had tried all the usual dealer's haunts, including a club owned by a friend of his. The club was a goldmine for his target, so if he were to find him anywhere, it would be there. Lennox had searched the whole place – the dance floor, the toilets, the mezzanine level chill-out zone, everywhere – and found nothing.

Earlier in the day he'd tried the dealer's flat. He hadn't answered, and his car hadn't been parked outside. After going to the club, Lennox had decided to try the flat again, and after seeing the car was back, he walked up to the front door to find it ajar, which it hadn't been earlier. He'd decided, reluctantly, to enter, putting on gloves before opening the door.

Inside he'd searched the flat room by room until he'd found the dealer's body sprawled out on the bedroom floor. He had been shot in the eye, through a pillow used to muffle the sound. The pillow had been left on the bed, a gaping hole in the middle of it surrounded by blood, the feathers from inside strewn all around and over the body.

Lennox had immediately taken out his mobile from his jeans pocket and dialled his boss's number. "I've found him. But we got a problem."

In code he'd relayed the situation to his boss, who told him to get out of there. He'd done as his boss had insisted and left the flat, leaving the door ajar as he found it. He'd then driven his Shogun back to Rothstein's home and the two of them had talked about possible reasons for the murder, and several suspects to look into. Rothstein believed this was just the beginning.

Three nights before he'd found the dealer dead in his home, Lennox had taken Rothstein's boat out to the rendezvous point, picked up the month's shipment, and the captain had steered the boat back to port under the cover of darkness. It was his uncle's consignment of uncut cocaine, and it was Lennox's job to collect it. Everything had gone like clockwork, as it did every month. He'd also handled other business dealings too.

His wasn't exactly a good life. It was the only life he knew, never having attended school in Jamaica – not properly anyway. He'd learned everything he needed from his uncle, who was more like a father to him, since his parents had been murdered in their home when he was just eight. He could vividly remember hearing the five shots fired, waiting by the stairway bannisters for a few minutes – his little heart racing – and then finding them sprawled out and bloodied on the sofa in the lounge. His father had been shot three times, twice in the chest and once in the forehead, while his mother had been shot once in the chest and once through the right eye. Lennox could remember the blood – there was so much blood. He had called his uncle – who'd come immediately – and ever since that day, Lennox had lived with him and learned from him.

Gemma turned over and cuddled up to him, her leg over his. He put his arm out and she accepted the invitation. He felt her hand stroking him. "Don't you want a shower first?" he asked. On the one hand he loved sex in the morning; on the other, he hated morning breath. When she kissed him, he reciprocated. It would be rude not to...

15

Nasreen Maqsood had had a busy few days with the stabbings cases, which had turned out to be gang-related, as everyone had assumed it was. They'd spent hours interviewing witnesses to the stabbings. It had been time-consuming and traumatic for all those involved, including her and Terrence.

For the first time in a few days, Nasreen found herself with a little time on her hands, so she sat down at her desk and took out her file on Danny's disappearance. As she'd added lots to it through her own investigating, she had to hide it from both Terrence and Adams.

As per Terrence's prediction, Danny's case had been dropped the day they had taken over the stabbings cases; no one had been assigned to it thereafter. As a result, his case had only six days of live investigative work attached to it, which made her angry. A person's life was apparently worth less than the force's clearance rate.

Carefully taking out the papers, she flipped through them one by one.

The forensics tests on the burnt-out van had turned up

nothing. There were no hairs, no fibres, no fingerprints, not even partial prints. There was no sweat or blood traces anywhere inside the van either, even though Danny had bled in the park. It was definitely the same van that had been used to abduct Danny though, as she had managed to catch the licence plate through cameras near the site of the burned van.

She had an even better picture of the driver – the man Valerie had described – and the passenger, which had been taken using the same camera near the scene of the burned van. So, Nasreen now had faces and a number plate, but all this proved unfruitful, as the facial recognition software they used had turned up nothing, and the van had been reported stolen from a house fifty miles away.

Nasreen typed "male escort agencies, UK" into Google and waited for it to load. She needed more knowledge of the industry if she was to carry on with her private investigation.

The first three entries were for agencies called Gentlemen4U.com, Beescorted.co.uk and the Beemanescortagency.com. Gentlemen4U.com was apparently a strictly "no extras" legitimate escort agency, promising escorts for dinner dates, weddings, work functions, and the like. The website looked professional and described how to become an escort by applying within. The men appearing on the website were advertised as real, and she found them appealing, yet none of them were as good-looking as Danny, not by a long shot. Although, of course, she was biased.

The second website, Beescorted.co.uk, was an entirely different service. It advertised the men on their site as being typical escorts, good-looking men willing and able to take their clients' fantasies and make them real. They were unabashed about advertising the fact that sex was on the table. She wondered how the website even stayed up, it was so obvious.

Continuing her search, Nasreen found that the majority of the sites were similar to Gentlemen4U – not actively advertising sex for money – however, she did wonder how true it was in the real world. What was advertised on their web pages wasn't necessarily what the users experienced, she suspected.

Out of interest she typed in "Nagel and Nagel Escorts" and waited for it to load.

To her surprise, their website popped up on her screen. A purple and yellow background framed a picture of Eric and Claire Nagel, with flashy writing of the company's name. The blurb beneath the name stated that theirs was a legitimate enterprise, with a strict "no sex" policy. Nasreen knew that was a lie, so she thought that they probably all had to say "no sex policy" on their site.

Nasreen knew that no more would be forthcoming from Eric or Claire Nagel; they'd already sent her their client list. She had already interviewed two of Danny's former clients and had another one booked in for that evening at seven. She hadn't learned anything new from the two she'd interviewed, but she was hopeful she might that night.

She scrawled down the numbers of the three agencies listed on the previous page and put them inside her suit jacket pocket; she would call them later and hopefully arrange interviews. She just wanted to gain an understanding of what really happened on these escorted dates.

When she heard Terrence's voice coming from a distance, Nasreen quickly shuffled the papers back into her folder and shut them away in her lockable drawer. He appeared in front of her. She'd managed to sneak them in.

"Hey, you ready?" he asked, beckoning her to follow him.

"When you are," she replied, standing. While his back was turned, she bent down and quietly jiggled the drawer to make sure it was locked.

Having pretty much achieved all they could with the stabbings, Adams had a new investigation for them to commence. All she wanted to do was look for Danny...

16

After fifteen days of captivity and being chained to his bed, Danny's first client as a "free" bee had been Donna, so he'd spent half an hour chained up again. She was certainly a creature of habit; she'd entered the room, dropped her robe, and climbed on top of him – no words, just in and out. The only difference between this time and the last was that she'd turned to him as she'd reached the door and said, "Thank you, Danny, that was wonderful."

He'd walked naked, under escort by Kimiko, to the toilet and shower area and had soaked himself for a good half hour. He'd thought about his former life, what he would be doing now if he was out. He thought about his clients, and then Kimiko crept into his head. Why was he thinking about her? He had no feelings for her; he was only getting close to her so he could persuade her to help him escape.

On the way back to his room – this time without Kimiko's aid – he observed the goings on outside. It seemed as though the guards spent all day by the bar – not drinking, just standing around – not good news for any potential escape. They were big blokes, and while Danny wasn't small by any means, he would have trouble with one of them, let alone six. He would have to bide his time.

Having dressed and eaten the gruel they called food, Danny spent the last hour sitting on his bed, meditating. He'd started meditating after his sister, his last remaining relative, had moved to Ottawa; it was his way of keeping calm when he felt anxious. And although he put on a brave face, he was always anxious in this room.

He opened his eyes when he heard the jingle of keys in the lock, and a second later the door opened. When Kimiko entered, he knew what time it was: client number two of six for the day. "That time already, huh?"

Kimiko replied, "Five minute," as she pulled his jumper over his head and unzipped his jeans, pulling them off his legs.

He lay back in just his underwear, watching as she folded his clothes and placed them neatly on the chest of drawers.

"You take off pants?" she asked politely.

"How about I let you do it?" He grinned as he lay still.

"Okay," she replied, pulling his pants down to his ankles.

Danny lay back with his hands behind his head – now at full attention – then watched as a woman came in and waited while Kimiko left. She was in her forties with shoulder-length curly brown hair. She was about five feet six. "Hi!" he said, stroking the sheets. "Come and join me."

She de-robed and stood for a second or two before joining him on the bed.

He moved onto his side as she lay on her back, and then he rubbed her belly, letting his hand move further south with each rub. "What's your name, sweetie?"

She closed her eyes, and he could hear her breathing getting deeper as she replied, "Grace."

"And what would you like me to do now, Grace?"

"Keep going," she replied through a delighted sigh, "please."

Using his skills, Danny carried out her wish until he heard her say, "Kiss my neck."

He leaned in and kissed the nape of her neck.

She leaned in too, her mouth just centimetres from his ear as she whispered ever so slightly, "Act normal, I have something to tell you. Cameras are watching, so please behave as normally as you can."

He gulped. "I'm listening."

"I'm an undercover police officer."

He wanted to yell with joy, almost forgetting where he was.

"Act normal, or they'll see us talking." She was still whispering. "Go on top; it's easier for us to talk. Keep your head in my neck."

He couldn't believe it! Was this really happening? Could he really be getting out of here? Did she have backup waiting outside, waiting for her signal? He'd watched too many cop shows maybe. Still, he could hope.

He took a couple of deep breaths before mounting her.

"We've been trying to penetrate Beatrice Harrison's operation for months, but we haven't been able to get inside her network until now." Grace pulled him closer. "We've been investigating multiple disappearances over the years and it's all led back to here."

He listened, while acting casual, wanting to snigger at the use of the words penetrate and inside, given where they were. It was too serious a situation.

"The only problem is we have no tangible proof, so I've had to come here as a customer and do this."

"How soon can you get me out of here? I've been in this place for over two weeks now... I *have* to get out," he added, kissing her neck for appearance's sake.

"It won't be long now – a couple of days tops, I promise," she said, her voice broken by an approaching fake orgasm.

"You're doing a great job," she whispered. "Now make it convincing when we finish. What do you do, cuddle up with your customers afterwards? Whatever you do, do it with me. If I get caught, Beatrice *will* kill me."

"They normally just get up and go. Say something nice and leave. And please give me a good rating, or my life won't be worth living."

She kissed him, then unwrapped herself from him.

"That was fantastic, Danny," she said as she stood up. "I'm going to book with you again, rest assured." She winked at him, picked up her gown, and wrapped herself up. "See you soon."

He watched her as she left the room, his mind all over the place. He knew he had to calm down. He so badly wanted out he could hardly breathe – how long would it be before the police raided this hellhole? Taking three long deep breaths, he lay back, staring up at the ceiling. He prayed to himself in his head.

A few seconds later the door opened and Beattie walked in, flanked by three guards. Behind the guards came Kimiko, and finally Grace. He was confused; what were they all doing here?

"Well, well, Danny," said Beattie. "Won't be having any trouble from you, huh?"

He saw the three guards start to move towards the bed. He sat up and, seizing his chance, jumped up and flew towards the open door. Unfortunately, he couldn't avoid one of the guards.

Two pairs of hands grabbed him and pulled him back to the bed. He fought them with every ounce of strength, screaming a feral scream. Then a third pair of hands grabbed him.

They were far too strong; as much as he struggled, they overpowered him, pinning him down and wrapping the cuffs around his ankles, wrists, and neck until he was in the same position he'd started this whole nightmare in. He struggled against the chains.

"You think you're really clever, don't you?" Beattie stared

down at him, her face angry and flustered. "I knew you hadn't adapted. Your transition was far too quick, Danny. No one comes to terms with it that quickly."

He watched as Beattie put her arm around Grace's robed shoulders. "She's wonderful, isn't she? Not bad for an amateur actor; worthy of an Oscar, I'd say."

"*Fuck you!*" he hissed.

Beattie stepped up to his bed. "I knew you were plotting to escape. I've been doing this a long time, so I know my bees and how they react. Now I've got to break you down. And I *will* break you down, you can believe *that*."

"I meant what I said, Danny, I'll be booking with you again real soon." Grace laughed. "You *are* a fantastic fuck. Though maybe you can choose the role play next time."

Beattie, Grace, and the three guards laughed. Kimiko had her head down, her hair covering her face. He fought against the chains again, as though sheer physical force would break them.

"Go ahead, Danny, get it out of your system," Beattie said. "By this time next week you'll be mine. As punishment, you're going to have the worst week of your life... and after the week's up, we'll see how compliant and grateful you really are. It's my biggest hate, you know, my bees being ungrateful."

Anger welled up in his chest. "Grateful? For this? You're a fucking psycho!"

One of the guards walked over and punched him on the cheek, snapping Danny's head sideways as blood sprayed the pillow.

"No! There's no need for that!" Beattie shouted, forcing the guard to back off. "I don't want my star bee all battered and bruised for tomorrow's clients."

When he turned his head back, Beattie was looking down at him with a grin he really didn't like the look of. It was devious, evil. "What's that supposed to mean?" he asked.

"You've had a taste of our classier, more sophisticated clientele, like Grace here; now I'm going to show you the other side of our business. And you're not going to like it, not one bit..." The grin got wider. "By this time next week, you'll be begging me for your old clients back."

Danny froze. The guards were there all day as far as he could tell, the door was always locked, Kimiko was too scared of Beattie to betray her and help him... the only way he was getting out of here was by being rescued somehow, or by death.

As he lay there, exposed – with Beattie, Grace, Kimiko, and the three guards watching him – he suddenly thought that death didn't sound like such a bad option after all.

Five minutes after being left alone, the air conditioning unit changed its whirring sound. It took him just a few seconds to realise it was blowing cold air...

17

Nasreen parked her red Ford Fiesta on the street outside Francesca Belmont's modern four-bedroom detached house. It was five to seven and she was off the clock. She took her badge and notebook with her to make it look official.

She'd had some luck phoning the escort agencies and had managed to talk the owner of Gentlemen4U.com into an interview. She'd told the owner, a woman called Theresa Gaffney, that she was looking to find out more about the industry – that she wasn't looking at her company for any wrongdoing.

She'd then mentioned the disappearance of Daniel Rose and that she was investigating the case. Theresa had told her it wasn't unheard of for male escorts to go missing; she alone had lost two very good-earning employees through mysterious disappearances. This had excited Nasreen, and she'd asked Theresa if she could take the details of the two escorts. Theresa had said she would have the information ready for when Nasreen came to her office the following day, though she did warn her that the police had already investigated.

Nasreen walked up to Francesca Belmont's blue front door, pressed the bell, and looked around at the other houses while she waited. It was dark, but the streetlights were good. Francesca Belmont's house was like every other house on the street, right down to the front porch. She wondered why people would want identical houses; her house was unique, and she loved that about it.

The door opened, and she was greeted by a very well-dressed woman in her mid- to late-sixties. She was surprised at how elderly she was; she'd expected Danny's clients to be a bit younger. The two previous clients she'd spoken to were in their fifties.

"You must be the detective," started Francesca. "I'm sorry, dear, I forget your name."

"Nasreen," she replied with a polite smile. "Nasreen Maqsood."

"Won't you come in, please?" asked Francesca, opening the door wider.

Nasreen stepped in and waited while the elderly lady walked along the corridor with her back slightly hunched, asking her to follow. Nasreen was offered a cup of tea, which she kindly refused, then she followed Francesca through to the lounge where she was offered an armchair.

"Now then, dear, what did you want to talk about?"

When Nasreen saw how black Francesca's teeth were, she couldn't help but flinch they were so nasty. And the smell! It smelt like rotting flesh; it was rancid and offended her nostrils. Hoping her face didn't give her away, she was surprised that this was one of Danny's clients. The old woman wasn't like the other two. Francesca even dressed like an elderly person; she was wearing a thick floral dress, stockings, and hideous slippers. A thinner Nora Batty sprang to mind.

"I'm looking into the disappearance of Daniel Rose,"

Nasreen started, "a friend of yours, I believe? I was hoping to find out a bit more about him."

"There's not a lot to say really." Francesca shrugged. "We went out on a dinner date not so long ago; he was great company. My husband died, you see, and I wasn't getting out much. A friend of mine gave me his number, said he was a lovely man."

Nasreen nodded. "So, where did you go? Some posh restaurant?" she asked, genuinely interested to see where Danny would take this old dear.

"It was lovely, a place on the high street... I forget the name. It's so annoying when you can't remember all the details. Anyway, he was just the perfect gentleman, and a hell of a looker too. I tell you, if I'd been twenty – or thirty – years younger." She winked.

"So, you didn't...?" Nasreen regretted asking straight away.

"Oh no, dear, I'm far too old for that. I invited him in for coffee – I remember because he was in here when he got a phone call – and then shortly after that he had to leave. Something about his mother having a fall and having to go to the hospital. That's right, I remember now, poor thing."

This neither confirmed nor denied anything. Francesca had invited Danny in for a drink, but then he'd lied about his mother having a fall – Nasreen knew this because she knew his mother had been dead for years. It sounded like sex had been in the offing and Danny had backed out. She wasn't surprised at that.

After a few minutes of chat, she decided she'd heard enough. It was another dead end, like the previous two clients. She'd not learned much more about Danny, other than there were limits to who he'd sell his body to. She was thankful for that, at the very least.

Nasreen asked Francesca if she knew of anyone who would

wish Danny harm. The old lady said that as far as she knew, everyone loved Danny. No help there either.

Itching to get away from the offensive odour surrounding Francesca, Nasreen asked a couple more questions, before needing to breathe fresh air. "Anyway, thank you for sharing that with me," Nasreen said as she stood up. "And if you think of anything else, please give me a call." She handed her a card.

When Francesca made to get up, Nasreen said, "No, please, Mrs Belmont, there's no need to show me out. I remember the way. You have a lovely evening."

It was quarter past seven by the time Nasreen got back in her car, and as it would take her an hour to drive home, she thought she might make it in time for Isha prayer at her mosque. Adding to that, she really wanted to see Mina too. She felt bad about how much time she was missing with her daughter. Work had to be a top priority though, especially now she was a single mother.

Although the meeting with Francesca had proven uneventful, Nasreen was still hopeful about tomorrow's meeting with Theresa Gaffney, of Gentlemen4U.com. As far as she knew, there were a possible two more missing persons cases.

As Nasreen drove through the dimly-lit suburban roads, she kept thinking there could be a link... or was she just hoping there was? At least if there was a link between Danny and these other two investigations, there might be more she could get from them to help her find him.

On the one hand, both the other cases had been investigated already and nothing had been found. But on the flip-side, *she* hadn't been on the other two inquiries...

18

Kimiko closed the hatch to Danny's room and sighed. Mrs Harrison had turned the air conditioning unit down to eight degrees, and she'd left him shivering, goosebumps all over his arms and legs. He would be left like that until the morning, when Mrs Harrison would switch it back up, ready for the first customer. She'd done this to several bees as punishment over the years, and mostly it was effective.

Kimiko hated seeing Danny suffer; she'd tried to comfort him for the past hour or so. He hadn't said a word to her. She guessed he was mentally adjusting to his situation.

With a letter in her hand, Kimiko walked down to the office and knocked on the door.

Mrs Harrison answered. "Kimiko, you're down here late."

"Excuse me, Bea, but I have letter to my family."

She handed the note – still not sealed – to Mrs Harrison. Each month Kimiko wrote a missive addressed to her father, as Mrs Harrison had suggested she do when she'd first arrived. All those years earlier she'd written a page a day, which soon went down to a letter a week, and now it was – if she could manage it – one a month. Mrs Harrison always read them before sending them. Sometimes Kimiko thought it was such a shame her benefactor could read and speak her language. It gave her no privacy. She wanted so badly to ask her father to come and get her. Time had taught her that it was impossible.

Mrs Harrison accepted it, waited a few seconds, and asked, "Is there anything else, honey?"

With her head down, Kimiko asked quietly, "Why you trick Danny?"

Mrs Harrison gently pulled Kimiko's chin up with her fingers, and smiled. "I didn't trick him, honey, I tested him." Then, opening the door wider and waving her in, Mrs Harrison beckoned her inside.

Shuffling her feet, Kimiko stepped into the office.

Mrs Harrison offered her a seat, which she accepted. Her employer pulled her chair close to hers so that they were staring at one another. "You see, Kimiko, Danny hasn't adapted yet. All New Bees need to have time to accept that they're here, that they work for me now. Danny failed the test; he just needs more time to adjust. But he will, you'll see."

"He a nice man," Kimiko said.

"You like him, don't you?" Mrs Harrison asked in a funny manner. "I understand. I know he seems like a nice man, but I'm warning you that he isn't what he seems."

"But–"

"No buts, Kimiko, he's not a nice man!"

Kimiko frowned. She didn't understand why Mrs Harrison was saying that.

"You know, all my bees are liars. It's what they do for a living; it's how they make money out there on the streets. They use their looks, and their... you-know-whats... to make money. And they do this by making innocent women believe they love them. It's why I chose them to work here; they're perfect for the job. I don't say this to be harsh, Kimiko, but Danny doesn't like you; he's using you."

Kimiko shook her head. "Danny would not–"

"He's using you!"

Mrs Harrison's tone changed, and Kimiko knew what that meant.

"Right now," Beattie continued, "he's probably thinking that he needs to get close to you, and soon he'll ask you to betray me. You're free to wander around here, you're not under guard, and you could certainly use this phone when I'm not around to phone the police... but it would be a mistake, Kimiko, a big mistake."

"I never betray you," Kimiko said, her voice frightened. "You been good to me."

She felt Mrs Harrison's hand rub her shoulder. "I know you wouldn't, honey, because you're loyal. It's why I love you."

Kimiko was lost for words.

"Come here, you." Mrs Harrison wrapped her arms around her.

They embraced. Kimiko's mind raced.

Mrs Harrison had never said she loved her before. Did she expect her to say it back? Would she take offence if she didn't reciprocate?

Finally, mid-embrace, Kimiko managed to say, "I love you too..."

19

Lennox opened the office door, greeting Zack and Neil Astor with handshakes before letting them in and ushering them through to their seats across from William Rothstein.

Lennox took his seat next to his boss, but further back and to the side; he wasn't considered equal to the other men at the meeting – he was just an employee.

Rothstein commenced the meeting with the usual "Would you like a drink" routine, talking about families and other inane drivel while he made them all Scotch on the rocks from the bar to the right of his desk. For some reason, Rothstein liked making the drinks.

After handing each of them a glass, he sat back down.

His boss was a tall man, about six-one, and thickly set with a full head of white hair, which belied his age – he was only fifty-eight. He'd had Beattie when he was fifteen, which had caused quite a stir back then. He was always immaculately dressed, just as he was that night. Lennox had heard so many stories about Rothstein from other employees – his colleagues – and none of them good either.

Back when Rothstein had been in his early twenties, he'd

already acquired a reputation as a prolific drug dealer. He'd pummelled his competition into submission, is the way he heard it. By the age of twenty-five, he had murdered six people, one of them – an innocent civilian woman – having died in the crossfire. People were so frightened of him that the police had never found anyone brave enough to testify against him.

He'd started importing when he was in his late twenties, knocking all the aggro that came with street dealing on the head. He'd started thinking smarter, had rid himself of his coke habit, and looked after his family. By this point in Rothstein's life, Beattie would have been about fourteen or fifteen, and she was beginning to ask questions about why people seemed so afraid of her.

In all the years Rothstein had been in business, he had not been sent down, charged, or even cautioned by the police. Lennox often wondered how he'd managed it, as psychotic as he was.

When he was in his forties, Rothstein had bought his first fixer-upper to renovate, which was how his property development business had started. By then he owned properties up and down the country: houses, blocks of flats, factories, office buildings. He outright owned two nightclubs, hotspots where the rich and famous went, safe they would not get bothered. Then, of course, Rothstein owned the blood bunker, as Lennox called it.

He observed the two guests as they continued.

Zack Astor was in his late fifties, about six foot with grey hair. He was huskier than Rothstein and might have one over on him in a fist fight – or he would if not for Rothstein's psychotic streak. Lennox would bet his money on his boss, every day of the week. Dressed in a light grey suit, Astor didn't spend as much money on clothes as Rothstein, though he still looked smart.

Lennox had heard stories about Zack Astor too. He'd grown up with an alcoholic father and a skaghead mother; not much of a start in life, but he'd gone on to be the biggest dealer in his neck of the woods, and like Rothstein, he had managed to stay out of prison.

He'd married a woman from a decent family, who'd managed to ground him, and Zack and Zoe had gone on to have two children, Neil and Olivia. Then they'd adopted their youngest, Ryan.

Lennox had met Neil on a few occasions and always found him friendly. He was quieter than his dad, more reserved. He was a plumber by trade, but outside of work he handled his dealers under a cloud of secrecy; he was the new breed, who knew that operating stealthily was the key.

Lennox met Neil's blood sister once, at a wedding of a mutual colleague, and he'd been smitten with her immediately. She was stunning, with long ginger hair, pale skin, and a killer body. He had had his fun with her in the toilets of the hotel. She was sweet.

But the real story was Ryan, and Lennox wished he knew more about that. He'd asked Rothstein what the deal was, but Rothstein told him that some stories should never be told – which, of course, had intrigued Lennox even more. All he knew was that Ryan knew nothing of their affairs and that the whole family did everything they could to shelter him from the truth, not even telling him that he was adopted. Apparently, Neil had hospitalised the one person who'd ever tried implying that he wasn't really an Astor. Lennox wished he knew that story.

"So, what's this proposition you have for me, Zack? It sounded interesting," Rothstein asked as he leaned forward, his elbows on the oak desk.

Zack Astor leaned forward too. "Shit! I don't even know where to begin. Okay, here goes. We got a visit from some bloke at the house, claimed to be some big-up cop, an assistant commissioner or some shit. Second in command of his area, he said, something like that."

"Right," Rothstein drew out the word as though he were confused.

"Anyway, he asks to come in, so I let him in, offer him a drink and all that..."

Rothstein raised his eyebrows. "This cop, you just let him into your home?"

"Wait, hear me out, you won't regret it," Astor insisted. "So, we're sitting at my dining room table, drinks in hand, and he starts telling me all about how he's devoted his life to law and order, and how he wants to leave a legacy after he's gone."

"Okay, so he's chatting you up."

"Wait! So, he starts telling me how the current system doesn't work, and how systems in other countries *do* work. And then he hits me with it... He wants to legalise drugs and prostitution."

Lennox watched as Rothstein leaned back in his chair.

His boss didn't look happy, not one bit.

"You what!" Rothstein exclaimed.

"He's going to start off small, which is why he's come to me, and others."

"What do you mean, start off small?"

"He wants to trial it in certain areas first, areas where he has colleagues with the same way of thinking. He wants us to work for the government; we'll carry on doing what we're doing, with no risk of getting pinched."

"And what does he get out of it?"

"Arrests, Will, lots of arrests. That's the best part – he wants us to drip-feed him our competition. He wants one dealer per area, that's it. Everyone else gets nicked. As far as the public's concerned the police look good, they get a percentage of our take, and we get to do what we do unhindered. It's a win-win situation. Well, win-win-win situation actually."

Lennox thought about the proposal for a minute: it was clever, it helped the police, it helped them, and what the public didn't know wouldn't harm them. Other countries had legalised drugs and prostitution, and they had some of the safest gear around. Not to mention that the prostitutes were safer in those countries than here in the UK.

"Let's say he's right, he's kosher... how's he going to do it without people finding out?" Rothstein seemed intrigued.

"I'm telling you, I asked him a bunch of questions; I thought he was taking the piss. He said this has been planned by the top people at the Home Office, the Department of Justice and other agencies, then it's been fed down to the most senior people in the police. His boss had to test him on the idea, and he's tested people under him. So only the big dogs know, not the rank and file pricks on the streets. He's promised that if we agree, they'll make sure no one pinches us for anything. We'll be above the law, Will, think about it."

Rothstein shook his head. "This sounds like bullshit to me, Zack. And what's more, you're falling for it."

"Hey, I'm not a stupid man."

"I know you're not, which is why this is so baffling. It's entrapment, mate, can't you see that? By having the conversation, you're all but admitting you're a dealer."

"This isn't entrapment, Will. You weren't there. He handed me this, for starters."

Lennox watched as Zack Astor pulled out a card and handed it to Rothstein. It had the police insignia on it and details of the card's owner.

"Look him up! He's legit, right up there, assistant commissioner. He's working for the Secretary of State for the

Home Department – or some nonsense – and the Minister of Justice."

"And when you say we, did you mention my name?"

Lennox watched as Zack Astor put his palms out in a placating manner.

"Hey, wait, hang on, Will, of course I didn't," he pleaded. "I wouldn't do that to you."

Rothstein sighed. "This all sounds too far-fetched. It makes sense, sure – to us. If we could do what we do without recourse, that'd be great, but it isn't going to happen."

"It is, Will, it really is. This *is* happening – not straight away, but it will. When this guy comes to see you, listen to him, for your own sake. If he decides to go with another supplier, well, it's curtains, isn't it! Your competition won't think twice about shopping you, will they?"

Lennox sat back as everyone went quiet.

Finally, Astor went to stand and said, "You can keep the card. Look him up, you'll see he's real."

When he reached the door, Zack turned and said, "I really hope you see sense, and get on board. We've been through a lot together; I don't want the journey to end here."

Rothstein closed the door behind them, turned around, and looked at Lennox. "What do you reckon, Lenny?"

"If it's real, you don't have a choice. Why? What do you make of it?"

Rothstein stared into the distance for a moment. "Zack's a lot of things, but he's not a liar, and he's not stupid..."

20

Day 16
Friday, 26th January

Beattie looked down at the monitors, noticing something strange in room eight. She heard raised voices outside. Christopher, one of her bees, was crouched in a ball on the bed, rocking back and forth, his knees pulled into his chest. Cara – one of her most regular customers – was standing there naked, shouting and pointing at him.

Beattie sighed as she muttered, "What now?"

Outside in the hallway that separated the two sets of rooms, one of her support staff, Enrieta from Romania, stood watching from the doorway. Pulling Enrieta out of the way, Beattie marched into the room. "What the hell's going on in here?"

"It's your bee," Cara said, naked save for the eagle tattoo on her left breast, "he can't get it up. Can you? You fucking waste of space! Look at you, all curled up like a fucking baby."

Beattie had to calm Cara down. Usually she was a

sweetheart, although she could certainly be a handful when angry. Beattie picked up Cara's white robe and held it out to her. "I'm so sorry about this, Cara. Put this on, and I'll see what I can sort out."

"It's not good enough! I pay a lot of fucking money for my time with you," she hissed at Christopher, "and this is how you repay me? Beattie should cut your cock off, you fucking piece of shit."

Beattie escorted Cara out of the room and shut the door, turning to Christopher. "What are you playing at, Chris? What have I told you, over and over again? If you have any problems, ask for the Viagra; Enrieta would've brought you some. Now you've gone and pissed off one of my best clients." Beattie turned away from him, placing her hands on her head in frustration. "Why don't you listen to anyth–"

"I took them. I took some a couple of hours ago and nothing's happening." Christopher started crying, big baby sobs.

Beattie turned to him again. He certainly was a sorry-looking state.

Christopher had been one of her bees for little over two years. He'd adapted pretty quickly and had been a good contributor to her bank account for the first year; he had not been the best, but he was still a good earner. It was why his room was so sparse; he had a TV, a DVD player and stereo, a good wardrobe of clothes, but very little else. He'd not been top of the leader board for well over a year.

Of her bees, he was easily the sweetest, which was probably why he'd never been her top earner; he was too nice to win. He had mousy brown hair and blue eyes, which the clients had loved a year earlier. Since then his ratings had dwindled, being rated on average with sixes and sevens. She'd spoken to him about his scores on several occasions, although it didn't seem to make a difference. "Here, take some more," she said, reaching for the pot of pills on his chest of drawers. "See if this will get you going."

"It won't work!" Christopher's bottom lip quivered.

"Take some anyway; you never know." She held out the pills.

"There's no point. Nothing's going to work. I'm so sorry, Bea."

A sudden pang of anger built up in her gut and she turned away, her hands on top of her head. What the hell was she going to do? She had Cara waiting outside and a useless bee... what *could* she do? Beattie mulled it over in her head for a moment.

There was no way Christopher would come back from this; he was done working for her now. She could auction him out to some of her dad's business colleagues... or she could...

"Enrieta!" she shouted, loud enough for the door to open immediately.

"Yes, Bea?"

"Bring Cara back in here, would you?"

Beattie saw Christopher stop crying for a moment and look up at her.

"What are you doing, Bea?" He was petrified; she could see it in his eyes.

Without responding, Beattie turned as the door opened and Cara entered, with a much calmer demeanour. She beckoned her client over with an outstretched arm.

"Is he ready now?" Cara asked.

"I'm afraid not." Beattie wrapped her arm around Cara's shoulder. "But I've got something even better for you. Normally I'd auction this off to my dad's friends, but because it's you, and because we've let you down, I'm giving you first dibs."

"Dibs on what?"

"I'm going to set Chris, here, up in a room on C Wi–"

"No, Bea, please," Christopher interrupted, his face pale. "It's working, it's working. Please, Bea!" He started crying again.

"And you can do whatever you want with him, okay?" She smiled at her client.

Cara stared at the bee, who was sobbing. "Whatever I want?"

"Whatever your sick little mind wants," Beattie clarified with a playful wink. "But it will cost you more than the standard five hundred."

"How much?"

"Two thousand. This will be Chris' last earnings, so I can't do it for any less."

"Done." Cara held out her hand.

With a smile, Beattie shook it and asked Enrieta to fetch two guards.

"Please, Bea, I'm sorry! Don't do this," Christopher pleaded through floods of tears. "I'll be your best earner, please! I'll do anything you want."

"It's too late for that, Chris, I'm sorry." She looked down at him with disgust. "And besides, a deal's a deal. You're in Cara's hands now."

The guards carried the screaming bee away, while she took Cara to the furnace room. Hung on the wall were all manner of tools. "Take whatever you need and when you're finished, the guards will dispose of the mess. I'm so sorry for the disappointment earlier; I hope this somehow makes up for it?"

She watched Cara pick out a knife and a machete. "Are you kidding? This is like all my Christmases and birthdays come at once!"

Beattie had known Cara for over ten years and had heard plenty of stories about her in that time. Cara had been sectioned under the Mental Health Act twice; once when she'd tried to commit suicide, and the second after she'd recently kidnapped her ex-girlfriend, in an attempt to carry out a suicide pact. Cara had suffered greatly at the hands of her father, who'd raped her regularly from the age of six, until it was her younger sister's turn, and she'd been overlooked.

According to Cara, she'd been groomed by a Pakistani man over the course of six years, and repeatedly raped by the Pakistani and his friends. It was little wonder that Cara was the person she was today; she'd stood no chance, being born into a family with a junkie mother and paedophile father. Beattie could see why men were drawn to Cara. She was extremely attractive.

After walking to room two of C Wing, Beattie could see Christopher tied to a chair, his back to her. He was crying and had urinated on the floor; a pool had formed around the chair. "Have fun!" she said to a smiling Cara.

"Oh, wait," said Cara, sliding the robe off her shoulders and handing it to her. "I won't be needing this; I'm going natural on this one."

Beattie watched a radiant and happy Cara, still holding the knife and machete, as she went inside and closed the door.

Beattie waited outside for a couple of minutes, thinking that Cara must be teasing her ex-bee, choosing her moment to commence dispensing the pain. That was when the screaming started...

21

Lennox Garvey hated the cold; he missed his country's weather. It was the end of January and about two degrees outside, and he was watching as a fat woman wearing a fur coat talked into the payphone across the street, *his* payphone. She'd been on it for twenty minutes already! What was she talking about?

He opened the door of his four-by-four and pulled himself out, feeling the bite of the cold at his eyes and cheeks. It might have been two degrees, but with the wind it felt like minus five.

He ran across the high street, dodging between cars, and as he approached the phone, the fat bitch in the furry coat hung up. Lennox used this phone every time he needed to speak to his uncle, as it was safer than using his mobile.

Once the woman was gone, Lennox took out a piece of paper and dialled the number in Jamaica. When a female voice answered, he said, "It's me."

It took a minute for a male voice to speak. "Lennox, it's good to hear from you, my boy. How's everything over there? You behaving?"

"Hey, Uncle, everything's fine here, but a situation's come up that I think you need to know about."

"Go on, what's on your mind?"

"Could be nothing, could be something."

He went on to inform his uncle of what had happened the previous night at Rothstein's home. It took Lennox five minutes to get everything out, and as he talked, he covered his lips with his hand.

"And you think this guy's telling the truth?"

"He's not a liar... but the cop could be lying, could be trying to entrap him. Rothstein's not convinced, but he's thinking on it, waiting to hear from this top cop."

"And you called me because you think he might try to fuck me? To go with another supplier?"

"Had crossed my mind, yeah. We didn't talk about it last night, but if he agrees to do it and the cops have their own supplier in mind, what do you think he'll do?"

"He'd be mad not to. Keep an eye on things for me."

"Will do. I thought you should know."

"Thank you for bringing it to my attention." There was a pause, then the uncle said, "Hey, Lennox, you still got that camera set up in his office?"

"Absolutely."

"If you ever meet this top cop, film it for me. I want to see what he's got to say."

Lennox agreed to record the meeting, said his farewells, and hung up. When his hands were free again, he cupped them together, breathing into them and rubbing them as he waited for a space between the cars. When one came, he ran over to his Shogun.

When he'd moved over here, his uncle had asked him to buy a covert camera and have it installed in Rothstein's office. He'd found the perfect place for the tiny recording device – up high and overlooking the desk and bar – and he'd used it a few times when Rothstein had business going on that conflicted with his uncle's.

After all, his loyalty was with his family, not Rothstein...

22

Beattie looked at her watch: 10:56. She could hear movement inside room two of C Wing, but so far Cara hadn't emerged. The screaming had stopped an hour earlier, so she assumed Chris was no more. He'd clung on for a good couple of hours, though, so Cara must've bided her time before moving in for the kill strike. She dreaded to think what horrors Cara was doing to Christopher's corpse; she had been in there a long time.

Eventually the door opened and out walked Cara, covered in blood.

Beattie could hardly see her skin; there was so much blood she looked like she'd bathed in it. As Beattie glanced past her client into the room, Chris's torso was still on the chair, his head nowhere to be seen. She could see two legs lying on the floor, but the rest of him was out of sight. She suddenly felt very queasy.

"Wow!" said Cara, clearly elated. "That was so much better than sex. Liberating! You should try it, Bea. You'll love it. I'm literally floating."

Somehow, Beattie knew that something had just been awoken in her client. Cara was radiant, glowing almost; her usual scowl and frown lines had all vanished. She watched Cara as she walked towards the shower area, dripping fresh blood across the floor. Beattie didn't want to admit it to herself, but she was turned on by her naked client, and as she watched Cara step into the shower, she turned to her and said, "Do you want to join me?"

Beattie declined, as tempting as it was. She wasn't afraid of lady play – in fact, she'd slept with a girl in college once and she'd enjoyed it. No, the reason she declined was because Cara was dangerous; she didn't want to give her the wrong impression and regret it further down the line. Cara had stalking tendencies, or so her dad had told her.

Two guards caught her attention as they carried various body parts to the furnace room. The last piece of Chris to be carried away was small enough to be carried in one hand, and it was then that she realised it was his penis; Cara had carried out her earlier threat.

When Beattie heard the water start, she walked through to her office next door, sat down at her desk, and watched the monitors...

Kimiko opened the door to his room and wheeled in her trolley loaded with his bathing equipment. She didn't believe Mrs Harrison when she'd told her that Danny wasn't a nice man. "Time get you ready." She wheeled the trolley to the side of his bed.

He lay there – no conversation, no bravado.

She didn't take offence; after all, he had a lot of thinking to do. He had to adapt and realise his situation was what it was. For the previous ten days he'd obviously thought there was hope, where there was none, and that was what he needed to understand. She'd taken months to truly realise that this was it for her. Now all she could do was get on with her life, awful as it was.

Dipping her sponge in the warm water, she squeezed it before wiping Danny's forehead. His eyes looked dead, lifeless; they just stared up at the ceiling. "Your next customer be here soon," she said, wiping his face. "You not want make Bea angry, do you?"

Kimiko continued the sponge bath, trying to make conversation with him.

He continued to stare up at the ceiling.

Kimiko, worried for Danny's safety, did the only thing she could: prepare him.

A knock at the door signalled it was time for her to leave. When she opened it, an old woman entered, wearing a white robe.

"Hello, Danny," said the old woman, ignoring her. "Fancy seeing you again."

Kimiko smiled, wheeled her trolley out, and closed the door behind her, hoping that Danny could cope with the horrible smelly old woman...

National Crime Agency Officer Steven Dyer drove his unmarked Volvo XC90 a hundred metres behind his target, Lennox Garvey's Mitsubishi Shogun. He'd been assigned to follow Rothstein's number two as part of an ongoing investigation into Rothstein's "businesses".

"Target's on the move," Steven said into his microphone.

Steven had worked for the NCA since its creation in 2013, when he'd been TUPE'd from the Serious Organised Crime Agency, SOCA. He'd been with SOCA for six years in various capacities, and prior to that he'd been a police officer on the beat for ten years. As he was now thirty-four, he'd been involved in law enforcement in one form or another for his entire working career.

The agency was set up in 2013 as a non-ministerial government department, replacing the SOCA and incorporating the child exploitation and online protection centre, among others. It had a wide remit; as it tackled human, weapon, and drug trafficking as well as chasing cyber and economic criminals both nationally and internationally, it was the UK's leading agency against organised crime. They worked in partnership with regional police forces, the probation service and CPS, Europol, Interpol, and others. The media had dubbed the NCA the UK's FBI; Steven hated that.

He'd been seconded to the Organised Crime Command Unit two days earlier to help with the Rothstein operation. Prior to that, he had worked in the Missing Persons Unit and the Modern Slavery Human Trafficking Unit, so he had a wide range of experience within the agency. While he didn't enjoy the intelligence gathering aspect of his job – such as following Lennox Garvey – Steven loved most of what he did.

This phase of the operation was to gather as much information as they could about their targets' movements, including where they went and whom they met up with. It mainly involved either driving around or parking up and waiting. It was laborious, but a vital part of the NCA's work. Steven had volunteered to babysit Garvey.

There were two other officers detailed with round-the-clock surveillance of Garvey, so at least he had help; they rotated in shifts of eight hours. They used different makes, models, and colours of cars to aid their concealment, and so far, none of them had been "made" – at least, as far as they could tell. Garvey seemed to be going about his business as usual.

He indicated right, then stopped at some traffic lights. Garvey was three cars ahead.

Being an NCA officer wasn't so different from the work he did in SOCA; he didn't really understand why they'd even created the NCA. They could have just kept the SOCA and extended its remit, but he didn't care for internal politics. Some top dog had come up with the idea, and now they had the NCA with all its bells and whistles.

During his ten years as an officer, Steven had been involved in some high-profile operations, including helping to apprehend and convict the Cahill brothers, which was actually a network of career criminals who'd committed the biggest diamond heist in history; that case had taken years to complete, and God knew how many man hours of investigative work. Then there had been the Wolfgang Affair, a bribery case that had dragged on for years too. The way politicians behaved baffled him. He'd never much liked politicians anyway.

The operation that gave him the most pride, however, was when he'd helped to secure the conviction of a gang of paedophiles who had used the dark web to hide their nasty pastime. They'd infiltrated hundreds of video games consoles, pretending they were teenage girl players in order to lure unsuspecting young teenage boys to meet them in secluded spots. Once there, they would assault the boys, take pictures, and upload them onto their hidden website. When Steven and his team had helped convict all twenty-six paedophiles, there'd been a party at HQ.

Steven could feel his Glock 17 digging into his back, so he adjusted the belt holster and settled back into his seat. His unit was one of only three in the NCA licenced to carry firearms. He'd had to go through vigorous testing prior to being given the licence.

When the traffic lights turned green, he slowly accelerated, watching Garvey's Shogun. Steven still had six hours left of his shift; it was going to be a slow and boring day.

He was looking forward to seeing his wife, Ashley, and their two children, Isabelle, eight, and Ben, six. The kids were at an age he enjoyed; they both had distinctive personalities. Isabelle was very self-assured and bossy, and Ben was a nutter – there wasn't anything he wouldn't try, which was why he'd had so many accidents. Ben had already broken his arm, so God only knew how many bones he'd break by the time he was an adult.

Steven smiled at the thought of his family. They brought him an immense amount of joy. He'd met Ashley back at college; they'd gone to different schools, but the college was the only higher education establishment around for miles. They'd met in their Sociology A Level class, and had smiled at each other across the room, a lot. They'd hit it off straight away, but it still took him a full academic year to ask her out, and on the last day of college in year one, she said yes. The next week they'd met in town and the rest was history.

The target indicated left.

Steven saw that Garvey was pulling into a petrol station, so instead of doing the same, he drove past and pulled up on the main road up ahead, behind a black BMW. "Lost visual on target. He pulled into a petrol station; I'll have him in a minute."

His radio crackled and a female voice acknowledged his transmission.

The Shogun drove past six minutes later, and after waiting for two cars to drive by, Steven pulled out. "I've acquired the target..."

23

"Hello, Danny. Fancy seeing you again." The old woman dropped her robe, and Danny watched in horror as she stepped towards him. The closer she got, the more he could smell a pungent odour filling the room. Why was she so familiar with him? he wondered.

This was Beattie's punishment, giving him the very worst of her clients. This woman was vile; she had grey stringy hair and a wrinkly face framing a set of yellow and black teeth. Her skin was like leather, probably from years of sunbathing.

Unable to stop her, she straddled him. He hesitated; he couldn't quite place her face.

"You don't recognise me, do you?" She looked down at him with a sly smile.

"I can't place you, no." He wrinkled his nose at the smell of rotting teeth; it was overpowering, noxious. He felt like gagging.

"You took me out on a date once."

"I did?"

"Oh yeah, you did. I'm surprised you don't remember me; most people do."

It hit him like a baseball bat to the forehead. "Francesca!"

"Well done, darling." She smiled. "I thought you'd forgotten me."

A sudden feeling of hope engulfed him. Someone from the outside was here, someone he knew. He could feel the hope rising to the surface. "Please help me, Francesca! I've been kidnapped; I'm being held here, tied up... Please send the police around!"

Francesca smiled wider, and as fast as it had risen, the hope sank. "But you're not here to help me, are you?"

"Just like you didn't help me," she replied, her face serious.

He frowned. "What do you mean?"

"I invite you into my home and you snubbed me. I was getting ready to fuck your brains out and you left me."

Holy shit! He had to think this through. He could try lying his way out of this, he thought – he just had to be careful. "I had to leave, Fran, I really did. My dad had a fall... I had to get to the hospital."

"Liar!" she spat. "You said your mum had a fall! I knew you were lying when you ran out on me."

He couldn't remember what he'd said; he only remembered wanting to get the hell out of her house. He couldn't sleep with her, not then. Not now. His skin crawled at hers touching his. "Mum, dad... I can't remember which one. But one of them had a fall, honest."

"They're both dead, Danny, have been for a long time. Since you were sixteen, right?" she asked, her face red.

She surrendered him, stepping off the bed, her rank nakedness burning into his consciousness forever. He would never forget that, would never be able to unsee it.

"I asked around," she hissed. "Do you know how that makes me feel? That you'd fuck all your other women, but not me?"

"I'm sorry, Fran," he gasped, "I didn't mean to hurt your feelings."

"It's too late for that," she said, her tone calm again. "Karma's a bitch, right?"

"What are you talking about?"

"Do you lie awake at night thinking how you got here? I bet you do, all chained up like that, women coming in here and using you." She was proud of herself, her black teeth on display again. "Well wonder no more, Danny. *I* put you in here..."

Beattie entered the room and closed the door behind her. "We go way back, don't we, Francesca?"

"Oh yes, darling," agreed Francesca, putting a saggy arm around Beattie's waist. "You see, Danny, I suggested you to Bea; I said you'd be the perfect bee for her hive."

Beattie loved the look of shock that appeared on Danny's face; it was priceless. "And you were right, of course," she replied with a laugh.

Danny exploded with rage. His chains sprung to life, preventing him from acting on his impulses. Beattie knew that if he got free, Danny would probably end up killing her. Give it a week or more of gruelling punishment, she thought, safe with him in chains, and he'd adapt to life here. She had time to break him down – she had all the time in the world.

Although Beattie had known Francesca Belmont for ten years or so, she hated her. She hated everything about her: the smell, for starters; she also hated her mannerisms, her personality, everything. To her, Francesca was a vile woman; she wasn't a lady. On the surface though, Beattie made sure to be a gracious and kind host, making Francesca feel extra special.

Francesca was married to a good and loyal friend of her

father's, Larry. Well, she used the term marriage loosely; Francesca was hardly ever indoors. She loved the pub scene and she often spent days away from home, getting drunk with friends. She had a massive drinking problem and a crippling gambling addiction.

Apparently, Larry had met Francesca as a prostitute on the streets, and what had started out as a business arrangement soon turned into true love and the couple married. The thought made Beattie want to vomit. Maybe she'd been prettier back then, because she couldn't see anything decent about Francesca's personality to make a lovely man like Larry want to marry this vile woman.

"I just thought you'd like to know who put you here." Francesca laughed. "And you're welcome, by the way!"

Beattie turned Francesca around and walked with her to the door.

"Oh, I forgot to tell you, I had a visitor round last night," Francesca said.

"Oh really? Anyone nice?" Beattie asked, not interested.

"Oh no, not like that. Some snoopy bitch detective came around asking me questions about my relationship with Danny."

Beattie froze as they reached the door. Danny had been missing for seventeen days, and ordinarily these investigations only lasted a couple before they were shelved. This bitch detective had been going for over a fortnight? That couldn't happen. After this long in business, there was no way she was going to let it fall apart because of some nosy cop. "Why didn't you tell me this last night?" Beattie asked.

"I thought I was coming here today anyway, not that I got anything out of *him*," Francesca replied, glancing over her shoulder to get one last look at Danny.

"Don't worry about that – I'll reimburse you, of course. Now, tell me more about this detective."

Francesca looked up at her. "She was about five-five, pretty, long dark hair, looked pretty fit. Indian, Pakistani maybe? If only I could remember her name… Began with an N… Nik… Na–"

"Nasreen," she heard Danny say.

Beattie turned to find that Danny had calmed down enough to listen to them talk. And he had a strange smile on his face; he looked relieved. Anger swelled up in her gut. "Don't go getting your hopes up, Danny. She won't be finding us any time soon!"

She turned to Francesca. "Have you got a surname for this Nasreen? I need to find out more about her. Is she going to be a problem for us?"

Francesca thought for a moment. "There was something off about her. She came alone. I've been around pigs long enough to know that they never travel alone, always in pairs. And she came to my house late."

In her experience that could mean only one thing: this Nasreen wasn't looking for Danny in any official capacity; she was investigating in her own time. It was worse than she feared. "Surname, Francesca, what's her surname?"

"Don't get shitty with me!" Francesca snapped. "I can't remember."

Without waiting for the vile old lady's memory to return, Beattie pointed at Danny. "What's her surname?" He didn't reply, just kept that stupid smile on his face. She stepped up to the bed and glared down at him. "What's her fucking surname? Tell me, Danny, or I swear to God I'll give you the worst two weeks of your fucking li–"

"Oh, wait, I've got her card in my bag," Francesca interrupted.

A wave of relief swept over her. "Let's go get it, then."

Beattie walked up to Francesca, linked her arm through the

old lady's, and helped her walk to the shower rooms, where her clothes and bag were kept. She made Francesca bend down and rummage through her bag until she found the card.

Beattie looked down at it. "Nasreen Maqsood. You've been a busy little bee, haven't you?" Beattie shook her head, smiling. "We're going to have to fix that..."

Kimiko looked at the time: it was half an hour until Danny's next customer was due.

She wheeled her trolley along the corridor, stopped at room two, and unlocked the door. When she pushed the trolley inside, she was surprised to find Danny looking up at the ceiling with a smile on his face. She'd expected him to be comatose. "Nearly time next customer."

"Come on in, Kimiko," he replied, pleased to see her.

They talked for twenty minutes while she bathed him, like before. Why was he so responsive to her? She didn't understand. Only a couple of hours earlier, he had been in a deep depression. What could possibly have happened in that time? Whatever it was, she was glad to have him back.

Seconds before a knock came at the door, he whispered, "Come stay with me tonight."

She hesitated. If she was honest with herself, she'd already thought about sneaking out after everyone had retired for the evening and going into his room. Now he was asking her to. "I like to, Danny, but Mrs Harrison no like it," she replied, her voice almost a whisper. "It make her angry." She looked down at his disappointed face. "Sorry!"

At four o'clock the inevitable knock came, and Kimiko wheeled her trolley over to the door, greeting Danny's next customer with a polite bow. His client didn't even acknowledge her; she stepped inside, dropped her robe on the floor, and straddled poor Danny.

Kimiko closed the door and wheeled the trolley back to the store area next to the shower rooms. As she did after every bed bath, she emptied the plastic basin of water down the sink and put all the dirty cloths and flannels in the laundry bin.

Poor Danny. Mrs Harrison was punishing him. It was then Kimiko realised how much she thought about him – it was all the time. She thought about him day and night. She had even thought about him the previous night, when she was under her duvet.

Mrs Harrison interrupted her daydream. "Kimiko, honey, can you come in the office, please?"

A sudden feeling of dread made her turn to Mrs Harrison with her head down. Kimiko walked into the office, expecting her employer to start shouting at her. She had obviously overheard her and Danny talking. "Yes, Bea?"

"Will you look up at me, please, Kimiko?"

Kimiko obeyed to find that her employer didn't seem upset or angry; on the contrary, she looked – almost – happy. "Sorry, Bea."

"We've got a New Bee coming in tonight." Mrs Harrison smiled. "His name's Thomas. Walter is bringing him in later, so I'll need you to help me, okay?"

"Yes, Bea."

As Kimiko walked back to the store area, she thought about Danny again. She couldn't get him out of her mind. And now that she knew he wanted her too, it would only get worse. She had to shake this – no good would come of it. If Mrs Harrison ever found out how she felt about Danny, she would be so angry she'd punish her as well. Her employer had already warned her against getting involved with him.

Realistic. That's what she had to be, realistic. Nothing would ever happen between her and Danny, it couldn't. He was one of

Bea's Bees and she was a member of the support staff. It wasn't like either she or Danny were ever going to leave this place alive, was it? Then again, if this was all they had, why shouldn't they be together? What was so wrong with them sharing their love with one another?

24

Nasreen was excited about this meeting. Between an estate agent and a betting shop was a brown door. On the wall to her right was an intercom system. There were several buttons with business names written on them, and after finding the button for Gentlemen4U, she pressed it.

The intercom crackled to life and a pleasant female voice asked who it was.

"Detective Constable Nasreen Maqsood, I have an appointment to meet with Theresa Gaffney," she answered, hoping she hadn't got the time wrong.

"Of course, detective," came the voice. "I'll buzz you in. We're on the first floor."

After the loud buzz, she entered, then walked up two flights of stairs, where there were three doors with company signs stuck on them to choose from. Picking the one with the Gentlemen4U logo on it, she knocked loudly.

A plump lady with dark curly hair and an attractive smile showing perfectly straight white teeth opened the door. "Detective Maqsood?"

She shook hands with the overweight lady. "Theresa?"

The woman stepped out of the way. "Yes, please come in."

Inside, Nasreen saw how small the office was. There were two desks sat side by side, and both desks had two chairs in front of them, for escorts and/or clients, she guessed. On the walls were shelving units filled with files – stacks and stacks of files. It was a dingy room with only one window behind the desks; it made sense to have the desks where they were, to make the most of the natural light.

"Please, have a seat, detective."

"Thank you." Nasreen sat on a chair opposite.

As she waited for Theresa to seat herself, Nasreen noticed that she had a wedding ring on, and that on the wall to her left was a picture of her and her husband on their wedding day. The couple looked very happy.

"An indulgence of mine. I really should have it on my desk, but I like my clients to see I'm quite normal, happily married," Theresa said. "Now, tell me what you need to know."

"I'd like to know how all this works. I'm investigating a missing escort and I need to know more about this industry – how it operates, what happens... to gain a better understanding. And I'm not looking into your company or anything like that, so you don't need to worry."

"That's fine, detective."

"Please, call me Nas," she said, hating formality. Her culture was very formal, which she'd rebelled against all those years earlier. She accepted British culture, and formality was so stuffy and unnecessary.

The woman nodded. "Okay, Nas, let me show you how it works for us."

Theresa turned her monitor slightly to give Nasreen a better view. The plump lady then took her through how the website and booking process worked. Once a booking was made, the two parties could communicate through a website-provided email service. Nasreen thought it looked simple enough and she understood why they didn't need a bigger office.

"This really is all the space we need," Theresa said, as if reading her mind. "It's only my partner and I in here. We have enough space to meet new customers and interview new escorts. All the work is done through the website, so there's no need for lots of admin staff."

"When you say partner, do you mean your husband? Or...?"

"No, business partner. My husband's an investment banker."

Nasreen needed to find out what happened on the actual dates. The website said the company had a strictly no sex policy, but she doubted that was really what happened.

"All I can tell you is that we, as a company, have a no-sex code," Theresa said when Nasreen asked about it, "which we instil into our escorts from the get-go. Now, if you're asking me if they disobey this policy... what can I say? Possibly. We don't ask the details of the dates or keep tabs on our escorts' whereabouts. If they end up going back to a client's house and having sex, that's up to them. They are two consenting adults. But that isn't to say that we're complacent about it – if we found out one of our escorts did have sex with a client, we would – under our policy guidelines – be obligated to terminate their employment with us."

Nasreen could tell that the questioning was bothering Theresa. "Please, I'm not judging you, or the company. This is just fact-finding for me."

Theresa sat back in her chair.

Deciding to take the conversation away from the day-to-day operations of the business, Nasreen asked, "Do you have the details we spoke about? The two missing escorts?" This was the real reason she'd come to visit.

Without hesitating, Theresa opened a drawer in her desk

and pulled out two A4 files. They weren't terribly thick with paper.

After Theresa had handed the files over, Nasreen opened the first and noted the name: Frederick Matthews. There was a missing persons form underneath his personal details page and she checked the date the report was filed – five and a half years earlier.

"Freddie was a lovely man, a real gentleman," Theresa said, reminiscing. "The clients went mad for him; he was by far the most sought after of our escorts at the time. Then one day, he just disappeared on us. He went out on a date one night, then he was gone."

"That's what happened to Danny," Nasreen said, then paused, realising that she'd been informal again. "I'm sorry. I'll be honest with you – Danny's an ex-boyfriend. He went missing over a fortnight ago and his case fell into my lap. After only a brief investigation, my boss shelved our inquiry, so now I'm investigating unofficially in my spare time."

She felt Theresa's palm on her arm.

"You poor thing, that's awful but not unexpected. The police filed away Freddie's case after two days too. They said they thought he'd moved away; they said it happens all the time. They checked his home, couldn't see any evidence of a disturbance... No blood... Nothing like that. They spoke to our client, who said he'd left hers in the early hours, and she was the last person to see him. It was all very sad."

"So, he wasn't abducted at home, and neither was Danny. We think Danny was abducted in a park on his way home, in the early hours."

"There's a park near to Freddie's too. The police checked it, apparently, but couldn't find anything."

"We found Danny's blood by accident. Luck on my part, really."

"They said they'd keep his case open, but nothing happened – just like with Julian fifteen years ago."

Nasreen shifted the files so the older case was on top, then opened the folder and saw the name: Julian Edwards. He disappeared fifteen years and four months earlier. Again, his body wasn't found; there was no sign of a disturbance in the home, no evidence of any description. He simply vanished one day.

Theresa explained what happened with Julian's case. Again, the police came up empty and shelved the investigation soon after commencing it.

"I can't help but think if they'd been children or teenagers, they'd have tried harder and kept the cases open longer, but because they worked in our industry, they don't think it's as important to find them."

Nasreen noticed that Theresa had said "in our industry" and not "the sex industry", which they were – it didn't matter how she dressed it up, Gentlemen4U was still a part of the sex industry. Nasreen didn't want to antagonise Theresa, however, so she refrained from commenting further.

It had been a very fruitful meeting, and Nasreen now had lots more to work with; she had a gut feeling that these two cases were somehow connected to Danny's disappearance. Other people might laugh at her – it didn't mean she was wrong. She was getting closer to finding Danny; she could feel it...

25

Lennox Garvey loved it when Beattie worked late.

She was busy on her computer when he walked in to count the day's take, and she was wearing a pair of jeans and a very attractive white V-neck long-sleeved top, so low he could see part of her cleavage. Plus, her long red hair was down, splayed over her shoulders. She looked amazing.

This had become his favourite part of the day, especially over the last ten days: he'd seen Beattie most nights that he'd come to pick up the money.

"Evening, Bea," he said, squeezing her shoulders as he brushed past her.

"Hi!" She turned in her swivel chair. "How're you?"

"All the better for seeing you." He smiled, setting his suitcase on the floor.

"Aw, you're such a smoothie," she said, her smile genuine.

He walked over to the wall safe, entered the code, opened the door, and took out the bundles of cash. When he'd placed the money on the desk, he stood and looked up at the picture of Beattie sitting by the pool. "I love that picture of you, up there."

Beattie turned her chair and looked up. "Oh, that – seems

like a lifetime ago now. Back when I was a hotty." She said it in a musing kind of way.

"Still are, if you ask me," he replied, suddenly realising what he'd said.

She smiled up at him. "That's kind of you to say – you can come back again."

He had to change the conversation. He was there to do a job, so he should sit down and count the money – stop flirting with the stunning owner of this blood bunker and get on with it. This was how it'd been for the last ten days, flirting with her, and he was sure he hadn't imagined their moments together. There had been times when she had squeezed his shoulders for a bit longer than she'd needed. She'd even rubbed his hair one night and their eyes had locked twice for a lot longer than was normal.

He had to shake it off. She was married, and more importantly, she was Rothstein's daughter. Lennox had been warned off her by her raging psychopath of a father, and he knew he had to toe the line; his life depended on it. Taking a deep breath, he sat down and started counting the money while she tapped away on her computer.

Halfway through counting fifties, she leaned back in her chair and stretched, her hand brushing his hair.

"Oh, I'm so sorry," she said, embarrassed.

She was so close, and he tried not to smell her perfume as he told her to forget about it. Going back to counting the fifties, he focused on what he was doing. Fifty, a hundred, fifty, two hundred.

"Do you fancy a cup of tea?"

He looked up at her.

"I can make you one if you want?"

She was so gorgeous in that low-cut white top and those tight dark blue jeans... He wanted to rip her out of them... Stop it! He shook his head. "No thanks, Bea. I'll be out of here soon, but I appreciate the offer."

"You sure? It's no trouble."

There was something so sexy about the way she stood looking down at him. And he'd lost count... again. "Really, no thanks."

He had to finish counting the money before she put him off again, or he'd never leave...

National Crime Agency Officer Steven Dyer had waited for Garvey to drive back down the country lane he'd driven up half an hour earlier. As the road he was on had no lights for miles, it was dark outside, which was good because that meant he would see Garvey's headlights coming, giving him enough time to switch his motor and own lights off.

He tapped the steering wheel while he listened to a song on the radio. He didn't know what song it was, not that he was listening. He felt the bass and drummed.

Following Garvey all day had been a laborious task, made all the more painful by pulling a double shift to help out one of his relief team; the officer who was supposed to take over from him couldn't make it, so Steven had had to call Ashley and let her know he'd be working all night and not to wait up for him. Ashley wasn't pleased.

He looked at his GPS again, hoping that the dirt track Garvey had driven up would somehow magically appear. It didn't. Whatever was up there was hidden, a secret from cartographers – who, to be fair, probably didn't think that whatever it was at the end of the dirt track was important enough to include. Steven was intrigued though.

Without radioing through his actions, he took out a small pair of binoculars, opened his car door, got out, and looked up the road into the darkness. With his eyes adjusting, he could barely make out the opening to the narrow track up ahead.

He hadn't seen any cars coming along this stretch of road for at least twenty-five minutes; it was the perfect place to have a covert business of some sort, being all quiet and secluded. He was more than a little interested to find out what lay at the top of the track.

With his Glock 17 sitting comfortably on his belt in the middle of his back, Steven felt safe, knowing that if he found trouble, all he needed to do was reach behind him to pull out the gun. He didn't feel the need to unholster it just yet.

When he found the opening to the dirt track, he followed it...

With her cup of tea in hand, Beattie walked back into the office, where Lennox was still busy counting the money – this time all the twenty-pound notes. She sat back down on her desk chair and blew her cup of tea before taking a sip.

She'd found herself staying late these past few nights. When she'd not been attending functions, she made sure she had plenty to keep her occupied in the office. She really looked forward to Lennox's visits, clearly a sign she was lonely – not that she ever felt lonely, as such.

Every night she'd been able to, she flirted with him when he visited to pick up the takings, and he had flirted back. They shared stories, laughed, flirted some more, and had even shared a drink or two at the bar on one occasion.

Lennox had phoned her father and told him that he'd bring the takings along in the morning, that he had some important "business" to take care of that was in her father's best interests. With her husband out for the night at one of his pressing engagements, she and Lennox had stayed up until the early hours talking and laughing. Beattie had enjoyed herself immensely; he was a very interesting man.

She liked him a lot, but more than that... she *really* liked him; he was so attractive. There was nothing, however, she could do about it. Her father had been very clear what his feelings were on "poking the payroll", as he put it. It wasn't good for business, he'd told her on many an occasion.

Sighing, Beattie went back to her computer and looked at her monitor: on the screen was Nasreen Maqsood's Facebook profile. Francesca hadn't been wrong when she'd said Nasreen was pretty. She had lovely chiselled cheekbones, a great smile, and going by her muscular physique, she worked out. It even said that her hobbies included kickboxing. There were photos of Nasreen with a young girl – whom she took to be Nasreen's daughter – and after reading the comments under the photos, she concluded that Nasreen's daughter was called Mina and that she was four years old.

Beattie felt Lennox's hands on her shoulders.

"I'm all done, Bea," he said in his lovely Jamaican accent. "I'll be back in tomorrow."

"Okay, honey." She turned the chair and stood up. "A pleasure, as always."

There was an awkward silence.

Her eyes locked with his for an uncomfortable amount of time.

Lennox finally broke it off by looking away. "I'll be off."

Another awkward silence sat between them.

"Yeah, I'll see you tomorrow."

Once he'd left, she closed the door, and leaning against it, banged her head three times. She felt so stupid, like a little schoolgirl. Why was she feeling like this?

Frustrated, Beattie slumped on her chair and went back to her computer.

The more she researched Nasreen Maqsood, the more she felt she needed to manage the situation. After putting Nasreen's name through Google, she'd sprung up on the screen in the form of several national newspapers covering a police investigation into the serial rapist Nasreen had helped apprehend. She was an up-and-coming detective, and Beattie didn't want a person like Nasreen looking into Danny's disappearance.

Picking up the receiver on her landline, Beattie dialled a familiar number. "Walter, when you get back tonight, I've got another assignment for you. I know I said I wanted you to find two New Bees, but something important has come up... I've got someone I want you to follow..."

Halfway up the dirt track, as he tried to avoid potholes and ditches, Steven Dyer saw the flash of headlights approaching through the trees and bushes.

He hid in the bushes while he waited for Garvey's Shogun to pass, then he waited for two more minutes before walking back onto the path. Fuck! He'd lost his target. He was going to get no end of grief for this. While he was here, he decided he might as well find out what was at the end of the road.

He carried on walking along the uneven road, mindful of any possible vehicles approaching, until he saw lights up ahead. There was a fenced-off farmhouse three hundred metres away, and in the two upstairs floors of the house, the lights were on.

Wanting to get a closer look – and still covered by darkness – he walked around the fencing, hiding in the bushes. He could just about make out a barn in the distance, and from what he could hear, it sounded like someone was coming out of it.

With much difficulty, he tried to observe the person emerging from the barn. He could see it was a woman with long hair, although from this distance – and in this light – it was impossible to make out any distinguishing features. He watched her get closer as she walked towards the large house.

What was Garvey doing here? It looked like a normal farm to Steven, but if Garvey had been here, there had to be a reason. Steven felt, in his gut, that the farm held secrets, and he intended to find out what they were.

After a few more minutes, he decided to head back to his car. He wasn't looking forward to telling HQ that he'd lost the target. In the grand scheme of things, losing Garvey didn't matter – they'd always find him again. Steven would tell HQ to look into the farmhouse and find out who owned it. He was positive it was a potential lead...

26

Day 27
Tuesday, 6th February

Nasreen leaned back in her chair and rubbed her face. She was exhausted. Running an unofficial investigation in her spare time was taking its toll on her energy levels; she hadn't been to a kickboxing session in almost a month; she hadn't been to her mosque in ten days, and was neglecting Mina, leaving her in the care of their live-in nanny far more than was normal. Nasreen felt guilty about the latter, although she knew – deep down – that it was worth it. At best, she was trying to save Danny's life. At the very least, she was going to find out what had happened to him.

"You look knackered, Nas," said Terrence, who, in contrast, looked full of energy.

"Thanks," she said, closing down the page she was on. "I didn't get much sleep last night; Mina's full of cold, so I had her in with me."

It was eight thirty, the day was young, and she felt like it was bedtime. She'd been in the office for an hour already and had drunk two cups of coffee. The only time she got to focus on finding Danny was either early in the morning, or after work. She'd opted for both, which was why her family life had been so badly affected.

"Looks like we've got another case," said Terrence, switching on his computer. "Adams texted me this morning. Briefing's in half an hour."

She reopened the page, safe in the knowledge there was a partition separating her and her supervisor. She couldn't risk him finding out she was still investigating Danny's disappearance, even if it was out of hours.

Since her meeting with Theresa Gaffney, Nasreen had managed to find out a lot more about Frederick and Julian's disappearances, and had even managed to discuss Frederick's case with one of the detectives who'd handled it. According to Lambert, the detective involved, there was no evidence of foul play, and no evidence of any actual crime being committed. He and his partner had concluded, therefore, that Frederick had simply skipped town.

They'd interviewed neighbours of the victim, and they'd also interviewed people in the park near his home, showing them his photograph. Some had recognised him – they hadn't seen him in the early hours of the morning. They'd spoken to a tramp who slept on a bench in the park, who'd drunkenly admitted to seeing two men attack Frederick and throw him in a van. The vagrant had been so drunk, however, that they'd dismissed him out of hand.

When Lambert had informed Nasreen of the tramp, she'd asked why they hadn't followed up on it, the conversation soon becoming hostile when Lambert sensed she was questioning the quality of his work. Fortunately, she'd managed to calm him down; the last thing she wanted was for Lambert to speak to Adams about it. The investigation needed to be covert, at least until she had some form of solid proof she could take upstairs.

She'd visited the park after work, in the dark, and had tried to locate the tramp, however she'd come up short. Another vagrant informed her that the tramp she was looking for had died four years earlier, found on his bench, dead. So, her one good line of enquiry was a bust.

The fact that both Danny's and Frederick's disappearances involved two men and a van made her even more convinced they were connected, which got her thinking: if there were two that she knew of in this area, what were the odds there were more, further afield? And did this just involve male escorts? Or could it involve female escorts too? And why should it be just this area? Should she widen her search parameters? There were so many questions.

Over the last ten days, she'd used the PNC, the Police National Computer, to help her with her research, conducting searches for male escorts who had been abducted all over the country. She'd painstakingly sifted through mountains of paperwork and police reports in the lonely office, after everyone else had retired to their homes. There'd been over a hundred male and female escorts/prostitutes abducted/missing up and down the country over the last fifteen years, and she thought there would be even more if she went back further.

While sifting through the missing persons reports, she'd sorted the cases into possible and not probable, then she scanned through eyewitness testimonials, looking for any mention of a man or two men with a van. All in all, she'd found five cases that had the same MO, in addition to Danny's and Frederick's. So, she now had seven cases that she felt were all linked. The only problem was she had no proof, so she couldn't go to Adams with it. Not yet.

She needed more. She'd phoned detectives who'd worked on

three of the five new cases, speaking to the ones who were still on active duty. A detective on one of the five cases sounded genuinely sorry that they'd never found out what happened to the victim, a petite twenty-two-year-old prostitute with three children under the age of five. The detective had known the sex worker, had tried to help her; he'd told Nasreen that he felt guilty for not putting more time and energy into finding out what had happened to her.

She'd asked the detective about the white van and he'd informed her that a lorry driver had admitted to seeing something near a park. He'd seen two men acting suspiciously, carrying something large wrapped in a white sheet and throwing it in a van, but admitted it could just have been a roll of carpet. He'd only seen it from a distance.

Even if she showed the photographs of the driver and passenger of the van to the lorry driver, there would probably be no way he could positively identify either of the two men. Although it was a dead end, it would add weight to her theory, if proven correct.

After work that evening, she was lined up to meet with another eyewitness from one of the five new cases she'd found. This case happened locally, so she would only have to drive forty-five minutes out of her way to meet him. Having occurred in 2010, it was eight years old. She was hopeful about this one...

27

Opening the office door, Lennox greeted the white-haired man wearing civilian clothing: a pair of jeans, black shoes, a blue and red striped shirt, and a beige overcoat. He guessed the visitor was in his late fifties.

He showed the guest to a chair in front of Rothstein's desk, and as the man sat down, Rothstein offered him a drink. The man refused.

"Let me give you my card," said the man.

Lennox waited slightly behind his boss as Rothstein took the card and read it.

"Well, excuse me, Assistant Commissioner of Police of the Metropolis, Peter Franks," exclaimed Rothstein. "Are you royalty round your way? Should I be bowing before you?"

"Something like that," Franks replied. "I've been authorised to come here and make you an offer, Mr Rothstein."

"You can call me Will," Rothstein said.

"Okay, Will. Do you mind if we discuss this in private?"

Lennox's boss looked over at him, giving him the signal to leave without saying a word.

Without hesitation, Lennox walked out of the office and closed the door behind him.

Earlier that morning, Rothstein had asked him to make sure the hidden camera was on for the meeting. He'd ensured it was, and he'd also ensured his uncle's camera was switched on as well. He was interested to hear what the offer was.

Outside in the hallway, Lennox pulled out his mobile phone and accessed the covert camera's app. A picture of the office quickly came up on his screen, and he could both see and hear the two men talking. He walked to the washroom at the end of the hall, closed the door and sat on the toilet seat, listening intently to his boss and the assistant commissioner.

"Good. Now we're alone, we can really talk," stated the senior policeman. "I understand from Zack Astor that he's explained the situation to you, am I right?"

"I understand that you're planning on legalising prohibited substances, yeah."

"That's an oversimplification, but not inaccurate. We're changing the system for the better, Will. That's how I see it. The system, the way it is right now, is rigged in favour of the drug dealers. That's not fair on anyone – except criminal gangs – and we want to right that injustice."

"Okay, but you being here means that you obviously believe I'm a part of that injustice," Rothstein pointed out.

"Absolutely. I truly believe that. But there are a lucky few, like yourself, who we need to distribute it. It's not like we're going to be asking our bobbies to deal on the street, is it? So, we need dealers, but we need our own chosen few to be distributing narcotics of our choosing, drugs that we can source ourselves and make sure are pure and safe for the users. That's our prime directive: to ensure that the population of users – if they're going to use – have access to safe products, not this crap your colleagues sell. God only knows what they mix in with it. It's shit!"

Rothstein nodded. "I'm with you on that; most of the shit out there is tainted, mixed with baking powder and all sorts of other crap."

"Exactly! Look, I'll be honest with you – we don't want to deal with you, but we need your expertise; you're the last piece of a very complicated puzzle. We have all our dealers in place, ready to go, but we need a good low-key importer we can rely on to ship our products safely and on time. We need you, Will. That's the God's honest answer."

"If I do it, do I get to choose the supplier?"

Franks shook his head. "We already have a supplier in mind – poised and ready to start – so no, your dealings with your current supplier will need to cease."

"I'm afraid that presents a problem for me."

The policeman shrugged. "It is what it is, Will. We can't negotiate on this, I'm not permitted. Like I said, you're the last piece of the puzzle, and changing suppliers isn't an option."

"I guess we have nothing to discuss then."

"Wait," Franks said, his hands out in a placating manner, "don't cut your nose off to spite your face, Will. If I leave here with a 'no' from you – which I'm prepared to do – then we'll approach your competitors. And since part of our deal with your colleagues is that they drip-feed us their competitors, how long do you think it'll be before your rivals finger you? Please, think about this."

"I have thought about it, and without my supplier, it's a no," Rothstein said firmly.

There was a long pause.

Then there was some shuffling.

Franks nodded. "And on that note, I thank you for your time. I'll let my superiors know you've declined."

"Like I said, if you accept my supplier, then we can have everything up and running as soon as you're ready to go."

"You know, I really thought you'd be smarter than this. We're giving you the chance to import for a huge portion of the UK, a far greater area than you supply to right now. And you'll be taking home your share of the profits without any risk. You'll have a get-out-of-jail-free card, if you ever get picked up. You'll be above the law, Will, how can you not want that?"

"To paraphrase you, it is what it is, Assistant Commissioner."

Another pause.

"Well, okay... I can't say I'm not disappointed, but I thank you for your time."

"You're welcome! Oh, and Commissioner, you see that? That's a camera filming you right now. If you think you're just going to try to get rid of me because I refused your offer, think about the shitstorm I can bring down on you with that footage."

The commissioner snorted. "Do you think we're afraid of this coming out to the public? We're going to leak it to the press when the time's right anyway, and we have enough tangible evidence of the good it's doing. None of us at the top – not my superiors, nor anyone at the Home Office or Department of Justice – will receive prison time for any of it. We're all coming to the end of our careers now, so the most we'll get is suspended or fired from our jobs. I've only got two more years until I retire. But we're trying to leave behind a legacy, a better Britain. So, I have something on you, and you have something on me, and yada, yada, yada."

"So long as we're both on the same page."

Another pause.

"Okay, I tried. Goodbye, Will. If you change your mind, you have my card."

Lennox heard the policeman walk past the door, and after closing down the app, he sat back to think. It seemed Rothstein had more backbone than he'd given him credit for. Lennox had been so sure that, had the police said they had another supplier, Rothstein would have gone along with it.

He'd gained a lot of respect for Rothstein in that short trip to the toilet. He would deliver the good news to his uncle later...

28

Beattie walked into Danny's room to find him dressed and lying on his bed. It was strange to see him wearing clothes; he'd spent the best part of a month naked and tied up. A couple of days earlier she'd seen enough of a change in her Star Bee to untie him. She still didn't trust him – as usual, only time would tell if she'd be able to in the future.

She'd been getting daily updates about Nasreen Maqsood from Walter, who was tailing her day and night. Poor Walter was always the one she chose for these kinds of details; he was the only one she trusted. So far, Nasreen was no nearer to finding Danny than she was to finding Lord Lucan. If, however, Nasreen got any closer, she had contingency plans.

Her plan was to let Danny keep earning her lots of money, and in the meantime, she would watch him closely, and how he was with Kimiko. She trusted that she'd broken Kimiko down enough, but she still had her doubts about Danny.

"So, Star Bee, are you ready for your first client?"

He told her he had showered and that he would prepare in five minutes. Beattie nodded her approval at his answer. He wasn't as cocky or self-assured as he'd been shortly after his arrival. Maybe he had adapted? The problem was, she couldn't know for sure. Still, so long as he performed and kept her clients happy, that was all she cared about.

When she'd agreed to untie him, she'd told him that he'd be getting her best clients again, that he was her Lucky Bee. For just over a week, she had given him nothing but the worst. He'd been bitten, slapped, punched, kicked in the face, spanked, and urinated on. She did have some very odd clients – with strange, twisted fetishes – who paid her well, so who was she to judge?

For the past ten days it had been a mixed bunch. She'd had problems with staff; she had a New Bee – Thomas – who was busy adapting to his new life. She had Danny back, hopefully. The best part of the past ten days was the time she'd spent with Lennox; she was growing fonder of him by the day.

The previous night, he'd held her hand for longer than was necessary, and they welcomed each other with a kiss on both cheeks. She longed for him every night when she went to sleep, sometimes next to Alan, but mostly alone. It was so frustrating that she couldn't act on her impulses, because given half a chance, she would have him – every last centimetre of him. All she could hope for was his company for half an hour while he counted the takings. That would have to do, for now.

When Kimiko came in to help Danny prepare, she wandered out of the room and along to room five, where Thomas was tied up. Peering through the peephole, she saw he was being prepared by Sofia – his assigned support worker – who was busy giving him a sponge bath and who would soon be working him up. His first client of the day was in half an hour.

With Alan away so much, Beattie was in charge of the whole operation, her Bees and his All-Stars. She'd thought about informing her father of Alan's absences. After all, it wasn't fair for her to have to cover for her husband so much. It was already a stressful business to run, always fraught with problems, and taking on Alan's responsibilities just added to the pressure. Two days earlier a fight had broken out between two of Alan's girls in the shower area, and it had taken three of her guards to pull them apart.

Satisfied that Danny and Thomas would be ready, she walked along the corridor to her office and closed the door. As she had a pounding headache, she took two paracetamols with the remainder of her tea.

Sitting back in her chair, she thought about seeing Lennox that night – he'd said he would be along as per usual. After a few moments she shook off her daydream and went back to her monitor...

Steven took a photograph of a thickly set man while he walked along the path to the barn. From his vantage point he couldn't see the man's face, but he took the photo anyway; he got the best shots when people came out of the barn and walked back to their cars.

Since he'd informed his superiors of what he'd found here, he'd been placed on surveillance duty. His bosses probably thought it was punishment for losing Garvey; the intel he'd managed to obtain from here was awesome – it was a who's who of villainy. They'd managed to film over a hundred criminals coming and going from the barn, probably more. Whatever was in that barn was big.

For most of the day there were around nineteen cars parked outside, and he'd counted that, on average, about nineteen people went into the barn an hour, generally coming out half an hour later. In terms of leads, he'd struck gold in finding this place.

In the office back at HQ, they had a dozen whiteboards full of photos he and his relief team had taken of these people. They had so many photographs, in fact, that the agency had had to purchase a dozen more boards. The sheer magnitude of this mystery was mind-blowing.

Without knowing what was so important about the barn, he and his team had floated numerous ideas about what was going on. The most widely believed idea was that it was used as a drug manufacturing plant and that these people were going in to buy the drugs they would later sell on; it seemed the most logical explanation.

They had found out that a man named Alan Harrison owned the property but looking into him had been tough. It hadn't taken long, however, to uncover that he was Vice President of William Rothstein's property development business. They'd also found out that Harrison had married Rothstein's daughter, Beatrice Rothstein – now Harrison.

Steven had managed to shoot some fantastic photos of Beatrice. She was a looker, with long red hair and pale skin. Some of his colleagues took just a bit too long looking at her pictures, he noticed – she'd caused quite a stir with his team when he'd pinned her photos up on the board.

The team back at HQ had already started hauling the barn's visitors in for interviews. The hope was that one or two of them would let slip what went on. So far, they had all remained tight-lipped. He found it interesting how many female visitors he'd filmed; it made him think they might be off base in their opinion it was a "meth lab".

Both the male and female visitors had form, their criminal histories reading like the worst kind of rap sheet. Their criminal activities ranged from assault, battery, and armed robbery to rape and murder. So far, they hadn't seen any paedophiles, but he knew these kinds of people loathed kiddy-fiddlers.

Steven took another photograph, this time a facial shot of a woman in her thirties with long dark hair and a fake tan; she was mostly orange. He watched her walk to her Toyota Land Cruiser and drive back down the dirt track.

Looking at his watch, he saw it was quarter to ten. His shift change was at 15:00, meaning he had just over five hours left on the clock. He couldn't wait – he was looking forward to seeing Ashley and the kids...

29

Assistant Commissioner of Police of the Metropolis, Peter Franks, had taken a rare day off work. His day was his own, and he'd planned it meticulously, choosing a day his wife, Ursula, had to work. He was going to have a nice relaxing day of doing whatever he fancied.

Deciding that he wanted to wash his Jaguar E-PACE, he got up from his comfy armchair and gathered up the bucket and sponge from the kitchen, filling the bucket with hot water and adding some detergent. He enjoyed washing his pride and joy, or rather he enjoyed having a clean car at the end of it.

He'd worked hard for everything he owned including his three cars – two Jaguars and a Land Rover. He had a lovely five-bedroom house in quiet suburbia, located in a good postcode and an even better school district.

His three kids had wanted for nothing growing up, he'd made sure of it. Oliver, his eldest, was a solicitor in a big law firm – so he was set for life. Vincent, his middle child, was a hedge fund manager, earning obscene amounts of money. His youngest, Annabel, was an OBGYN nurse and was doing very well for herself. He doted on his daughter – maybe a little too much – but she was so lovely he couldn't help it.

His retirement would come in a couple of years or so, after this project was leaked to the press and after the fan had stopped spraying the proverbial shit. He'd spent his entire career fighting criminals – fighting a losing battle all the way – and it always made him angry whenever he thought of the scum out there, getting paid for their misdeeds. It made him so angry, in fact, that when the commissioner, his boss, had come to him with this brilliant idea, it hadn't taken long for him to fight his conscience and climb on board. When he heard the benefits and weighed them against the costs, it really was a no-brainer.

Would people call them corrupt police officers? Probably, at first. But after they'd demonstrated the benefits, they would eventually be called heroes. It wasn't like he was the mastermind behind the whole thing; the true engineer of the project was the Home Secretary and the Secretary of State for Justice. Having cabinet ministers backing the project made it easier to agree to; none of them would receive custodial sentences. When the shit did hit the fan, the government machinations would probably hide it and brush it under the carpet, like they normally did.

Franks carried the bucket of water out to his wide driveway, put it on the ground, and wiped his windscreen. It was cold out – about six degrees – yet the sun was shining and his overcoat protected him from the chilly wind.

His mobile rang in his coat pocket, and after wiping his hands on his trousers, Franks retrieved his phone and answered it. "Peter Franks."

"Peter, it's Will. We need to talk. Can we meet?"

"Changed your mind, have you?" Peter asked with a smug smile.

"Can we meet or not?"

He replied that they could and suggested meeting at a park

nearby in two hours. There was a bench overlooking the central bandstand. He said farewell and put his phone back in his pocket. He had not rung the commissioner to inform him of the bad news yet, and by the sound of Rothstein's voice, it was lucky he hadn't.

Although his boss was adamant they needed Rothstein, Franks didn't like the fact they were dealing with him. Back when he was a young police officer, he'd heard horror stories about the young Rothstein. And he'd been part of a task force set up to investigate the man, back when he was in his late thirties – the bastard was slippery. No one had ever agreed to testify against him. That's how he'd escaped punishment; he made them fear for their lives.

Franks wiped the left side of his Jaguar.

So, yes, there were downsides to the project, but he was happy that the benefits were far greater. He was certain they were doing the right thing...

Kimiko placed another pint glass on the tray, then slid the tray of glasses into the glasswasher. She pressed the green button and the machine started whirring. Beattie had asked her to tend bar for the day.

Even though she'd tried everything she could think of, Kimiko couldn't get Danny out of her head. It didn't help having to prepare him four times a day, having to touch him and taste him. Every night she went to sleep thinking about him and every morning she woke up with him on her mind. He'd asked her to sneak in to see him twice, and she'd said no on both occasions. She didn't know how long she could keep saying no for. It would be so easy to creep into his room under the cover of darkness. So easy, she'd dreamt of it:

In her dream she hides in the shadows, narrowly avoiding the guards, quiet, stealthy. She opens the door to find Danny tied to the bed. In her dream she unties him, and he sweeps her up in his strong arms before kissing her, his smooth tongue massaging hers. Then he places her – so gently, like she's a porcelain doll – on the bed and he kisses her all over.

Every day she looked forward to preparing him. She shouldn't feel like this; it wasn't how she was brought up to behave. She was a simple village girl – her father would be so ashamed if he could see her now.

The machine stopped whirring and she pulled the tray out, placing it on the bar top, waiting for them to dry. Picking the tray up, she lowered it to the floor and started putting them on the shelves still wet. Even when she was supposed to be concentrating, she thought about him.

She silently cursed when she spotted she'd put a highball glass in with the pint glasses. It was Danny's fault! Lovely Danny, she thought, a smile creeping over her.

"Kimiko!"

She jumped. Kimiko hadn't noticed Mrs Harrison and a client stood at the bar. Bowing, she forced her smile to vanish; she couldn't afford to give herself away.

"Honestly, what is the matter with you at the moment?" Beattie asked. "Mr Edwards would like a drink, if you can manage that?"

Kimiko listened as Mrs Harrison apologised on her behalf, saying that good staff were hard to come by these days. The client asked for a vodka tonic, so Kimiko obliged, handing him the glass and asking for payment. The man paid her with a ten-pound note and she gave two pound coins back. He then went and sat down on one of the soft sofas with Mrs Harrison.

With her employer busy talking to the client, Kimiko wiped down the bar and attempted to busy her mind, trying not to think about lovely Danny. The edges of her mouth rose again. But she caught herself just in time, hiding her lust. It wasn't easy.

What could she do about it? She couldn't sneak into his room at night and make love to him, could she? No, there was too much at stake... Their lives, for one. Mrs Harrison would kill her if she found out, and Kimiko had no idea what Danny's punishment would be. She couldn't afford to think like this... it was madness...

Danny looked up at Donna. His wrists, ankles, and neck were chained to the bed again. Because it was just for one client, he didn't mind. Donna was a five-minute wonder, which was great because it meant it was over about as soon as it started.

Unusually, she smiled and collapsed on top of him, spent, and he accepted the kisses she bestowed on his neck.

Eventually she released him, standing up and wiping herself with a tissue. "Thank you, Danny, that was marvellous," she said, her cheeks rosy.

"You know, I'm really good with my hands and tongue, if you want to try that next time?" It was the first time he'd spoken to her, more than to say, "You're welcome!"

He watched as she considered it, and when she nodded her approval, he breathed a sigh of relief inside – no more chains. If he never saw a set of chains again, he would die happy.

Donna approached him, bent down, and kissed his cheek, before wrapping herself in her robe and leaving him helpless on the bed.

Two guards came in after a couple of minutes to release him, after which he got up and walked with one of the guards – he didn't know them by name – to the showers. Stepping under the showerhead, Danny felt the strong jets of water on his shoulders and face.

He'd endured eight days of hell at Beattie's hands. For one thing, whenever he'd been alone, she'd left the air conditioning on low, making him shiver all night, every night.

But more than feeling the cold, the most savage part of his punishment had been servicing all the freaks Beattie let in. He even had a scar on his shoulder from a nasty client who'd bitten him – it had actually drawn blood, which she'd then proceeded to lick. He'd been slapped so hard his ears rang, and he'd been punched hard in the face. He'd had to endure so many humiliating fetishists.

It hadn't been all bad, however. After all, he'd found out that lovely Nas was out there looking for him. If there was one regret he had in life, it was dumping her. She was the best girlfriend he'd ever had, and she'd been besotted with him. He was, however, a walking hard-on; the grass was always greener with him, and still was. It was why he made such a good escort; it gave him the variety he craved. Though after this experience, he was starting to think otherwise.

Back when they had been really tight – before the beginning of the end, before he'd cheated on her with five different women – they'd confessed their dreams to each other. He'd told her about his fantasy of becoming a famous painter, and she'd confided in him her desire of becoming a police officer. That was how he'd known it was Nas that nasty old hag, Francesca, was talking about.

He often thought about Nasreen and what she was doing, though he'd never summoned the nerve to call her up unexpectedly, not wanting to drag up the past and hurt her again. He wasn't good enough for her anyway; he wasn't a good man, full stop. She deserved someone who would treat her right, and unfortunately, he didn't qualify.

He often wondered why he couldn't remain interested in one person for long, especially with Nas, who'd been the whole package: she was lovely-looking, had a great smile, a good body... There he went again, thinking of physical attributes first. She was smart, funny, kind, generous – things every guy needed in a girlfriend – so why couldn't he have just been satisfied? He knew the answer to that question: boredom.

Danny poured shower gel in his hands, lathered it up, and rubbed it over his face, under his armpits, and between his legs. As the jets washed it off, he stood there, feeling the heat, leaning forwards against the wall as the water probed his back.

He was glad it was Nas looking for him. She wouldn't give up – she didn't know how. His ex-girlfriend was the single-most stubborn person he'd ever met, which was good for him.

Turning the tap to the right, Danny stopped the shower and stepped out of the cubicle. As he dried himself off, he saw a woman drying herself to his left. Their eyes met briefly, before he heard a guard tell them to turn away. He turned and continued drying himself.

He couldn't, however, bank on Nas being able to find him. From what he could make out – from what Kimiko had told him anyway – this place had been going for at least sixteen years, and bees had come and gone... and by gone he meant been killed. No, he had to accept the fact that he might have to get himself out of here, so he'd just have to wait and see if an opportunity arose. Failing that, he was making headway with Kimiko; she could still be his escape to freedom...

30

Assistant Commissioner Peter Franks saw William Rothstein walking past the bandstand, approaching the bench he'd suggested they meet at. He was stood in a clearing of a wooded path, and after reaching into his pocket and pulling out his mobile, he dialled Rothstein's number and waited. When Rothstein answered, Franks told him where he was.

Whenever Franks looked at Rothstein, he felt failure; Rothstein was everything he despised in this world, and he had failed to put this sociopath inside. He profited off everyone else's misery, but more than that, he was responsible for six murders that Franks knew about – not that anyone was willing to testify against him – and one of those six had been a civilian woman, who'd been in the wrong place at the wrong time and caught a bullet in the chest.

When the project was finally up and running, they were going to put so many of these people away, it would almost make up for Rothstein's freedom. Almost. They might even have to build more prisons just to house the dealers they would incarcerate. Franks smiled at the thought.

"Peter!" Rothstein said in greeting.

"Let's walk and talk," Franks said as he turned.

They walked side by side through the wooded section of the park. There were fewer people around, which was good. The last thing Franks wanted was to be seen with Rothstein. "What's on your mind, Will?"

"I've had a change of heart. I'm on board, but first I have some concessions."

That was about right, thought Franks – Rothstein believing he could bargain his way in. The nerve of this guy! "Glad you're with us," he replied, remaining nonchalant. "What about your supplier? I thought you said you wouldn't do it without him."

"The guy you met in my office, who greeted you at the door?"

"The black guy?"

"Yeah, him. He's my supplier's nephew. I couldn't be honest with you earlier, not with him around."

"But you sent him out of the room."

"He's bugged my office; he thinks I don't know. I went along with the meeting at mine so when Lenny reports back to his uncle, I'm in the clear."

"Okay," Franks said quietly, still confused.

"Which brings me to my first concession. When this thing starts, I'm going to get blowback from Lenny and his uncle, which is why Lenny's got to go... if you know what I mean."

Franks stopped walking.

Rothstein followed suit, and they stared at one another for a second.

"You can't mean you expect us to..."

"Relax! I don't mean kill him. I have an idea what to do, but I'll need your help when the time comes."

Franks listened as Rothstein explained his plan in detail, nodding at the right times and making the correct comments. He was listening, while also thinking about all the things this guy had done – it wasn't fair.

"Okay," Franks said once Rothstein had finished, "when the time comes, call me and I'll sort it. The place you're talking about is in another force's district, but the chief constable there is one of us, so it's no problem." After a brief pause, he said, "And the other concession is?"

Franks watched as Rothstein looked down at the floor, sighed, and looked back up.

"I have a real problem with the NCA, one you'll need to fix."

Who the hell did this guy think he was! The project really wasn't worth helping this guy keep his criminal empire, but as much as he detested Rothstein, the commissioner had been clear about how important he was for its success. He had to swallow his pride and deal with it. "What kind of problem?"

"The kind only top dogs can sort." Rothstein was as cryptic as ever. "They're probing my businesses and they have their eye on one in particular that they can't look into. I can't afford to lose it. The investigation has to disappear."

"And how are we supposed to do that?"

"My insider tells me the Assistant Director General is into all sorts. Maybe you can talk to him, see if wants to come on board? You get him onside, maybe he can terminate the investigation?"

"Yeah, well, we won't get far with the Director General, that's for sure. He's as straight as they come. Believe me, he won't be swayed, no matter how much you throw at him. And he's good friends with the prime minister."

"So, maybe the Director General should go? Replace him with one of our own?"

Franks couldn't believe he was talking about killing the most senior officer at the National Crime Agency with a known thug and murderer. The commissioner said the project must proceed, but he hadn't said anything about offing people in its name. This wasn't what he'd agreed to. "Let me talk it through with the commissioner, see what we can sort out," Franks told Rothstein.

"The NCA operates under a different remit than we do. The commissioner will know what to do, though..."

"So, you're just a pawn, huh? People upstairs pulling your strings?"

"We're all pawns, Will. We all answer to someone."

Rothstein shook his head. "Not me. I don't answer to anyone."

Franks stepped back a pace and stared at Rothstein. He was trying to goad him into agreeing to assassinate the DG of the NCA in order to save his own arse. Rothstein answered to people; he answered to his suppliers... Oh wait, no he didn't. It must be nice not answering to anyone, Franks thought, leaving a bitter taste. "Good for you," he said, "but I have to discuss it with my boss."

"Hey, you're helping me out with my first problem, so it's only fair that I help you out with this, right? Your lot don't have to do anything; leave it to me."

"No, Will, leave it," Franks insisted. "Whatever you're planning, hold fire until I've spoken to the commissioner, okay?"

"There won't be any problems, Peter, I promise," insisted Rothstein. "You don't have anything to worry about. You don't even need to call the commissioner; just be ready to have the Assistant DG promoted."

"Why wouldn't I need to speak to my boss?"

"People will just think he's died in an accident, so there's no problem." Rothstein shrugged. "People will cry, but the world carries on spinning and we'll have a new Director General in our pocket."

They spoke for a while longer.

Franks still couldn't believe he was planning the assassination of a high-ranking law enforcement official with a known drugs importer and murderer. This was not how he'd intended his day to go, not at all... How had it come to this...?

31

"Please come visit me tonight," Danny begged. "Come after everyone's gone?"

Kimiko shook her head. "I tell you before, I want to, but can't," she whispered back, as she dusted his chest of drawers. "I sorry, Danny, but no. Too dangerous. Mrs Harrison kill me. She kill us both."

In case Mrs Harrison was watching, Kimiko made sure to face away from the camera when she spoke. Her employer was so smart, she could probably read lips. It was infuriating how smart Mrs Harrison was, as it meant she couldn't get away with anything. What had ever made her think she could get away with sneaking into Danny's room and making love to him?

"I want to be with you," he whispered. "You're amazing, I want you... please come."

"No, Danny!" Her whisper sounded angry.

Kimiko watched as he splayed his arms out in surrender, saying, "Okay," before lying back on his bed in a sulk. If he wasn't careful, Mrs Harrison would know what was going on; she always knew.

Having finished her cleaning duties, Kimiko said goodnight

to Danny and closed the door, locking it behind her. She carried the cleaning supplies to the store area and placed everything in their designated spaces. On her way back out, she stopped outside the office.

The door was open and there was no one inside. Looking around, she saw that the guards had all left for the evening. Mrs Harrison was nowhere to be seen. Kimiko looked up at the clock on the wall and saw it was half past seven.

Stepping inside the office, she stood looking at the phone on Mrs Harrison's desk. How easy would it be to call the police right now? There was no one around, and the phone was right there. She could pick it up, dial nine-nine-nine, and say she'd been kidnapped, please help. Even though she didn't know where she was, the police would be able to trace the phone number, wouldn't they?

She stepped closer to the desk.

It could all be over in less than a minute. She could phone the police now, and they could burst through the hatch and down those steps in less than an hour.

She could save all these people with one simple phone call.

She could help put Mrs Harrison in prison, where she belonged.

Kimiko reached the desk and stared down at the phone.

Silence.

There were no guards, no Mrs Harrison, no Mr Harrison.

Her lips tightened as her hand reached out for the life-saving communication device. It felt like her arm was elongating, or the phone was getting further away, she wasn't sure which.

One phone call, that was all it would take.

Pick it up! she told herself. *Dial the number and say you've been kidnapped!*

She heard voices in the distance.

With haste, she stepped into the hallway, stopping when she saw two guards.

Kimiko closed her eyes and breathed a sigh of relief as she leaned against the wall.

"Hey, Kimiko, make us drinks."

Obediently, she hurried behind the bar and made the two Croatians vodka rocks, their favourite tipple. The guards – she didn't know or want to know their names – stood at the bar, talking and laughing in their own language, while she finished cleaning up after them...

Nasreen had called her next eyewitness and asked him if it was okay to meet at half eight. He'd agreed and suggested meeting up in a local pub called the Squid and Rabbit.

The office was quiet, with just a couple of detectives still at their desks. Adams' office door was still open, which meant he was milling around; he had a literal open-door policy in his office, which she admired. She'd worked a couple of jobs in her younger days and the owners/managers would sooner spit at you than talk to a mere mortal member of staff. No, Adams was good like that – whatever you needed, he was there to help.

Adams had briefed them on their new case earlier that morning, and they'd travelled to a shopping high street, where the body of a woman had been dumped behind some wheelie bins. They'd had to walk down an alleyway between two department stores to see what they were dealing with. The woman had looked to be early- to mid-thirties with long brown hair, and she'd been dumped face down, naked.

After the crime scene unit had carried out their role, Nasreen and Terrence had turned the poor woman over, identifying the cause of death immediately: her throat was slashed, with what looked like a serrated knife – the flesh was torn, rather than cleanly sliced. Because the victim had been dumped naked, they had no means of identification. Fingerprints might help them, but only if she was in the system.

They certainly had their work cut out for them. They'd managed to identify her, which was a start. As it turned out the victim was a nurse, they'd spent a good few hours that afternoon interviewing colleagues and friends of Phoebe Lockhart at the hospital she worked at.

Glancing at the clock, Nasreen saw it was quarter to eight. So she grabbed her jacket from her chair, put it over her white blouse, and picked up her black bag.

As she was running late for meeting Ian Rowbotham in the Squid and Rabbit, she quickly shut off her PC, poured her paperwork into the drawer, remembering to lock it, and rolled her chair under the desk, all neat and tidy. No one was going to call her slovenly.

Once she'd walked through the double doors to the landing area, she had to decide whether to take the lift or walk it down four flights of stairs. Deciding the stairs would be faster than the lift, she opened the emergency exit doors and trotted down two steps before hearing a voice. It was an angry voice.

She looked over the railing. Adams was on his mobile; his back was to her. To be safe, she crept back up the steps and loitered, listening to Adams' conversation.

"And you're telling me this now?"

She'd never heard Adams talk like this.

"And you think this is a good idea?

Pause.

"The man's a menace; he represents everything we despise."

Pause.

"I don't think it's worth the price. Having to deal with him isn't what I signed up for."

Nasreen frowned. What was he talking about? *Who* was he

talking about? She only wished she could hear the other side of the call. Whatever they were arguing over, it sounded serious, and dodgy.

"So, you're pulling rank on me?"

Pause.

"And what if I quit?"

Nasreen audibly gasped, but not loud enough to interrupt her boss.

"I know what's at stake, sir."

Pause.

"Okay, but I want it on the record that I don't agree with this choice."

Pause.

"Jesus, another thing? Wasn't that enough?"

Pause.

"No way. You're wrong. She's a great investigator, a great officer. Nasreen wouldn't do that."

Upon hearing her name mentioned, Nasreen gasped again. Was this about Danny? It was just too creepy; she wished she knew who Adams was talking to.

"If she's been investigating Rose's disappearance under the radar, I'd know about it."

Nasreen's stomach lurched.

"I can't argue with that. I'll talk to her in the morning, size her up. If she has, she won't be going anywhere near it anymore, I promise."

Pause.

"Okay, I'll speak to you soon. And please, no more surprises?"

When Nasreen heard Adams start to walk up the stairs, she crept up and around the next flight of steps, then watched as he walked back through the double doors and into the office. She sat on the top step, leaning on her knees, her mind racing.

What was Adams thinking? From that conversation, it sounded like he was involved in something shady. And how did the mystery caller know she was investigating Danny's disappearance? The respect she'd had for Adams not five minutes earlier was now gone, evaporated. Was her super corrupt?

When she was positive he had gone, she rushed down the five flights to the ground floor and flew out of the rear fire exit. Her car was parked two spaces down, and she jumped in and accelerated away.

Once on the road, she thought some more about what she'd heard. Could she be reading too much into this? Could there be a simple and rational explanation? She shook her head when she realised that her gut had, up to that point, always been the best judge of any given circumstance, and it usually proved to be correct.

Her gut was telling her that Adams was on the make...

32

Beattie had taken ages getting ready for Lennox's visit. She'd showered, shaved her legs and armpits, and carried out the usual hygiene musts, but choosing her outfit had been the tough part. She thought that Lennox would probably prefer her buck naked, as most men did.

She'd decided on a maxi dress, mid-grey, which went down to the floor on her. She could almost be mistaken for floating when she walked. She'd meant to have it taken up a bit; unfortunately, she'd not found the time. She looked amazing in it, though, even if she did say so herself. The shop assistant's jaw had all but dropped on the floor when she'd tried it on.

Looking up at the clock, Beattie saw it was two minutes past nine.

All day she had waited to see him, and for just thirty minutes. She had to find a way of getting more time with him – ask her father if he could work here, maybe? No, that wouldn't work. She could tell her father about Alan's long absences, though, maybe request some kind of help in here, at least temporarily? There must be something she could do.

"Hey, Bea."

Standing, she greeted Lennox with their newly customary kiss on both cheeks. She could hear her heartbeat; it was so strong. "Hi!"

"You look nice," commented Lennox. "That colour suits you."

"Thanks. It's just an old dress I haven't worn in a while. Laundry day."

There was no way that was going to fool him – she could tell by the way he raised his dark eyebrows and nodded slowly. Her dress practically screamed "brand new".

"Old or new, it looks good on you."

She sat, watching him open the safe and transport the cash to the other desk. He looked great, too. "It's warm in here, isn't it? Do you want me to take your coat?"

"Take it where?" He turned to her with a grin, before taking it off. "Just put it in the corner, Bea. I'm not going to take long with this."

"Oh? Do you have plans tonight?" she asked, trying to sound casual. "A hot date, perhaps?"

"Nope. Your dad has another job for me. He wants to go through it with me tonight."

Damn her father! He was always getting in her way. "Drink before you go? Cup of tea?"

"Yeah, that would be great, thanks," Lennox replied, sorting the cash into three denominations.

Beattie walked through to the bar and made two cups of tea, using the professional coffee machine she'd had installed two years earlier. She was more of a tea drinker, whereas her clients generally appreciated a decent cup of coffee when they visited.

She placed one cup on the desk in front of him – almost spilling some on the fifties he was busy counting – and stood watching him, holding her drink and occasionally sipping.

He was so cute, she thought, observing how muscular he

was. She could see the muscles on his back through his white T-shirt. His biceps were rock hard too; she could tell how firm they'd be to the touch. She could imagine how safe she'd feel in his arms, and...

"Bea, everything all right?"

"Huh?"

"You've been standing behind me for a while. You okay?"

With her daydreaming, she hadn't noticed that he'd finished counting the fifties and was halfway through counting the twenties. Embarrassed, she turned and cursed under her breath, not loud enough for him to hear.

"Alan still away, is he?"

"He's never in these days," she replied, sitting back down at her desk. "Not that I mind. We've grown apart, is all. Happens to lots of couples, I guess."

She noticed he was counting the tens – soon he would be finished, and she'd have to wait another twenty-four hours for his company. What was wrong with her? She was a strong woman, independent, self-assured. So why was she pining after a man like some love-struck teenager? No! This wouldn't do!

"Right, that's me done."

She rose up to say goodbye too quickly, and before she knew it she had tripped and fallen into him. His strong arms steadied her, and then she looked up, into his beautiful brown eyes.

She heard him say, "Ah, why not," a moment before their lips met...

Nasreen arrived late to the Squid and Rabbit. When she looked at her watch, she saw it was twenty-five past nine. She hoped he was still here.

Walking up to the bar of the gastro pub, she ordered a soda

and lime, or as she called it, a slime. There were lots of tables filled with groups of people at various stages of eating; some on starters, some on mains, some on desserts. It was busy.

At the far end of the pub was an area with seating, a pool table, and a darts board. A man in blue jeans, white trainers, and a mid-brown jumper stood up and caught her eye, before waving her over. He was fat – she estimated him to be about twenty, maybe twenty-one stone – and most of the flab fell over his belt. He had a tiny little moustache, topping off the ensemble.

"Are you the detective?" he asked.

She reached into her jacket pocket and pulled out her badge, showing it to him for confirmation. "Detective Constable Nasreen Maqsood," she affirmed. "Ian Rowbotham?"

"Take a seat," Rowbotham said, pulling out a chair. "My mate was just here, but he's got to get home to the missus."

Nasreen placed her drink on the table and sat down next to him, not opposite. She figured he wouldn't want anyone knowing he was talking to a police officer.

"So, what can I do for you, Detective Maqsood? Maqsood... where's that from?"

"Pakistan," she answered, with a fake smile. She hoped he couldn't tell. "My family's from Pakistan."

"Whereabouts? I visited a few years back. Lovely country, really friendly people."

"A small town near Lahore. You won't have heard of it."

"So, what're you doing in this shithole then? I mean, don't get me wrong, England's all right, but it's nothing compared to your country."

"I was born here; this is home," she answered, hoping this wasn't going to end up being a racism-laced interview. Why couldn't people understand that just because her extended family lived in Pakistan, it didn't mean she had to as well? She had as much right to live in "Engerlaaand" as anyone else born here. She tried to keep her temper in check.

He nodded and said, "Right," but in a weird way, like he didn't quite understand.

"Sorry I was late getting here; traffic was a nightmare," she said, changing the subject. "Are you still all right to talk now?"

"I'm not going to tell you anything I haven't said to your lot already."

"My lot?" she repeated, her temper rising slightly.

"Detectives."

"Oh, right, from before, you mean?" She knew she was being super-sensitive, but it was only because he'd put her on edge with his demeanour.

"You have to understand this was eight years ago, and my memory's not great."

"I understand, Mr Rowbotham," she replied. "If you can just talk me through what you saw on May nineteenth, I'd appreciate it."

Nasreen listened as the witness described seeing two men carrying what looked like a body across a road from a park, before dumping it in a white or cream-coloured van. Rowbotham had been out driving his lorry in the early hours that day and estimated the time to be about half three in the morning. It mirrored the testimony of Valerie Chapman, right down to the colour of the van. Her gut told her that these two cases had been committed by the same abductors; she had no doubt in her mind. She bet that if she scoured the PNC she'd find that a white van had been torched near that abduction site too.

"I have a photo in my bag of the two men we suspect abducted Daniel Rose," she explained, reaching into her handbag. "Do you mind taking a look at it for me, and seeing if you think these are the two men you saw?"

Rowbotham nodded and she passed the photograph across the table, turning it the right way for him to see.

Nasreen waited while he picked his glasses up and put them on, which made his face look even rounder. "Take your time."

"It was eight years ago, so I can't be a hundred per cent certain." He picked up the photo and stared hard. "I don't know, maybe."

"Your best guess?"

"One was butch and the other skinnier. I'd say... yeah, it's probably them."

She could feel the excitement building up inside her, and although there was no way he could be certain, it was a start. "Thank you, Mr Rowbotham. You've been a big help," she replied, taking the photo from him and sliding it back in her handbag.

When she said her goodbyes to the witness – after asking him several more questions – she left the pub and walked back to her car. There was no way these two cases could be separate. Both abductees were male escorts, and they'd both been abducted in parks near to their homes. The MO was identical in both investigations. She believed wholeheartedly that the other missing persons cases had been due to the same two suspects as well, but to what end? What could these perpetrators want with male escorts?

33

Passion overtook them. They kissed vigorously, as though it was the one and only kiss they would ever get.

"Wait, wait," said Lennox, as he pulled away abruptly.

"What? What's wrong?"

"We can't be doing this, Bea. It's not a good idea."

She knew he was right, no matter how much she wanted him to be wrong. "I know… Daddy will kill us if he finds out," she added, her legs dangling off the desk.

"I'm sorry. It was my fault. I got carried away."

With a half-smile, she said, "It does take two, Lennox."

For a few moments there was an awkward, frustrated, and disappointed silence.

She slid off the desk and stood facing him. There were no words to describe her sadness at not being able to kiss him anymore. It wasn't fair. What did it matter to her dad if she had sex with him? Why could her husband go out and do whatever he wanted with whomever he chose, when she had to stay in and be good? Why couldn't she have some fun for a change?

"I'm so sorry, Bea. I've got to go meet your father."

Beattie accepted Lennox's farewell kiss on the lips and then watched as he picked up the suitcase, put on his coat, and walked out, closing the door behind him. He didn't hide his disappointment well.

Alone in the office, Beattie stamped her foot as tears of sorrow flowed down her cheeks. She sat down on the chair, bent forwards, put her head down, and sobbed, the sad sound filling the air.

The landline phone rang.

Beattie wiped her face and straightened up, trying to hold back the sobs, and when she picked up the receiver and said hello, her voice sounded strained.

"It's me," came Walter's voice. "I followed that bitch to a pub tonight. She met a fat man who saw me. It was eight years ago."

She sniffed audibly. "How can you be so sure it was the same person?"

"You not forget a man like him... he's fat, very fat. He drove a lorry past us; he saw us. It was why I had to burn the first van."

Beattie sighed. "Yes, I remember."

So, the persistent detective was still out there investigating Danny's disappearance? She didn't like committed people, especially not committed detectives. As careful as they'd been for the past sixteen years, if left unchecked, this detective could end up finding her quarry, which would lead her back here. There was no way Beattie could let that happen. "Okay, Walter, let's pay this bitch a little visit. Give her a warning."

"This I can do," replied the Bavarian guard...

Having said goodnight to Mrs Harrison over an hour earlier, Kimiko slipped on her plimsolls, wrapped herself in a floral sky-blue kimono, and looked at the clock next to her bed: 23:36. She tiptoed to the door, opened it a crack, and looked through the gap. The landing was empty, and she couldn't hear anyone upstairs. The guards were either out or upstairs asleep, or watching television. She held her breath as she slipped out onto the landing.

Still on her tiptoes, she descended the stairs, walked to the front door, and opened it, slipping out into the cold black night. She waited for her eyes to adjust to the dark, even though she knew the way to the barn well enough – she'd walked it enough times. Turning, she checked no one was behind her. If she couldn't see two feet in front of her, there was no way anyone would be able to see her.

When she reached the barn, she unlocked it, lifting the wooden locking planks and placing them on the floor. She opened the barn door just a crack, enough for her to creep in, and then closed the door behind her. She froze for a second, deciding to go back out, pull in the locking planks, and bring them inside. To anyone who might pass, the doors looked shut.

Fortunately, the Land Rover wasn't parked over the hatch, so she didn't need to worry about moving it. It was one of the obstacles she'd been concerned about. Mrs Harrison sometimes parked it over the hatch, and sometimes she didn't.

Being careful not to make a sound, she opened the hatch in the darkness and descended the thirty stairs. She was scared, but she also felt alive. Kimiko could feel how excited she was getting in anticipation of finally seeing Danny alone, with no one watching them on the monitors.

Downstairs, the only light available was coming from the bar; the lager pumps and fridges were lit, though they didn't give her much visibility.

She crept through the bar seating area and into the corridor where the rooms were located, not stopping until she reached Danny's room.

Using her set of keys, she quietly unlocked the door.

"Danny," she whispered, closing the door behind her. She could just about make out his shadow on the bed.

"Kimiko, you came," Danny whispered.

She took small nervous steps towards him.

"Come here, beautiful," he said, his voice soothing. "I've been looking forward to this for ages; I can't believe you're actually here."

She joined Danny, sitting on the edge of the bed. "I very nervous," came her small voice. "I not done this before."

His hand found her waist.

Finding the courage from deep inside, she stood and flipped her plimsolls off before letting her kimono drop to the floor. She knew he couldn't see her properly, but it still felt invigorating to be naked with him.

He patted the bed and she joined him, lying back with her head on the pillow.

It was really happening...

34

Day 28
Wednesday, 7th February

Kimiko felt safer in Danny's arms than she had in a long time, longer than she could remember. She knew she shouldn't, given where they were. Sharing her first night of passion with Danny was as delicious as in her dreams. And now it was over. She had to get back to her bedroom before she was found. "I got to leave now, Danny. Mrs Harrison be up soon."

"Come back tonight, will you? Please?"

"I try," she replied, sitting up and feeling the carpet with her toes.

Danny sighed. She could tell he was disappointed, although there was nothing they could do; if they didn't want to be found by the guards – or worse, Mrs Harrison – Kimiko had to get moving. "I be back tonight," she whispered.

"You promise?"

"It depend on guards and Mrs Harrison, but I promise I try."

"That's good enough for me."

Kimiko found her robe and slipped it on, then did the same with her plimsolls. She didn't want to leave him, yet their circumstances dictated she must. It took her another ten minutes of kissing him goodbye before she finally opened the door and left the room, locking it behind her.

Fortunately, she'd left just in time; none of the guards had awoken, and there was no sign of Mr or Mrs Harrison. Kimiko crept up the stairs to her room, slowly closing the door, making sure it didn't creak.

When she closed the door, safe in the knowledge that no one had seen her, she leaned back against it and smiled.

What a night! She was finally a woman. She had made love to a beautiful man. And Danny really was beautiful, from his lovely dark hair all the way down to his cute toes and everything in between, including his... She giggled for the first time in years.

The clock next to her bed said 04:45, and although she had enough time for a tiny nap, she was far too excited to sleep. She couldn't wait to see her Danny again, and she would in just a few hours, when she had to clean his room, and prepare him.

She had time for a long soak in the bath, and knowing that she would have to wash her kimono before Mrs Harrison smelt it, she took it along the landing to the bathroom, turned on the taps in the sink and soaked it, while she drew herself a hot bubbly bath.

She stepped in, then gradually eased her way under the steaming water. As she lay back, caressing her legs, she thought about her most amazing night. Just thinking about him excited her. Was this it? Was this love?

. . .

Beattie awoke to the sound of her burner phone ringing, and she reached across the bed, feeling Alan's empty pillow. Away for the whole night again, even though he'd told her he'd be back in the early hours.

She sighed as she picked up her phone, looking at the caller before answering it. "Hello, Daddy," she said, as normally as she could. She'd cried herself to sleep, her voice was coarse.

"Morning, princess. An acquaintance of mine is on his way to the farm. He'll be with you in twenty. The usual deal, usual price, okay? Oh, and make sure they back their motor into the barn; our law enforcement friends are taking pictures."

Beattie sat up suddenly. "They're taking pictures? Of what, the farm?"

"Relax, princess, relax! I've got a source inside; he tells me they're just gathering intelligence. They haven't got anything on us. And besides, I've got something in the pipeline that'll make them call off the investigation altogether."

"But still, Daddy, shouldn't we cancel all our appointments until–"

"Not a chance. It's business as usual until I say differently. Now, go meet my colleagues and make sure they back into the barn. If the NCA see what they have in the boot, they'll have all the intel they need."

"I'll be ready when they get here."

She hung up and pulled herself out of bed. All she wanted to do was lie there, feeling sorry for herself. Now, she had to worry about the bloody National Crime Agency outside, taking photos of the comings and goings here? She trusted her daddy, and felt uneasy, knowing that law enforcement agencies were on her doorstep – literally.

Beattie decided not to shower and got dressed, choosing a pair of dark jeans and a cottage rose tunic. Not bothering to apply any make-up, she brushed her hair quickly in front of her full-length mirror, noticing the bags under her eyes. Awful. She looked awful.

Downstairs, she walked into the kitchen and switched the kettle on, before getting her mug prepped for her first cup of tea. When she opened the refrigerator, she noticed they were almost out of milk, so she made a mental note to have a go at Kimiko for letting supplies get so low. It was yet another example of Kimiko's new scatterbrain. It hadn't gone unnoticed.

The clock above the refrigerator said it was 05:55.

With five minutes before her visitors arrived, she was quick making her drink.

After putting on her green Parka jacket, she walked outside into the freezing blackness, armed with only a torch, walking along the two hundred-metre pathway until she came to the barn.

The headlights of an off-road vehicle bathed her in light as she unlocked the doors.

Turning around, she walked up to the Range Rover driver's side and said that they had to back into the barn, though she didn't say why, not wanting to spook them. She opened the barn doors, waited while the driver reversed his vehicle inside, then closed the doors from the inside. When she was sure that the NCA couldn't see what they were doing, she switched on the lights.

The two craggy-looking visitors exited the Range Rover and the passenger went around to the boot and opened it. She looked inside and could see a body shaped object wrapped in a sheet. At one end – she assumed the head end – blood had seeped through the sheet and soaked through to the interior of the vehicle.

As the driver approached her, he reached inside his thick black leather jacket and pulled out an envelope. "Your dad said two gs? That right?"

"If that's what Daddy said," she replied, taking the fat envelope from him.

Without talking to them any further, she showed them down the stairs – wishing her father would budge on getting a lift installed – through the bar, past the rooms, and over to the furnace room, where they stopped. She then opened up and led them inside, where the furnace was roaring away.

"What do we do? Just bung him in there?"

"That's the plan."

The passenger – who'd carried the body downstairs – dumped it on the floor, took off the sheet, and stood there for a moment, staring down at it. "Should we say something?"

Beattie studied the dead body. Half his face was missing – whoever had shot him had done it with a shotgun, by the looks of it; half of the dead man's jaw was missing and the rest of one half of his face was pulp, bone, and red tissue. She felt queasy.

"Nah, let's just get this done and get out of here," replied the driver.

Judging by the way the passenger had his head down and his hands clasped in front of him, like he was at the man's funeral, Beattie assumed the dead man used to be a friend of theirs. She could have been wrong.

She stood back as the two men picked up the body, one at either end, and lifted it into the furnace. The fire appeared to go out, but she insisted it would be roaring in a matter of minutes. She closed the furnace door and led the two visitors back upstairs to their Range Rover, where they each shook her hand. She then opened the barn doors for them and watched as they drove away.

These visits were commonplace for her. In the sixteen years that she'd lived here, her dad had probably sent over a hundred visitors to her farm for this very purpose. Over a hundred bodies had been incinerated, never to be seen again. It had made her dad a small fortune and was a very handy service to be able to offer his colleagues.

The first couple of times it had bothered her, but by the time she'd seen three or four disposals, she'd become desensitised to it. Now, none of this stuff bothered her; she still felt queasy, sure, but she felt queasy around blood anyway. The worst body she had seen was a man who'd died from an acid attack; his face was melted. The smell had been awful too...

35

Clive Adams frowned. "Please tell me you haven't been running around asking potential witnesses about Daniel Rose, Detective Maqsood. Please tell me that."

Nasreen didn't know how to respond. She had both Adams and Terrence glaring at her. While she was looking at Adams, she could feel Terrence's stare. "I've been making some enquiries, yes," she replied.

Adams looked up at the ceiling.

"I did it off the clock, sir."

He glared back at her. "And that's why I just got a call from the IOPC! Someone you interviewed said you were questioning them out of hours. And what's more, they said they saw you drive away in your red Fiesta. So, investigating a case out of hours is fine in your humble opinion, is it?"

"Well, no, but I'm showing initiative," she said, knowing the rebuke would come. "And can I ask who complained, sir? And why?"

"Jesus Christ, Detective Maqsood! Showing initiative is clocking up extra hours when asked, or volunteering at schools as a police liaison. And no, you can't ask; it's not my place to say."

"But, sir, no one's actively looking for Danny," she said, suddenly realising she'd done it again. She really was in the shit now.

"Excuse me, Danny? Do you know the victim, Detective Maqsood?" His voice was getting louder and angrier with every word.

What should she do, lie? Why should she justify her actions to a dirty cop? He was the one who should be justifying *his* actions, not her. At least she was out there trying to do some good – unlike him, trying to impede her investigation.

"So, do you know Daniel Rose or not, detective?"

"Yes, sir, I know him," she answered. "I went to school with him."

"Oh my God! It gets worse." Adams turned his back on her, his hands clasped on top of his head.

"Tell him the rest, Nas," she heard Terrence say. "It's cards on the table time."

Yeah, thanks, Terrence, thanks a lot, she thought as she turned her head to look at her supervisor. She thought she could trust him.

"Tell me the rest of what?" Adams had turned to her again, his face even more flustered.

"Go on, Nas, tell him!"

"...He's my ex-boyfriend."

Adams' silence said it all. He stood there staring at her, his face getting redder by the second. She thought his head might explode, it was so red. "Your fucking *ex*?" he said eventually. "Are you fucking kidding me right now?"

"It's why I have to find him, sir, don't you see? I've already made progress–"

"Stop right there!" he yelled, before shaking his head and taking a deep breath. When he spoke again, his voice was quiet, yet full of anger. "I don't want to hear what you've got, not one word. You've broken God knows how many rules and regulations, codes of conduct... you've put yourself and everyone you've talked to in danger... Fuck! You'll be lucky if you only get suspended for this, you do realise that, don't you!"

"Please, take a look at–"

"One more word from you and you'll be suspended immediately! I knew appointing you was a mistake from the start. I knew choosing you to bolster our ethnic intake would result in something like this. Now shut... the... fuck... up!"

Nasreen stood up straight. There was nothing he could do to stop her from continuing her investigation. She might lose her job, but she didn't care. This guy was a crooked cop. She wasn't going to let him win. Even so, she kept her mouth shut.

"And as for you, Detective Johnson," he said, turning to Terrence, "did you know about this?"

"Well, sir, I didn't know Nas was investigating this on her own, no."

"But you clearly knew she had a relationship with the victim, didn't you?"

She could hear Terrence squirming next to her. Good, she thought, backstabber! A smile almost crept over her – almost; inside she was crowing that Terrence was now on the receiving end of Adams' rage.

"Um, yes, I knew," Terrence replied, eyes down.

Adams closed his eyes and sighed, and when he opened them again, he asked, "Right, is there anything else I need to know? Anything else you can tell me that will help give me an ulcer?"

They shook their heads.

"Okay, I need to think what my next course of action's going to be. You two have fucked up on such a monumentally epic scale that I'll need to speak with the IOPC about this and see what they say. You two are grounded until further notice."

"Yes, sir," they replied.

"Now get out of my fucking office, the pair of you!"

Nasreen followed Terrence out of Adams' office, along a corridor, and into an empty conference room. She was in for it with Terrence now. She heard the door slam, it closing so violently she felt the air brush her cheeks.

Here we go, she thought, round two.

"Thanks a fucking bunch, Nas!" Terrence boomed. "I'm in the shit for something you did! And now the IOPC's going to investigate me and everything I've done!"

"He said they received a complaint against me, not you! And you got yourself in the shit, so that's on you!" she shouted back, her temper rising by the second. "If you hadn't said anything it'd just be me in the shit."

"What?"

"You heard me. If you'd kept quiet you could've denied knowing anything, but you didn't – you just wanted to get me in deeper, so no, thank you."

That shut him up. Terrence paced back and forth over the same stretch of blue carpet.

"Why did you lie to me?" he asked finally. "I'd have told you to stop, to leave it, and we'd both still have our jobs!"

"I never lied to you!" She pointed at him. "I didn't say I'm not continuing the investigation. You never asked, and I never told! When we got given this case I told you I was going to find him. I'm surprised you didn't know I was doing it outside of work hours. Did you think I'd really just drop it because Adams told me to? Danny's my friend, and that's what I do for friends, and what I'd do again if I had to."

Another long silence enveloped them.

"He's crooked, you know," she said eventually, her voice cool and pointed.

"What? Who?" Terrence asked, in a calmer voice. He had his back turned to her.

"Adams. I heard him in the stairwell last night. I overheard him talking to someone on his mobile. He's on the take."

"Don't be so stupid." Terrence turned back to face her.

"It's true; I heard him talking to someone about knowing what's at stake, about having to deal with someone who represented everything he hates, and whoever he was talking to warned him that I was investigating Danny's disappearance. Adams told them I wouldn't be after today. He's right so far, except that I'm going to carry on."

"Stop it, Nas." Terrence held his hands up. "This has gone far enough. If you want to get fired, that's your business, but I want to keep my job."

"Even if it means working for a corrupt super?"

"You have no proof of that. All I've got to go on is your word, and right now your word means fuck all to me."

Nasreen turned her back on him. It was frustrating, but she hadn't expected him to believe her straight away; it was a lot to take in. If she hadn't come to terms with it yet, she couldn't expect Terrence to have accepted it.

Another silence fell over them.

Finally, after a few minutes of quiet, Terrence opened the conference door and she followed him into the corridor. She looked back down the hallway at Adams' office and saw him talking on his mobile phone.

"Look," Nasreen whispered to Terrence, "he's probably talking to his co-conspirator right now, telling him how he's grounded us, congratulating himself."

"Nas, stop it now, okay? I've had enough. I'm going to go back to my desk and start looking at transfer options. God knows we're done here."

With the partition separating them, Nasreen switched on her

PC and waited for it to boot up. It was only now, in the silence, that she realised the gravity of her situation. Everything she'd worked so hard to achieve was falling apart before her very eyes, and on top of all that, she was about to be investigated by the IOPC, which no police officer wanted on their record.

The Independent Office for Police Conduct was a non-departmental public body which, since 8th January 2018, was responsible for overseeing the system for handling complaints made against police forces in England and Wales.

The functions of the Independent Office for Police Conduct were previously undertaken by the Independent Police Complaints Commission, the IPCC, which had been established in 2004 and abolished upon the creation of the IOPC.

No police officer wanted to have dealings with the IOPC, and most officers' careers never fully recovered after they were made the target of an IOPC investigation. That was all Nasreen had to look forward to.

That being said, she was still determined to find Danny, no matter what the cost; it was her duty as both a police officer and a friend, a duty she took with the utmost seriousness...

36

Steven Dyer couldn't understand why his superiors hadn't ordered a search warrant for the farm. They had enough evidence that something big was happening to order one, and he was positive the warrant would prove fruitful.

According to his team, the visitors of the barn they'd interviewed had given them zero information to go on. None of them were talking, much less offering to testify, and even though his agency knew Rothstein owned the farm, they had their hands tied by the burden of proof and probable cause. These were shitty lawyer terms – unfortunately his agency had to abide by these laws, or risk losing in court when they came to charge Rothstein. After all the work and all the hours they'd put in, the last thing they wanted was to have Rothstein's case thrown out because they didn't meet the criteria needed to prove he was a criminal deserving of incarceration.

Not that he knew the Director General, Steven had heard that Michael Wells was a big picture thinker; he would rather sit back and wait until he had an airtight case than go in on a hunch. So far, this approach had served him well; Wells had a distinguished career, with not a single blemish to his name, and Steven knew he intended to keep it that way.

He took a photo of a man he'd not seen before. The man was tall and lean – so lean, in fact, that he thought the man might disappear if he turned sideways.

Steven shivered as he took the photo. It must have been minus six outside, and he was on surveillance duty again. It was lucky he was wearing a puffer jacket over a thick jumper. He also had on two pairs of socks under his thick leather boots, and he was wearing a beanie hat.

And so it was his team's job to remain hidden outside the farm, taking more and more photos of the visitors without knowing what was happening inside. It was becoming a laborious and painful task, but an important one. Without the intel they provided, the agency wouldn't be able to interview them and possibly break one down enough to make them give up what was going on in the barn. While he certainly didn't enjoy this aspect of his job, he carried on taking snaps of these ever-increasing criminals like the truly dedicated professional he was.

He saw Beatrice Harrison (formerly Rothstein) emerge from the farmhouse, flanked by the petite Japanese girl he'd seen on a few occasions. Looking through his binoculars, he watched Beatrice as she walked along the path towards the barn.

His relief team member had told him that a Range Rover had pulled up outside the barn and reversed inside. He'd apparently taken note of the number plate and had also taken photos of Beatrice talking to the driver.

Steven sighed at the thought of another seven hours watching the visitors coming and going. He so badly wanted to find out what was happening in there; he was tempted to creep around and take a look inside. However, he knew he couldn't, not until he was given the authority to do so...

37

"Last night was great," Danny whispered.

"I know," Kimiko replied as she swept the floor. "I enjoy very much."

As soon as Kimiko had appeared to clean his room, Danny had noticed the natural smile she wore, like a woman freed of her shackles. She was beautiful, he thought, kind and sweet. He watched her vacuum, tempted to walk up to her and kiss her on her gorgeous lips.

"Guard be here soon," she warned. "Better get out of clothes."

Realising what time it was, Danny unbuttoned his jeans and took them off while sat on the edge of his bed. Then he pulled his jumper and T-shirt over his head before whipping off his underwear. It was shower time.

He stood naked in front of Kimiko, who had a lovely smile for him while he waited for the guard's arrival. He wanted her badly – he could have taken her right there and then on the bed – but he'd have to wait until later for that.

One of the guards entered.

Danny took a step forwards, meeting the guard's stare. After a while, he started feeling uncomfortable. The foreign guard was staring at him for too long. "Are we going, or what?"

The guard turned and stood in the doorway.

Danny heard raised voices, followed by screaming and shouting coming from outside. A male voice shouted for assistance, and the guard turned to him and said, "You wait here," before rushing off in the direction of the showers.

Danny stepped into the doorway and looked to his right. He couldn't see anyone.

He looked to his left, and while it was all clear at the bar, he couldn't be sure whether all the guards were down in the shower area or not.

Deciding it was now or never, he turned to Kimiko, kissed her on the lips and said, "I love you, but I've got to go."

Without thinking, he ran towards the stairs in front of him. He heard Kimiko shout, "Danny, wait!" Adrenaline drowned out everything after that.

As he ran towards the steps, he heard a guard call after him.

Although his legs felt like jelly, he was sprinting.

He flew up the stairs – his feet barely making contact with the carpet – and he could see the opening getting closer with every step. He was almost at the top, almost there.

By the time he reached the top stair, he could hear one of the guards right on his tail.

When his front foot made contact with the barn floor, a searing pain shot through his heel as something sharp tore through his skin, causing his foot to erupt in a pool of blood.

Before he could stop himself, his other foot met the same fate, the skin tearing and a gush of blood pooling on the floor.

With a scream, he fell backwards, shards of glass piercing his back.

The guard behind him grabbed his hair and pulled him down the carpeted stairs, a line of blood pouring out of his skin.

Danny was dragged through the bar area, along the corridor – past his room and all the others – and then over to the left, stopping outside the second room of five.

"You on C Wing now," the guard said in his broken English. "You just made big mistake."

Opening the door to the second room, the guard pulled Danny in by his hair.

He crouched into a ball as the guard kicked him hard in his ribs, his boot connecting sharply with Danny's ribs. He felt the air vanish from him in an instant.

"Bea here in minute, you piece shit," said the guard, before he left the room and locked the door behind him.

Danny felt faint as he looked around the room and saw how red it was – there were patches of red all over the floor and walls, but the deepest red patch was beneath where he was lying, right in the middle of the room. He knew it was blood, and this blood looked fresh.

He gulped. He was about to enter hell...

Courtesy of the PNC, Nasreen copied down some addresses of the missing sex workers' families she'd found while screening the cases, dating back ten to fifteen years earlier. Then she unlocked her drawer, pulled out her file on Danny's disappearance and slid that into her bag, along with her notebook.

"Adams wants to see us in his office," said Terrence solemnly.

"You go ahead; I'll be there in a sec."

She quickly closed down her PC, locked the drawer, and pushed her chair under her desk. The desk probably wouldn't be hers for much longer, so she picked up the picture of her and Mina – the one her husband had taken – and placed it in her bag, along with the other bits she needed.

Putting on her suit jacket, she picked up her bag and walked back along the corridor to her inevitable suspension. Considering her career was in tatters, she didn't feel too bad about it, not really. Adams was in the wrong, putting Danny's case on the shelf like that. No one could make her give up looking for him.

"Detective Constable Maqsood, please take a seat," Adams said as she entered his office. "This won't take long."

Nasreen placed her bag next to the chair and sat down. "Yes, sir."

"I've spoken to my contact at the IOPC and they are pursuing their investigation into your recent behaviour. In the interim, you are suspended on full pay, pending the outcome of the enquiry. You are to make yourself available to the officers at the IOPC at any time of their choosing. Is that clear?"

"Yes, sir," she replied, without flinching.

"Do you have anything you wish to add at this time, detective?"

She had plenty she wished to add, not that it was worth repeating to a bent police officer. As far as he was aware, she knew nothing of his corruption, and that was the way she wanted it to stay. She would make it her own personal mission to find out how dirty he was. First, she had to find Danny. Then, once she'd completed her mission, she would focus her energy on Adams. It was a promise she made to herself in that moment. "No, sir, I have nothing to add."

"Don't you want to apologise for your behaviour? Don't you want to save your career?"

"I said I have nothing to add, sir," she replied, ignoring his incredulous look. "Are we done here? Am I allowed to go home now?"

She picked up her bag and left Terrence awaiting his sentence from Adams, and as she walked out she muttered, "Dirty bastard," under her breath, barely audible even to her. If there was one thing in life that she detested it was people abusing their power. Corrupt police officers were right at the top of that list, along with dirty politicians, and while she wasn't naïve – she knew corruption went on – she'd never observed it in any of her other colleagues before.

Maybe she'd chosen the wrong career; maybe she should've applied to the Independent Office for Police Conduct. Maybe she would get greater job satisfaction working there, helping bring these people to justice.

Knowing she wouldn't be back in the office for a while, she picked up a few more trinkets from her desk and then did the walk of shame, with most of her colleagues watching her as she left – word travelled fast, but nowhere faster than at police HQ. The rumour mill would be turning, and before long, her indiscretion would transform into something much bigger. "Did you hear? Nas got suspended for conducting an unofficial investigation!" would turn to, "Did you hear? Nas got suspended for shagging Terrence!" – or something along those lines. It was annoying, yet inevitable.

She made her way down the stairwell and out to the car park at the rear of the building and had just got to her red Fiesta when Terrence ran up to her.

"Nas, wait! I'm glad I found you before you disappeared."

"What, Terrence? What do you want?"

He looked sorrowful. "I'm sorry this happened, sorry I yelled at you earlier. You were right, I should've kept my mouth shut."

"It doesn't matter now, does it? It's over!"

"It doesn't have to be. Tell the IOPC that you were in the wrong and beg for leniency. You don't want this to be the end of your career – the end of *us* – do you?"

"Of course I don't," she sighed, "but I can't see any way out of this. No one recovers after being investigated by the IOPC, you know that. I'll be lucky if I get demoted back to a uniform."

"Look, you broke a code of conduct, sure, but it's not like you're being investigated for corruption or anything like that, is it?"

"No, I was just doing my job."

"Come on, Nas, be reasonable here. You were in the wrong, and you should've told me what you were doing. I'd have talked you out of it."

No, he wouldn't! Sometimes she thought no one knew her. Or rather, people thought they knew her, but didn't. She couldn't be persuaded to do something if she didn't want to; she was headstrong and independent. Some people called her stubborn, and they may be right. At least she wasn't a sheep, or a kiss arse. "All right, Terrence. Enough said. I've got to go now."

"Listen, you can always call me if you need to talk. You know I'm a good listener, and you never know, you might find I give good advice too."

She got into her car, started the engine, and backed out of her space. She then moved forwards a little way, stopped suddenly, and wound down her window. "Hey, Terrence, I forgot to ask: what did Adams say after I left? Are you suspended too?"

"Not a chance," he replied with a smile. "They can't suspend me; I'm too important to their ethnic statistics. I've been given a formal written warning. One more and I'm out."

Nasreen nodded. "I'm sorry I got you into this."

"Don't worry about me, I can take care of myself. See you soon, Nas."

She thanked him, then drove out of the staff car park.

Glancing at the digital clock on her dashboard, she saw that it was 09:56, which was great – she had the rest of the day to plan her investigation. She also decided to give Mina's nanny the afternoon off and pick up her daughter from school herself; she hadn't done that for a long time...

38

Beattie watched one of the guards as he bandaged Danny's feet. "Make sure it's nice and tight; if he bleeds out, he's no good to anyone."

Outwardly she was calm. Inside she was seething; there was no other word to describe the rage she felt for her "Star Bee". He'd waited for his chance, and he'd taken it – at least temporarily – when two of Alan's girls had started fighting. Well, fighting wasn't exactly the right word for it: scrapping was far more appropriate. They'd punched, kicked, bitten, pulled hair, and spat at one another.

Beattie looked down at a semi-conscious Danny, willing him to wake so she could show him just how angry she was with him. At least he hadn't managed to make it too far past the top of the stairs. Her idea of throwing shards of glass on the barn floor was genius; the bees weren't allowed outside of their rooms clothed, so they could only make a run for it naked. Bare feet plus glass... it had certainly put paid to Danny's escape attempt. "Chain him up!" she ordered.

Danny groaned, and Beattie watched as two of her guards pulled him to his feet, placing his hands in cuffs that dangled from the rafters in the ceiling. When they let go of him, Danny slumped a little, the cuffs around his wrists keeping him upright.

"What you want us do to him?" one of the guards asked.

"Leave him be for now." She was going to wait until he was awake before she unleashed her fury. He was going to pay for this, but he was going to pay when he was fully conscious. "I'll come and get you when it's time."

Nodding, the two guards left room two of C Wing, leaving her alone with Danny. She walked around him, staring at his half-conscious face, waiting for him to open his eyes. Although he'd lost a lot of blood, she knew he'd wake soon, and then she would show him what true pain was. Around and around she went, hoping his eyes would open.

Finally, she decided to leave him for a couple of hours and check on him later.

Outside, she walked past three support staff trying to mop up the trail of Danny's blood that stretched the length of the carpet – from the top of the stairs, all the way through the bar, past the rooms, to room two of C Wing. The entire carpet was ruined, and she'd only had it fitted a year earlier. It was yet another reason why she was so furious with him.

Still seething, she took three long deep breaths, attempting to calm her mind, not that it worked. When she saw one of her support staff putting no effort with her cloth, she told them, "Make sure you really get in there and soak it up."

All she wanted to do was go back to bed, but with Alan still away, it wasn't an option. She'd already had a crap morning – what with Danny's escape attempt, the two girls fighting, and having to cancel Danny's clients at short notice – and that wasn't even including her dad telling her the NCA were outside the farm taking photos for their investigation.

It was little wonder she wasn't rocking back and forth,

drooling, with the amount of pressure she was under.

Beattie wandered into her office and closed the door behind her, needing a couple of hours to rejuvenate. Sitting on her chair, she stared at the PC monitor, thinking maybe some retail therapy might help. She needed some new clothes, so she clicked on her favourite online store icon and scrolled through tops and underwear.

In a couple of hours, she would be ready to see Danny...

Lennox watched as the Director General of the NCA, Michael Wells, walked from his home and headed along his drive to his Mercedes SLC Roadster. He continued watching as the lean grey-haired man stepped inside his car and backed out of the long gravelled driveway.

Sighing, Lennox observed the decadence that law enforcement had bestowed upon Wells. The Director General's home was spectacular from a distance. He expected it would be as lavish on the interior as well. Maybe obeying the law wasn't for suckers; it seemed working for the NCA had its perks, he thought, as his target turned at the end of his driveway and sped off down the winding country road. After waiting for five seconds, Lennox followed.

The previous night he'd met with Rothstein, who had assigned him with this detail. He was told he must run Wells off the road, killing him. If the crash didn't kill him, then he was to finish it himself. He didn't ask Rothstein why; it wasn't his place to question his boss's orders. All he'd managed to get from Rothstein was that it was of the highest priority.

Lennox had driven along the road Wells lived on a number of times and knew all the steep turns well. He knew, therefore, exactly where to bump the old boy off the road. It was going to be a long boring day of mostly waiting in his motor, a stolen

Ford Ranger 4x4 that Rothstein had provided especially for the job. It was a beast to drive.

As Lennox followed Wells along the curvy country road, he thought about Beattie. He'd noticed how hurt she looked when he'd backed off and told her he couldn't go through with it, though he'd wanted to. He could feel how much she'd wanted it too; she'd been pulling him to her, gripping him through his jeans. She wanted it as much as he did.

Without thinking Lennox slowed, following Wells' lead. They came to a junction, and he had no choice; he had to pull up behind his target's car. A sweet ride. He liked Mercedes, especially the Roadsters. He'd thought about buying one himself, although he'd ended up settling for the Shogun for practical reasons.

After forty-five minutes, the Director General pulled in at a hotel miles away from the NCA HQ building. The hotel – an independent boutique – was situated along a busy A-road, out in the middle of nowhere.

Lennox pulled into a conveniently placed lay-by over the road from the hotel and watched Wells enter the reception through the revolving doors.

Lennox rested his head against the seat and sighed. Now all he had to do was wait...

Assistant Commissioner Peter Franks picked up his disposable pre-paid mobile phone and answered, cutting off the shrill ringtone. He was sitting at his desk, the door to his office closed. "Clive, I was expecting your call. How did it go with Detective Maqsood this morning?"

"It went as expected," Adams replied. "She's suspended pending an investigation by the IOPC."

Franks leaned back in his chair with a smile. "The IOPC?

How did that happen? I was only expecting an internal disciplinary hearing."

"Blind luck. It turns out she pissed off someone she interviewed, and they twigged that she must be off-duty. They said they saw her drive away in a red Fiesta."

"That's perfect." Franks turned his chair a hundred and eighty degrees and looked out of the window at the tall buildings in the distance. "Very fortuitous for us, I must say."

"Anyway, she's out of the picture, so are we all square?"

"Yeah, that's all I need from you, Clive. Thank you for your co-operation." He hung up and placed the phone in his uniform jacket inside pocket. Then he turned back around and stared at his monitor.

Franks' meeting with the Assistant Director General, Graham Holmes, had gone well. Holmes was a pragmatist and believed in what Franks had proposed; it had taken him all of half an hour to get Holmes to agree to his plan. As soon as the DG was out of the way, Holmes would step up and replace him. Franks had spoken to Holmes about having to put a hold on the Rothstein operation, and he'd accepted that too. It couldn't have gone any better.

Of forty-one police and crime commissioners in the UK, he had fifteen ready to go for the project. Each PCC had a chief constable under their influence, and every chief constable had their subordinates. Franks had his supplier ready and Rothstein would run logistics on importing the narcotics. He also had his dealers waiting and poised to take over sections of the UK. The country's drug trade would be split up into the South East, the South West, London, the Midlands, the North West, and the North East. It was all starting to come together.

Taking out his disposable phone again, he dialled the commissioner's second number. "We are a go," Franks said, before flipping the phone shut with a smile...

39

Cara Mooney rolled over and felt the pillow next to her. Lucy – her one and only true love – had left her over a year earlier, yet it still took a while to remember in the mornings. Rolling back over, Cara stared up at the yellow-stained ceiling.

The feeling of elation she'd felt after butchering Chris had waned, and now all she was left with was a numbness she couldn't exorcise. She needed to get that feeling back. The previous night she'd sent Beattie a text saying she would definitely be interested again, any time another of her bees needed taking care of. Beattie had sent a reply, saying that next time she would let her join an auction. An auction was out of the question; Cara couldn't afford it.

She had tried a number of remedies. None of them worked. She'd tried drinking away the feeling, smoking it away, and the previous night she'd tried getting so smashed on heroin that she couldn't remember anything. She'd fucked her drug dealer and his two friends the night before, but even that couldn't compare to the feeling of liberty she'd found in slaughtering that Bee, Christopher. She would do anything to feel that way again.

Deciding to get up, she pulled the duvet off her and sat up, naked. Her head was groggy, but she felt fine, which surprised her considering she'd pumped her veins with all that vile shit. The needle was on the floor on top of her dress, next to the rubber tourniquet.

She walked naked through her flat, which was a fucking dump. Her bedroom had clothes all over the floor, and her lounge looked like a party had just finished, with bottles of spirits and cans of lager everywhere she looked. There were packets of crisps and pizza boxes covering the coffee table and she couldn't see the sofa for some nasty bastard lying on it.

"Get the fuck out of my flat!" Cara shouted at the naked guy. "I know you can hear me – get the fuck up and get out!"

She looked down at the man. He was skinny, with greasy dark spiky hair and a weaselly face. She couldn't remember a thing from the previous night. The last thing she did remember was getting home from the pub, pissed off at feeling shit, before she'd sat on her sofa and injected herself. When did this loser get in her flat? She couldn't work it out.

The unwanted guest rose, rubbing his face and eyes. Finally, after taking off his rubber tourniquet, he said, "Come on, Cara, I haven't got anywhere to go."

"Not my fucking problem, mate. Now, get the fuck out!"

She grabbed him by the arm and dragged him to the front door, opening it and pushing him out before slamming the door in his face. She heard him shout, "What about my clothes?" Irritated, she found his dirty clothes, picked them up, and carried them to the door where she flung them at him. "Just be grateful I gave them back, now fuck off!"

The smell emanating from the kitchen was putrid; she thought someone must've died in there. Someone had to clean this shit up, and it wasn't going to be her.

About the only room she could stand was the bathroom, and after heading inside she looked in the mirror at her reflection. Considering the battering she'd given herself, she didn't look bad at all. She still had nice, long blonde hair and a pretty face – albeit with more bags under her eyes than she wanted – but overall, not bad. She was just the right weight, and she still had a nice flat belly.

The most attractive thing about her though, was her eagle tattoo on her right breast. It was a full-frontal picture of the bird landing, about to grab something with its talons. She loved it – she had an affinity with birds of prey – and, since Beattie had let her butcher Chris, Cara felt like an eagle. After all, she *was* a bird of prey.

She stepped into the shower cubicle and turned on the taps, feeling the jets of warm water prod and probe her head, shoulders, and neck, as her thoughts turned to her gorgeous Lucy, the bitch! It amazed Cara how quickly she could go from pure love to pure hate while thinking about the same person.

Lucy Davis was the only person Cara had ever truly loved. She'd never loved her dad – he was in prison for raping her and her sister – and she'd certainly never loved her druggie mum, who'd sat back and let it happen, so long as she got her fix, she didn't care.

Cara shook her head. That was enough thinking about them; they didn't deserve her thoughts, not one.

When she'd met Lucy during her first spell in a rehab clinic, she'd been smitten immediately. Lucy was everything she'd ever desired in a person; she was cute, kind, and smart – the whole package – and it didn't hurt that she was sexy as hell too. They'd hit it off straight away, and once they'd both completed their stint at rehab, they'd started a romantic relationship A year after that they'd moved in together, to this shithole flat.

She thought back to how the flat used to be. Lucy liked it tidy, where she was more carefree about cleanliness. It had caused a few arguments in their four-year relationship. They'd christened the lounge on their first night by making love on the floor. Cara had been genuinely happy for the first time in her entire life in this shithole of a flat, but of course it hadn't been a pit back then.

She stepped out of the shower. Drying herself, she thought back to how Lucy had changed. Her work as a *Daily Telegraph* columnist had Lucy working stupid hours, which left little time for her, and eventually the bitch had chosen a career over her. She'd tried to get Lucy reinvested in their relationship by making sure Lucy knew she was around. She used to bring her lunch at the office, and wait for her to finish work, but Lucy hadn't liked her doing that, and it had caused huge arguments. Ungrateful bitch!

And then, one day, Cara came home to find that Lucy had packed up all her stuff and disappeared. Lucy had left her a note saying she needed help, that she was stalking her, and Cara couldn't believe it. She couldn't believe the love of her life had just left without so much as a goodbye.

Of course, she'd gone looking for her only love, but when she'd finally managed to pluck up the courage to speak to her, Lucy had called the police. The next thing Cara knew, she had a county court injunction against her – stating she must stop her harassing behaviour – and Lucy took out a civil court action against her. All this, just because she wanted to talk to her! That was all – she wanted to talk and gain closure. Bitch!

A sudden feeling of panic overwhelmed her and a second later she realised she was going to throw up. Crouching over the toilet, she threw up three times, nothing but black liquid appearing in the toilet bowl. She was coming down.

When she felt able, she wearily walked back to the bedroom, lay down on the bed, and curled up in a ball under the duvet. She felt terrible. She was shivering, while dripping with sweat. Maybe she'd caught something?

As she drifted off to sleep, she started thinking again of ways to get that feeling back...

40

Nasreen parked her car outside Mina's school gates, got out, and stood and waited for the bell to ring. She was wearing her mid-grey and blue salwar kameez. She was taking Mina to the mosque straight after school, so she'd brought Mina's salwar kameez to change into. Mina's little suit looked so cute on her, Nasreen thought she would burst with pride. Her husband would have been so proud of their baby too.

She felt embarrassed when, standing with all the other mums, she realised she couldn't remember any of their names. Her nanny would know. It illustrated just how much Nasreen worked, and how much of Mina's life she'd already missed out on.

Finally, the bell rang, and all the small children came running out to meet their parents. Nasreen saw her baby running towards her, and she bent down and greeted Mina with a big hug and kiss.

"Where's Katerina?" was the first question Mina asked.

"I've given her the afternoon off, sweetheart," Nasreen replied, hurt that her daughter wanted to see her nanny when she was here. "It's just you and me this afternoon. We're going to the mosque for an hour, and then – if you're a good girl – I'll take you to McDonalds after, okay?"

That certainly got her daughter's spirits up; Mina shouted, "Yay!" and jumped up and down. Mina was so cute when she was excited, Nasreen thought, as she led her daughter to the car.

On the way to the mosque, Nasreen listened to Mina rabbit on about what she'd done in class, watching her through the rear-view mirror while also focusing on the chaotic roads. At the same time, Nasreen was thinking about the meeting she had arranged for the following morning, with the mother of a prostitute who went missing ten years earlier.

After Nasreen had returned home from being suspended, she'd sorted all the files out on her dining room table, going through the case files she'd fortuitously photocopied the previous week – as though she'd known she would need them – and finding two disappearances with similar circumstances to those of Danny and Julian. If she had to, she'd speak to every single family member of these missing sex workers. She was getting close to finding Danny, she knew it.

"Mummy, will Katerina be picking me up from school tomorrow, or will you?"

"I don't know yet, baby. I've got some unexpected time off from work, so I'll be around more for a few days," she replied, not sure what the expression on Mina's face meant. "Don't you like Mummy picking you up from school?"

Mina said that she loved it when she picked her up, but the question still bugged her. What she was really saying was that she wanted Katerina to pick her up, and while it hurt, Nasreen couldn't be too surprised. She hadn't been around enough, she knew. Some days Mina was lucky if she saw her mother for an hour a day. It was like that with her line of work, though – long unsociable hours.

Nasreen parked the car, let Mina out, and then took her

daughter's change of clothing from the boot before walking with Mina, hand in hand, to the mosque's lavatories, where she waited for Mina to change.

When the little girl came out of the cubicle, Nasreen wanted to cry with joy. Mina had lovely long shiny black hair and a cheeky round face, and she looked so cute in her navy blue and rose-pink salwar kameez. Mina had said it made her feel like a princess when she'd tried it on in the shop, and she certainly looked like one.

Looking at her watch, Nasreen saw it was four o'clock. In her mosque, Asr was prayed at 17:09, so she had just over an hour to socialise with the other mosque visitors. She knew about ten people in the foyer, and she'd been meaning to catch up with them for some time. One friend of hers, Ghayda, an Indian woman, had a daughter the same age as Mina, so she would let her daughter play with Ananya while she chatted with Ghayda.

So far, not being at work was working out great...

"Good! you're finally awake," said Beattie, observing Danny's rolling eyes. "Focus, Danny, focus!"

She watched until they stopped rolling and she realised he could see her. She'd been waiting for him to wake for hours, and it was now 18:15. He'd lost more blood than she had thought. It didn't matter; he was alive, so she could administer his punishment.

Danny didn't say anything; he just stood there with his arms up in the air, tightly chained to the ceiling cuffs, his ankles chained to the floor.

When she walked around him, she could see his back was still bleeding, although mostly scabbing over. "You've really gone and done it this time, haven't you? Because you know I've got to punish you, and it won't be like before, Danny. No, this time I'm going to give you the real dregs of society."

One of her guards stood in front of Danny and punched him in the gut. She heard him groan in pain, which made her smile. That was just for starters. "Again!"

The guard punched him hard on the left cheek and Danny's head snapped left.

"Not in the face, please," Beattie told the guard. "We can still get decent money for him, but not if his face is pulp."

"Is slapping okay?" The guard looked at her for confirmation.

"I don't see why not," she replied, then the guard slapped Danny hard.

She imagined his ears would be ringing, and his face was turning redder by the second. She walked up to him and grabbed his chin, shouting, "Look at me!" When she saw his eyes focus, she added, "You're in hell now."

Beattie listened as he tried to speak. It came out all garbled. "What was that, sweetie? Speak up! We can't hear you."

When she pulled her hand away, his head fell; he was unconscious again.

The second guard approached Danny, poured some liquid on a handkerchief, and smothered his face with it. She watched as Danny woke up again, startled.

"You're back with us then? Good."

She stood back and let the guards take it in turns punching him in the stomach, and after five turns each, she signalled for them to stop. "You see, Danny, this is what you get for trying to escape. Do you understand now?" she asked. "You're *never* leaving here. The only way out is death, and I'm not forgiving enough to give you that; I'll keep you alive for as long as I want you to be alive, and you're going to suffer along the way, you can believe that."

She nodded at the guards, who carried out five more turns of stomach punches.

"This is just the start of your punishment," she said. "I'm going to leave you in a minute in the care of my guards, who are going to see to it that you behave in the future. It won't be pleasant." She grinned. "And after you've convalesced for a bit, you're going to be servicing the vilest creatures known to man, but don't worry – if he," Beattie pointed to Danny's groin, "doesn't want to work, I'll fill you with Viagra to make sure he does." She paused for a moment before adding, "Believe me when I say you've made the worst mistake of your life today."

Feeling the rage inside her taking over, Beattie excused herself, and as she left the room, she heard the guards beating Danny. They were well trained, and they enjoyed their jobs. She smiled as she closed the door behind her…

Nasreen opened Mina's bedroom door a crack to check she was asleep, and when she heard her daughter's heavy breathing she smiled, thinking it would probably turn into full-blown snoring as she got older – that was, if her dad was anything to go by.

Nasreen left the door ajar, as Mina liked, and walked along the landing to her bedroom. Inside, she took off her salwar kameez and changed into her satin pyjamas; she loved the feel of the fabric, and although they were expensive, she thought they were well worth the money.

Once in bed, she lay awake, looking up at the ceiling. The television was on in the background. She could hear the news presenter talking about Brexit, the usual nonsense with politicians from both sides arguing about how the country would fare once the UK had left Europe. It bored her; the whole thing was a farce and had been handled astonishingly badly by both sides – the UK government and the rest of Europe.

It was on nights like these that she most missed Ashraf. Had he been alive today, she'd have chewed his ear off about how she'd been suspended, and he would've had her back all the way; he wouldn't have played devil's advocate, he'd have been shouting about suing the police force. She loved him so much.

A tear rolled down her cheek as she thought back to when Mina was born. Ashraf had just arrived home from work that fateful night to find her on the lounge floor, in labour, her contractions two minutes apart. He'd panicked so much she'd had to calm *him* down and tell him to phone for an ambulance. Because they were in the middle of nowhere, however, the ambulance hadn't arrived in time, and she'd given birth to Mina in their lounge, Ashraf encouraging her as he delivered their daughter with his own two hands. He was amazing – as good as any doctor or midwife.

And she so loved this house too. It was a white painted country cottage with half an acre of land, which should've been awesome to behold, but neither she nor Ashraf were keen gardeners, so it was just a big back garden and a huge driveway and lawn. She wished she had time to get her fingers green – her job wouldn't allow it.

It was the shock of Ashraf's death that had been the hardest part. One day he was going about his daily routine – as normal as anyone else's – and the next he was dead, and she was being asked to identify him at the morgue. If only she'd had time to say I love you, or even just goodbye... It wasn't fair!

Nasreen had already endured enough heartache, what with the deaths of both her parents six months apart; her mother had died from a heart attack when she was twenty-eight and her father was going through chemotherapy for prostate cancer, and six months later, he passed away from the disease. That had been a horrible time in her life.

Now all she had left – apart from Mina, of course – was

Ashraf's mother, Yasmin. She was really great and understanding about her career. It wasn't the same as having her parents to talk to and confide in. Although she had rebelled in her late teens and early twenties – which was how she'd got together with Danny – she'd found her way back and married a true Pakistani man, which had thrilled both her parents. She knew they were proud of the person she'd become.

She sat up, hearing a strange sound, like something clanking.

It sounded like it came from the kitchen.

Using the remote, she switched the television off and listened again.

Another loud clank.

It could have been Hugo, their cat, jumping on the kitchen counter and knocking things off as he walked by.

Nasreen's adrenaline told her differently.

She got out of bed, and crept over to her bedroom door, opening it a crack and listening.

There was no one outside the bedrooms, so it hadn't woken Mina, or Katerina, if her nanny was back from her night out.

Shit! What was it?

Slowly, Nasreen opened her door and edged her way along the wall to Mina's bedroom, sneaking inside and waking her daughter. She put a finger against Mina's lips and whispered, "Shhh! We're going to play a little game, sweetheart. I want you to lock your door after me and I want you to stay really, really–"

There was another bang, louder this time.

"Quiet!" She put her finger against her lips. "Stay really quiet. In fact, put your fingers in your ears and count to a hundred in your head, okay? Mummy will be right back."

Her daughter did as she was told; she heard the bolt as her daughter locked herself in. "Good girl," she whispered, as she crept along the hallway.

It wasn't pitch black in her house, but it was dark enough, and as she crept through to the lounge, she saw nothing untoward. She walked through to the dining room, finding nothing, then continued. It was the kitchen she was more interested in.

When she reached the kitchen, the door was closed. Ever so slowly, she opened it, the wood creaking under her weight. She made a note to get the flooring fixed.

Her breath came out in rasps.

She breathed a sigh of relief when she saw their cat, Hugo, on the countertop. It was exactly like she'd said to herself.

Smiling, she went and picked up Hugo, giving him a kiss on the head. "You scared the shit out of me, little man," she said, kissing him again.

It was only when she put Hugo down on the floor and looked up that she noticed the back door was open.

As she stood there, the hairs on the back of her neck stood up.

There was someone behind her – she could feel it.

A sudden burst of adrenaline gave her the boost she needed to spin round and attack whoever it was, her fist connecting with a black mask.

The man wearing it was big and broad-shouldered. She was no match for him.

The masked man groaned in pain for a brief second before countering her punch and rushing forwards, pushing her backwards until her head hit the bottom of a kitchen cupboard.

She heard a ringing sound as the wind got pushed out of her, the pain in the back of her head immense.

Next, the masked man grabbed her by the neck and threw her across the room until the top of her head smacked against one of the lower cupboards.

Slightly dazed, she rolled onto her back, as the man reached her, and she kicked upwards at the right time for her bare foot to strike him in the face.

She needed a weapon!

Using the time she'd gained by kicking him, Nasreen pulled herself up enough to grab a saucepan she'd washed earlier.

As she went to pull it back, however, she felt his powerful hand around her wrist, and when he squeezed, she involuntarily let go of the pan.

He was behind her, and he had the advantage; she knew this because she felt his other hand as he placed it around her neck.

Finding energy from wherever she could find it, she put her spare arm around his leg and pushed back as hard as she could. His leg straightened, his kneecap locking, and he yelled in pain before throwing her sideways, away from his leg.

She utilised the space and ran through to the dining room.

He was limping – right behind her.

Before she could move out of his way, he pushed her into the dining room table.

When she was on the floor, he stooped down, grabbed her by the collar, and lifted her up and onto the table with such ease that she was momentarily awed by his power.

A second later, she kicked him in the face again and rolled to the other side of the two-foot wide table. She had a barrier between them, and she utilised it by switching one way, then the other.

He moved every time she moved.

She had to jump back when he yelled in frustration, grabbed the table, and upended it, almost throwing it on top of her.

Making her first mistake, she saw a space and tried running past him.

He easily reached out and grabbed her by the neck.

She found she couldn't breathe as he lifted her up off the

ground, her legs flailing in the air and her head almost reaching the dining room light.

"Daniel Rose is dead," the man said, his accent unusual. She couldn't place it.

The pressure in her head was truly intense, but with all the force she could muster, Nasreen kicked him in the groin. It was such a hard kick that the man instantly dropped her, bending over in agony while she lay on the floor, trying to get her breath back.

"Ahhh, fucking bitch!" he yelled.

Nasreen still couldn't catch her breath; all she could do was crawl away from him while he stumbled after her, letting her crawl as far as the middle of the lounge. When she gave up crawling, he bent down and turned her onto her back.

He sat down on top of her, then with a groan of pain, pinned her wrists down with his powerful, slab hands. "I like it when they fight," he said, wincing. "Feisty ones are the best."

She strained to get him off, but it was no use; he was too strong.

"Mummy?"

Nasreen's heart stopped for what felt like eternity. She felt her head tilt backwards. She wasn't doing it herself, and the next thing she saw was the silhouette of her daughter, upside down.

"She is beautiful," she heard him say.

While looking at her upside-down daughter, Nasreen rasped, "You remember what Mummy said? Go back and lock your bedroom door, sweetheart." She tried to keep her voice level, though there was such rage inside her. How dare this man do this to her, to her daughter!

Nasreen watched Mina run away, then she pulled her head back so she could see the man's eyes and smile through the mouth hole in the mask. He had dead eyes.

"I'll have to make acquaintance with little girl," he said smugly.

"You touch her, and I'll fucking kill you."

The masked man's laugh was twisted, powerful.

"I came to give you message," he said, no smile this time. "Daniel Rose is dead. Don't keep looking him, or I come back for little girl. Understand, bitch?"

He made a horrible grating sound with his throat, before slowly letting a big goblet of saliva ooze out of his mouth and drop down onto her face. She tried to get away from it – the speed was so slow, it would have been possible. He kept matching his pace with hers, mirroring her actions. Finally, it landed on her cheek.

"I go now, but remember what I say," he said, easing the pressure off her body. "I come back and kill you both if you continue; I be watching."

Groaning, he picked himself up and Nasreen watched as he hobbled out of the living room. She heard him in the kitchen, and then nothing.

She lay there on the living room carpet for several moments, feeling his warm saliva dripping – sliming – down her cheek. There was something stopping her, however, from instinctively wiping it off and washing her face; she had the masked man's DNA...

41

Day 29
Thursday, 8th February

Beattie yawned and stretched. The PC monitor told her it was 12:32. She'd been in the office all night, partly because she had paperwork to catch up on, mostly because she'd been waiting for Lennox to arrive. He hadn't, so her dad had sent some other associate to come and pick up the day's takings.

Disappointed was an understatement; she'd really wanted to see him.

"Hi! How've you been, honey?"

She turned around to find Alan leaning against the wall by the door. "How long've you been standing there?"

"A couple of minutes. I think we need to talk."

She groaned inwardly. It was the last thing she needed. She sighed. "Not now, Alan. I'm really tired; I was just about to turn everything off and go to bed."

"We need to clear the air."

"You mean *you* need to clear your conscience."

Alan frowned. "What's that supposed to mean?"

"What do you think it means? You're going to tell me how sorry you are about being away for so long, and I'm supposed to just say, 'Ah, Alan, that's okay,' but the truth is, it's not okay. You're out there fucking who knows what every n–"

"Hold it," he interrupted, "wait. Back up a bit, honey. I haven't been fucking anyone," he insisted.

"Of course you have," she replied, confusion etched in her brow. "Haven't you?"

"No! I haven't fucked anyone while I've been away."

"Then where have you been all this time?"

Alan stepped forward, then crouched so his eyes were on the same level as hers. He reached out, taking her hand in his. "I've been trying to find the right moment to tell you this for a while, but there never seemed to be the right time... So, here goes..."

Beattie waited for what felt like forever, and she was about to say, "Come on, spit it out, I haven't got all night," when he announced, "I've got a daughter."

What the actual f...? No, she meant what the fuck? Was he admitting now that he *had* cheated on her? Her brow furrowed even more. "I'm confused, what do you mean?"

"*You're* confused?" He shook his head. "Try getting a text from a girl you had sex with at school, saying you have a daughter, and that she's thirty. That'll confuse you."

"Wait, if she's thirty, then you mean her mum is..."

"Someone I went to school with, yes. I didn't cheat on you, if that's what you thought I was going to say."

Her head was spinning; this was definitely not how she saw her day going.

She was too confused to speak.

"I'm so sorry I didn't say anything sooner," Alan said eventually, breaking the awkward silence.

"Yes, you shit, why didn't you?" Beattie spat. "You should've told me the moment you found out! I mean, you *could*'ve told me; I'm understanding, aren't I?"

He smiled at her. "Honey, of course you're understanding... and beautiful... and intelligent."

"Keep going," she said. A smile crept over her.

He almost laughed at that, but stopped himself at the last second, shaking his head. "If I'm honest, I didn't want to tell you until I found out if it was genuine or not."

"What do you mean? Why wouldn't it be genuine?"

"Well, look at what we've got: the wealth, the power... Hannah could've been lying about Samantha being my daughter. She could've been trying to get money from me."

"So, your daughter's name is Samantha?"

He nodded. "Yep, Samantha Browne."

"Samantha Brown," Beattie said out loud, trying it for herself.

"With an E," he added.

"Samantha Brown with an E. It's very pretty, Alan."

His smile got wider. "You should see her, Bea. She's gorgeous. Looks a bit like me too – well, as much as a daughter can look like their dad, I guess. But you know what I mean."

"I do," Beattie replied, with a smile. "Have you got any pictures of her?"

Beattie waited while Alan found the photos on his mobile, and she looked – really looked – at her husband for the first time in years. He was a good-looking forty-five-year-old man. He also had all his hair, which was more than most wives could say. He didn't have a hideous beer belly, and he still had a sparkle in his eyes.

She took hold of his phone and scrolled through reams of photos dating back three weeks, smiling as she looked. Samantha was every bit as beautiful as Alan said. She had lovely shiny shoulder-length brown hair, blue eyes, and an attractive smile complete with dimples. She had a dainty little button nose too, which suited her chiselled cheekbones.

"That's Hannah, there," said Alan, pointing to a woman in a wheelchair.

"What's wrong with her?"

"Multiple Sclerosis, final stages. She can't walk."

"That's terrible," Beattie replied, her voice genuine, which surprised her.

"She's been given six months, tops."

"Is that why she contacted you now, and not years ago?"

"I guess so," he said. "It was Sammy; she talked Hannah into contacting me. She wanted to find out what her daddy's like."

Beattie handed him the phone back and they remained silent for a couple of minutes; she was trying to get her head around Alan's surprise, and Alan was scrolling through the photos, smiling.

"Do you want to meet her?" he asked after a few moments.

"Of course I do; she's your daughter. But do you think she'll like me?"

Alan bent down, staring into her eyes. "She'll love you as much as I do, I'm sure."

"You still love me?" Beattie asked him, her voice quiet. "But we've been so distant for so long."

"I know, and I want it back; I want us to be the way we were before, honey."

She smiled as she leaned forwards for an embrace. She wanted the same thing, or at least she thought she did. Beattie was so confused. For years they'd drifted apart, had become more like friends than husband and wife, so why now? Why would he want to start afresh now?

"This whole experience has taught me to appreciate what

you've got, while you've got it," he said, as though reading her mind. "I love you, Bea, I always have."

"I love you too," she replied, before *really* kissing him for the first time in months.

Maybe this was what she needed, she thought as their kiss deepened. Maybe her infatuation with Lennox was just her unconscious telling her she was lonely? Maybe she didn't need Lennox after all? Maybe she still loved her husband?

"Bloody hell, Nas, what happened to you?"

Nasreen had an ice pack on top of her head. Her left cheek was swollen, and her neck was red from where the masked man had picked her up and choked her. She had lumps and bruises everywhere. For the most part, though, she'd come away relatively unscathed.

Katerina had come back from her night out a few minutes after the attack to find Nasreen lying on the floor, and as soon as she was able, Nasreen had phoned Terrence, not wanting to officially call in the attack. After all, she trusted Adams about as far as she could throw him.

She'd asked Katerina to find a receptacle, something she could put the saliva in, and her nanny had come back with a small Tupperware cylinder. She'd managed to scoop the saliva off her cheek and wipe it into the cylinder, sealing it with the lid and making it airtight. Then she'd limped over to the kitchen sink and washed her face with Fairy liquid. She could walk – or rather limp – but she still felt like she'd been in a kickboxing match. One she'd lost.

Mina was sitting on Katerina's lap, crying.

"We had an intruder," Nasreen replied. "A masked man came in through the back door and attacked me." When she saw the concern on her partner's face, she added, "Don't worry – I'm fine, really. Just a few cuts and bruises, nothing serious."

"We need to get you to the hospital, get you checked out."

"No! There's no need for that, please." She touched her head, feeling the lumps that were starting to swell. "I do need a couple of things, though, if you can help?"

"Sure, whatever you need."

Nasreen asked Katerina to take Mina to her bedroom and help her pack some of her things. Katerina was to do the same. Once they'd gone, it was just her and Terrence.

"What's going on, Nas?" he asked gently. "I'm getting the feeling there's more to this than you're telling me."

Nasreen took a deep breath before replying. "It was the driver from the picture. Danny's abductor. He told me that Danny's dead and he warned me not to keep looking, or he'll come back here, rape and kill my daughter in front of me, and then kill me."

"Fuck!" was all Terrence could manage.

"He said he'll be watching me, so I can only assume he's been watching me for days already – maybe even weeks. He knew I'd been investigating Danny's disappearance."

She paused, catching her breath before asking, "When you drove here, did you see any cars nearby?"

She waited while Terrence thought back to arriving.

"There's a car just down the road from here, on the other side of the street, yeah. I thought it was one of your neighbours' cars."

"Shit! Then he's right outside."

"I'll go get this prick."

"No! Wait a sec. Let us get our stuff together first. I'm going to go off-grid for a while, but I'll need your help, if that's okay with you?"

Terrence nodded his understanding. "What do you need?"

"I need to get that guy away from me, so I can disappear. I need a gun, and I need you to get this analysed for me. Do you think you can do that?"

Terrence took hold of the Tupperware container and stared at it.

"The intruder spat on my face. That's his saliva."

Terrence raised his eyebrows in salute. "His DNA, more like. Well done, Nas. I'll get on this first thing in the morning. Not too bright, this guy, is he?"

She smiled. Generally, they weren't too bright, she thought. "You understand that this needs to be analysed on the quiet though, right? I don't want Adams finding out."

"Of course," Terrence whispered. "I know you don't trust him. I'll let you know who this guy is."

"And I'll need you to access the PNC for names and addresses of his family and any known associates."

"No problem," Terrence replied, much to her surprise.

After everything that had happened, she hadn't been sure he would want to help her out.

"Anything else?"

"The gun, it has to be small enough to fit in my bag." She'd trained with firearms at the academy, so she knew her way around weapons.

"I know just where to go for that, no problem. I'll bring a couple of clips too." Terrence looked at her like he wanted to say something.

"What is it?" she asked, beyond tired.

"I was going to try to talk you out of–"

"Don't even. Danny's still alive; I know it."

Terrence shook his head. "I said I was going to *try*. I know you well enough to know that when you set your mind on something, there's nothing anyone can say to stop you. Just be careful, yeah?"

She agreed to be as careful as she could, given the circumstances. "Now, how are we going to get rid of this bastard outside?"

"Leave that to me."

Nasreen and Terrence packed some of her clothes, then helped Mina and Katerina with their packing. When they were all ready, they stored the suitcases in the boot of Nasreen's car. Mina and Katerina got in and waited, while Nasreen and Terrence walked to the end of the driveway.

"Be careful," she said to Terrence, as he walked across the road toward the masked man's car.

Nasreen watched as Terrence pulled out his police warrant card, holding it up. She heard him say, "Get out of your vehicle, you're under arrest..." when the headlights of the car – she couldn't make out the make or model – came on, the driver speeding off in Terrence's direction, the tyres screeching.

"Terrence, watch out!" Nasreen screamed.

With adrenaline spiking, she watched Terrence dive out of the way, narrowly missing being hit. The car shot past her – so fast that she still couldn't get the full registration, only a partial– and she ran over to where Terrence was picking himself up.

"Don't worry about me, get in your car and go!" he said, brushing himself off.

"Thank you so much for your help. I'll be in touch – I'll let you know where to meet me with the stuff I need."

"Get going. He could double back on us any second."

Nasreen ran home, got in the red Fiesta, and sped in the opposite direction.

She was going under the radar, and she *would* find Danny...

42

Lennox accelerated his Ford Ranger and pulled up beside the Director General's Mercedes. As he glanced to his left, he saw Michael Wells looking at him, shocked, and knowing there was a curve coming up, Lennox turned his steering wheel sharply, smashing into the side of the Mercedes.

He managed to correct his car, as the Director General lost control of his and careered off to the left, into a bank of trees. When he heard the crash, Lennox slowed down and looked in the rear-view mirror. He could see smoke.

Lennox stopped, then reversed. Considering there were no street lamps, it wasn't too dark – the whole area was brightly lit by a supermoon.

As he got out of the Ranger, he could smell the stench of burning rubber and metal. And as he approached the crash site he stepped on broken glass and other debris. He could hear moaning in the distance, meaning the NCA officer was still alive. For now.

Lennox reached inside his coat pocket and took out a pair of black leather gloves, pulling them on one at a time.

The Mercedes hadn't fared well against the mature hundred-year-old oak tree; the bonnet of the car was wrapped around it, and as he peered inside, he could see blood on the windscreen. The Director General was semi-conscious and leaning back in his seat, blood pouring from a huge gash on top of his head, as well as out of his mouth. Lennox knew it wouldn't be long until the man died from blood loss, but he had his orders from Rothstein; there could be no chances taken with this.

The dying man groaned as Lennox reached in through the broken window, pinched Wells' nose, and covered his mouth. When Wells realised he couldn't breathe, he tried to fight back but he was no match for Lennox's strength.

It took no more than a minute for the NCA officer to stop flailing and go limp.

Lennox kept his hand covering Wells' mouth and nose for another minute, to make sure, and when he was certain the man was dead, he walked back to his Ranger, got in, and drove off. He'd done it all without having seen a single passing car. There was no way anyone had seen him.

Once he was past the Director General's home, Lennox picked up his burner phone and dialled Rothstein's burner number. When Rothstein picked up, Lennox said, "It's done," and hung up...

43

Day 33
Monday, 12th February

Nasreen peered through her hotel room's net curtain to see Terrence getting out of his car, dressed in jeans and a bomber jacket and carrying a heavy-looking rucksack. She waited by the door for him to knock, dressed in light blue jeans and an acorn brown jumper.

When she'd left her house that night – which was a few days earlier – Nasreen had checked in to a Premier Inn a few miles away from her home. It was an average hotel, with no frills or excess; she had a room with a bed, a desk, a television, and a small refrigerator. The bathroom and everything else about the room was basic, and so was the price.

She'd left Katerina and Mina at Yasmin's house until Nasreen knew she could return; what she had planned was going to be dangerous and she didn't want them anywhere near it. If the masked man did return to her house, he'd be out of luck.

Although she didn't think she was being followed, she still checked behind her wherever she went, to be sure.

In an attempt to stop the masked man finding her, she'd left her car in a long-term car park and had rented a nondescript common Ford Focus from an Enterprise Rent-a-Car nearby, using a fake passport Terrence had managed to get her at very short notice. The day after she'd left her home she'd emptied her bank account, and she had over ten thousand pounds on her in cash. No one was going to be able to locate her.

For the past three days she hadn't done much. She'd spent her time convalescing, getting fit again for when the analysis of the masked man's saliva came through. Although Terrence had told her that he'd asked for the results to be expedited, the forensics officer responsible was really busy, and doing Terrence a favour – especially one off the books – wasn't a top priority.

The only thing keeping her sane was being able to chat to Mina on her burner phone every evening, just before bedtime. Ashraf's mother always ended the call asking her – pleading with her – to be careful, and Nasreen always swore she would, saying that she aimed to be back home soon.

Nasreen wasn't a naturally patient person. Ashraf had always told her she needed to relax more, and not get impatient; it wouldn't make things happen any sooner. Waiting for Terrence – and more importantly, the DNA results – therefore, was killing her; she wanted to be out there, chasing down leads. Doing *something*.

There was a knock on the door, and she opened it a crack, checking it was indeed Terrence, even though she'd seen him arrive in the car park. After all, she couldn't be too careful. "Come in," she said, allowing him inside.

She joined Terrence by the bed, waiting as he emptied the

contents of his rucksack. There was a brown A4 envelope – she assumed the results of the DNA test – and there was also a gun-shaped object wrapped in a couple of white handkerchiefs. It looked small enough to fit in her handbag.

"First off, let's get this out of the way." Terrence picked up the handkerchiefs and uncovered the Remington RM380 matt black pistol and two fully loaded clips.

Nasreen took hold of the gun, sliding one clip inside the butt. She locked it, then chambered a round by sliding the top chamber back and forth. "The Remington RM380 has a 410 stainless-steel barrel with an oxide finish and a glass-filled nylon grip. Six rounds per clip and one in the pipe, plus a long, smooth, light, double-action only trigger."

Terrence whistled. "The girl knows her stuff. I don't know whether to be scared or turned on right now."

Nasreen smiled. Terrence knew how good she was with a gun; she'd blown him away – figuratively – with her shooting when they'd had to renew their firearms training three months earlier at the police target range. "Where'd you get it?"

He shook his head. "You don't want to know. One of the advantages of growing up where I did, you get to know some wrong 'uns. The disadvantage is... you get to know some wrong 'uns. That pistol's had the serial number filed off, so it's untraceable."

She placed the gun and the extra clip in her bag, and Terrence passed her a couple of boxes of thirty-eights, which she put in there too. Now that she felt sufficiently armed, she was interested in the DNA results – more than interested.

"And here's what you've been waiting for." He opened the envelope and slid out the contents. "Take a look for yourself. This guy's got one hell of a history."

She took the papers from Terrence and skimmed through the information. The masked man's name was Walter Gebhardt, an immigrant from Bavaria. She'd known he was European by his accent when he'd threatened her and Mina, though she hadn't been able to place it entirely. Bastard!

She continued reading the official forms.

Walter Gebhardt was fifty-two and had moved to the UK eighteen years earlier. He'd had numerous jobs around the country, had a National Insurance number, a UK driving licence, and a European passport. He'd only been picked up once, for assault, which was why he was in the system. She looked at the photo of the two abductors in the van, then at the photo Terrence had brought in his envelope. They were definitely one and the same person. "Have you seen this?"

Terrence nodded. "It's definitely him."

Included in the stack of papers were also several known addresses where Gebhardt had resided, and most importantly, the address of his wife. Nasreen knew that was where she needed to start. She was going to have to drive for hours up north, but she had been prepared for that possibility. Now that she had everything she needed – cash, a fake passport, a car under her assumed identity, a gun, and the file – she was ready to begin the hunt for Walter Gebhardt...

44

Beattie, wearing a pair of dark blue jeans and a long-sleeved black and silver stud lace top, opened the hatch to Danny's room and watched him lying there, chained to his bed. Her guards had done considerable damage to his body; he had broken ribs, fractures to his arms and legs, and even a fracture to his collarbone.

It would take him months to recover fully. It wouldn't stop her from putting him to work in a couple of weeks. The way she saw it, if his "little man" still worked – albeit with medicinal aid – then her clients could still make use of him, and she could still make money. Which was all that mattered.

It was such a shame he couldn't be more like her other bees, she thought. He was far more talented than the rest – and had the ability to really show her customers a good time – he just seemed incapable of transitioning, of adapting to his new life. He was probably still holding on to hope, hope that that bitch detective would somehow find him and rescue him.

Beattie had thought about telling him that Nasreen was no longer a detective – Beattie's dad had informed her she'd been suspended from her job and that she was no longer seen as a threat. Plus Walter had paid her a visit. That should be enough to keep the bitch away, she thought, watching Danny squirm as he tried to get comfortable.

With a sigh, she closed the hatch and walked through to her office, where Alan was busy on his computer. He was wearing a pair of black jeans and a dark grey zip-up sweater over a white T-shirt.

"I don't know what I'm going to do with Danny," she said as she sat down at her desk.

"He can still earn, can't he?"

"Yeah, I guess so. I'll just dose him up."

"There you go," Alan said, not really paying her any attention. "Problem solved."

Beattie felt like she had her old life back again. Alan was where he should be – here, where he belonged – and their relationship had improved no end. That being said, it didn't stop her from thinking about Lennox.

The previous night she'd met Samantha "Sammy" Browne for the first time. She'd asked Alan to invite her over for dinner, and the three of them had sat down and talked, eaten, drunk, and laughed. It had been a great night for them, and Beattie had found Sammy to be great company too. She was charming and funny, just what she needed from a stepdaughter. And Sammy was even prettier in person than in her photos.

Despite feeling that her life was back to the way it used to be, Beattie still couldn't get Lennox out of her head. She wanted to – she didn't want to keep obsessing over him – but she couldn't do anything to prevent it. She couldn't forget that kiss, and she wanted more.

"I've got to go out tomorrow, honey," said Alan. "It's Hannah's birthday. She's invited me to join her and Sammy for dinner. You don't mind, do you?"

Beattie *did*, not that she could show it. She'd spent more than enough time on her own already. In spite of this, she replied, "No, that's fine. Are you coming back home after dinner?"

"Yeah, should be about half eleven."

Beattie gave her blessing, then she turned back to her computer and the spreadsheet she was working on...

Kimiko wheeled her trolley into Danny's room and closed the door. He was in pain, twisting and writhing as much as his chains would allow, trying to get comfortable. Mrs Harrison hadn't given him any pain relief.

It had upset Kimiko, watching him run off like that. She'd tried to warn him that there was glass on the floor, that he wouldn't get very far if he tried to flee. He'd sped off before she could get the words out. After it had all happened, she wondered why she hadn't told him about the glass before, to prevent him from even trying. But how could she have known?

Just before he'd run, he'd turned to her and said, "I love you, but I have to go now." Had he truly meant it? *Did* he love her? She'd tried asking him, the previous day, but all he did now was stare up at the ceiling, a dull blankness in his eyes. He hadn't spoken to her once since the incident, since the guards had beat him.

She took out her sponge, dipped it in water, and gave him a sponge bath. She was very gentle, especially over his ribs, arms and legs, which had taken the worst of the beating. He continued to lie there, eyes up, staring at the ceiling. "Why you not talk to me?" she whispered, thinking Mrs Harrison was likely to be listening, watching.

Nothing.

He winced when she touched his knee, making Kimiko jump.

"I sorry," she said, bathing him with more care. "I must wash you."

"Help me," he said, his voice barely audible.

She stopped bathing him and looked into his eyes.

He was watching her, only his eyes moving, while the rest of his face remained upright.

"What did you say?" she whispered again, still bathing him.

"Beattie will kill me soon," came his quiet voice. "Please, help me."

Kimiko paused for a moment, thinking. She wanted to help him – she wanted to help all the bees and all the support staff in this horrid place – and she could, if she picked up that phone and called the police. If she wasn't interrupted again. But that was easier said than done. "I cannot, Danny, I sorry," she whispered. "Mrs Harrison kill me."

"Phone police, please."

There was a pleading look in his eyes, and Kimiko felt so guilty that she wasn't strong enough to help him – to help all of them. The risk was too great. If she betrayed Mrs Harrison, she would be killed, and she wanted to live. Then again, what kind of life was she living here? She was as much a prisoner as the bees were. The dilemma made her brain hurt.

Having finished washing him, she wheeled her trolley to the door and turned to look at him. "I sorry, Danny," she whispered.

As she wheeled the trolley back to the store cupboard, she walked past the office and saw Mr and Mrs Harrison kissing, like they'd done when she arrived here.

Kimiko smiled at one of the guards outside the showers as she wheeled her trolley past him. She had some serious thinking to do. Should she risk her own life to help Danny? Did she love him? And if so, did she love him enough? She thought she might; the feelings she had whenever she saw him told her she did, but was she being foolish? Did he really love her? Would he risk *his* life to save *her*, if the situation were reversed?

There was no denying that she had to leave this place. Mr and Mrs Harrison were evil people, who allowed unspeakable things to happen here. Kimiko, on the other hand, wasn't a bad person. No, she was a good person.

Being a good person, however, wasn't enough.

She wanted to be – had to be – a *strong* person...

Steven was two cars behind Garvey, stuck at some traffic lights. He could see his target's Shogun with its indicators blinking left.

Since the Director General's sudden death in a car accident, a lot had changed at HQ. The first thing that happened was that his team had been pulled off surveillance detail at the Harrison farm, which had frustrated him immensely. Steven knew something big was happening in that barn – and the vast majority of his colleagues believed so too. Now they might never know.

The operation investigating William Rothstein seemed like it was crumbling, not because there was insufficient evidence – on the contrary, there was a mass of evidence – but because of other forces at work. If Steven didn't know any better, he'd say that someone didn't want Rothstein investigated.

Steven hadn't heard it himself; a colleague had informed him that the new Director General had said the target was Lennox Garvey. While it wasn't official, Steven believed his colleague. The whole situation left a bad taste in his mouth; he knew that Rothstein deserved to be sent down. Now it looked like that wouldn't happen.

It was true, he had a personal reason for wanting to raid the farmhouse, and in particular, the barn. It was *his* find, and he had a vested interest in ascertaining what was going on in there. But more than that, he wanted to shut it down, to help stop whatever was going on there. That was what the NCA did: it stopped criminals from carrying out their foul deeds. And whatever was happening in the barn was big, he knew it. It wasn't fair for the new DG to pull them off the surveillance detail. Something was going on.

He followed Garvey as he turned left and then continued his pursuit. He was back to the dull task of tailing his target, which was disappointing. He might have been warmer in his car, but following Garvey wasn't going to yield as much intel for the agency as photographing the visitors at the barn. He would rather be cold and hungry getting results, than warm and bored following a car around all day.

He took a deep breath and focused on the task at hand. Getting angry at the situation wouldn't alter the fact that the barn surveillance had been axed. Maybe Garvey would meet someone interesting, giving him something he could take to the top brass. He wasn't all about personal glory, but – in his opinion – there was nothing wrong with wanting it. Everyone wanted to get noticed at work; it was perfectly natural.

"Following target along Churchill Road," he said into his microphone.

The voice acknowledged his transmission.

There was something about the new Director General that Steven didn't trust. Graham Holmes was a weasel – a brown nose, through and through. Steven had never met the man himself, yet he'd heard enough stories in his time to know he didn't like him. He hadn't met Michael Wells either, but he knew the deceased Director General had been a straight arrow – everyone said so.

Steven had spoken to his wife about the whole situation, and although it was just talk at this stage – him letting off steam mainly – he'd told her he was thinking about applying to a different agency. He felt so strongly that the NCA would suffer under Graham Holmes' leadership. And Steven wasn't the only one; he'd spoken to three colleagues so far who'd said the same as him. Director General Graham Holmes was a tosser, plain and simple. Still, it was only talk at this stage. He would give it a few months under Holmes before even looking at vacancies in other law enforcement agencies.

"Target's approaching the Rothstein residence," he said into his microphone.

The team at HQ had pulled in over fifty of the barn visitors and spent hours upon hours interviewing each of them. Of those fifty plus interviewees, however, not one of them had given even a hint as to what was happening there. The cloak of silence was all encompassing, and it pissed him off something awful. He'd thought about requesting a transfer to HQ, to have a crack at getting one of them to talk himself, but the way everything was going, permission to transfer wouldn't be forthcoming.

Steven pulled up a little way down the road from the entrance to Rothstein's home, in a place where he'd be able to see visitors as they came and went.

He was in for a long boring shift...

45

Rothstein held out his hand. "Lenny, come on in."

Lennox shook Rothstein's hand and sat down on the chair in front of his boss's desk. He noticed how happy and carefree Rothstein looked, and he didn't trust it. His boss was also looking very dapper in his three-piece tailored suit, in contrast to Lennox's dark blue jeans, navy blue zip-up jumper, and black leather jacket.

"It's payday, my man," said Rothstein, opening his top desk drawer and pulling out a wedge of cash wrapped in cellophane. "I know how much we agreed on, but I put a little extra in there, by way of showing you how grateful I am for what you did. Seventy-five Gs."

Lennox reached across the desk and accepted the money, placing the fat wedge of fifties in his rucksack. "Thanks, but you didn't need to do t–"

"Rubbish!" Rothstein exclaimed, interrupting him. "Of course I did; because of you, the farm is now officially out of the NCA's sights and the overall investigation is slowly going to be grounded. Plus, now I have someone in the NCA looking out for my interests, so it's a win-win all round. Let's have a well-deserved drink, yeah?"

Never one to pass up a free drink, Lennox stood and walked over to the office bar. Taking down two tumblers from the glass shelf, he was about to pour two large Macallan eighteen-year-old triple cask malts when Rothstein shook his head.

"It's time we pulled the big boy out," he said, taking down the slender bottle of Macallan Reflexion Single Malt Whisky. "I've got to know what a nine-hundred-quid whisky tastes like, and this seems like the perfect time, don't you think?"

Lennox agreed, pouring two large shots in each glass and handing one to Rothstein.

"To you, Lenny." Rothstein smiled, holding up his glass in salute.

Lennox watched Rothstein take his first sip.

"Fuck me, that's a good fucking whisky," his boss said, savouring every drop. "Hints of vanilla, fresh apples, and apricots, if I'm not mistaken."

He was right; it was the tastiest whisky Lennox had ever sipped. At that price though, it needed to be tasty. Personally, he thought it was ridiculous paying that sort of money for a drink, even if it was for a special occasion.

"Who the fuck am I trying to kid? I just read the label on the bottle when I bought it." Rothstein laughed. "I can't tell the difference between this and Bell's – apart from the price."

Lennox continued to sip at his drink and chat with his boss until both glasses were almost empty, and although he was listening to Rothstein, Lennox wasn't really hearing him; he was daydreaming about his boss's daughter, which he knew was dangerous.

"Anyway, enough of this bullshit." Rothstein placed his empty glass on the bar. "Back to the business at hand."

Lennox sipped the last few drops of the delicious whisky,

placing his empty glass on the bar next to Rothstein's before walking over to the desk and sitting down in front of his boss again. Lennox thought he knew what this was about.

"Due to family sickness, Yusef won't be able to drive you this time," Rothstein explained. "I'm trialling a new captain, and I'll see how he goes, so you'll need to bring him up to speed next week, okay?"

This wasn't good news. Yusef was the captain of the fishing trawler Lennox travelled on to pick up his uncle's shipment. It had always been steered by Yusef. Lennox couldn't remember a single occasion, in fact, when someone else had steered the trawler, and all of a sudden, something felt off. "Can we postpone picking it up until he's recovered?"

"I'm afraid not, Lenny. It's okay, though – this new guy will be good for us. We can't always rely on one person, can we? This way I can rotate boat captains, give one of them a rest while the other works. It'll be good, trust me."

Lennox's uncle had always said, "Don't trust anyone who says 'trust me'," and while he wouldn't exactly say he trusted Rothstein, his boss had never done anything to make him distrust him either. Even so, something about the switch of captains didn't sit right. "In that case, I want my own people on board with me when I make the pickup."

"However you want to play it," Rothstein yielded. "It's your gig."

Lennox had three friends he called on from time to time. They were what the English would call "Yardies", and they had all worked for his uncle when they'd lived in Jamaica. Barkley, Bembe, and Khenan were his best friends here in this shithole of a country, and they helped remind him of his own country, his home.

Whenever they got together, Lennox felt as though there was nothing they couldn't do; they were untouchable when they were in a group. He was closest to Barkley, having spent his childhood growing up with him – after his parents had been shot dead and he'd gone to live with his uncle. Bembe and Khenan were best friends, but the four of them together were solid.

"It's like you don't trust me... or something, Lenny." Rothstein sounded hurt.

"It's not that... It's just that in all my time here–"

"Yusef's always steered the boat. I know, I know. It can't be helped. His wife's been taken really ill." Rothstein shrugged. "There's nothing I can do. I mean, I can't cure her cancer, can I? Though I wish I could; I'd be rolling in it."

"Okay, I'll call my brothers in to give me a hand. It's not a problem."

"Good. That's sorted then. A week today."

Lennox studied Rothstein for a second, and thought he seemed genuine. Fuck it! It was probably just him being paranoid. So far, Rothstein had been good to him. He'd even passed the real test when he'd been asked to join the Assistant Commissioner's conspiracy. If he'd heard Rothstein accept the invitation, it would be a whole different story. So, instead, he tried to push his misgivings to the back of his mind.

"We're back in business, Lenny." Rothstein held out his hand, signalling that the meeting was over. "Smile – it's a good thing."

Lennox smiled half-heartedly...

46

"Sorry to bother you, Bea, but my van's stuck in the slush," said a voice from behind her. "Don't suppose I could use your guards for a push, could I?"

Beattie turned around to find her last client of the day stood in the doorway. She had been serviced by the New Bee, Thomas, and she certainly looked happy enough. "Of course you can," Beattie replied, getting up and walking over to her.

Mrs Reid was a fifty-six-year-old cleaner by trade, though she looked about sixty-five in Beattie's opinion, with wispy dyed red hair and wrinkles belying her age. Although she looked older than her years, she was fit from cleaning homes full-time. She also walked dogs for money in her spare time. She certainly was a strange one, Mrs Reid; by all accounts, she wasn't the normal demographic for Beattie's business. The majority of her clients were hardened career criminals, who came here to relax and have sex with her bees. Mrs Reid wasn't, but her husband was in prison for armed robbery, and he'd told his wife to get in touch with Beattie.

"So, how was my New Bee? Was he to your liking?" Beattie asked politely as she walked out of the office with her client.

Mrs Reid replied that she was entirely satisfied with Thomas' performance and would give him an eight out of ten; the only reason it wasn't higher, she said, was because he was tied up, and she liked fingers and tongues. Beattie assured Mrs Reid that Thomas would be out of his restraints by her next visit.

Out in the corridor, Beattie went along each room on both sides, making sure all the doors were locked. When she came to Danny's room, the door was still open, and she could see Kimiko finishing her cleaning duties. Danny stared up at the ceiling. "Kimiko," Beattie said, "please can you make sure you lock this door when you're finished? We're all going upstairs to help push Mrs Reid's van out of the slush, okay?"

She heard Kimiko say, "Yes, Bea," and then carried on walking along, continuing to check all the other doors were locked.

All five of her guards – minus Walter, who was still out trying to find her a New Bee – were stood around the bar, enjoying a drink and a laugh in their own languages.

"Come along, boys, we need your muscle," she ordered.

Once upstairs and out of the barn, Beattie saw the problem: the van's rear tyres had sunk into the grass, which had become mud and slush. It was freezing out – below freezing, in fact – and she wished she'd brought her jacket with her...

"Now, Kimiko, please!" pleaded Danny, in a whisper. "They've all gone upstairs."

Kimiko froze.

Was now the right time to phone the police? She knew she had to do it, although she hadn't expected to be able to do it quite so soon. She was frightened; if she got caught talking on the phone, Mrs Harrison would kill her. She'd end up burning in the furnace, just like all the others. "I cannot, Danny, I scared."

"I know you're scared, sweetheart. I'm scared too. You have to, *please*. It's the only way for all of us to get out of here... I know it's shitty. You're the only one who can do it. I would, but look at me: I can't even walk."

"Please don't make me."

She knew – deep down – however, it had to be done right now, or it never would.

Kimiko walked out of Danny's room.

"Thank you," she heard him say.

She didn't reply.

In the hallway, she checked left and saw that the bar was empty.

She checked right and couldn't see anyone there either.

All the doors to the bees' rooms were closed.

Every step she took towards the office felt heavy, and time felt like it was slowing.

The office door was open, and after stepping inside she did another check to make sure no one was coming down the stairs. The coast was clear, but she knew she had to hurry; she had no idea how long it would take for them to push a van out of the snow.

The phone was right there on Mrs Harrison's desk. All Kimiko had to do was pick up the receiver and dial those three magic numbers. That was it.

She was still listening out for any movement outside when she finally picked up the receiver.

Nine. That was one done. Her hand was shaking.

Nine. That was two.

Nine. She felt nauseous.

The ringing tone sounded, and she listened to it while also

trying to listen outside for any voices. She really needed to pee, badly. She'd never been this scared before – ever.

"Emergency services," came the female voice, "what service do you require?"

"Police, please," came Kimiko's tiny voice. She didn't know how the person on the other end of the phone had heard her; she could barely hear herself.

Somehow, however, she did. "One moment, please."

There was a moment of silence, and then another voice – male this time – asked her what the situation was.

"I need help," she said, her voice still small and scared.

"We're here to help. Can you tell me what the problem is?"

"There are... about twenty-five of us... being... held... prisoner..." Kimiko gasped, unable to believe she was actually doing this.

"I'm sorry... did you just say there are twenty-five of you being held prisoner? I can't hear your voice very well."

"Yes, twenty-five here, prisoner... please help!"

"What's your name, please?" asked the voice, sounding remarkably calm.

"I Kimiko, please send police," she pleaded.

She wanted this phone call to end. She wanted to be anywhere but here.

"Okay, Kimiko, we're going to help you. Just tell me where you are."

Kimiko cringed. She'd been held prisoner for sixteen years and didn't have a clue where she was. She never got to see any of the mail, she never got to see anything that would give her what she needed. "I... don't... know, I sorry."

"It's okay, Kimiko. Have you seen any landmarks, anything nearby that we can use to locate you?"

"Can't you use phone number?" she asked, desperate to hang up.

Just then she heard voices in the distance, and panicking, she dropped the phone back on its cradle, looking for a way out. She had to get out of the office before anyone saw her.

Without thinking of the consequences, she walked up to the office door and peeked out towards the bar. She could see two of the guards – their backs to her as they leaned against the bar – and seizing her opportunity, she snuck out while they weren't looking, tiptoeing back to Danny's room.

She'd done it – the police would be on their way soon...

47

Nasreen looked at the clock on her dashboard: 20:46. She'd been waiting in her car, across the road from Lina Klugheim's two-bedroom terraced house, for over two hours. Nasreen was wearing her dark blue jeans, her black cashmere turtleneck sweater, her black leather jacket, and her dark brown ankle boots, yet she was still cold. Walter Gebhardt's wife hadn't returned home from wherever she was. The lights weren't on.

Klugheim's home was the second of four in the terrace, and it had a bay window next to the white PVC front door. There was a small garden outside the front, which she – or he – tended to regularly, by the looks of it. The white fence was newly erected and painted; they obviously looked after their home.

This was Gebhardt's last known address, and Nasreen hoped he still lived here; she wanted to catch him unawares. She could have continued searching for Danny at her own house, waiting for him to return to her home, but that would have been on his terms. She wanted to find Gebhardt on *her* terms. By hunting *him*, it put *her* in control – he certainly wouldn't be expecting her to turn up on his doorstep with a Remington RM380 in her hand.

A tall woman with long brown hair walked along the road toward Klugheim's house, Nasreen watching as the woman – who had a cigarette hanging out of her mouth – stopped and reached into her handbag. She pulled out a set of keys, opened the gate to Klugheim's garden, walked up to the front door, and then opened it, flicking her cigarette butt into her next-door neighbour's driveway before stepping inside.

Nasreen waited for Klugheim to close the curtains and turn on the lights, giving Nasreen ten minutes to settle down before she reached into her bag and felt for the pistol, making sure she had backup – if needed. She got out of the car, hooking the straps over her shoulder.

Nasreen stood at the side of the road, waiting for the traffic to clear before she crossed. She wasn't leaving here without either Walter himself, or an address where she could look next.

She knocked on the door, her hand around the butt of the Remington inside her bag, and waited. After a few seconds, she could hear movement inside.

The brown-haired woman opened the door enough for her face to peer out.

Nasreen immediately noticed that she had a black eye and a cracked lip.

"Who are you? What you want?" asked Klugheim, with a heavy European accent.

"Lina Klugheim? I'm looking for your husband, Walter Gebhardt."

"I not know him no more. Go away and leave me alone."

Klugheim went to close the door, but Nasreen put her boot between the frame and the door. "I'm afraid I insist on seeing him," she said firmly, pushing hard.

When Klugheim staggered backwards, Nasreen took the opportunity to step inside, closing the door behind her. She still had her hand on the butt of the gun; while she didn't want to produce it, she would if she had to. "Now, tell me where your husband is, and I'll leave. But I'm not going anywhere until I get what I came for."

"He not my husband no more. It why I Klugheim, not Gebhardt."

Nasreen looked around the house, which was as orderly, clean, and tidy as her front garden; Klugheim was clearly house-proud, making her stock go up in Nasreen's estimation. There were two lovely soft burgundy sofas and an armchair in the lounge, set around a mahogany and glass coffee table. There was a huge fifty-inch flat-screen television mounted on the wall above the fireplace, and several pictures adorned the walls. "And how long have you been divorced for?"

"Not divorced, separated. Bastard won't give me divorce. Separated fifteen years. Now get out my house before I call the cops..."

"I am the cops," Nasreen said, immediately wishing she hadn't.

"Show me badge, prove it," said Klugheim, holding her hand out.

"I should've said I *was* a cop," she muttered, letting go of the pistol and rummaging around in her bag until she pulled out a business card. "I don't have my badge with me, but this is my card, okay?"

Klugheim took the card and read it. "You far away from here. I call real cops."

As Klugheim went to walk towards the telephone next to the sofa, Nasreen said, "Please, wait. Your ex-husband has kidnapped my ex-boyfriend. I'm just trying to find Walter so I can get him to take me to Danny. Please, Lina, I'm not here to cause trouble."

Klugheim turned back to Nasreen. "Kidnapped? That sounds like Walter, bastard."

Nasreen put her hand out placatingly. "Yeah, over a month ago. And I think he's abducted many more, not just Danny... Please, I really need your help. I need to know where I can find him, that's all."

When Klugheim gestured towards the sofa, Nasreen sat down and waited for her host to talk.

Klugheim looked tired; she had droopy eyes, like she was about to fall asleep, but most of that was because her left eye was badly bruised. She was attractive in a wrinkly "had a hard life" way, and her teeth were yellow, probably from smoking for decades.

"I not seen Walter for five years." Klugheim lit another cigarette. "Last time I see him, he gave me worst black eye. I in hospital for two weeks. He a bastard! He left me pregnant, then, when I eight months, he beat me up, I lost baby."

"I'm so sorry," Nasreen replied genuinely.

Klugheim shrugged then stared at the floor. "It not matter, I always meet bad man. I got this yesterday from man I throw out. This his leaving present."

"It's hard these days, meeting the right man."

"You meet bad man too?"

"What this?" She pointed at her bruised cheek. "No, Walter gave me this. He came to my house and threatened to hurt my little girl if I don't stop looking for Danny."

"I sorry, like I say, he bastard."

After a long silence, Klugheim said, "I not know where he is now, but I have address of girlfriend he left me for, if you want."

"Yes, please, if you don't mind." Nasreen nodded, hopeful.

Standing up, Klugheim walked over to a bureau in the corner of the lounge, next to the fireplace, and after opening it, she took out an address book. "I not know if she live there now."

"If I have her name, I can find her."

"But be careful, she a nasty bitch. If you think me hard, she worst."

"I can look after myself."

"I not doubt it. But if you find Walter, take care; he a dangerous man."

Nasreen took the piece of paper from Klugheim, shook her hand, and thanked her for her help. She looked down at the paper – the woman's name was Petra Farkas.

As she walked to her car, Nasreen pulled out her disposable mobile and called Terrence.

"Hey, Nas, what do you need?"

"Anything you can give me on a Petra Farkas..."

48

Day 36
Thursday, 15th February

Kimiko couldn't understand why the police hadn't arrived yet. It had been three days since she'd phoned them and explained what was going on, so where were they?

She pulled off her duvet and got out of bed. The floor was cold, so she slipped on her plimsolls and wrapped herself in her bathrobe.

When she stepped into the shower and turned on the taps, the hot water instantly warmed her. Showering was one of the highlights of her day.

It was also a time for her to think. Why had they not found them? She couldn't phone them again; the only reason she'd managed to before was sheer luck. Mrs Harrison or the guards were always there. In fact, it was strange that she'd had two occasions recently where she'd had the opportunity to use the phone without anyone being around. Maybe Mrs Harrison was getting complacent with security; maybe she had other things on her mind?

Kimiko washed her hair with shampoo before rinsing it out thoroughly.

If the police weren't coming, what else could she do? She could try running away. If she got caught, Mrs Harrison would kill her, and then she'd kill Danny. Kimiko had to think of a way out of here, and soon. Danny was in a bad way, and Mrs Harrison was already talking about giving him clients to service despite the fact that he was still in a lot of pain. She was a cruel woman, Mrs Harrison.

Kimiko stayed under the shower for fifteen minutes, letting her body soak up the heat. Whatever happened, she was looking forward to the nicer weather coming; this winter had hit her hard.

So, what else could she do? How could she possibly get her and Danny out of here? She couldn't carry him out, and he couldn't walk, which didn't leave much in the way of options. She had to think things through. She also had to be quick about it. After all, Mrs Harrison would end up killing Danny in the end – of that she was sure – so she had to get him out sooner rather than later.

Kimiko stepped out of the shower, dried herself, wrapped herself up in her robe, and then walked back to her bedroom. As it was seven thirty in the morning she'd be the first person in the kitchen, which was good as she was hungry.

Dressed in a kimono, as always, she went downstairs.

In the kitchen, Kimiko set two eggs to poaching before placing two slices of bread in the toaster and taking a plate out of the cupboard. Poached eggs on toast was her favourite breakfast meal; it was very English. Over the years she had found that she liked a lot of English food, such as shepherd's pie and roast dinners.

The toast popped up. Kimiko placed both slices on her plate before walking over to the counter and taking a knife out from the block. It was seven inches long and serrated.

She looked at the stainless-steel blade, the ceiling light glinting in the metal.

The water was boiling over by the time her attention returned, and after cutting the toast with the knife and placing the eggs on top of it, she took her breakfast over to the table.

She had to eat and wash up quickly, before Mr and Mrs Harrison and the guards came down for their breakfasts. Looking up at the clock while she ate, Kimiko saw it was already approaching eight o'clock.

Kimiko washed up as she listened to the stirrings of the guards and the Harrisons, getting more and more nervous as the seconds ticked by. She washed and rinsed her plate and cooking utensils, leaving the cutlery until last and placing them in a mug to drain.

She looked behind her, then picked up the knife and slipped it inside her sleeve.

"Morning, Kimiko," came Mrs Harrison's voice.

How much had she seen?

Kimiko waited for a couple of seconds before replying, "Morning, Bea."

As Mrs Harrison didn't say anything else, Kimiko dropped her arms down beside her and turned to face her boss, the blade of the knife just touching her arm underneath her kimono.

"Are you all done in here?"

"Yes, I wash up and leave to dry," Kimiko replied.

"Okay, then," said Mrs Harrison with a smile.

Kimiko walked through the kitchen toward the stairs.

"Oh, Kimiko..."

All she wanted was get away from her captor.

Slowly, she turned to face Mrs Harrison. "Yes, Bea?"

"Can you focus on rooms one, three, four, and five today please?" asked Mrs Harrison. "Leave room two; it doesn't need doing while Danny's convalescing. Thank you."

Kimiko nodded before turning and walking slowly up the stairs, passing two of the guards on the way. She smiled politely at them and then walked along the landing to her bedroom. She felt like she hadn't breathed for the entire length of her walk.

Once inside she closed the door, leaned against it, and let out a long breath. She'd done it now; she had crossed the point of no return. She didn't even know why she'd taken the knife, or what she was going to do with it. It had been an impulsive act, and a dangerous one.

She took the knife out of her sleeve and stared at it. It was the only weapon she had...

Nasreen had finally tracked down her target, Petra Farkas, and was sitting outside her house in her car. The clock read 08:15.

Nasreen could see movement in the kitchen, could see Petra moving about through the curtain-free window. It looked like there were a couple of kids in the house too; she'd seen the tops of their heads in the kitchen.

Since being given Farkas' name by Walter Gebhardt's ex-wife, Nasreen had travelled over a hundred miles to two different addresses looking for her, only to be given yet more forwarding addresses. This was the third address she'd driven to. She'd checked into three different Premier Inns, and she was tired.

Terrence had provided Nasreen with some information about Farkas: she was a Hungarian-born immigrant of eight years, she'd never married, and she had two children, daughters. Petra Farkas worked from home as a freelance accountant, and she moved around, a lot. Nasreen didn't know what to expect from Farkas, but she was going to proceed with caution; after all, Lina Klugheim had warned her of how tough she was.

As it was a weekday – and as the kids would, therefore, be leaving for school soon – Nasreen decided to stay put until Farkas was alone.

Farkas lived in a three-bedroom semi-detached house, one that had an identical design to every other house on the street. None of these houses were especially expensive; there weren't many expensive homes in the area. The whole suburb looked run-down and tatty, with graffiti everywhere.

The front door opened and a tall lean man with a beard came out, dressed in a grey suit and carrying a briefcase. He had greying hair, and he looked to be in his late forties; it clearly wasn't Walter Gebhardt. It must be Farkas' new man, or not so new – Nasreen didn't know how long Farkas had been with Gebhardt. The mystery man got into his grey Honda Civic, reversed, turned, and accelerated past her.

Five minutes later the door opened again, and the two girls walked out in their red jumpers and grey skirts. Farkas, wearing a beige dressing gown, came to the door with two jackets in her hands, and Nasreen heard the mother order her girls to wear their coats. Farkas seemed like any other caring mother. Maybe Lina Klugheim had it wrong; maybe Farkas wasn't going to be a handful. Maybe she'd calmed down over time.

Nasreen waited five more minutes before getting out of her car, handbag over her shoulder. She crossed the road, walked up Farkas' driveway, and knocked on the door.

"Yes? Who are you?"

Nasreen noticed the scar on Farkas' neck first of all. It was an angry red line, and it looked like it had been made recently.

Petra was a tall woman with dark curly hair and deep brown eyes. She looked to be in her mid-forties.

"Ms Farkas?" asked Nasreen.

"Yes, and you are? If you're selling something, I'm not interested..."

"Ms Farkas, I'm Detective Constable Nasreen Maqsood, from the–"

She didn't get to finish her sentence before Farkas slammed the door in her face, and letting out an audible sigh, Nasreen bent down and opened the letterbox. "I just want to talk to you about your ex-boyfriend, Walter Gebhardt, Ms Farkas, that's all. I'm not here for you."

Nasreen stood up, then turned and looked across the road. This wasn't what she'd expected. Now she knew how door-to-door salespeople felt.

"What do you want to know about *him*?" Petra asked eventually, her voice muffled by the door. The way Farkas had said "him" made Gebhardt sound like a monster.

Nasreen turned back to face the door.

A second later, Farkas opened the door.

"I'm looking for him in connection with several disappearances of sex workers up and down the country," Nas explained. "I heard from someone that he was your boyfriend."

"Huh, some boyfriend. He did this to me last year." Petra pointed to her neck. "I called the police then, and you know what they did about it? Nothing... not a thing. A man cuts your throat, and the police can't even be bothered to look for him."

"I'm sure they did their bes–"

"They did *nothing*!"

Nasreen put her hands up in surrender. "Look, Ms Farkas, I understand you're angry – I would be too – but I'm not here about that, I'm sorry. I'm just here to see if you know where he might be. Do you have a forwarding address for him? Or do you have any of his family's addresses? Please, this is really important – people's lives might depend on me finding him."

"You'd better come in, detective." Farkas huffed, opening the door for her.

When Nasreen was inside and Farkas had closed the door behind her, she followed the woman through to the lounge/dining room, where the dining table had been set up as a makeshift office; her laptop was parked at one end, wired to a scanner-printer. The house smelt amazing – of cooked breakfast with bacon dominant. Nasreen didn't eat bacon, although she did love the smell.

She was offered a seat on one of the two L-shaped sofas, which was so comfortable she fell into it. "Can I ask what happened with..." Nasreen asked, gesturing at the woman's neck.

"It was partly my fault. He dumped me, and I didn't take it very well. I hit him, he pulled a knife on me... he went berserk and sliced my neck. He said I was lucky he was feeling charitable, lucky he didn't slice me deeper." She shook her head. "He's an animal."

Nasreen was beginning to see that. "And how long were you together for?"

"On and off for twelve years," she admitted. "He never live with me though. He came and went when it suit him. When I ask where he's been, he tells me to mind my own business. I was lucky if I saw him once a week; would be better maybe not to see him at all."

"And in those twelve years, did he ever mention anything–"

"About kidnapping people? Ha!" she spat. "He wouldn't talk business in front of me..."

Nasreen sighed. It had been worth a shot. "Did you ever meet any of his relatives?"

"He has brother, but I never meet him. He supposed to be worse than Walter; he told me stories about Conrad. I not sorry I never meet him."

"Conrad Gebhardt? That's Walter's brother?"

"That's what I just say."

"Sorry, I'm just saying it out loud, so that it sticks in my mind. I don't suppose you have an address for him, do you?"

"No, I don't, I just tell you… Oh, wait…" Farkas paused. "A friend of mine went out with Conrad a couple times. Hang on, I'll get you her phone number."

Finally, Nasreen was getting somewhere. In all her time on the force, she had learned that families could be relied on to know the whereabouts of other family members. Even if there'd been a big rift between siblings, they generally knew where the other sibling lived. If she could find Conrad, chances were high that he would be able to point her in the right direction. "Thanks," she said, accepting the piece of paper from Farkas.

The name on the piece of paper was Zuzanna Jankovics, and Farkas had also written down her phone number and address. Jankovics lived two towns away – Nasreen could easily drive there in less than an hour…

49

Beattie was in the mood for a big cooked breakfast. Generally, she would just have a bowl of cereal and a couple of slices of toast, but this morning she was in the mood to cook, and she would cook for the guards as well. They all sat down around the table while she prepared their breakfasts.

Alan was already at work – so she didn't need to worry about meeting and greeting the clients – and Kimiko was upstairs, getting ready for work, and would soon be helping Alan. Beattie wasn't really needed, so she told Alan she was taking the day off, to make up for all the time he'd had off lately. Alan had happily agreed to this.

In the refrigerator, she took out the bacon, sausages, and tomatoes. Then she went to the cupboard and took out the baked beans. The hash browns she fetched from the freezer, and the bread from the bread bin on the work surface. Then she took out all the utensils she needed and started cooking.

One of the guards offered to help. She insisted she was more than capable of making seven breakfasts. She would call Alan in when it was ready.

While everything was cooking, she looked at the bacon, and

seeing how fatty it was, she went over to the block of knives, taking out the long meat knife and noticing that a smaller knife was missing. She paid it no mind, however, thinking it would be in the sink.

The kitchen smelt amazing as the bacon fried and the eggs and sausages sizzled, but there was a lot of smoke, so she opened the window in front of the sink. She waited until everything was ready, then plated up. She was famished, and couldn't wait to start eating. Turning to the guards, she asked one of them to go and get Alan...

"Go ahead, I've pulled over onto the hard shoulder." Nasreen spoke into her simple mobile. "What've you got for me?"

"Conrad Gebhardt, forty-three, moved to the UK five years ago. He was questioned over the death of a Russian diplomat back in 2015. He was never formally charged. He has ties with the Bavarian Brotherhood, as does his brother, Walter. The Brotherhood has a branch here, in the UK, and although it's never been confirmed, apparently it deals in all sorts: extortion, protection racketeering, drugs, prostitution, and human trafficking. All that good stuff."

"Have you got a last known address for him?"

"It's a YMCA up north," he replied. "As far as I can see on the PNC, he's a ghost, Nas. The only reason we know *anything* about him is because he got picked up that one time; since then, nothing."

"Okay, thanks."

There was a slight pause before Terrence continued, "I know you don't want to hear this, but I'm going to say it anyway... be careful out there; this guy's the real deal, a nasty bastard by all accounts."

"You know me, I'm always careful. Plus, you forget: I've got a friend with me." She looked over at her bag. "She's been looking forward to getting out, and now it looks like I've found the right guy to show her off to, huh?"

"Okay, just saying."

Nasreen smiled. "Anyway, how's everything in the office?"

"Adams is spitting acid. It was your first scheduled interview with IOPC yesterday. I'm sure I don't need to tell you he wasn't happy you missed it."

Nasreen smiled again. "He'll get over it. I'll call you later."

She put her phone back in her bag, pulled out onto the motorway, and accelerated to get ahead of a lorry that was rapidly catching up with her.

Her rental car had a GPS installed, so she followed the instructions to get to Zuzanna Jankovics' flat...

The blade of the knife scraped Kimiko's arm as she descended the stairs.

She didn't know what to do with it.

As she left the house, closing the door behind her, she decided she would hide the knife in her trolley for now.

She walked along the paving towards the barn, passing Mr Harrison and one of the guards as she went. She was paranoid they would see the knife through her kimono. Neither of them said anything. Once clear of them, she continued into the barn and down the stairs to the bar before walking through the bar, past the bees' rooms, and turning right, past the showers and toilets. She stopped in the storage room.

With adrenaline coursing through her veins, she slid the knife out from under her sleeve and stored it on the bottom level of her trolley. Knowing she couldn't keep it there indefinitely, she tried to think of where else she could hide it, but after five minutes, she still couldn't think of a safe place.

There was no point giving the knife to Danny; he was tied up permanently, with little chance of that changing. No, she had to have it within reach; it was going to be all down to her when they finally managed to escape...

"Hi, Will, I'm just checking in," said Assistant Commissioner Peter Franks into his mobile. "Any idea when we're doing this thing?"

Franks was sat in his study. His wife had left for work, so he had the house to himself, and he'd finalised the date for the big meeting, the big reveal. He had access to a warehouse in the Midlands; there he would gather his troops and divulge how the project would proceed. As the warehouse would be integral to it, he thought it best that his troops at least know where it was.

"I said I'll call you when it's time," Rothstein snapped.

"I know what you said, but I have a timeline here, Will. It's not only you in this, you know."

"Look, you've got someone tailing him, haven't you?"

"The NCA have, yes."

"When the time's right, I'll call you, and then you can call the Director General, okay?"

"Can you be any clearer than that? If it's in the next couple..."

"In the next few days, yes."

"Well, all right then," Franks said, hanging up.

He really couldn't stand Rothstein. There were many things he had to do as part of his job that he hated, but this topped the list. When the project was finished – when they'd leaked it to the press and when they had their evidence of all the good it had done – he was going to enjoy putting Rothstein away. It was all part of the Commissioner's big plan: use them for as long as they served a purpose, then put them down.

He had twenty-nine Police and Crime Commissioners in favour of being a part of the operation – that was twenty-nine police forces out of forty-one. He felt sorry for the few he hadn't approached, as their crime stats would pale in comparison to those involved; when the dealers started drip-feeding their rivals it was going to be payday, and those poor few commissioners he hadn't approached would be left out of the raids, left out of the headlines.

That was what the project was for: high-profile detentions. Before they leaked the details of it, they had to have enough media coverage of the police forces making drug seizures – and prosecuting those responsible – so that the public wouldn't forget why they'd gone ahead with the project in the first place. It was about making the drugs, and the streets, safer for everyone.

Franks was, and always had been, a big believer in legalising drugs. It made sense to him to give people choices in life. Prohibiting the use of anything drove up the black market value and gave the criminal gangs something to offer their customers.

He didn't understand the government's stance on drugs and prostitution. Other countries had legalised both. Amsterdam in particular had made a lot of money.

He picked up his phone again and dialled. "Graham, it's Peter. How's everything going your end? Rothstein's no nearer giving us a date."

"We have Garvey under twenty-four-hour surveillance, as you asked. I'm getting some blowback from some of the officers, but nothing I can't handle."

"Good, good. Rothstein did tell me it would be in the next few days, so keep your phone handy. I've got a rough date in mind for the primary meeting, I'll text it to you."

"Okay, I'll be expecting it."

Franks hung up, but as soon as he'd put his mobile down, it rang.

"Peter, it's Clive, I thought you should know that we've lost Nasreen Maqsood."

"Now, how'd you manage that? I thought you told her to make herself available for the IOPC?" Franks rubbed his temple with his free hand. He had a lingering headache.

"I did. She missed her first interview yesterday. Her partner says he doesn't know where she is. I've sent a couple of uniforms to her house, but her car's gone and there's no sign of life."

"And you believe him?"

"Terrence isn't going to lie for Nasreen. She's the one who got him in trouble; there's no love lost there. One of my admin team heard them arguing in a conference room right before I suspended her."

Franks sighed. "Clive, is this going to be a problem for us?"

"All I can say is we're looking for her."

"Okay, keep me posted," Franks said before hanging up.

He had far more pressing matters to deal with than the disappearance of Nasreen Maqsood. Hell, she might have just gone away for a while, to gather herself. She wasn't going to be a problem, and what could she possibly do anyway? She was suspended...

50

Alan placed his knife and fork together. "That was excellent, honey."

"Glad you enjoyed it." Beattie received five more complimentary comments from the guards before she shooed them off to work, then she started washing up. She was looking forward to a relaxing morning.

Collecting the plates and cutlery from around the table, she stacked them up and carried them over to the sink. After a few moments, she noticed that the smaller knife wasn't in the sink. It wasn't on the counter, and it wasn't in with the bits Kimiko had washed up earlier.

Beattie actively looked for it. She couldn't have a missing knife in her house; not with the kind of work she did. Who would want to take a knife? That was too obvious to answer, but who would want to take a knife, and actually had access? Access was the key. The only people who had access to the kitchen were Alan, herself, the guards and Kimik–

Oh shit! Beattie's face went pale, quickly draining of its blood.

She had to be sure, so she looked in all of the drawers and

cupboards, and in the sink again. She turned the kitchen upside down looking for the seven-inch blade; there was nothing. Could one of the guards have taken it? She doubted it – she needed to know for definite before she confronted her top suspect. She didn't want it to be Kimiko.

Grabbing her coat, Beattie wrapped herself up and walked along the paved path to the barn, where all five guards were stood chatting before the customers started arriving. She assumed Alan was already downstairs getting the bar ready, and Kimiko would be downstairs cleaning the rooms she'd been instructed to service. "While I have you all here, I need to ask if one of you have taken a knife from the kitchen for any reason?"

She watched their heads shake, receiving five "no"s.

Shit! It was looking more and more likely that it was Kimiko, but why would she do it? What was she thinking? Did she think she could use a knife to escape? And where would she escape *to*? It wasn't like she had any family in the UK. And then it dawned on her... she probably wanted to get the police involved, to have her and everyone else here arrested.

Ungrateful bitch, Beattie thought, instructing the guards to follow her downstairs...

Steven watched Garvey get into his Shogun, then looked at his dashboard clock, noting it was 08:40. "Target's on the move," he said into his microphone.

His shift had started forty minutes earlier. The officer he'd relieved – a friend of his – had passed the clipboard and camera to him and told him that Garvey hadn't done much in the preceding eight hours. Steven's friend had had a very boring shift.

Steven's friends all thought his work was so glamorous; they didn't realise just how dull it could be. The majority of what the NCA did was surveillance, which involved following people either in cars or on foot and setting up cameras and microphones. So, it really involved listening to, and watching people. When his agency thought it had enough intel and/or evidence of wrongdoing, they would arrest the target. It was rare that they got to catch their mark in the process of committing a crime.

"Target's turning right onto Station Road," Steven reported, receiving a crackly acknowledgement in return.

Garvey's Shogun turned left and parked at the side of the road, next to a park. Steven drove on and found a space further down the road, all the while keeping an a eye on his target, walking along a path. "Target's on foot through Bellfield Park," he said, as he exited his car. "I'm on foot, following."

He kept Garvey in view, remaining a distance behind him, carrying a dog lead he'd picked up when he'd got out of his car – it was a way of making his presence look more normal. Even though there was no dog, he could call out for it if he thought Garvey was onto him. As a last resort, he could ask Garvey if he had seen his dog.

In the distance, he saw Garvey stop and talk with three black men. After a couple of minutes, the four guys carried on walking through the park together. "Target's on foot with three unknown associates."

"We need visual confirmation," came the voice in his earpiece.

"Copy that..."

Kimiko was busy putting cleaning supplies on her trolley. She'd hidden the knife between boxes of tissues – she still hadn't been able to think of a decent place to hide it, at least not one that was accessible at a moment's notice.

Turning off the taps, she lifted up the plastic bowl and placed it on the trolley, steam rising from its surface. Checking she had the sponges and everything else she needed to service the rooms Mrs Harrison had asked her to, she turned to start pushing her trolley when she heard Mrs Harrison's voice.

"Here she is."

Kimiko turned to find Mrs Harrison and the five guards stood in front of her.

Something was wrong.

Why did Mrs Harrison have all the guards with her?

Realising that Mrs Harrison knew about the knife, Kimiko felt sick.

"What the matter?" Kimiko asked, her voice sounding smaller than it had earlier.

"Oh, nothing to worry about, Kimiko." Mrs Harrison smiled. "I just noticed we have a knife missing from the kitchen and I was wondering if you'd seen it anywhere?"

Mrs Harrison didn't sound mad, but Kimiko had seen this performance before. "Um, no, I not think so." She bowed her head. She was a terrible liar; she always had been. If she couldn't convince herself, how could she expect Mrs Harrison to fall for it?

"You won't mind if I take a look on your trolley, then, will you?"

There it was: the tone Kimiko had expected, the one she'd been waiting for.

Mrs Harrison knew about the knife, and she was about to find it.

Kimiko held her breath.

As Mrs Harrison stepped up to the trolley, Kimiko shoved her employer, hard, before bending down, grabbing the blade's handle, and pouncing up with a speed and agility she was unaware she possessed. "Get away from me!" Kimiko yelled.

She'd found her voice; it was steely and strong.

Mrs Harrison stepped back.

"Get back! I stab you with this!"

"What's gotten into you, Kimiko? It's like you're a different person."

"I prisoner here, for long time! But not no more. I leave now, I take Danny with me too!"

Mrs Harrison took a step forward, trying to scare her, but instead of backing off, Kimiko matched her employer's step forwards, stabbing the air with the blade. "I mean it, I stab you!"

"Come, now, Kimiko, we can talk about this," Mrs Harrison said gently, as the guards started separating, attempting to surround her.

She was impossibly outnumbered, six to one.

Without thinking, Kimiko pushed the trolley at Mrs Harrison and ran towards her.

Before she knew what she was doing, she was behind Mrs Harrison with the knife under her chin, pressed against her skin. The other arm was wrapped around her employer's shoulder and neck. "You all back off or I cut her!" Kimiko screamed.

"Don't be silly, Kimiko, it's not too late to stop this." Mrs Harrison moved back with each of Kimiko's tugs.

Kimiko watched as the guards formed a single line in front of her, sweat pouring from her forehead as she walked backwards.

What was she going to do now? She thought she could bring Mrs Harrison to the top of the stairs, walk her to her car, and get her employer to drive her away from here, all at knifepoint.

But then what about Danny? She hadn't planned for this!

How had Mrs Harrison found out about the knife so quickly? "You all stay here, do not follow!" Kimiko screeched.

She was nearly at the doorway to the storeroom, but as she turned to look behind her, she saw movement. Before she could react, a long object hit her on the top of her head...

51

Steven saw Garvey and his three companions stop at a bench. While the associates sat, Garvey remained standing, like he was lecturing them or performing a speech in front of them.

There was a row of bushes across from them, flanked by a row of trees, which was good news for him; there would be plenty of cover for him to take photos of them all.

He was still a hundred to a hundred and fifty metres from his target, and none of them had looked over in his direction.

The row of trees started a hundred metres away from the bench, so he entered the woods away from their line of sight, walking through them until he came to the bushes directly in front of the bench. Crouching, he found a good vantage point to take photos from. The only way they would see him was if they happened to catch the sun reflecting on the glass of his camera. Thankfully it was a cloudy day with very little in the way of sunshine.

Peering through the lens, he took five photos of the three black men sat side by side. In two of the photos Garvey had moved in the way of his three associates...

. . .

With relief, Beattie waited for Kimiko's body to hit the floor, grabbing the knife from her ungrateful support worker's tiny hand as she fell. "Pick her up!" Beattie hissed at the guards.

"That was a close call," said Alan, holding the baseball bat.

Beattie stared at her husband with rage-filled eyes. "What the fuck took you so long?" she spat. "She could have slit my throat by the time you came in!"

She stared down at Kimiko as the guards picked her up; she was semi-conscious. Alan had hit her hard enough to stun her, but not hard enough to knock her out. When she heard groans coming from the dainty Okinawan, Beattie ordered, "Take her to Danny's room; I want him to witness this."

For sixteen years she had looked after and nurtured Kimiko. When she'd first arrived here at the farm, when Kimiko had been a tiny twelve-year-old, an innocent, meek, mild-mannered little girl. Now all Beattie saw was an ungrateful, manipulative, sneaky, conniving bitch being dragged to her demise. And it was all thanks to Daniel Rose. He'd sucked her in with his charm and good looks; he was going to pay for corrupting her Kimiko!

Beattie followed Alan and the guards into Danny's room.

"Kimiko!" Danny yelled, before shooting a glare in Beattie's direction. "What the fuck've you done to her?"

There was only one thing Beattie could say in response to that. "Nothing... *yet*." She smiled when she saw the glare turn to fear in his eyes, as he lay there helpless. His body was still bruised, slowly turning from blue to a funny yellow colour. "You know, Danny, I've just realised that this is all your fault. Kimiko wouldn't have dared to even think about pulling a knife on me until you arrived. I blame you for all of this."

"It *is* my fault, all of it. Please, punish me – leave Kimiko alone. I asked her to help me escape, it was me. Please, Beattie, please, don't take it out on her; she's innocent."

"Enough!" she retorted, noticing Danny wince in pain. "I'll

deal with you another time, Danny. Right now though, I've got to think of how I'm going to deal with her."

Two guards were holding Kimiko upright, and though her head was down, she was moaning – her support worker was still conscious. Beattie grabbed Kimiko by the chin, yanking her head up, so she could see Kimiko's eyes rolling.

"Danny," Kimiko mumbled so quietly it was barely detectable.

"Kimiko, I'm here, honey."

"Shut up!" Beattie yelled, an unequalled fury biting through her as she looked over at Danny's concerned face. She held Kimiko's head up, looked into her rolling eyes, and said, "I trusted you," before quickly plunging the knife into Kimiko's belly. Beattie heard her gasp at the same time she heard Danny yell, "No!" Then she pulled the knife out and plunged it in again. She heard Danny crying. She plunged it in a third and fourth and fifth time. Blood had soaked her hand and the handle of the knife by the time she stopped. When it was done, the guards dropped Kimiko's body to the floor.

Beattie looked down at her corrupted helper's body; there was a big red hole where she'd repeatedly stabbed her, and blood was pooling around it. "Take her to the furnace," she ordered, hearing Kimiko groan. She wasn't dead, yet.

Then Beattie turned to Danny. "I'll deal with you later. But for now, I'll be sure to turn on the intercom in the furnace room so you can hear her scream." She grinned. "I hope they haunt you for the remainder of your short life…"

"So, tell us what you need, mate." Barkley covered his mouth as he spoke.

"I need your help with a collection." Lennox stood in front of them, his hand over his mouth. It was a tactic they'd devised together for avoiding lip reading. The only way law enforcement could hear them was if one of them was wearing a recording device, and Lennox trusted these three men with his life.

"Why now? You've never asked us before, Len. What's up with that?" Bembe was the direct forthright one of the trio.

"I'm not sure," Lennox replied, "but there's something not right about it. Rothstein's pulled his captain, saying he has family issues so he's unavailable to steer the boat."

"And you think your boss is... what? Setting you up?" Khenan was also pretty direct.

"Nah, Rothstein's got a good thing going with my uncle, why would he set me up?" Lennox asked, sounding like he was trying to convince himself. "It's probably nothing, just my paranoia. I'll feel safer having you boys with me, is all."

"I'm in," Barkley replied, as Lennox knew he would.

"That's you, through and through, Bark," Bembe interjected. "I'm in. No thinking, no arguing, just, 'I'm in'."

They all laughed.

"Look, if any of you don't want to, say so now," Lennox said. "I'll understand if not, but just so you know, the money's good. It'll be worth your time."

"I'm in," replied Khenan.

"Bembe? You in or out?"

"Nothing like putting a man on the spot. Oh, fuck it! Anything happens, there's nothing we can't get out of."

"We coming tooled up?" asked Khenan.

"Nah, we won't need them," replied Lennox. "We haven't before, can't see why we would now. It'll be a simple collect and drop job, and then we get paid."

"Sounds perfect to me, brother." Barkley smiled...

After locking Kimiko in the furnace, Beattie looked down at her bloody face.

She could hear a faint whimper. "You betrayed me, Kimiko," Beattie said with acid in her voice. "I warned you. I warned you not to let him in your head, didn't I? You brought this on yourself. Well, now you have to pay."

She stood back and glanced at one of the guards, who switched the intercom on dutifully. "And this is what you get, Danny," Beattie snapped, before looking over at Alan, who pushed the red button a second before the furnace roared to life.

The screams were blood curdling as the flames spread around Kimiko's small broken body, first melting the clothes to her skin, then licking the flesh from her bones.

It took an agonising two minutes for the screaming to stop.

Beattie watched in silence as what was once her innocent little Kimiko gradually succumbed to the biting flames, every second becoming less Kimiko and more ash. She watched the furnace for a further fifteen minutes...

"Let go of my arm!" Zuzanna Jankovics squirmed as she tried to release her arm from Nasreen's grip. "I tell you what you want know."

Nasreen had Jankovics on the carpeted floor of her flat. She had her quarry's right arm behind her back, and her thumb pulled back as far as it would go. "First off, why did you just attack me?" Nasreen asked. "I'm not here for you; I'm only interested in finding Conrad Gebhardt."

"I not trust police. I thought you want arrest me."

"Well, it's your lucky day, Zuzanna. Today I'm not a police officer." She put her full weight on Jankovics' back. "Tell me where I can find Conrad, and I'll be on my way."

"If I tell you, he kill me," Jankovics said amid groans of pain.

Nasreen pulled her thumb back, but it couldn't go any further. "Wrong answer, Zuzanna. I'm not leaving here until you give me an address."

After a couple of seconds, Nasreen lessened the pressure a little on the woman's thumb. "I tell you what: I'll promise you that when I find him, he won't bother you again."

"You not know what you dealing with! If he not kill me, the Brotherhood will. These bad people."

"The Bavarian Brotherhood, right? I've heard of them, Zuzanna. But you know what? I'm not interested in them either. Just tell me where I can find Conrad, and I won't bring you into it, I promise."

"If not the Brotherhood, why you want Conrad?"

"I don't want Conrad; I want his brother, Walter."

"I not know him."

"Okay, if you can't help me find Walter, tell me where I can find Conrad." Nasreen reapplied the pressure, plus a little extra.

Jankovics cried out in pain. "Stop, stop! You breaking my arm!"

Nasreen crouched until she was almost touching Jankovics' face. "Tell me what I need to know, and I'll let you up."

"Okay, okay, I write down address of warehouse he use for business, but please, you not break my arm."

"Good, Zuzanna, good," Nas said, gently easing the pressure. "Now, I'm going to let you up, and then I'll walk with you to where you're going to write down the address, got it? Don't try anything stupid; we both know I can kick your arse."

The two women stood up, then with her arm still pulled behind her back, Jankovics led Nasreen to the dining room.

Nasreen waited – making sure her interviewee's arm was still locked – while Jankovics bent down, opened a drawer of a cabinet, and pulled out an address book. Nasreen continued to watch as the woman pulled out a piece of paper with a handwritten address on it.

"Here, this is where Conrad does business; it warehouses not far from here. You make a bad mistake, he kill you."

Nasreen had a decision to make. Jankovics was a hostile witness, so she couldn't be trusted not to phone Conrad the minute Nasreen left the flat, in which case there were two options: either tie her up here, in her flat, or take her along for the ride. The former wasn't an option. Jankovics might be found sooner rather than later.

She took the piece of paper from Jankovics. "Here's how we're going to play this. You're coming with me for the ride, and if it turns out you're lying about the address, I'll do more than put you in an armlock, do you understand me?"

"You a bad policewoman."

"Police officer, and I already told you, I'm not with the police today."

Nasreen marched Jankovics out of the ground floor flat and across the car park before helping her into her car. Nasreen made Jankovics drive, while she rode as passenger; it was the only way she could be sure Jankovics wouldn't try doing something stupid...

52

Day 38
Saturday, 17th February

"Bea, I'm all done," said the carpet layer, a friend of her dad's.

Beattie nodded. Having the bar area, corridors, and Danny's room re-carpeted was costing her a fortune, and while it wouldn't break the bank, it was another cross against Danny's name. He was responsible for the trails of blood down the stairs and through the bar, and he was also responsible for the pool of Kimiko's blood in his room.

"Thanks, Mark," Beattie said. "I appreciate you coming at such short notice."

"Hey, who can say no to your old man?"

Mark had laid the original carpet in 2002, and he'd laid new carpets five years earlier too. Beattie had known him for that long and she genuinely liked him; he was affable, friendly, and – most importantly – professional and tidy. Beattie shook his hand

and then walked him up the stairs, through the barn, and to his van.

After she'd waved him off, she went into the house, up the stairs, and into Kimiko's room, where she was in the middle of packing Kimiko's belongings into boxes. She would burn them in the furnace later.

She picked up the last of Kimiko's kimonos, put it under her nose, and sniffed. It still smelt of her. Beattie was so conflicted; on the one hand, she was angry that Kimiko had betrayed her, while on the other, she was sad that Kimiko was gone.

Beattie felt like a part of her was missing. Why would Kimiko betray her like this? She'd been treated very differently to the other support staff and had been given more freedom to come and go as she pleased around the farm. She even had her own room with access to the kitchen.

Of course, Beattie knew why: Danny. He was responsible for turning Kimiko against her. And to think she had thought Danny was special, gifted. How could she have been so wrong about him? She'd specifically warned Kimiko about getting involved with him, and what had she gone and done? Her naïve helper had fallen in love with him.

"Bea, I'm off out, okay?"

She looked up at Alan as she placed the last kimono in a box with the others. "Is it that time already?"

"Yeah, afraid so. I can cancel, stay home tonight, if you want company?"

"No, it's fine, go and have a nice time with Sammy and her mum." Beattie saw the look of concern on Alan's face and added, "Really, Alan, I'm fine. Say hi to Sammy for me."

Alan's attempted reconciliation had failed. She knew it, and he knew it. She didn't love him anymore. He'd become more of an annoyance to her than anything else. Things couldn't go back to the way they were before. There was too much history between them. Her heart belonged to someone else now. Lennox was coming over that night to collect the day's takings, and she intended to be there to see him.

Picking up two boxes, she carried them to the furnace room. When she opened the oven door she saw the remains of Kimiko's blackened skull, and a tear rolled down her cheek as she removed the contents of the two boxes and threw them inside.

On her way out, she pressed the button and heard the flames roar to life, burning the remaining evidence that Kimiko had ever been here.

When she'd closed the furnace room and locked it, she walked to room three of C Wing and opened the door. Danny was chained to the ceiling and floor, his body held up only by his wrists, his head down. His body looked like one big bruise of varying colours, ranging from black to blue to yellow.

After Kimiko had been taken care of, she'd instructed the guards to place Danny in this cell and beat him regularly. For two days he'd been subjected to hours of torture, a painful battering by a mixture of the five guards.

"I know you can hear me, Danny," she said icily, pulling his head up by his hair. "Was it worth it, huh? Did turning Kimiko against me bring you anything other than pain? Well, I'm here to tell you that I've not even begun yet... You'll be begging me to kill you by the time I'm through, and even then I won't let you die. Killing you would be too kind." She narrowed her eyes. "And you won't be getting that from me..."

"Target turning left towards the farmhouse." Steven was following Garvey's Shogun along the country road.

He slowed his car to a stop, parking a hundred metres away

from the road leading to the Harrison farm, then he switched off the engine and sat back in his seat.

He knew something suspicious was going on with the operation.

William Rothstein was no longer being watched, and all resources were being reallocated to Lennox Garvey.

The farmhouse, it seemed, was no longer a target.

Ever since the Director General had been killed and the new DG had been sworn in, the whole operation had changed. Steven knew that Garvey wasn't worth the effort they were putting in – what with bugging his car and house and putting twenty-four-hour audio and visual surveillance on him – so why were they doing it?

Somehow, Rothstein had managed to worm his way out of an NCA investigation, and while Steven wasn't saying Graham Holmes was corrupt exactly, it did seem suspect that as soon as he took over, the operation had changed.

If Wells were still alive, he'd put money on the fact that they'd still be investigating Rothstein. According to a colleague, Holmes had told him that the change of target was a direct order from the Home Secretary.

Steven didn't buy it, and neither did his team.

It was dark outside, and cold, so he switched the key slightly to allow the heater to come on. He was looking forward to the warmer weather coming, but it still seemed a long way off. The clock on the dashboard read: 20:55.

The previous day he'd spent some time looking into changing agencies; he hadn't applied to any vacancies, although he'd had a preliminary search to see what he might fancy. After all, the NCA was tainted in his view. He wouldn't ever consider police work. There were other agencies he could look into. He'd seen some roles in immigration, and also revenue and customs, for instance, so if he saw a role he liked, he might apply for one of them. Then there were always private security firms he could try.

According to HQ, the audio and visual surveillance hadn't picked up on any criminal activities from Garvey, which was both irritating and understandable. The man was far too smart to discuss work at his home or in his car. Steven knew they would have to catch him with his hand in the jar, so to speak, or they'd need to find a witness willing to testify against him on past criminal deeds, and neither of those were very realistic...

Peter Franks was alone in his study, sat at his desk in front of his PC with the radio on in the background. His wife was out with a friend – at a pub having dinner – and he'd already eaten his steak and kidney pie, mashed potatoes, and vegetables.

He was getting impatient waiting on Rothstein's phone call; it was bad enough dealing with the man in the first place, but having to jump to his tune was even worse. He thought they should have gone with the original importer. Not the Commissioner, he was adamant that it had to be Rothstein. His boss had explained that they'd never been able to infiltrate his network before, and that was exactly the kind of person they needed as part of the project.

When his mobile rang, he looked at the caller: Rothstein. He picked it up and answered, hoping it was finally time to set their plan in motion. "Will, I was just thinking about you," Franks said, leaning back in his chair.

"It's happening tonight. Write down this address..."

Franks did as instructed.

"He'll be there around midnight; when he returns, you know what to do."

"You're going to owe me one. And what do we do with him once we have him?"

"Process him as you would any other collar, and I'll deal with it once he's banged up, okay? You don't need to do anything beyond arrest him. It'll be a good day for your lot, I promise."

Franks hung up, smiling. The first of the high-profile arrests was coming their way – the project was about to start. He thought about the headlines, the publicity. It would, of course, be a joint effort between the appropriate Force and the NCA, but the media would eat it up.

Once this was over, he would finalise the preliminary meeting of all those involved in the project, and they could get the logistics sorted out properly. He hoped they'd be able to start the project within a month, two tops.

Looking at the address he'd scribbled – the location of a marina down south – he checked the force to see if the Police and Crime Commissioner, and hence, Chief Constable, was one of his or not. He smiled, realising it was. He picked up the phone and made the call, telling the Chief Constable to have uniforms near the area; they weren't to be visible until the suspect returned.

Once he'd terminated that call, he phoned Graham Holmes' mobile. "Graham, it's Peter. It's happening tonight. Have you still got him under surveillance?"

"Round the clock, like I told you before."

"Good, write this address down," he added, telling Holmes and spelling certain words. "Have your officers nearby, but don't spook him. We have to wait until he returns."

He hung up, satisfied.

All his pieces were in motion. All he had to do now was sit back and wait...

53

Lennox walked through the bar, noticing there was a new carpet – it had that new carpet smell too. The lights were already on when he arrived, so he knew Beattie must still be around. He'd not seen her since their brief sexy encounter, and Lennox hoped it was her and not that dickhead husband of hers.

As he walked up to the office he noticed that the door was open and the lights were on, and when he went inside, he saw Beattie sat on her chair, her back to him. "Hi, Bea," he said, as normally as he could.

When she turned in her chair, he noticed how amazing she looked in a white sleeveless blouse with plunging neckline and a pair of dark blue jeans. She looked stunning.

"Hi!" she replied with a half-smile, her voice hoarse.

He walked to the desk, placing the suitcase on the floor and his torch on the wooden surface. When he heard her sniff, he asked, "Are you okay?"

She nodded, her back still to him.

"It's good to see you; it's been a while," he said, trying to break the awkward silence.

"You too," she replied, her voice gruff.

He walked over to her then, gently rubbing her bare shoulder. "Hey, are you okay?"

When she turned to him, he could see her red puffy eyes, and her face crumpled as she gently sobbed. She put her arms around him and cuddled his waist.

"Hey, hey, what's up?"

Beattie wouldn't answer him; she just continued to gently sob.

He waited for her to unwrap herself, to release him, and finally, she did.

When she turned in her chair and sat facing the wall again, he asked, "Do you want to talk about it?"

Beattie shook her head.

Lennox didn't know what to do, what to say. He'd never seen her like this – he'd always thought she was a hard cold bitch – and seeing her look so vulnerable was a massive turn-on.

He finally saw her as a human being, with feelings, and she looked so sweet, so innocent. Who'd have thought teary eyes could excite him?

He watched Beattie shake her head, like she was shaking off the blues, willing them to go. Then she stood and turned to him.

"Can I get you anything? Tea or coffee? Something stronger?"

"No, I'm good, thanks. You look like you could use something stronger though."

She didn't reply to his last comment; instead, she walked out of the office to make herself a drink. He sat down to start counting the fifties, and when she returned, she brought him a glass of whisky that she left on his desk, next to the pile of tens.

"A little something to say sorry," she said in a deflated voice. "I shouldn't have cried in front of you; it was very unprofessional of me."

He looked up at her, frowning. Whatever it was, it was upsetting her.

Lennox stared at her cleavage, at the top that left little to the imagination, and saw she was wearing a chain that dangled between her breasts, accentuating them. In addition to looking great, she smelt great too.

Beattie leaned on him, putting her arm around his shoulder.

"You don't have to apologise, I don't mind." He looked up at her. "You sure you don't want to talk about it?"

"No, it's nothing, forget it happened."

"Okay, but I'm a good listener." He raised his arm and rubbed her cheek.

Their eyes locked.

Then their lips met...

"Is that him?" Nasreen handed the binoculars to Jankovics, who used her free hand to spy on the driver of the van that had stopped outside the warehouse. She'd tied the Hungarian woman's other hand to the steering wheel with plastic cable ties.

"No, that not him." Jankovics handed back the binoculars.

From their vantage point across the road, Nasreen had the perfect view of who came and went from the warehouse. For two days she'd been spying on the building, so it was fortunate that the business park they were in was largely deserted, probably why Conrad Gebhardt had chosen it to conduct business.

By day the warehouse was a mailing house, a legitimate business with fifteen tax-paying employees enrolled on PAYE. By night, it was frequented by suspicious-looking white van drivers, none of whom had been Conrad Gebhardt, at least not according to Jankovics.

Nasreen had asked Terrence to conduct a background check on the business, and he'd confirmed that the company was above board, had a Company's House number, was VAT registered and that the CEO was a seemingly upstanding member of the community. However, subsequent searches of Alexander Rohr, the CEO, had led to further discoveries: he was the second cousin of Walter and Conrad Gebhardt. There was no evidence to suggest that he was involved with the Bavarian Brotherhood, but the fact he let suspicious men use his warehouse after hours told Nasreen a lot.

"I hope he kill you." Jankovics sulked.

"Mmm hmm." Nasreen watched the driver's shadow in front of the well-lit door of the warehouse. "I'm sure you do. You're just upset because I kicked your arse all over your flat." She smiled at the memory as Jankovics muttered something in Hungarian under her breath.

For two days Nasreen had had to endure Jankovics' winning personality, and while she had wanted to punch her in the face on a number of occasions, she'd opted for making sarcastic quips at Jankovics' expense instead. For the past two nights they'd stayed in a local Travelodge, with the Hungarian tied to the bedpost. The poor woman had had her hands tied to either a bedpost or the steering wheel ever since they'd left Jankovics' flat.

Nasreen watched the driver of the van as he turned off the warehouse lights and closed the metal shutter. He then opened the driver's side door, stepped in, and reversed out of the forecourt.

Nasreen was pretty sure she couldn't be seen; she'd parked in an abandoned warehouse car park, which had some bushes for cover. She'd chosen the spot specifically because she could see what was going on over there, but anyone at the warehouse would have to look hard to see her.

She was hungry. "You want one of these sandwiches?" she asked as she reached behind her and pulled out two cardboard sandwich containers from Waitrose. "Seafood or tuna mayo?" As soon as she'd asked, she heard Jankovics' stomach rumble. "I'll take that as a yes," Nasreen said, with a smile. "Which one do you want?"

"Seafood."

Ripping open the seafood sandwich box and pulling out one triangle half of the sandwich, Nasreen held it in front of Jankovics' mouth and waited until she took a bite. Then she ripped open her tuna mayo sandwich box and took a bite of her own sandwich.

In spite of how long she'd waited, however, Nasreen still felt she was close to finding Walter Gebhardt, and consequently Danny. She'd also had time to think about her situation.

There was nothing she could do about the IOPC investigation; it was happening, and no amount of apologising or grovelling for forgiveness would prevent it from going ahead. She didn't want her career to be over, but that looked more and more certain with every passing day. She'd wondered, while sat in the car, what she would do next? She couldn't think about it too hard, not yet; she still had to find Danny and bring him home...

54

"What the fuck is this?"

Lennox heard Beattie gasp.

"Alan! It's not what it looks like… I can explain!"

That would teach him for having his back to the door. Fuck! He'd just been caught with his pants around his ankles, literally. Lennox bent down and pulled his jeans up, turning to find Alan's angry red face marching towards him. He backed a pace until he reached the desk and couldn't go any further.

"You fucking arsehole!" Alan cried, pointing at him.

He waited for Beattie to intervene; after all, he was her husband, her responsibility. He hadn't just cheated on Alan, she had. Beattie was busy pulling her jeans up and trying to find her top.

"I'm going to fuck you up for this!" Alan yelled.

"Alan, wait, please let me explain," pleaded Beattie, fully dressed and trying to pull her husband back.

"Explain? Explain what, how you fucked the help? I've just seen how you did that, and on my fucking desk too, you bitch!"

Lennox stood still. He didn't want to incite the husband; his temper was wearing very thin. If Alan called him "the help" again, he'd nut the bastard, Beattie's husband or not. He didn't need this shit. He had to be careful though; Alan had Rothstein's ear. Let Beattie sort her man out, he thought, putting on his T-shirt and jumper as he listened to her attempting to calm her husband down. It wasn't working.

"I can't believe I blew Sammy and her mum off to come back and make sure you were all right, and I come home to this? To find you fucking a ni–"

"I wouldn't do that if I were you," Lennox warned.

"Who the fuck do you think you're talking to! You're the one in the wrong here, not me. I'm not the one who's just been fucked by..."

"By what?" Lennox couldn't help himself.

He watched as Alan stopped, then he took two steps forwards. He was three inches taller than Alan, and broader. Alan looked like he was shitting himself. He'd seen it many times with arseholes like this – when he stood up and faced them, they shut up, fast. "Come on, Alan, what were you going to say?"

He took another step forward until he was nose to nose with Beattie's husband.

With a sneer Alan replied, "Oh, fuck off back to your own country!"

Alan spat in his face.

Lennox saw red; his vision clouded, and he headbutted Alan's nose, which exploded over his face. Before he knew it, Lennox had Alan on the floor, pummelling him with his fists.

"Lennox, stop! Stop it!" Beattie's desperate cries were wasted on him.

He couldn't hear her; he was so focused on punching Alan in the face.

Having the upper hand, being on top, Lennox knocked out

three of Alan's teeth, broke his nose, and probably fractured his cheek too by the time he stopped hitting him.

Lennox's breath came in rasps.

"I told you to stop hitting him, didn't I? For fuck's sake, Lennox, look at him! You've beaten him to a pulp!"

Lennox looked down at Alan's broken face. Had he just done that? His knuckles were red raw, bloody. Alan had deserved it though, he thought, as his breathing stabilised. "Fucking prick shouldn't have said that," he said, standing up.

Beattie stooped, pressing her palm to Alan's cheek before putting two fingers to his neck. Looking up at Lennox, she said, "I can't feel a pulse."

"The fuck you say? I didn't beat him that hard. He can't be dead."

It didn't register for a couple of seconds, but Lennox watched in shock as Alan's arms came to life, his face becoming focused and enraged as he grabbed Beattie's neck with both hands and strangled her. He'd never seen a man so determined before.

He could hear Beattie fighting for breath.

Panicking, he scanned the room, spotting a fire extinguisher hanging on the wall.

He went to it, picked it up, and carried it to the middle of the office, where Beattie was turning purple. Grabbing the extinguisher by its sides, Lennox brought it crashing down on Alan's head.

The first blow cracked Alan's skull, but somehow he still had hold of Beattie, so Lennox brought it down a second time.

With Alan on his back, spluttering, Lennox pummelled Alan's face with the metal cylinder. Beattie's husband's face was smashed, his left eye red from a brain haemorrhage. He was still alive, coughing and talking gibberish.

The second and third assaults smashed his face more,

contorting it, but it was the fourth that killed him, splitting his skull down the middle.

Lennox took a step backwards, trying to regain his breathing, and then looked over at Beattie, whose colour was returning to normal.

His mobile phone rang in his jeans and taking it out he looked at the caller: Rothstein. "Fuck! It's your dad," Lennox said, putting his finger to his lips, telling Beattie to be quiet. She was too busy studying her dead husband. "Yeah?" Lennox asked once he'd answered the call.

"Lenny, I need you to do me a favour. They've had to bring the pickup forwards."

Lennox looked down at Alan's smashed head. "To when?"

"Tonight. I know it's short notice, but there's nothing they can do."

Lennox's head was spinning; what the fuck was he going to do? He'd killed Beattie's husband, and he couldn't leave her here to deal with the mess. "That's not possible, my boys can't make that; it's too short noti–"

"I've already sorted three of my own associates to go and give you a hand. It's tonight, or wait until next month, Lenny. Can you make it by midnight?"

He put the fire extinguisher down and looked at his watch: 21:43. Fuck! "I'll try to make it, but the bunker's takings will have to wait."

"No problem, we'll do a double pickup tomorrow. Thanks, Lenny."

Lennox hung up and dropped the phone back in his pocket, swearing under his breath, then he knelt down and looked at Beattie, who seemed to be in shock. She had tears rolling down her cheeks. "Bea," he said gently, "we need to deal with this before I go, baby. I won't leave you to deal with this alone, but I really need to get going. I've got something to do for your dad."

Nothing. She was just staring down at her husband's bloody corpse.

Knowing he had to do something, Lennox moved behind Alan, picked him up from under his armpits, and dragged him backwards out of the office and into the corridor.

"Wait! What are you doing?"

He continued dragging the body as Beattie trailed after him, asking him what he was doing over and over again. "We've got to get rid of the body, Bea," he said, tugging Alan along. "We'll use the furnace. It's perfect."

Outside the furnace room, Lennox dropped the body and opened the door, stooping down and dragging it inside until he was right in front of the huge oven. "Give me a hand, will you? He's heavier than he looks."

Nothing. She was still in shock, which wasn't surprising.

Although he managed to hoist Alan up and into the furnace, Lennox did it with difficulty. He was a physically fit guy, but lifting the deadweight of bodies was hard work. Finally he managed to push Alan in, then he closed the door, breathless again.

Lennox stood back and sighed. This was *not* how he'd seen his evening going. He was only supposed to come to the farm to collect the takings.

"Bea, I'm so sorry," he said, to a catatonic Beattie. "I would stay with you – help you get through this – but I've really got to go. I'm sorry!"

She didn't reply.

Not wanting to go, Lennox turned and walked up to the button on his way out. Pressing it, he heard the flames eat her husband. He turned as he reached the door to find Beattie stood there, watching the flames...

. . .

"That him!" Jankovics was looking through the binoculars Nasreen was holding up for her.

Nasreen looked for herself. This van was bigger than the one from earlier, taller and longer. The driver – Conrad Gebhardt – looked short and squat, from what she could tell from his silhouette. He was probably about the same height as her, maybe a bit taller, but a lot more heavily built. She would have to be careful; he looked like he could be a handful.

As she watched, as far as she could tell, people were getting out of the van. It looked like multiple people, but by the way Gebhardt herded them and threatened them, they didn't seem to be part of his group. Terrence had told her that the Bavarian Brotherhood were into people trafficking, so maybe these were victims? From the look of their silhouettes, they were all women, and small women at that. They cowed when they passed him.

Glancing at the clock, Nasreen saw it was 23:38. The adrenaline was kicking in, a feeling she lived for. It was how she felt before a kickboxing match, the feeling of dread and excitement in the pit of her stomach, the feeling of anticipation, of not knowing what was to come. She both loved it and hated it in equal measure.

"Be careful," Jankovics said, to Nasreen's surprise.

Nasreen looked over at the Hungarian. "I thought you hoped he kills me."

"I got big mouth. You not so bad, he a bastard!"

Nasreen took a deep breath, trying to keep her fear in check. "You don't need to worry about me, Zuzanna; I've got lots of tricks up my sleeves." She reached behind her for her bag, put it on her lap, and pulled out the pistol. "And if my tricks don't work, I've got this as backup." Leaning forwards in her seat, she reached behind her and put the Remington RM380 in the top of her jeans, right in the small of her back, before covering it with her jumper.

She got out of the car and walked around to the boot, which she opened, taking out some rope. She had a serrated pocketknife in her bag, which would work wonders cutting it. After closing the boot, she went back to her side, opened her door and reached for her bag. After stuffing the rope inside, she was ready.

She took another deep breath, then said, "And you, you stay here."

Jankovics held her hands up as far as the cable ties allowed. "I go nowhere."

Nasreen closed the door, said a small prayer to Allah, and felt behind her for the pistol as she walked towards the warehouse. At the bushes, which still gave her a modicum of cover, she crouched and navigated between two horizontal fence posts. Once out on the pavement on her side of the road, she crouched again, and with speed and agility, crossed the road before sneakily making her way to the front of the van. Conrad had reversed in, so that the rear doors were closest to the warehouse metal shutter.

There was a man talking, not yelling.

Nasreen heard a woman yelp.

She reached behind her for the Remington and pulled it out, switching the safety off so she'd be ready for action. With only six rounds per clip she was limited on firepower, but she didn't anticipate using them anyway. If she fired even one she'd have to make a run for it – the police would be on her in no time. She needed to obtain information from Gebhardt, and that could take time, time she wouldn't have if she fired her weapon.

She gripped the gun with both hands, and as she turned to try to see down the side of the van, a shadow appeared. Before she consciously knew what had happened, she'd kicked the shadow in the balls, grabbed his head, and smashed it into the passenger's door. The shadow fell in a heap on the floor.

Looking down at the face, Nasreen saw it wasn't Gebhardt. She hadn't been aware there was another man present; it was lucky her reflexes were so quick.

"What the fuck was that?"

Hearing Gebhardt coming her way, Nasreen backed up and turned so that she was covered by the front of the car, her pistol poised.

"God damn it, Jimmy," she heard Gebhardt say, mere inches from her.

Seizing her opportunity, she shot out from the cover of the van and faced Gebhardt, her gun aimed at his chest. "Well, well, Conrad Gebhardt, I've been waiting a long time to meet you..."

55

Day 39
Sunday, 18th February

"Following target on foot," Steven said into his microphone.

He'd driven at a safe distance behind Garvey for a little over two hours, and the last place he expected to pull into was a marina. Garvey wasn't aware of his presence; he felt confident he hadn't been made. But why here? Why this marina?

In the distance, he could see Garvey walking along a dock, past lots of fishing vessels of varying sizes. The expensive recreational boats were along a different dock. On any normal day he would love coming to a marina, having a walk with his family and admiring the exclusive yachts, boats, and occasional cruise liner, but tonight was different. He had no idea what Garvey was doing here, and it made him nervous.

He watched as Garvey met and shook hands with an older white man wearing yellow fishing overalls, long, thick boots, and a beanie hat. The mystery older man had white hair and an impressive white beard. He looked like a fisherman, or more accurately, a fishing boat captain, which was what Steven guessed he was.

Through his binoculars, he saw Garvey step into some similar-looking yellow overalls and black boots. As the two men engaged in conversation, Steven saw three more men on the boat. He adjusted the binoculars, looking for the boat's name. He could only see the words *Sea Fisher*, the number 2608, and the type of boat it was: Purse Seiner.

Steven frowned. Garvey didn't strike him as the fishing type.

Steven watched as the boat's engine started up, Garvey shaking hands with the three passengers in turn; going by Garvey's body language, he didn't know any of them.

There had to be more to this than a night fishing trip – *had* to be. Maybe that was all there was to it? He shook his head. No way!

"Officer Dyer, please be advised that local police are present, joining the NCA in apprehending the target upon his return," came the female voice. "You are to report to the Metropole Hotel for a briefing."

Steven frowned again. "Can you elaborate on that, Control?"

"You are to report to the Metropole Hotel," the voice repeated. "A half mile from your current location, for a briefing. The NCA have received new intel concerning the target's activities; local police and the NCA are conducting a joint operation to apprehend the target when he returns... please acknowledge."

What new intel? They hadn't been able to record him discussing his criminal activities at home, or in his car, so how had they come by this new intel? "Acknowledged, Control," he said reluctantly, "on my way."

When he turned to walk back along the promenade, he saw the joint task force. In fact, everywhere he looked, he saw police.

There were no blue lights flashing, but there were at least fifteen police cars parked in and around the main car park to the shopping market.

Steven glanced at his watch: 00:04. At this time of night the marina was largely deserted by civilians, yet there were a few people hanging around. He could see the main pub was still open as was a twenty-four-hour supermarket with late-night shoppers milling around inside. The bowling alley and cinema still had their lights on, though they would be closing soon.

When he reached his car, Steven sat on his seat and found the Metropole Hotel on his GPS. He could probably have walked it, but he didn't want to leave his car.

He sat back in his seat and sighed. Something was definitely going on; it was suspect, this new intel. He was interested to find out where it had come from.

It reeked of a set-up...

Lennox was in dangerous waters, both literally and figuratively speaking. It was a choppy night for a pickup, and he was being steered by a man he'd never met before, in a boat with three of Rothstein's guys he had never clapped eyes on. And, to make matters worse, he'd just fucked Rothstein's daughter, killed her husband, and then left her without knowing how she was going to react or what she was going to do. Beattie could be on the phone to her dad right now, he thought.

On the way over to the marina, Lennox had phoned Barkley and informed him of what was happening. He'd asked Barkley to meet him at the marina when he arrived on shore. With a feeling of being set-up, he'd asked his friend to stay back, not wanting him to get collared, if that was what Rothstein had planned.

Why was he so distrusting of Rothstein? Lennox kept asking

himself. Rothstein had been good to him, for the most part; he'd given him a good job, and had given him the chance to prove himself – which he had. Rothstein had also proven himself by turning down that commissioner's offer. It didn't make sense for Lennox to feel like this – to doubt his boss – but even so, he couldn't shake the feeling. It didn't help that in the ten years he'd been making this trip, he had never had a different captain steering the boat. That was his main doubt; he didn't trust change.

As the boat cut through the waves, Lennox held on to the bannisters inside the cabin, visions of Alan's face flashing through his mind – images of his face after one hit from the fire extinguisher, then the second, the third, the fourth. By the time he'd finished, Beattie's husband had been unrecognisable; his face had caved in and his skull had cracked under the force and weight of the blows.

Why had Rothstein phoned him that night of all nights? Did Rothstein know about him and Beattie? Had she told him already? Maybe she'd picked up the phone as soon as he'd left the bunker? Lennox had to stop thinking like this. Rothstein had his reasons for moving the date forward – the captain he'd come to respect had family problems – so Lennox had to stop obsessing over it.

The boat ride would go as smoothly as it always did, he kept trying to tell himself. He was just being paranoid; it was the cannabis he smoked regularly messing with his head, that was all. He gripped the bannisters harder as the waves increased in size...

56

"Bring your friend inside," Nasreen ordered, her gun pointed at Conrad Gebhardt.

Nasreen walked around her target, the gun trained on him every second; if she lost focus, she was sure he would lunge for her.

She watched as he mumbled something in German, grabbed the shadow's arms, and pulled him towards the warehouse door.

"That's it," she added, "pull him inside."

Walking backwards, her gun never swaying, she was inside the well-lit warehouse. Then she reached inside her bag and pulled out two lengths of rope. "Tie him up, nice and tight." She threw him the rope. "Tie his wrists behind his back and his ankles together. Leave him face down."

"You don't know what you get involved in here, lady."

Gebhardt tied his associate up the way she'd ordered.

Studying him, Nasreen noted how stocky he was. He was only about five foot seven, but he was almost as wide as he was tall. Underneath his jumper, she could clearly see his toned arms, the biceps defined even through the fabric. If she wasn't careful, he would overpower her. It was simple physics – he was a lot bigger and heavier than she was.

"Aww, you're looking out for me. That's sweet."

"Who the fuck are you anyway? What do you want with me?"

"All in good time, Conrad. All in good time."

She was stood with her pistol pointed at his back as he stood up and turned to face her. He wasn't a bad-looking man – with his wide face and big cheeks – but his pleasant features belied his underlying sickening actions. "Before we get to that," she said, "let's see what horrors you have hidden out back, shall we?" She found the shutter control panel, pressed the red button, and waited for the door to close with a squeak.

She could hear crying and whimpering in the background, coming from multiple women, and she stood to the side, letting him walk past her after she signalled with her gun for him to move. They were in the delivery point of the warehouse, surrounded on both sides by heavy-duty shelving units piled floor to ceiling with boxes of envelopes and other sundry products required on a day-to-day basis.

Never being more than two feet behind Gebhardt, Nasreen walked through the warehouse floor, scanning the large room. The main area of the factory housed four large tables with eight chairs around each, set off to the left of the room. This, no doubt, was where the inserting happened, where employees were paid to stuff inserts into magazines before the machine at the other end of the warehouse wrapped the magazines in cellophane. There were two of these machines to the right of the factory floor. There were also four large cages dotted around the factory, three half-filled with sacks, the other empty.

As she adjusted to her new environment, Nasreen looked upstairs at the mezzanine level, where there was a kitchen to the right and a storeroom to the left, with more boxes piled floor to ceiling. The main office was to the right of the kitchen.

"You're one sick bastard, Conrad," she said, observing five petite Chinese girls tied to the shelving units at the rear of the warehouse. "How old are these girls? They can't be any older than twelve or thirteen?"

Feeling rage building up inside her, Nasreen reached into her bag and pulled out the serrated pocketknife. With one hand holding the gun, still trained on Gebhardt, she used the other to hold the knife as she walked up to the terrified girls. "Do any of you speak English?" She waited for a response, studying each of the pretty girls in turn.

"I… do," came a tiny voice.

Nasreen went behind the girl who could speak English and cut the rope she was shackled to with her knife, still pointing her gun at Gebhardt. "I'm here to help, sweetie. Take this knife and free the rest of the girls, okay? Then I'm going to need your help with something." She noticed a pile of clothes and shoes on the floor to her right. "Get everyone dressed, then come over and join me when you're ready."

The girl nodded, still petrified.

While the English speaker was busy cutting her friends free, Nasreen focused her attention back on Gebhardt. They were stood next to the four tables with a cage nearby, Nasreen three feet away from Conrad, giving her enough room to manoeuvre if he decided to lunge at her. "So tell me, do you just rape them, sell them, or what? What's your set-up?"

"Why you so interested in what I do?"

"I'm not interested in what you do."

"What is it you *do* want to know? Why are you here?"

"I'm asking the questions here, not you, so shut your mouth and strip."

"What? No fucking way."

Nasreen pulled the hammer back on her pistol.

"Strip now, or I'll do it for you... after I pistol-whip you... your choice."

"You fucking bitch." Gebhardt undressed.

Nasreen listened as he moaned something in German. She so badly wanted to pull the trigger, to wing him, to hurt him. He was scum – there was no better word to describe him – and he wasn't fit to lick these girls' feet. Nasreen had a mind to leave him tied up with the girls, to let them do to him whatever they wanted. She still might, she thought, watching as he slowly stripped.

"There," said Gebhardt, in his underpants. "I strip, now what?"

"And the pants, Conrad, don't be shy," she said, motioning with the pistol for him to pull them down. "You had these girls tied up naked; it's only fair that you do the same in return."

She beckoned the small English-speaking Chinese girl over, taking the knife back. "Now, do me a favour. Take these," she said, handing the girl four lengths of rope from her bag, "and tie him up tight." Then she found an old wooden chair, picked it up with her free hand, and placed it in front of Gebhardt. "Sit!"

With her gun poised to fire, Nasreen waited for Gebhardt to pull his pants down and sit, grumbling to himself. She watched him sit down, trying not to notice how small his penis was. And she'd been wrong about his physique earlier; he was fat, with a big belly that nearly hung over and covered his tiny limp appendage. When he'd had clothes on he'd looked quite muscular, but it was all a façade; he was fat with muscly biceps. "Tie a knot around each wrist, and tie that to the chair," she told the Chinese girl. "Good, that's it. And now the other one."

She instructed the girl on how to tie Gebhardt's legs to the chair, then went and checked that he was bound tightly. When she was satisfied Gebhardt couldn't escape his restraints, she walked over to the clothed abductees and made sure they were okay. Then she went over to Gebhardt's clothes, rummaged through his jeans and pulled out his keys, handing them to the English-speaking girl. "Take these, and go wait by the door. I'll be along shortly. First, there's something I need from *him*..."

"Excuse me, sir, but where did this *intel* come from?"

Steven was in a conference room along with a mixture of police and NCA officers. At the front of the room stood Director General Graham Holmes and Police and Crime Commissioner Philip Byrd, the two highest-ranking personnel there. Sitting around the table were several senior members of the police force and Steven's seniors at the NCA. Half of the room was awash with police uniforms, while the other half was swamped with varying coloured suits. Steven was one of only three officers wearing plain clothes.

"Officer Dyer," said the tall lanky Director General, "I'm glad you could make this briefing, but you were late getting here, so I'd appreciate it if you'd leave the questions until after we've finished."

"Well, you haven't answered my question, sir." If Steven wasn't careful, Holmes would ask him to leave; the way he'd said "intel" had been scornful, like he didn't believe it. Which, of course, he didn't.

"The intel comes from an extremely reliable CI," Holmes replied. "Now, do you mind if we get back to the briefing? Is that okay with you?"

There was another awkward silence while everyone waited for him to speak.

"This covert informant, who is he, or she? And how do you know they're reliable?"

He'd done it now. He'd just questioned Holmes' integrity and judgement.

"He's reliable, but I'm not at liberty to divulge their identity, you know that. That's *why* they're covert."

"So, it's not William Rothstein then?"

The room erupted in murmuring and whispering, and Steven felt all eyes on him again as he waited for the inevitable admonishment from Holmes.

"Of course it's not Rothstein, don't be absurd. William Rothstein is a secondary target, Officer Dyer."

"He was the primary until Director General Wells died, sir," Steven blurted out without thinking. "Why is he only secondary now? He's the mastermind we should be targeting, not Garvey – he's Rothstein's right-hand man. Garvey's not important in the grand scheme of–"

"Enough!" Holmes snapped. "Our orders come directly from the Home Secretary; we don't decide targets autonomously. We work together with the Home Office to decide who we investigate, and we all decided Garvey was the primary we should be seeking to apprehend. Our intel tells us that Garvey isn't working for Rothstein at all; he's actually a partner of Rothstein's. But, in fact, he's more than that: he's the mastermind of a drug operation with a street value of over fifty million a year in cocaine and heroin."

Steven couldn't speak; he wasn't in full receipt of the facts.

It was plausible that Garvey was partners with Rothstein, and it was also plausible that he was, in reality, the head of the drug empire they were seeking to destroy.

It was plausible, yes, but not likely. He knew Rothstein was the head of said drug empire. Anyone could see that.

"Are you going to come back with something, Officer Dyer, or can I get on with the briefing? I was going to give your team the honour of bringing Garvey in, but it doesn't sound like you'll consider it an honour–"

"We'll do it," he said, cutting Holmes off mid-sentence.

"Are you sure?"

"I'm sure. Can we interview him first too, please?"

"Your team has contributed a lot to this operation. It was your lucky find with the Harrison farm that gave us leads to pursue, and for that, we're thankful. If you want first crack at Garvey, who am I to say no?"

"Thank you, sir," he replied.

As Holmes and PCC Byrd continued briefing the officers, Steven tuned their voices out. He was positive Rothstein had rolled over on Garvey, just given him up, but why? Maybe there was a rift between the pair? Without solid proof, all he had was a theory. The fact that the operation had changed targets midway through was alarming enough, but now they were supposed to believe that it was Garvey controlling the drugs, and not his boss? Holmes must've thought they were all born yesterday.

Being the first to interview Garvey, when they apprehended him, would be the only chance he'd get to prove his theory that Rothstein had sold him down the river...

57

"Wrong, wrong, wrong!" cried Nasreen as she cracked Gebhardt over the head with the butt of her pistol. "That's not the answer I'm looking for. Telling me to go fuck myself isn't going to get you out of this... so, I'll ask you again, where is your brother?"

She watched as Gebhardt swore in German, a look of pure hatred in his eyes. For the past three hours she'd interrogated him over the whereabouts of his brother, and she was getting bored of asking the same questions – not to mention getting the same "fuck you" reply.

"I'll tell you the same thing I just told you: go fuck yourself."

Nasreen's temper was fraying. The longer she spent with this fat vile man the more she wanted to put a bullet in his head. She lifted the pistol, then brought it crashing down onto Gebhardt's shoulder.

"Ahh, you fucking bitch!"

"I can carry on doing this all night, Conrad." She walked round to face him, then bent down and stared into his dark eyes. "The thing is though, I don't want to. I don't want to be anywhere near you – you disgust me to my core. Now, tell me where he lives, or this interrogation is going to get more severe.

I'm not talking pistol whippings, or ear twisting, Conrad, I'm talking bone breaking, limb severing... You don't want that, and I don't want that. So, do yourself a favour and give me what I want."

"And you do this over a male prostitute?"

Nasreen stared into Gebhardt's lifeless eyes. "I do all this for a friend, and you better believe I'll break your bones for him. Here, let me show you..."

Gebhardt tried to move in his chair but couldn't.

She bent down and grabbed the little finger of his right hand. "Tell me where he is, Conrad. Don't make me do this," she said, tightening her grip on his littlest digit.

"You a police officer," he said, bracing himself for pain. "You not allowed to do this."

"You're wrong about that," she replied, snapping bone as she pulled his finger back; she physically felt and heard it snap. "I *was* a police officer. Now I'm just a member of the public you really don't want to piss off."

She listened as he cried in German, swearing probably.

The pain had turned Gebhardt white, and sweat was beading on his brow and trickling down his face. His breaths came in rasps as he tried to fight the need to vomit. "You fucking whore, I fucking kill you for this! I never tell you where Walter is, *ever*. Do whatever you want; you not getting nothing from me."

As soon as he'd finished telling her he wouldn't help, she grabbed the little finger on his other hand and broke that too, the pain causing Gebhardt to practically spasm in his chair.

He spat as he yelled out, his face and chest covered in sweat.

"Two down, eight to go, Conrad." She grabbed his left ring finger. "You know you can end this right now by telling me where he is. It's up to you how much pain you feel."

"Fuck you!"

Nasreen sighed as she yanked his finger back and felt it break, hearing him cry for the first time since she'd abducted him.

This wasn't getting her anywhere.

He might not crack even after all eight fingers and two thumbs had been broken.

She stood up, went over to her bag, and took out her serrated pocketknife. It had a six-inch blade and was perfect for cutting and slicing into things. Standing in front of him, she bent down so that her eyes were level with his. "This really is pissing me off now, Conrad, so I'm going to give you one last chance to tell me where he is."

"Or what? You break another finger? I from Bavaria, you not break me."

"Or I cut off something no man wants to lose, do you understand what I'm saying?" she replied, her eyes steely and cool. "One last chance."

"Fuck you! You won't do that, bitch!"

Without thinking – and without flinching – Nasreen placed the knife underneath it. "Are you ready to test my resolve? In a couple of seconds, I'm going to start sawing away."

She heard him audibly gulp. He clearly believed her by the way his eyes were bulging.

She waited for five seconds, then she pulled back the knife enough to scratch.

"Okay, okay, stop, stop! I tell you what you want know! Please, take knife away, I need it. Please, please, please."

She didn't take it away immediately. "If you lie to me, if you give me the wrong address, I'm going to come back for you and cut this tiny thing off, do you understand?"

"Yes, yes, I understand. I won't lie to you. Get a piece of paper, I give you his address. Please, just take knife away, please."

Nasreen sighed. She should have threatened to cut his penis off three hours earlier, saving her a lot of time and hassle. Why hadn't she done that? She wanted to slap her forehead, Homer Simpson style – instead she took out a notepad and pen from her bag. "Go ahead. What's the address?"

He couldn't have been more helpful, telling her the address of a farm in the South West. He told her that Walter lived with the Harrisons. He told her that Beatrice Harrison was the daughter of William Rothstein, and about how they'd converted a World War Two bunker into an underground exclusive brothel, where only career criminals were invited to pay to have sex with prostitutes and male escorts they'd abducted from around the country.

Nasreen couldn't believe it. Finally – after almost a month and a half – she knew why Danny had been abducted; he was being used as a sex slave. It all made sense. That was why there had been so many sex workers disappearing over the years.

She'd also found out that Walter had worked for Rothstein for sixteen years or so, which fitted with the timeline of the missing persons cases she'd found. She'd been right all along; they were all connected.

With the address in her bag, she walked towards the door.

"Wait, where you going? You can't leave me here like this!"

"You're kidding, right?" she said, turning to face him. "Do you think I'm going to let you go? You're going to prison, Conrad. Human trafficking and sexual slavery will get you about twenty years. Thanks for the information. The police will be here in about five minutes. Have a nice life, and I'll be sure to tell your brother you gave me his address."

"You fucking bitch!" he spat, straining against his ropes.

Nasreen walked towards the five girls stood by the door, now all fully clothed, and when she got to them, she pulled her mobile out of her bag and dialled 999. She informed the police –

anonymously – that she'd heard a gunshot in the retail park, then she hung up before telling the English-speaking girl that she had to go, asking her to keep her friends there at the warehouse until the police arrived. The girl agreed and said "thank you" for saving them.

Back at the car, Nasreen cut the cable ties and set her Hungarian hostage free. She then asked Jankovics to go over to the Chinese girls and stay with them until the police arrived. Jankovics agreed, saying that if needed, she would testify – especially if it meant she would never have to deal with Conrad again. Nasreen assured her that with her testimony, Conrad would get twenty years plus in prison.

With a sense of real hope, Nasreen started her car, glanced at the clock on the dashboard, and accelerated, heading off on her way to find Danny.

It was 03:45. She estimated it would take seven hours to reach the farm, according to the GPS, so she should be there around eleven...

The pickup had gone like clockwork, as usual. The sixteen ice boxes – containing two kilos of cocaine each – were on board the boat like normal, covered with ice and fish of varying types. To anyone passing, it would look like they'd caught a good haul. It would take the four men two trips to load all the merchandise on the van, and in total the shipment had a street value of six hundred and ten thousand quid. Not bad for a night's work.

As the boat docked, one of Rothstein's guys jumped off and tied it to the post, then Lennox picked up two ice boxes by their handles, stepping off the boat and onto the dock. It was still dark at quarter to six, and as he looked out at the marina he couldn't see anything suspicious; he couldn't see any police cars or anything else that gave him cause for concern.

Lennox waited for Rothstein's guys to pick up their ice boxes and step onto the dock, then when they were all ready, he led the long walk down the dock, passing several fishing boats along the way. He was vigilant about looking for suspicious figures; he still couldn't see anyone he thought might be a police officer. His heart was racing – like it did every time they docked. This time it was more severe; he was really worried.

When they reached the van and put the ice boxes in the back, Lennox closed and locked the door behind them. One down, one to go, he thought, following Rothstein's guys back to the boat. The three men in front of him were a distance away, yet he didn't think anything of it.

As he got near the boat, he saw that the eight remaining ice boxes were already on the dock. He couldn't see Rothstein's three guys anymore.

He looked at the post and saw that the boat wasn't tied to the dock.

"See you later, Lennox!" came a voice, followed by laughter.

A second later the boat's engine started, and before Lennox could run to the boat and jump aboard, it set sail, leaving him stranded there with sixteen kilos of product.

The dock suddenly flashed blue.

Fuck! He *had* been set up, and there was nothing he could do, nowhere he could run.

"Lennox Garvey, turn and face us with your hands up," came a male voice over the metallic-sounding handheld microphone. "You're under arrest!"

When he turned, Lennox saw just how many police cars he'd missed. How could he have possibly missed that many? There must have been a dozen blue flashing lights there.

There were four armed police officers walking towards him, their Heckler and Koch MP5s aimed at his chest, their infrared dots showing him exactly where their bullets would go.

This was it.

"On your knees!" shouted the first armed policeman.

Lennox did as he was told; there was nothing else he could do. He'd thought briefly about running and diving over the dock, but that was a stupid idea – he didn't know how deep the water was, and he'd be fished out of there in no time. No, it was better to let them take him in, where he could thrash out some sort of deal. After all, he had some leverage; he had a lot of information on Rothstein that he could use to his advantage. That fucking treacherous prick, Rothstein.

Lennox vowed, right there on his knees, that he would get his former boss for this.

Once he'd been searched for weapons, handcuffed, and pulled to his feet, a man in jeans, a jumper, and a thick coat stood in front of him, his ID wallet held out for him to see.

"Lennox Garvey, I'm NCA Officer Steven Dyer. And you're under arrest..."

58

"Go ahead, Terrence," said Nasreen, as she pulled her car over onto the hard shoulder. "Tell me you've got something on Beatrice Harrison and William Rothstein, *please*."

"Not as much as I should."

"What do you mean?"

"Most of it's been redacted. There's tons of material here – reams of paperwork – but most of it's been blacked out, Nas," he said, his voice concerned. "There's nothing on here that'll be of any use to you, sorry."

"Shit!" She thought for a second. Why would their records be redacted? The only reason for redacting something was to prevent knowledge of illegal activities because they were helping the police with their enquiries. "You don't think that means they're informants, do you?"

"This is just Rothstein's file. There's nothing on Beatrice Harrison; she's never been in trouble with the police, never had her fingerprints taken, or even a swab taken. She's clean, as far as I can see."

"Just because she's not in the system, doesn't mean she's

clean. Gebhardt's brother assures me she's running this thing for her father."

"I'm just telling you what I see on the PNC, Nas."

Nasreen sighed. "I know, I'm sorry, but I'm getting so close."

"You know what I'm going to say..."

"Don't say it! There's no need, I'll be careful."

Nasreen thanked her ex-partner and hung up, trying to think. There was so much more to this situation than she knew. When she thought back to Adams' conversation in the stairwell, she started tying it all together in her mind. She couldn't find the bow to top it all off. It was there though. She was missing a vital piece of information. Whatever it was, she knew she had to be careful.

As cars whizzed past her, she switched her engine on and indicated right, moving out when it was clear.

When she was up to speed with the rest of the cars and lorries, she thought about Danny, about her childhood growing up with him. She thought about how they'd bumped into each other when she'd returned from university for the summer holidays, and about how giddy she'd felt after their first kiss.

And then she thought about how he'd been kidnapped and made to have sex with paying criminals. She was going to get him out of that bunker, no matter what. Despite what she'd been told, Nasreen knew he was still alive; it was a gut feeling she had, and she'd come to trust her intuition. She stepped on the accelerator...

Assistant Commissioner Peter Franks awoke to the sound of his burner mobile, and looking over at his alarm clock he saw it was 07:02. It had taken him a long time to get to sleep but he'd eventually fallen into a deep slumber, so when the mobile shouted its shrill tone it startled him. He picked it up and answered.

"Peter, it's Graham," said the soft voice. "Thought I'd let you know we have Garvey in custody. He's being processed now."

"That's great news. Hold on, let me get up."

Franks glanced briefly at his wife, still fast asleep next to him, then carefully pulled himself out of bed and put his slippers on. He took his dressing gown from the hook on the bedroom door, wrapped himself in it, and tiptoed onto the landing, closing the door behind him. "Sorry, Graham, I just had to find a quiet place. Go on. What about the others?"

"The boat's captain and the three others slipped past us." The way he'd said "slipped past us" insinuated that there was no chase made.

"Good, that's exactly the way Rothstein planned it. When are you interviewing Garvey? I think I'll come down and listen in, if that's okay with you?"

"Sure, that's not a problem for me."

"I'll be there as soon as I can. Hold off interviewing him until I get there; I want to see what he has to say. I should be there around eleven."

Franks hung up the call and then walked through to the bathroom across the hall from his bedroom, where he closed the door, stepped over to the toilet, pulled his pyjama bottoms down, and sat on the seat. He made a call.

"Yeah, Peter, is it done?"

"We have him in custody, Will, thought you'd like to know."

"Great news," Rothstein replied. "Thanks for the heads up."

"He's being processed as we speak. Once that's taken care of, we can get on, yes?"

"Absolutely. Set up the initial meeting and I'll be ready to go when you need me."

Franks hung up, showered, brushed his teeth, and shaved in

a record twenty minutes; he was excited to get going, now that the last hurdle to the project was about to be successfully navigated. All he needed to do was make sure Garvey was incarcerated and Rothstein would do what he had to do to make the problem go away.

Garvey had been arrested with thirty-two kilos of white powder in his possession, so there was no question he'd be imprisoned, but Franks still wanted to be there to see how the interview went down; they couldn't just arrest and charge the man without due process, so it was Garvey's right to have an interview.

If Garvey had information they could use for future arrests, they could offer him a deal, but Franks' boss, the Home Secretary, and everyone else involved couldn't have Garvey offering up Rothstein, so Franks wanted to be there to make sure that didn't happen. It was a risk, because Garvey was integral to Rothstein's current organisation, not his future one.

It was a complicated web Franks was weaving. He knew what he was doing, knew which pieces needed to be where and when. He was the real mastermind behind the project, not the Commissioner and certainly not the Home Secretary.

He dressed himself in his uniform – complete with hat and shiny shoes – kissed his wife goodbye and left the house. As he got in his prized Jaguar and drove away, excitement crept over him...

Lennox paced back and forth in his windowless white-walled holding cell. He needed time to think everything through.

He knew that Rothstein had set him up, but didn't know why. It couldn't be because Rothstein had found out about his extracurricular activities with Beattie; the boat trip had been planned way before he'd fucked Beattie. He also knew it couldn't be about his work with Rothstein. The only reason he could think of was that Rothstein had decided to accept the Assistant Commissioner's offer and therefore needed to get rid of him because his uncle wasn't going to be the supplier anymore. It had to be that, *had* to be.

After he'd been processed – including his fingerprints and picture being taken – the NCA officer had allowed Lennox to make one phone call, as per his rights. He'd phoned the number Rothstein had given him if this situation ever arose; his boss had told him that the number would always be answered, no matter the time of day, and he'd had the number in his wallet for the past ten years, never needing to use it, until now. He'd only used it to test Rothstein, and lo and behold, it had just rung out – no one had answered. That proved Rothstein was behind it.

As his boss was behind his current predicament, Lennox knew he was in imminent danger. Rothstein couldn't leave him alive; he knew far too much about his boss's operation, about his day-to-day activities. He also knew that Rothstein had a network of lackeys inside; he'd be shanked as soon as he arrived in general population.

His only way out of this mess was to secure a deal with the NCA, the police, or whoever else he needed to barter with. And on that subject, he needed to consider his options.

What did he really have on Rothstein? He thought about the recording he had on his mobile of Rothstein meeting with the Assistant Commissioner. He had the Commissioner clearly conspiring with Rothstein to legalise drug use without the public's knowledge. It was unethical, illegal, and if found out, it would be the single biggest scandal to hit the UK's media in decades.

He'd heard the Assistant Commissioner clearly talking about that, and he thought he could use it in the interview, but then he considered that, to his knowledge, the conspiracy hadn't started yet. All he really had were two men talking about doing something illegal. Plus, the recording clearly showed Rothstein declining the offer. That was no use.

What else did he have? He needed something strong enough to convict Rothstein, to put him inside for a long time. He needed… He had it!

"Hello?" he shouted through the thick locked door, banging on it with his fist. "I'm ready to make a deal… hello…?"

59

Steven was sat beside his colleague, Howard Greene, and opposite Lennox Garvey, watching as the latter bit his nails. As his colleague had set the camcorder to start recording, Steven went through the motions, stating the date and time and who was present, and then asking Garvey to confirm his name and age. Garvey obliged.

This was their third interview since bringing Garvey in earlier that morning. The first interview had been a total bust; Garvey had said nothing but "no comment" throughout the entire forty-five-minute questioning. Steven had, however, noticed how jittery Garvey was – clearly, he was scared.

The second interview hadn't gone any better. The "no comments" had been mixed in with lots of "fuck you" and "go fuck yourself". He'd asked Garvey to confirm his name and age, to which he'd answered truthfully, but as for the rest of the answers, they'd gained nothing of use. It was the way Steven had expected it to go. After all, Garvey wasn't going to roll over on someone like William Rothstein, unless he had good reason.

Five minutes earlier, Garvey had banged on his cell door, saying he was ready to talk, to make a deal, and Steven had felt excited when he'd opened the cell door and led him into the interview room. "You said you're ready to make a deal?"

"If you promise me immunity from prosecution, I'll give you what I have."

Steven noticed how strong Garvey's Jamaican accent was. He'd never actually heard him speak until the first interview, and he thought it was a cool accent. "Why don't you tell us what you know, and we'll tell you if we can."

"Don't treat me like a prick, Officer Dyer," he said, leaning in for effect. "You confirm I get immunity and I'll serve you up Rothstein on a platter."

"Rothstein? We're not after Rothstein," said his colleague. "You're the one we're after. All we want to know is where you get your product from, Garvey. We caught you with thirty-two kilos of cocaine; you're not going to get immunity from that."

"Yeah, on Rothstein's orders. I'm a little spoke on a big wheel, and I know you want the heavy hitters."

"That's bullshit! We know you're the brains behind the drug trafficking; you're partners with Rothstein. Tell us who your source is, and we'll talk about a deal. And it won't be immunity, I can tell you that much."

"Listen, Garvey, give us what you have, and I promise we'll see what we can do for you." Steven said, to which Garvey shook his head. "However, we all know that what you're expecting isn't going to happen. You can't get immunity after being caught with that much coke."

"When you hear what I've got to say, you will give me immunity."

Garvey was messing with them. He was wasting their time for a reason Steven couldn't fathom. He looked over at Howard Greene and the two of them stood up at the same time. "We'll come back to this when you're really ready to talk."

Steven reached the door and touched the handle.

"The Harrison farm," Garvey said, his voice raised. "I know what's going on down there. I know you NCA guys were set up there taking photos, and I know you have no idea what Rothstein and his daughter are doing there. If you did, you'd have got a search warrant and raided the place weeks ago."

Steven stopped. Finally, there was someone who could tell him what he needed to know. He'd stumbled onto the farm himself, and he had to know.

He turned to Garvey. "And you want immunity for telling us that the barn's being used as a drug distribution centre?"

"Good guess, but wrong. I'm not only offering to tell you what's happening there; I'll testify to it in court too."

Greene looked at him. They needed to get permission from higher up to deal with a suspect.

"We'll be back in a minute, we need to confer with our superiors."

"Don't take too long, Officer Dyer – people's lives are at stake. Twenty-four lives, to be exact. Tell your superiors that if you don't deal with me, I've sent instructions to a friend of mine to inform the media of what's going on down there. If he doesn't hear from me at a certain time... and, well, that time's near."

"We'll be sure to inform them."

Peter Franks had been observing the interview on a PC monitor, and he watched as Officers Dyer and Greene left Garvey alone in the interview room. Franks was in a quandary: he was supposed to prevent Garvey talking about Rothstein, but having heard that lives were at stake, he wanted to know what Garvey had to say. He was pretty sure the Commissioner would want to know too. He waited for Steven and Greene to enter the room.

The two officers entered and stood in front of him and Holmes.

"We're finally getting somewhere with him now," Franks said.

"Do you believe him, sir?" Greene asked Holmes.

"I don't know... it sounds like the rantings of a desperate man to me."

"I'm not so sure. I think we should hear him out." Franks made his feelings known.

"He's not going to say a word until he has a deal."

"Agreed," Franks said. "Tell him he has a deal, if the information is accurate and we get to apprehend William Rothstein."

"Peter, you can't make that kind of decision," said Holmes. "Dyer, Greene, leave us for a moment, will you?"

Franks waited for the two NCA officers to leave the room.

"Peter, what are you doing? Have you forgotten what we have planned? We need Rothstein. And don't tell my officers what to do either. I'm their boss, not you."

"Oh, do shut up, Graham, and don't forget who put you here. You didn't get to where you are now on merit. And we don't *need* Rothstein; we have other options available to us." Franks sighed. "I hate having to deal with that prick. If what he's got going on at his daughter's farm is as bad as Garvey says it is, we're not missing the opportunity to put this scumbag behind bars. Get them back in here and tell them to make a deal with Garvey. Go on!"

He watched as Holmes walked to the door, his proverbial tail between his legs, and let the two officers back in. He hoped he was making the right decision, hoped the Commissioner would see his way of thinking. Rothstein wasn't the be all and end all of the project – they had other importers they could use...

. . .

"Okay, Garvey, we've been given the authority to grant you a deal." Steven passed an A4 piece of paper over the table then watched as Garvey picked it up and read it.

"So, what's so important it merits an immunity deal?"

Steven glanced over at Greene. He was trying to make out he was nonchalant about what Garvey had to say. He was excited inside, really excited. "Let's have it then."

Garvey nodded, taking a deep breath before starting his explanation. "For sixteen years, Rothstein's been abducting male and female prostitutes from up and down the UK and forcing them to work for him at the farm. Underneath the barn – the one you were so interested in – there's an old World War Two bunker. Rothstein's renovated it into a kind of exclusive club. It has twenty-five rooms, twenty of which are used for the prostitutes and five are torture rooms. It has a bar inside and a lounge area. It's also got a huge furnace, which Rothstein rents out for disposal purposes, if you know what I mean."

Steven couldn't believe what he was hearing. "So, right now, there are twenty prostitutes held captive under that barn, is that what you're telling us?" He was about ready to leap up and run out of the door to his car. This was massive, and he had to be part of the raid team on this one.

"That's exactly what I'm telling you, except it's more than twenty. There's five support workers there too. They're foreign, and they're being used as glorified cleaners and helpers. They help the prostitutes get ready for their customers... if you understand what I'm saying when I say help?"

Holy shit! Steven thought. When his team had speculated about what they thought was going on in the barn, they'd never have guessed this. "And how have they managed to get away with this for so long?"

"Because they're not stupid; they kidnap the prostitutes from all over the country, never from the same place twice. You police guys don't talk much between forces, do you? Rothstein knows this. He knows it's easy to get away with it, if you kidnap one from down south, the next one from up north, and the one after that from the Midlands."

"So, if there's twenty sex workers there now, how long have they been there?"

"It all differs. Some make it about five years before they wear themselves out, others aren't fortunate enough to live that long..."

"Live that long? You mean they're killed if they're not useful anymore?"

"Fuck yeah; that's what the furnace is used for..."

Steven tried not to imagine the furnace Garvey kept speaking of. "So, if the longest they live for is five years – or thereabouts – how many do you think have been in that bunker over the last sixteen years?"

"I call it the blood bunker, if that gives you a clue. It's hard to say, but it's easily over sixty."

Steven sat back in his seat, reeling from the information Garvey had given them. Those poor bastards, he thought, kidnapped and forced to have sex until they couldn't anymore, and the best they could expect after was to be incinerated. "And you're willing to testify to all of this, are you, Garvey?"

"If it's part of my deal, I will. But it gets worse. Beattie – sorry, Beatrice – auctions them off when she can't get them to work anymore."

Steven was starting to feel a little sick. "What do you mean by that?"

Lennox explained the situation.

Steven looked over at Greene, who was speechless, then back at Garvey. "We'll be right back. Do not move!"

60

Nasreen slowed down, looking for a turning on the left – she couldn't see one; all she could see was what could only be described as a dirt track. It was about big enough for a car, although she didn't want to risk it with a rental – she didn't want to have any more problems to deal with on top of everything else that was going on. It was the only kind of road in the area though, so it had to be the place. Gebhardt hadn't warned her of the narrow lane. Then again, why would he?

She slowed to a stop, pulled up the handbrake, and switched off the engine. It had taken her longer than she'd thought to get here. She'd had to stop at a service station to fill up the tank and get something to eat, the traffic had been horrendous, and she'd taken a wrong turn earlier. Her dashboard clock told her it was 15:03.

There was no turning back, she thought, reaching across for her bag and pulling out the Remington. She held it in her lap while she thought about her next course of action. Beneath the trees it was getting dark, and she would have to wait until then before going inside, which was fine – she had to do a bit of surveillance first anyway.

Stepping out of her car, Nasreen went to the boot to retrieve her flashlight and binoculars; walking along the dirt track was going to be dark. Gebhardt had informed her that the bunker's customers came and went at all times of the day, but were largely gone by eight, so she'd need to stick to the treeline for cover.

After locking the car, she crossed the road, sticking to the embankment until she came to the turning. She wondered if she was being stupid – careless – by going it alone, but she couldn't go to Adams, not when she was suspended and still investigating Danny's disappearance. No, this was her only course of action.

As she walked along the track, she pulled out her pistol and held it by her side. After five minutes of walking along the track, she heard a car approaching, then saw its lights through the trees. With haste, she climbed up the bank and hid amongst the trees and bushes while the car passed, confident she hadn't been seen.

Having walked a little further, Nasreen finally reached the gates to the farm, and up ahead she could see the farmhouse with a smaller house situated next to it. There were five cars parked out the front.

She turned right at the gate, following the perimeter fencing until it turned left, then she continued until she had a good view of the house and barn behind it.

She crouched and observed through her binoculars.

After a while she saw a woman coming out of the barn, though with how dark it was getting it was difficult to make out any facial features. Two men in black trousers and white shirts under their coats followed the woman. Could that be Beatrice Harrison? Nasreen put the woman in her late thirties – early forties maybe – and she certainly looked in control, confident.

Shivering, Nasreen put the binoculars down, cupped her

hands, and breathed hot air into her palms. She wished she'd dressed for this. It was too late for those kinds of thoughts.

Picking up the binoculars again, she continued to observe...

"Officer Dyer, get back here!" Graham Holmes ordered.

Steven continued walking; there was no way he was going to let twenty-five innocent people die in that bunker. He'd spent quarter of an hour arguing with Holmes about raiding the Harrison farm, and he didn't want to waste any more time.

He couldn't understand, knowing what they did now, why Holmes and the Assistant Commissioner didn't order a raid immediately. They'd said they'd requested a search warrant, but he didn't believe them. There was something very suspect going on with Holmes and the Commissioner, and while he didn't know what it was, he knew it had something to do with this whole situation.

As he rushed through the police station, he noticed the NCA officers and uniformed officers alike moving out of his way. Maybe it was his purposeful stride, or maybe they had overheard him arguing with their seniors.

Outside, he got in his car, checked his Glock, and sped off; he had to get to the farm as quickly as he could. If the seniors had actually requested a search warrant and were going to raid the farm, he wanted to get there before them. He wasn't going to have someone else raid the bunker; he'd found it, and he wanted to be part of the team to arrest the Harrisons – and Rothstein.

"Officer Dyer, this is Control," came the voice in his ear. "Director General Holmes has requested that you return to the station immediately. Please acknowledge."

He pulled the microphone lead out and threw his earpiece behind him onto the back seat. He had a two-hour drive ahead of him and he didn't want to spend it arguing with the control room...

Peter Franks closed the door of the empty interview room behind him. He pulled his burner from his pocket and dialled.

"Yeah," came Rothstein's voice.

"You absolute bastard!"

"Hey, hey, what the fuck kind of way is that to start a conversation?"

"Cut the bullshit, Will, we know what's going on under that barn now, you fucking sick maniac. Garvey's just spilled his guts securing a nice little deal."

"What the fuck? Why are you even interviewing him? I gave him to you on a silver thirty-two-fucking-kilo platter. All you were supposed to do was book him and send him through to nick. Why the fuck did you question him?"

"Um, there's a little legal term called due process, but don't worry, I wouldn't expect you to understand that we have certain ways of doing things."

"This isn't what we agreed to, Peter! Jesus fucking Christ, this could fuck everything right up. How much has he said?"

"A lot. You've been doing this for sixteen years? All those innocent people you've had locked up down there, all those fucking dead..." He had to stop himself. There was a rage inside him that he needed to expel.

"Oh, fuck you, Peter. I'm not going to let you judge me, you hypocrite. Those people aren't innocent; they sell their bodies for money, for fuck's sake. Anyway, I'm not justifying myself to you, you bent piece of shit."

"Fuck you! What we're doing is going to help a lot of people; it will actually save lives. What *you're* doing is abducting prostitutes, forcing them to have sex with people until they can't anymore, and then butchering them, you fucking psycho."

There was a long pause.

Franks tried breathing deeply a couple of times. "Why the fuck did you set Garvey up anyway? Why not just kill him? It seems you're pretty good at that."

"Because, you idiot, I'm going to get blowback from his uncle either way, but if he gets pinched and sent to prison, and someone shanks him while he's in there, his uncle can't blame me for it, can he? If he just went missing, his uncle would send some heavies over and I can do without that."

Franks considered Rothstein's reply. He had a point.

There was another long pause.

"Look, this is getting us nowhere fast," Rothstein said finally. "What's your next move, Peter, huh? What're you going to do? You coming after me? Because if you do, you'd better bring a fucking army. And when push comes to shove, you should know that if I go down, you're coming down with me."

"Don't threaten me, scumbag! When we invited you to participate in this project, we didn't know you were a complete psychopath. I mean, we had our suspicions you were importing, but we had no fucking idea you were doing this. As far as I'm concerned, our deal is nullified."

"No, no, Peter! You don't get to decide that for me; the project goes ahead as planned. It's up to you to find a way out of this, and if you say no, just remember I've got the fucking recording of you coming to me with your little plan."

Franks sighed. That God damn recording. Rothstein was right; he had no choice but to attempt to brush this under the carpet. But how the hell was he going to do that? He paced back and forth, going over his own footsteps time and again.

Taking another deep breath, he said, "All right, let's calm down, shall we?" What the hell was he going to do? He had to think. "Right, you've got an NCA officer on his way to your farm as we speak. I'll get Holmes to call him off – that'll give me some time to think things through."

"Hey, I don't give a flying fuck what you do," Rothstein said, calmer. "This is your ballgame, do whatever you have to. But if an NCA officer comes anywhere near my farm, he's going to wish he hadn't. Do you understand what I'm saying?"

"Yes, I understand," Franks said before hanging up, adding, "Prick!" when the line had been severed.

Shit! He had some real thinking to do, but first he had to pressure Holmes into making sure that Officer Dyer didn't breach the farm. And then Franks had to deliver the bad news to his boss. He wasn't looking forward to that, not one little bit...

61

Beattie couldn't believe how much pain Danny could tolerate.

Hung by his wrists, his body battered and bruised and his head down, she watched as he opened his one good eye, the other so swollen flesh covered it.

She walked around him, observing the bruising. His ribs were a bluish grey, his back was covered in bruising and deep red welts from where the guards had burnt him with cigarettes, and his lovely face was swollen and contorted. He'd lost five teeth.

"I see you're still with us then?"

She gripped his hair and pulled his head up so she could look at him directly without crouching. There was nothing she wanted more than to see him die – except, of course, to cause him pain, both physically and mentally.

Since Kimiko's death, he would be hearing her screams, over and over again, haunting him. He'd defiled Kimiko, and turned Beattie's beautiful support worker against her, and now he was paying the price. "You've exceeded my expectations, Danny," she said as his eye rolled back. "I thought you'd be dead by now. But don't worry, it won't be long; the guards will be in shortly... and I've given them instructions to end it today."

As soon as she'd finished speaking, she heard him try to speak.

It came out low and muffled.

Not being able to understand, she put her ear closer to his mouth.

"F-fuck... y-you," came his garbled response.

"Fuck me? *Fuck me?*" A deep rage filled her as she slapped him with both her forehand and backhand. With his head slumped, she grabbed his hair again, lifting his head up and punching his cheek with her free hand. It felt so good to take her pain out on him – and she had so much pain.

Her mobile phone chimed, and taking a deep breath, she pulled it out of her jeans pocket and answered it, still watching Danny. "Hi, Dad," she said as nonchalantly as she could.

"We've got problems, Bea," came her daddy's voice. "An NCA officer is on his way over to you. I'm trying to fix it, but it will be a good idea to prepare. Get the guards to fetch the arsenal."

"How bad is it?"

"Lenny's been arrested. He's given up everything in exchange for a deal. They know about the bunker, they know about the abductions and how we get rid of your bees... They know everything!"

"Shit!"

"Yeah, right, shit. We might have reached our end game, like we talked about. I'm still trying to sort it out – so we're not there yet – but get the guards to arm themselves, just in case."

"Wait, why haven't they raided us already?"

"It's a long story, and I haven't got time to go through it with you now, but don't worry: I have things in the pipeline that will prevent the police from raiding us."

"What kind of things?"

"Look, sweetie, I already told you, I don't have time to go through it. Where's Alan? I need to speak with him."

Beattie's heart started thudding. "I, er, don't know. He went out last night and hasn't come home yet."

"Jesus Christ! He's never around when I need him. Get him to call me when he graces you with his presence, will you? Oh, and Bea, I'll be in touch if it's time for the end game, okay? And when it is, be sure to press that button when I say."

"Of course, Daddy, just like we talked about."

She hung up and stared at the floor for a moment.

Holy shit! If things weren't bad enough already, now she had to worry about the police and the National Crime Agency raiding the farm. With more rage filling her, she punched Danny's face, hard. "This is all your doing, you bastard!"

She didn't have time to continue pummelling him, although she wanted to. Her knuckles hurt anyway. She left room three of C Wing and walked through the corridor to the bar, where some guards were stood having a drink.

As calmly as she could, she asked them to go into the house and fetch the pistols...

As Steven approached the lay-by, he noticed there was a car parked where he used to park his. Fortunately, the lay-by was large enough for two cars, so he carefully pulled in behind the Ford Focus and switched off his engine. It wasn't quite dark – by the time he reached his old surveillance spot, it would be. It was 18:10 by his watch, and according to his timepiece, he had about six minutes until sunset.

He walked around to the rear of his car, opened the boot, and took out his flashlight. Before he crossed the road, he checked his Glock and holstered it on his hip. Once he'd crossed the road he walked along until he came to the narrow dirt track.

Switching on his torch, he started walking the half-mile to the gates of the farm.

If he had a normal job – an office or factory job – he'd be tucking into a lovely Sunday roast about now, he thought, as he followed the torchlight along the muddy frozen path, his breath visible in the white light. Or maybe he'd be at his local enjoying a pint before dinner.

After ten minutes, he found himself at the gates to the farm. He turned right, following the perimeter fence to the end, and then turned left, heading towards his usual surveillance spot...

62

Nasreen watched through her binoculars as a silhouette walked out of the barn and headed towards the house. She hadn't seen any activity for over half an hour, until now.

The woman – who'd walked out of the barn earlier – had walked back in, so if it was Beatrice Harrison, she was still in the bunker. Nasreen hadn't seen Walter Gebhardt yet, but in the darkness she wasn't able to make out any facial features through the binoculars.

Deep down, she knew she was in the right place; Danny was here.

She had to decide her next move.

She thought she'd counted five men – whom she'd taken to be guards – but there was no way to be sure of the number, given her distance from the barn and how dark it was. With odds of five to one – her being the one – she had to be extra vigilant and make the right choice; she couldn't go in there, gun blazing. That wouldn't help anyone.

Suddenly she heard rustling to her left, the hairs on the back of her neck standing to attention.

Putting the binoculars down, she picked up her pistol and

torch, then looked into the blackness, hoping she was imagining someone there.

When a twig snapped, she raised her gun and shone the torch in the direction of the sound. "Identify yourself!" she said in a shouted whisper. "I'm armed, I *will* shoot you. Identify yourself!"

"Jesus Christ! Put that gun down and get that torch out of my face," snapped a man, his face turned away from the glare of the torch and his palm out, trying to deflect the bright light. "I'm Steven Dyer, NCA. Turn that torch off before they see us."

"Show me your warrant card," Nasreen insisted, the torch still in his face.

She waited for him to reach into his jacket and pull out his identification, then she shone the torch on the wallet and saw that he did indeed work for the NCA. Her nerves started to calm once she realised she wasn't in imminent danger. "Sorry!" she said, between deep breaths. "I thought you might be one of the guards."

"That's all right. I'd have done the same thing."

Feeling a lot calmer, Nasreen went back to her original position, gun and torch on the mud in front of her, her eyes staring through the binoculars.

"You've seen my ID," said the uninvited guest crouching next to her. "Who are you?"

Nasreen turned to face him. "Sorry, I'm Detective Constable Nasreen Maqsood," she said, telling him which force she worked for.

"And you expect me to take your word for it, do you? Where's your warrant card?"

She didn't have time for this. "Me? I don't have one. I'm on suspension." There was no reason for her to justify herself to this NCA officer, so she didn't; she went back to watching the barn through her binoculars.

"Okay, so you're a suspended detective," the annoying man clarified. "Why is that?"

"For shooting a suspect who asked too many questions."

"That'd do it, I guess. Can I ask why you're here – without you shooting me? I'd like to know who I'm dealing with."

"I was suspended for investigating the disappearance of a friend in my spare time." Nasreen sighed. "My friend was abducted over a month ago, but my bosses gave the investigation just five days before they shelved it for more important cases. I carried on the investigation in my own time, and it got me suspended. But it also brought me here."

"And where's here? What I mean is, how much do you know about this place?"

He really was getting on her last nerve. "I probably know more than you do actually."

"Doubtful, but I'll play along."

"My friend, Danny, was abducted by a man called Walter Gebhardt, who lives here at this farm. Underneath that barn there's an old World War Two bunker that Beatrice Harrison and her husband have converted into a kind of brothel-cum-torture house. That's where they've got Danny, down there in that bunker."

"Along with twenty-four more hostages. This is so much bigger than the disappearance of your boyfriend, detective."

"It's Nasreen. Call me Nasreen, or Nas," she said, hating the formality of titles. "And I know how big this is – my source told me how many they have down there. I'm not stupid."

"Hey, I don't think you're stupid, Nas, I just need you to know what you're getting yourself into. This farm is owned by William Rothstein, have you heard of him?"

She shrugged. "My partner looked him up, but his file's been redacted."

"Redacted? Why?"

Nasreen looked at the officer in the darkness. He was asking a rhetorical question; he didn't expect a response, so she didn't give him one.

"My agency has been investigating Rothstein for a good month," the man explained. "He's just your typical gangster. Well, I say typical... he's anything but typical. We've not been able to pin a single thing on him... until now. Finally though, we've got a witness willing to testify against Rothstein, hence why I'm here."

She looked around her pointedly. "Just you? Where's your backup?"

"Waiting on a warrant."

"Uh-huh!" This guy was full of shit, she thought, picking up the binoculars once again and studying the barn. It was nearly time for her to go in and get Danny out, and this NCA guy could come with her or not – she didn't care. She had to do this, for her friend, for her Danny. The adrenaline was starting to kick in.

"What're you doing?"

She felt his hand on her shoulder. "I'm going in." She picked up the pistol and switched off the safety.

"Hell no, we're not!" he said in a forceful whisper. "I'm calling this in. The search warrant might have come through by now."

"*We're* not going anywhere." She shook his hand off her shoulder. "My friend's in there and I'm going in to get him. Come with me or don't, it's up to you."

"Do you want to get yourself killed, huh? Because that's what's going to happen."

There was a pause.

"Look, Nasreen," the NCA officer said, his voice softer, "let me call this in and see where the land lies, okay?"

Nodding, she waited for him to put his earpiece in before she stood and ran up the bank. She navigated the perimeter fence by going over one beam and under another, and within seconds she was on the Harrison property.

The last thing she heard was Steven calling for her to return...

~

"Nasreen, come back!" he growled, watching as she bent down to get under the top fence beam. When he realised she wasn't going to, he called through to Control and asked to be put through to Director General Holmes.

Nasreen was out of sight by the time the director answered, so Steven picked up her binoculars and tried to find her shadow in the darkness. The light of the barn made it possible, but he couldn't see her.

"Officer Dyer, where the hell are you?"

"I'm outside the Harrison farm. Have we received the warrant yet, sir?"

"That's a negative on the warrant. You are to wait right where you are until I say so, is that clear?"

Fuck! He couldn't leave the detective out there on her own; she was going to get herself killed. He couldn't, in good conscience, sit here and let it happen. "I'm afraid I can't do that, sir," he said. "There's been a complication..."

"What? What kind of complication?"

"I've just met a detective; she's breached the Harrison farm, sir."

There was a pause, and then a different voice came over the radio.

"Who, Officer Dyer? Who was it?"

"Nasreen Maqsood, sir? Who the hell is this?"

There was another pause.

"This is Assistant Commissioner Peter Franks. Did you say Nasreen Maqsood?"

"That's affirmative, sir. She's breached the farm perimeter. She's after a friend of hers called Danny. She's very focused... what do you want me to do? Shall I go after her?"

There was a longer pause.

"Sir? Shall I assist Detective Maqsood?"

"That's a negative, Officer Dyer. Nasreen's not a detective anymore. She must be apprehended at once, is that understood? Do whatever you must to ensure she doesn't breach that bunker."

That was Assistant Commissioner Franks giving him orders. Steven wasn't about to go and arrest Nasreen. After all, her goal was the same as his: they both wanted to save the abductees. He searched the darkness for her shadow. He still couldn't see her through the binoculars. This detective was stealthy, he had to give her that.

"Officer Dyer, do you understand what I've just said? Nasreen Maqsood is a rogue police officer; she must be apprehended immediately. Officer Dyer?"

Steven let Franks and Holmes sweat while he located Nasreen in the shadows and watched her creep closer to the barn. She was brave; she might even be the bravest cop Steven had ever met – and feisty too. He couldn't let her go in alone, but if he breached the farm now, without a warrant, it could blow any case they might have against Rothstein.

"Detective Maqsood's at the barn now, sir," he replied finally. "She's about to enter; I won't reach her in time..."

Nasreen was shielded by darkness. She crept up to the barn, her pistol poised and ready for action, the light from the barn drawing closer with each footstep.

Sweat formed on her brow.

She knew how dangerous her mission was – one wrong move could be the end of her – and as she reached the barn door, she tried not to think of Mina, of what would happen to her.

Holding her pistol out in front of her with both hands, Nasreen turned right and entered the barn, moving her arms to cover the whole area quickly. She saw the Range Rover parked at the back of the barn, and after checking that no one was behind it, she decided it was clear. In front of the Range Rover was the opening to the bunker.

Taking a deep breath, she approached the hatchway and looked down the stairs; there was a man walking up, his head down. He was humming to himself and hadn't seen her yet.

She held the gun on him, hoping he wouldn't look up.

As he reached the fourth step from the top, he looked up, as she kicked him square in the face, the heel of her boot smashing his nose in a torrent of crimson. His head snapped back and he tumbled down the stairs, turning and hitting every part of his body as he rolled down all twenty-six steps.

Nasreen quickly followed the fallen guard – her gun still out and ready to fire – and as she reached the bottom, she knew she was in enemy territory – there was no turning back.

She didn't know how many guards were down here.

So far, it looked like only the one, a crumpled heap on the floor behind her.

He was out cold, so she didn't have to worry about him.

Looking around, she first noticed the plush bar to her left.

In front of her were what appeared to be twenty doors, ten on either side. Danny had to be in one of these rooms, she thought. Right at the farthest end of the bunker were two doors, one big heavy and metal, the other smaller and open.

Needing to check that the area was clear, Nasreen approached the bar.

As she leaned over, a white-shirted man jumped up and knocked the gun out of her hand with his elbow.

He grabbed her head, and slammed her forehead down on the bar surface.

It was so quick, she had no time to react.

On the floor, dazed and confused, she felt her arms being pulled as her body was dragged through the bar area and along the corridor, past the doors...

63

"Well, well, if it isn't Detective Maqsood."

Beattie crouched and stared at the semi-conscious police officer.

She was prettier in person than in her Facebook feeds, Beattie thought. "Or should I say ex-detective?" she added. "You have no right to be down here, Nasreen; you have no powers of arrest anymore."

Standing back up, she looked at the guard. "Put her in C Wing, room two..."

Steven spotted headlights to his left, and a few seconds later a large-set man opened the gate, got in his four-by-four, and drove into the farm, getting out and closing the gate again before driving up to the house. He watched the stocky man walk up to the farmhouse as three men came out, carrying something between them. He watched the four men carefully, trying to see what they were holding. It was too dark.

The four men chatted briefly before the stocky man seemed to take control, and when the stocky man took a long thin object from one of the others, Steven suddenly realised what it was. "I can't wait any longer," he said into his microphone. "Four men have come out of the farmhouse carrying a fucking arsenal. I'm going in!"

He unholstered his Glock and climbed the bank to the perimeter fence. He was shielded by darkness, so he was safe to approach the men – at least, until he got closer to the barn.

"Don't breach that farm, Officer Dyer," came Holmes' angry voice. "Listen, if you breach it now, any case against Rothstein will be forfeited, do you understand? We don't have a search warrant yet."

"Nasreen's in there," Steven replied, crouching under the top fence beam and then heading over the middle beam. "They're going to kill her."

"That's not your concern," came the irate voice. "I repeat, do not breach that farm!"

"Fuck you, sir!" Steven snapped, watching the four men in front of him as they started walking towards the barn.

"What? What did you just say to me?"

"Fuck you very much," he replied, having always wanted a reason to say it.

He took out his earpiece and threw it behind him.

He had to focus; he was about to engage four heavily armed men, by himself, with no backup on the way. How had it come to this?

He took a deep breath. This would probably be his last act as an NCA Officer; he would surely be fired the next day, if he survived the night...

"What the fuck are we going to do now? We can't just leave him to face them alone, Peter!" said Holmes. "We have to send backup."

Franks nodded in agreement.

The farm was officially breached; there was nothing they could do to prevent that now. Rothstein's time was over. He had to think his next move through. "Fine, I'll send the most local armed response team. Leave it with me."

Phoning the local Police and Crime Commissioner, Franks explained the situation, gave him the address, and ordered a fully armed assault team to assist Officer Dyer and Detective Maqsood. This whole situation was unravelling faster than Franks could think; before he knew it, Rothstein would be arrested and then they would all be screwed.

There was only one solution to this: Rothstein had to go. They couldn't risk him exposing the project, and that was exactly what he had threatened to do.

First things first: he had to warn Rothstein to flee, so that the local police didn't arrest him at his home or any other known residence.

With only Holmes in the room with him, he took his mobile out of his jacket pocket and dialled Rothstein's number. "Will, it's me. Everything's gone south. The farm's being breached as we speak. Do whatever you need to do to get out of harm's way, I'll be in touch shortly." Franks cut him off, not giving Rothstein the chance to react.

Franks imagined Rothstein would be putting together a suitcase and fleeing his home. By the end of the night, the gangster would be the most wanted man in the UK.

Now Franks had warned Rothstein, he had to put the last act into play...

Nasreen came around slowly. Her head was pounding and she felt nauseous.

What the hell had happened?

She tried to think back to the last thing she could remember: a sudden flash of white, then being pulled by her arms.

It suddenly dawned on her where she was.

When she opened her eyes, she found her hands were bound to something – she couldn't move them – and when she tried moving her legs, they were bound too.

Looking down, she realised she was tied to a chair.

Peering around the room, she saw the red-brown stains on the concrete floor around her – there were blotches everywhere – and when her head finally cleared, she knew they were bloodstains. There were so many... there were even stains on the walls. When she looked up and saw chains dangling from the ceiling, she felt very, very sick. She was in one of the torture rooms that Conrad Gebhardt had told her about.

From behind her, she heard a door open and the sound of footsteps.

Then she heard the door close. She was finding it hard to stay awake, but while she was suffering from concussion and wanted to sleep, the fear kept her alert.

"Has anyone ever told you how troublesome you are, huh?"

She turned her head left, then right, trying to catch a glimpse of the voice's owner.

"You wanted to find out what happened to your precious Danny, yes?"

A woman appeared before her.

She had long red hair, a good physique, and green eyes.

Beatrice Harrison.

"Where is he? What have you done with him?" Nasreen rasped, her voice strained.

"That's what you're here to find out, isn't it? Let me show you," replied the psychotic bitch, bringing a knife out from behind her back.

The woman stepped towards her.

Moving as much as she could tied to the chair, Nasreen tried to get away from the knife.

She moved her head back as far as it would go just as the knife touched her right cheek.

A burning sensation gripped her cheek, as the woman swiped the serrated knife through her flesh, splitting it open.

Blood gushed down her face, neck, and chest.

"And that's just for starters..."

64

Steven had to get to the barn first, to cut them off.

Fortunate to still be shrouded in darkness, he ran low, trying to make himself as invisible as possible, watching as they walked slowly towards the barn.

If he kept the same pace, he'd reach the barn first and be able to engage them, having the upper hand. He could see the stocky man had a shotgun, but the rest only had handguns. They hadn't seen him yet, so he kept going, gaining on the barn.

He was about fifty metres from the barn when he heard someone yell in a foreign language – possibly German – so he sped up, reaching the safety of the outhouse where he turned to face the guards. "Put your guns on the ground! You're under arrest!"

The first gunshot came from the stocky man.

The shotgun reverberated through the floor.

Steven fired a single round and shot the stocky man, watching him fall to the ground, the shotgun falling by his feet.

Unsure if Stocky Man was out for good, he didn't have time to check.

A second later, the three other guards opened fire with their handguns.

Steven ducked inside the barn, taking cover as the bullets hit and cracked the wood.

In return, he fired two rounds by swerving around the door frame and hit the nearest guard in the chest.

The guard fell back and lay still.

Two down, two to go.

He hid behind the barn wood again – waiting for the returning fire to cease.

Finding his moment, he went to move just as a bullet cracked the corner of the barn door frame, causing splinters to fly out and hit his face and eyes.

Momentarily blinded, Steven continued his assault, firing in the general direction of the guards. Then, after five shots, he hid behind the door frame to load a new clip. He wiped his face, trying to get the splinter out of his eye, with no idea of whether his bullets had hit their targets...

Peter Franks opened the door to the interview room where Garvey was sat at the table. He walked over to the camera and switched it off.

No one could hear what he was going to say.

Before he'd gone inside, he'd phoned Clive Adams and asked him to meet him in a couple of hours. Then Franks had requisitioned an unmarked police car. He knew what he had to do. First, he had to get Garvey out of the station. "Garvey, I'm here to take you into protective custody, as part of your deal to testify against William Rothstein. Get up!"

He handcuffed Garvey and led him out of the interview room, taking him along the corridor and then out of the station via the fire exit stairs. Outside in the car park, he opened the rear passenger door of his car and let Garvey get in, closing it after him.

Getting in the driver's seat, he closed the door and started the engine.

"Where are we going, Commissioner? Where are you taking me?"

Franks didn't answer. Instead, he stepped on the accelerator and followed the GPS instructions.

He had a plan, and it had to work.

There was no room for failure on this one...

Having taken cover again, Steven crouched down, peeked out from behind the door frame, and fired five more shots, watching as the fourth and final guard fell, slumping down onto the floor. He'd managed to get the third guard after he'd been hit in the eye with wood splinters.

Knowing he had successfully taken out the four guards, Steven ran out to make sure they were incapacitated, which they were. He then collected their weapons and walked with the cache into the barn, leaving them in a corner before descending the stairs down into the bunker.

When he reached the bunker floor, he looked around, seeing the bar and the luxurious seating area, and then the doors spreading out along the corridor. This was where the abductees had to be held, he thought, his gun still out in front of him, ready to discharge at the slightest provocation. "Nasreen?" he yelled out...

Nasreen flinched as she felt the tip of the knife digging through her blouse, into her left breast.

The woman in front of her relished taunting her, threatening her with painful torture.

As Nasreen felt the blood dripping down her cheek and neck, she shouted, "Tell me where Danny is, you bitch!" She was trying to ignore the scratching of the knife near her nipple.

"Oh, he's around here somewhere, not that you'll get to see him. And if I were you, I'd be more worried about your own predicament than his. You're not in a good place right now, you know?"

Nasreen closed her eyes and prayed to Allah under her breath; if she ever needed His help, it was now. Her lips moved but no words came out. She could feel the knife directly under her nipple.

Nasreen kept her eyes closed, expecting to feel a sudden sharp pain in her breast.

The door burst open behind her.

"Drop the knife, bitch, I mean it! If you hurt her, I'll shoot you in your face, do you understand?"

Nasreen opened her eyes to find Beatrice Harrison backing away.

She still had the knife in her hand.

Beatrice slowly bent over and placed it on the floor.

Nasreen had never felt such relief before. Another hour or so, maybe less, and she'd have been dead. From what she could tell, Beatrice enjoyed – no, relished – torturing people, so it probably would have taken even longer. No matter how long it took, however, the outcome would have been the same.

"I've never been so pleased to see anyone," she said as Steven untied her wrists. "Thank you."

"You're welcome," she heard him say as her hands became free.

She quickly put them to work untying her ankles.

She stood and turned to Steven, who had his back to the door.

"Get over in that corner, now!" Steven barked at Beatrice.

Nasreen watched as Beatrice walked over to the corner of the room, to the left of the door. She herself remained facing the door, feeling her cheek pumping blood down her face and neck.

"That's a really bad gash – we've got to get you to A&E," said Steven, his gun by his side. "You've lost a lot of blood."

"I'm fine. We need to get these people out of here."

A figure appeared in the doorway.

A white-shirted man raised a pistol.

"Steven, behind you!"

The two gunshots happened so fast, she didn't have time to react; she stood there as the white-shirted man shot Steven in the belly and Steven returned fire, shooting White Shirt in the chest.

White Shirt's gun slid across the floor, landing near Beatrice.

Nasreen saw Beatrice staring down at the gun.

As the owner of the bunker bent down to pick up the weapon, Nasreen instinctively rushed her, colliding with Beatrice and sending her back against the wall with a loud thud.

A red haze of rage engulfed her as she headbutted the redhead before punching her in the stomach, then in the face. She rained down blow after blow on the evil woman, pummelling her face as she fell to the ground, and by the time Nasreen stopped, she'd knocked out four of Beatrice's pearly whites.

With her chest heaving, as she tried to regain her composure, Nasreen suddenly felt her body get lifted from the floor as the redhead kicked her off before crawling towards the gun.

Still on her arse, Nasreen didn't have time to get up and get to the gun before Beatrice had it in her hand...

65

Steven couldn't feel his legs. He'd seen the women fighting and he knew he had to get to his gun before it was too late.

It was easier said than done. After he'd been shot, his gun had fallen from his grip and had slid to the back of the room; how it had managed to end up there, he didn't know.

He instinctively crawled over to retrieve it.

Picking it up, he raised the gun with as much effort as he could muster and fired it three times, just as Beatrice raised hers. The first shot struck her in her left breast; the second struck her in the chest; and the third hit her centrally in the forehead. The third bullet had both an entry and exit wound, spraying brain matter over the wall...

The deafening sound of the three gunshots left Nasreen's ears ringing.

She couldn't believe it – she thought she was dead! She'd seen the smile on Beatrice's face as she'd raised the gun, had thought for sure it was the end for her.

But now it was over.

Beatrice and the guards were dead!

She rushed over to Steven, going to his aid. Fortunately, the gunshot wound wasn't as bad as she'd first thought; he'd been hit in the side, not in the belly. However, his face was pale and he was sweating profusely.

"We've got to get you help," she said, holding her hand over the wound.

"Call for ambulances, it's more important than staying here with me," Steven said through grimaces.

"Haven't you got your earpiece?"

"I threw it away," he replied, in pain. "Find a phone."

She rushed out of the room, running along the corridor until she came to an open door. It looked like an office inside, and she could see a landline phone on the desk. As she picked it up, she dialled 999.

Having rung for help, she went back out into the corridor.

Five heavily armed policemen entered, all wearing bulletproof coveralls, helmets, and cameras. They were carrying Heckler and Koch MP5s.

"I need help down here!" Nasreen cried, asking the armed policemen to help Steven.

Back inside the torture room, Nasreen bent down and searched Beatrice's dead body, finding a set of keys in her jeans pocket, each one numbered. Two of the keys looked like they might open the cell doors, so Nasreen took them and open the twenty doors – one by one – each time hoping to see Danny's face.

Her heart sank when she realised she'd opened the last one and still hadn't found him. Where could he be? Could they have killed him already? Was she too late? Had Walter Gebhardt meant it when he'd told her Danny was dead?

"Detective, you've still got four more doors down here," one of the armed police officers pointed out.

She looked back at the corridor as the abductees came out of their cells. Ambulance workers were busy dealing with them on an individual basis, and while it was a chaotic scene, it was a delightful one too. She'd helped free these people from a life of sexual slavery and eventual death at the hands of some of the most evil people she'd ever come across. She had done a good thing.

Focusing back on her task, Nasreen took the key and opened the first door on the separate wing. It was empty. The second room was the one Steven was being aided in. She turned the key in the third door and opened it.

"Danny!" she yelled in delight, before observing his broken body, hanging from the ceiling by his wrists. His torso was one big bruise and his mouth was swollen, as were both eyes. He could just about see out of one of them. "I've been looking for you for so long!"

He said something indecipherable, and then he broke down in floods of tears.

Nasreen lifted him so that his wrists weren't bearing his weight anymore and hugged him tight for what felt like an eternity...

It was five to twelve when Lennox watched Franks get out of the unmarked police car. He was still cuffed in the back seat, and he didn't know where they were – except in a dimly lit multi-storey car park. Another unmarked police car had parked next to this one.

He watched as the Assistant Commissioner approached the other car, and after a man with white hair got out, the two men stood there chatting for a couple of minutes. Then Lennox watched as the Commissioner got back in again and turned to speak to him.

"I've got a proposition for you, Garvey. It's more of a deal actually."

"I'm listening."

"Rothstein's a problem for us now. We can't arrest him – not with how much he knows about our project – so I need you to kill him for me. In return I'll let you go, never to set foot in this country again. I'll pay for a one-way ticket back to Jamaica. How does that sound?"

"Tempting, Commissioner, but I've got a better idea."

"Go on, I'm all ears."

"How about I take care of your Rothstein problem tonight, and you give me the contract to import, with my uncle as the supplier… He's good, and the product's good too."

The Commissioner turned around and sighed.

Lennox didn't think that was a good sign. "It's a good deal," he insisted. "My uncle's a good man to do business with. He doesn't sell shit."

"I'm not sure I can sell it, but I'll try."

Lennox watched as the Commissioner got out of the car, closed the door, and got onto his mobile. He talked animatedly for a few minutes before he got back in and turned to face him again. "Well? What's the verdict?"

"You've got a deal. If you take care of Rothstein, you'll be our go-to guy in a couple of months, when the project starts."

"And what about my uncle?"

"Your uncle will be our go-to supplier."

Lennox waited for the Commissioner to unlock his door and uncuff him, and to his surprise, the senior policeman even gave him a pistol to carry out Rothstein's execution with, as well as the keys to the unmarked police car.

Before the Commissioner left in the other car, he made Lennox promise to phone him the minute Rothstein was out of the way, informing him that they'd meet up afterwards at a place of the Commissioner's choosing...

66

Two Days Later
Tuesday, 20th February

Nasreen looked at her angry scar, at her cheek stitched together, and sighed. The stitches looked awful, but she'd been told by the surgeon that, over time, the scar would fade to a dull red, which wasn't much in the way of consolation. She would always sport this hideous reminder of her time spent in the company of Beatrice Harrison.

Nasreen was enjoying spending time at home with Mina, who kept staring at her scar. When she'd gone to collect her daughter after her ordeal, she'd had to hide the scar as much as she could. After all, her mother-in-law had practically wept when she'd seen it, and if an adult wept, how could she expect a child not to?

After the siege at the Harrison farm, once Nasreen had climbed the stairs and had emerged outside, she'd been confronted by a dozen reporters, who were all keen to get her story in their papers. After much consideration, she'd decided to give exclusivity to Wanda West with the *Daily Telegraph*; she needed the media support to help get her job back.

The IOPC were still going ahead with their investigation, but that day's papers were full of support for her, even the papers she hadn't given an interview to. They'd all come out in support for the detective who had gone above and beyond the call of duty to break a sex slave network of unprecedented size and scale.

One newspaper had worked out that the Harrisons, under Rothstein's guidance, were probably responsible for the abductions of over a hundred and fifty sex workers over a sixteen-year period, and at least a hundred and thirty murders, given that there were only nineteen abductees saved.

It was such a huge story for the tabloids, and the manhunt for William Rothstein was well under way – he'd made it to the top of the Most Wanted list in the United Kingdom.

Nasreen dressed after showering. She was going to visit Steven Dyer in hospital later on, for the first time since he'd saved her life – twice.

He'd undergone major surgery in the early hours of the previous morning to pull out the bullet, and thankfully the surgery had been successful.

Nasreen had soon been informed by the nurses that he'd be available for visitors later that day. Before she went to visit Steven though, she had to visit Danny, who unfortunately hadn't fared as well as Steven.

Danny was in a psychiatric hospital, being treated for severe PTSD. Once he'd started crying on Nasreen's shoulder, he'd not stopped; he was so deeply traumatised that the paramedics had had to sedate him to get him to the hospital.

She could only imagine the kind of trauma he'd gone through, as there was no way of knowing what that bitch,

Beatrice Harrison, had made him do. If it wasn't bad enough forcing him to have sex with people he didn't want to, the bitch had tortured him too.

The physical results of the torture would heal far faster than the mental anguish caused by it. She only hoped he'd be able to recover some day.

After changing, she went down to the kitchen and made herself some breakfast. She'd already fed Mina and taken her to school, having to brave the reporters outside her house in order to do so. They were vultures, the lot of them, out there to pick at her bones, but at least she knew they wouldn't be there forever; they'd eventually get bored, finding a newer story to claw into. She didn't have much respect for journalists.

When she'd finished her breakfast and had washed up, Nasreen grabbed her car keys, bag, and leather jacket, and headed for the front door.

She took a deep breath before opening it and was immediately confronted by a wave of questions as she made her way through the throng of news-hungry writers, eventually getting to her car.

She didn't say a word; she unlocked her car and got in...

Lennox had waited for Rothstein to emerge from his isolated log cabin for over twelve hours, and while he hadn't seen him, he knew his ex-boss would be inside – it was the only place Rothstein could go to escape the police, as only Rothstein, Beattie, and Lennox knew of the cabin's existence, hidden deep in the Welsh forest.

He was cold and hungry. More than that, he was eager to conclude his business with his former boss. Now that Beattie was dead – an unfortunate by-product of Lennox's confession to the police – Rothstein wouldn't know what to do with himself.

He couldn't escape via plane or boat; his face was too well known after two days of intense media coverage.

Having found a row of thick bushes to hide behind, Lennox was watching the front door of the cabin, waiting for Rothstein to show himself. It was dark in the forest, and as the lights were on, every now and then Lennox saw Rothstein's silhouette in the windows.

Crouching down and peering through holes in the branches, he finally saw his former boss open the door and step out onto the porch. He was carrying a suitcase.

Without a moment's hesitation, Lennox stomped out between the bushes until he was in full view of Rothstein, his gun down by his side.

It took Rothstein a moment to see him, but when he did, his face dropped.

"Lenny?"

"What? You weren't expecting me, *boss*?" Adding the boss on the end was a nice touch, he thought. It was the way he'd said it; it resonated with disgust. "You thought I was in prison, didn't you?"

"Hey, Lenny, I didn't have anything to do with you getting nicked, you have to believe me. It was just bad luck."

Lennox nodded, as though he believed him. "Yeah, sure, just bad luck. A bit like this then," he added, raising his arm, the pistol aimed at Rothstein's chest.

"Hey, put that down," Rothstein said quietly. "We can talk like adults, can't we?"

"You heard about Beattie? I suppose that was just bad luck too, huh?"

"I tried everything I could to warn her to get out of there. She was my only daughter, damn it, my only child."

Lennox thought Rothstein's voice sounded strained – he'd even say choked, if he didn't know any better. Rothstein had always been a good actor, and Lennox didn't believe for one moment that he loved Beattie. He didn't believe a narcissist like Rothstein could ever love anyone, except himself.

"She should never have been involved in any of that," Lennox said. "You were supposed to protect her from the vile things you do, not make her a part of it."

"I know, I know, I was a crap dad, but I did love her, more than anything."

Lennox felt a chill cut right through him. He took two steps forwards, gripped the handle of the gun tight and squeezed the trigger three times.

The first shot made a hole in Rothstein's shoulder, the second hit him centre mass in the chest, and the third in the stomach.

Hearing Rothstein gasping for breath on the porch, Lennox walked up to his fallen bloody body and looked down at the man's wide begging eyes. He couldn't speak; his throat was filling up with blood.

"Say hi to Beattie for me, in hell," he said, pointing the gun at Rothstein's forehead and pulling the trigger.

Once the deed was done, Lennox reached into his jacket pocket and pulled out a handkerchief. Then, after wiping the handle of the gun and the trigger, he threw it on the porch next to Rothstein's corpse.

Feeling a little relief that Rothstein was no more, Lennox pulled out his mobile and checked the reception. He only had one bar, but he hoped it would be enough. He dialled.

"It's me. It's done."

Assistant Commissioner Franks told him where and when to meet him, then Lennox made a second call to Barkley.

As Lennox trusted Franks about as far as he could throw him, he wanted Barkley to remain hidden; he had a feeling he would need him close by...

67

Nasreen held Danny's hand and smiled.

"I knew you'd find me." Danny spoke as best he could.

The psychiatric nurse had warned Nasreen that Danny might be drowsy and unresponsive as he was currently dosed up on sedatives; it was the only way to prevent him from going into shock, not surprising, given the trauma he'd been through. Nasreen thought about all the pain he'd endured throughout his imprisonment; no one should ever be subjected to that level of torture, ever.

"It was the only thing that gave me hope," he added.

"You're welcome," she replied, her eyes welling up.

"Is she dead?"

Nasreen frowned. "Who? Beatrice? Oh yes, very. She won't be hurting anyone anymore. All you need to do now is concentrate on recovering. No one's going to hurt you again, I promise."

Her voice had come out hoarse, and she suddenly felt a lump in her throat.

Although their relationship had ended badly, she felt so much love for Danny. He had his flaws, as did everyone, but deep down he was a good man. And more than love, she felt protective of him.

"Did she give you that?" he asked, pointing at her scar.

Nasreen put her fingers on her cheek. "This? It'll heal in time, so don't you worry about me, yeah? I can take care of myself. The main thing is you're safe, so stop thinking about her and focus on getting better, okay?"

She watched as his eyes drooped, and two minutes later he was asleep. It was quiet, save for the humming and occasional bleeping of the machines he was hooked up to – and she could hear the rain outside as it patted against the window. It was such a depressing place to be. The main thing was that Danny was on the road to recovery; it would take a long time, but she had confidence that he would heal...

It was 21:30 when Lennox parked the unmarked police car in the multi-storey car park he'd chosen to meet Franks in. It was cold, dank, and dimly lit.

On his way up the last ramp, Lennox spotted Barkley's car on the level below, and while he hadn't seen Barkley himself, he knew he was crouching down, trying not to be seen. He felt safe knowing his friend was nearby.

Five minutes later, two more cars pulled up next to his. Franks was driving one and two men in plain clothes were driving the other.

Alarm bells went off immediately.

Franks hadn't mentioned bringing along anyone else when he'd spoken on the phone.

Lennox opened his car door and pulled himself out.

The three officers did the same.

Lennox's adrenaline kicked in. He was about to be double-crossed again, he could feel it. It was lucky he had backup.

"Well done, Garvey." Franks held out his hand. "I thank you for helping me out."

While he was shaking the senior police officer's hand, the two men in plain clothes walked behind him and grabbed his arms. A second later, he felt the cuffs wrap around his wrists. "You motherfucker! You said we had a deal!"

"We don't deal with drug smugglers, you should know that by now. These detectives are going to take you back to your cell. You're going to prison for a very long time."

"You're going to fucking regret this, Franks! I promise you that!"

Before he was ushered into the plain-clothed officers' car, one of the detectives searched him for the keys to the other car, then got in it and drove off. Lennox watched Franks drive off in his own, leaving Lennox alone with the remaining detective, who then drove him towards the police station.

With his hands cuffed behind his back, Lennox watched as the detective drove them down the three ramps to the ground floor, and while he looked behind him, out of the rear window, he couldn't see Barkley's car.

There was no way Lennox was going to spend years in prison, no way! He wrestled with his cuffs, trying – fruitlessly – to free his wrists, but it was no use; they weren't coming off.

"Relax, fella, you're not getting out of those."

The detective was looking at him in the rear-view mirror.

Lennox leaned forward, noticing a bulge in the back of the detective's jeans. Detectives in the UK didn't carry firearms.

Oh fuck! He wasn't being driven to any police station.

Franks had ordered his assassination.

He looked behind him through the rear window again, desperately searching for Barkley's car. When he saw it three cars behind, he turned back around, relieved. “Where are you taking me?”

“The police station, like Commissioner Franks told you.”

“Which police station?”

The detective remained silent, all the confirmation Lennox needed that he wasn’t being booked that night. The man driving him probably wasn’t even a detective; he was probably one of the dealers’ guys involved in the project.

“Hey, since when do detectives carry guns?”

Silence.

He caught the “detective’s” glare in the rear-view mirror and started wriggling his cuffs again, although he wasn’t sure why; there was no way they were getting loose.

After five more minutes of driving, the “detective” turned left into a narrow woody lane, making Lennox more certain than ever that he wasn’t heading for a police station.

The car continued along the narrow lane until it stopped outside a field, where the “detective” got out, opened a gate, and then got back in before driving into the field.

A few seconds later, the “detective” stopped the car, got out, pulled out his gun from behind him, and opened Lennox’s door, the gun pointed straight at him.

Reluctantly, he got out of the car.

“On your knees, fella,” said the “detective”.

Lennox got down on his knees and waited while the driver went to the boot, pulling out two cans of petrol and placing them on the roof.

He could smell the strong odour of petrol immediately.

If he wasn’t going to end up in the boot of a burning car, he had to do something – now.

The “detective” walked up to him, raised his arm, and brought the pistol down hard on the top of his head.

Lennox was dazed, like he’d just been hit by a truck.

"It's nothing personal," said the "detective", grabbing Lennox under his armpits and dragging him to the rear of the car. "In you get, yeah?"

Lennox tried using his weight against the "detective", but the man was strong enough to lift him up and force him into the boot of the car. Still concussed, Lennox tried to fight with his legs, but it was no good – before he knew it, he was inside the dark confined boot.

He could hear the "detective" pouring the petrol over the car, could smell the fuel all around him, and after what he took to be two minutes or so, he heard a whoosh. He felt the heat surrounding him. He coughed, the petrol tickling his throat.

When he thought his time was up, he heard two loud bangs.

A couple of seconds later the boot popped open.

He felt two strong arms grab him and pull him out, then he fell to the ground, his jeans smoking.

"You okay, Len?"

Relief swept over him. "I'm fine; better than fine."

Barkley pushed Lennox onto his side, then used the key from the "detective's" pocket to unlock his cuffs.

When his hands were free, he stood for a moment looking down at the corpse lying on the ground, then he hugged Barkley. "Thanks, brother."

He bent down and grabbed the corpse's arms, signalling for Barkley to grab his legs. Then, trying to avoid getting burnt, they both threw the body in the boot.

Covering his hands with his jumper sleeves, Lennox closed the boot and stood back, watching the car burn. "It looks like I'm a dead man," he said with a smile.

"Come on, Len, we'd better get out of here."

"Yeah, you're right," he replied, thinking he had better contact his uncle.

As he walked through the field to Barkley's car, Lennox

started thinking how he was going to get even with Assistant Commissioner Peter Franks and the rest of the conspirators.

He wasn't going to let this slide; he had vengeance on his mind...

Nasreen looked over at her alarm clock: 23:33. She couldn't sleep. Too wired; her brain wouldn't shut down. It always happened after a big case, and this was the biggest case she'd been involved with so far. Although the bunker was gone, Beatrice Harrison dead, and William Rothstein a very wanted man, there were still several missing pieces Nasreen couldn't put together. She knew she didn't have the whole picture.

Clive Adams was involved somehow, of that she knew, and if she managed to miraculously get her job back, she vowed to investigate him. If she could find out how he was involved, she could find out more about other players, like whomever he'd been talking to on the phone in the stairwell. He'd said "sir", so it had to be someone higher up on the Force. Whoever it was, why did they want her off Danny's case?

As she closed her eyes, she kept thinking of other loose ends, though she knew she had to stop doing it – at least for now.

The first thing she needed to do was focus on getting reinstated.

At least Steven was okay. She had visited him in hospital while his wife and kids were off getting something to eat and drink. He'd been in good spirits considering the surgery he'd endured, and he was happy that the NCA had paid for a private room – it was the least they could do.

Over the next few days, she had lots to focus on.

The following day she had her first interview with the IOPC, something she wasn't looking forward to. She was hoping that the positive media coverage of her bravery would convince the IOPC to drop her case. She would have to wait and see.

Sighing, she tried again to get to sleep.

Though she didn't know what her future held, she was hopeful...

ACKNOWLEDGMENTS

I'd like to thank, first and foremost, you, the reader, for taking a chance on reading my book. Without you picking up and reading it, there would be no need for me writing it, or the publisher releasing it. So, thank you. If you enjoyed No Way Out, please consider leaving a review. And if you'd like some behind the scenes information, please follow me on Instagram: @dcbrockwell or my Facebook page: DC Brockwell Author. In addition to writing, I like gardening and making cocktails, so you'll find quite a mixed bag on my Instagram account.

I would also love to thank the team at Bloodhound Books. Betsy and Fred, for taking a punt on my story, thank you so much for this opportunity to showcase my work; it's more appreciated than you know. Morgen Bailey, my editor for shaping it up, ready for publication. Also Heather Fitt and the publicity team. Thank you all for your contributions. I hope I don't let you all down.

And I can't sign off without thanking my beta readers, who often pull me up on poor choices with storylines, especially Jayne

Tanner, who I can rely on to give it to me straight. You helped give me the confidence to submit 'No Way Out'. Thank you!

DC Brockwell can be found here:
Instagram: @dcbrockwell
Facebook Page: DCBrockwell Author
Twitter: DCBrockwell